THE ILLUSTRATED TREASURY OF
AUSTRALIAN STORIES

CHOSEN BY GEOFFREY DUTTON

THE ILLUSTRATED TREASURY OF
AUSTRALIAN STORIES
CHOSEN BY GEOFFREY DUTTON

NELSON

Nelson Publishers

Thomas Nelson Australia
480 La Trobe Street Melbourne

Designed and produced by
Mead & Beckett Publishing
139 Macquarie Street Sydney

First published 1986
Copyright in this selection © Geoffrey Dutton 1986

Picture research by Joanna Collard
Designed by Barbara Beckett

National Library of Australia
Cataloguing-in-publication data

The illustrated treasury of Australian stories.

Bibliography.
Includes index.
ISBN 0 17 006757 2

1. Short stories, Australian.   I. Dutton, Geoffrey, 1922–

A823'.0108

Typeset by Asco Trade Typesetting Ltd., Hong Kong
Printed in Hong Kong by Mandarin Offset Marketing (H.K.) Ltd.

CONTENTS

CONTENTS

CONTENTS

INTRODUCTION

THE SHORT STORY has always been important both to Australian writers and readers. It has been like a conversation between them and the country, informal, humorous or sad. There is the conversation that is getting-to-know-you, and the conversation that is between old friends, where a word or an image is enough to recall years or places.

There is an immediacy about the short story that, like the informality, is deceptive. There is considerable art needed to get the conversation going, to convince the reader that this is a situation that matters, without making the reader feel that he or she is being manipulated. And the boredom threshold is very low; with a long novel one is prepared to hang on and see what happens, but a short story by its very brevity has to make a quick connection.

Nobody understood this better than J.F. Archibald and his colleagues on the *Bulletin* of the 1880s and 1890s. Louis Becke, Henry Lawson, Steele Rudd and others are masters at quickly capturing the reader's attention so that the ensuing conversation seems inevitable and not forced. The *Bulletin* made them keep it short, and often one longs for more, but maybe the writers' talents were best suited to a form that let them hint rather than expand. One could make one's own imaginary feature film that could run for hours from the short footage they provide, glimpses of lives and landscapes, moods and convictions.

There were many short stories written before those that appeared in the *Bulletin*, some of them by important writers like Marcus Clarke, but they did not find either an Australian or an individual voice. The conversation was conducted not only in an English accent but in words and terms that are now sadly dated. The voice from the past may be from a greybeard loon but if it has a certain quality it is like that of Coleridge's Ancient Mariner: one 'cannot choose but hear'.

The first five writers in this anthology, Louis Becke, Barbara Baynton, Henry Lawson, Steele Rudd and Henry Handel Richardson, were all born within fifteen years, between 1855 and 1870. It is an interesting comment on both life and literature that two of these were pseudonyms and that Becke's names were George Lewis, rather more prosaic than Louis. Arthur Hoey Davis called himself 'Steele Rudder' in his first writings, which were skits about rowing contributed to the Brisbane *Chronicle* in the 1890s. When his first story of selection life appeared in the *Bulletin* in December 1895 he had contracted the pseudonym to 'Steele Rudd'. Ethel Florence Lindesay Robertson's father was Dr Walter Lindesay Richardson; her husband was Professor J.G. Robertson. In London she published her first novel, *Maurice Guest*, (1908), under a man's name, Henry Handel Richardson, so that her work would be taken more seriously, a sad comment on the times. Barbara Baynton made up a romantic biography for herself in which her mother became an Englishwoman who eloped with an Indian Army officer, instead of the wife of a carpenter from northern New South Wales. Lawson was the son of a Norwegian ex-sailor, Niels Hertzberg Larsen, who changed his name to an easier and more Australian Peter Lawson.

So there is something strange about all of them; they are not quite what they seem. Perhaps there is something symbolic in this, in the difficulties writers had in depicting subjects that often had never been written about before, and at the same time making them recognisable through their impact on the eternal verities of human nature.

The immense range of the new subject-matter is one of the most exciting ingredients of the Australian short story. The writer as explorer has never been in danger of doing a perish in Australia. For Becke there was also the Pacific; for Lawson and Rudd and many others the bush in all its variety; for others there was the beach, country towns, motels, and the migrants who give such warm flesh and blood to Judah Waten's story of the 1920s and to those of the youngest writers in this book, Angelo Loukakis and Tim Winton.

Of course every writer who is any good sees something new in what he writes about, however old and familiar it may be, like Shakespeare writing about Julius Caesar. Sheer novelty can be highly dangerous to writers, who have to create as well as report. Many of the early Australian stories not included in this book were breathless accounts of a strange new world where there was a platypus in every creek and a kangaroo snoozing under every bush. One of the mysteries about good writing is in the paradox that the new becomes familiar and the familiar new, but that novelty is never there for its own sake.

Such discoveries of subject-matter were for those who settled in Australia. They were already familiar to the Aborigines, for whom the country was also populated by spirits and ancestors. In Paddy Roe's story the old man whose wife has been stolen can make the lightning blow her alone to pieces in a cave where she is sleeping with three other women. In Kianoo Tjeemairee's story told to Roland Robinson the girl who is being chased by a man climbs a bottle-tree, and when he tries to climb up to her 'the girl in the branches sang the tree and the bottle-tree began to get bigger and bigger and grow up more and more', and she escapes him. The imagination is real for the Aborigines in a different way from the white man, adding another strangeness and richness to the Australian short story.

There is a characteristic lilt and melody to Aboriginal speech, which Stephen Muecke has with some success endeavoured to reproduce in his record of Paddy Roe telling his story. Roland Robinson edited it to be more familiar to English readers. The idiom of the non-Aboriginal Australian is much more complex and varied, and one of the great successes of Australian short-story writers has been to understand its rhythms and phrasing, and convey it so that the language of the conversation of the story becomes authentic. This is not just a case of getting the dialogue right, in its various nuances, as for instance Lawson, John Morrison, Dal Stivens, Frank Hardy, Nene Gare, Morris Lurie and Helen Garner do, but in keeping the reader in undisturbed communication with what is happening.

The individual voice, in life as in the short story, is what is immediately recognisable. Perhaps Australia's greatest master of it in the short story, Hal Porter, is represented here by a perfect example of sympathy and irony, 'Francis Silver'. But much the same could be said of Patrick White's 'The Letters'. Where does one stop? Unfortunately, the anthologist has to stop, even with the generous space here of forty-three stories. One only mourns all the good stories for which there was no room.

GEOFFREY DUTTON

A TRULY GREAT MAN
A Mid-Pacific Sketch

LOUIS BECKE
1855–1913

THEN the flag of 'Bobby' Towns, of Sydney, was still mighty in the South Seas. The days had not come in which steamers with brass-bound super-cargoes, carrying tin boxes and taking orders, like merchant's bag-men, for goods 'to arrive', exploited the Ellice, Kingsmill, and Gilbert Groups. Bluff-bowed old wave-punchers like the *Spec*, the *Lady Alicia*, and the *E. K. Bateson*, plunged their clumsy hulls into the rolling swell of the mid-Pacific, carrying their 'trade' of knives, axes, guns, bad rum, and good tobacco, instead of, as now, white umbrellas, paper, boots and shoes, German sewing-machines and fancy prints – 'zephyrs', the smartly-dressed supercargo calls them, as he sub-mits a card of patterns to Emilia, the native teacher's wife, who, as the first Lady in the Land, must have first choice.

In those days the sleek native missionary was an unknown quantity in the Toke-laus and Kingsmills, and the local white trader answered all requirements. He was generally a rough character – a runaway from some Australian or Amer-ican whaler, or a wandering Ishmael who, for reasons of his own, preferred living among the intractable, bawling, and poverty-stricken people of the equatorial Pacific to dreaming away his days in the monotonously happy val-leys of the Society and Marquesas Groups.

Such a man was Probyn, who dwelt on one of the low atolls of the Ellice Islands. He had landed there one day from a Sydney whaler with a chest of clothes, a

musket or two, and a tierce of twist tobacco; with him came a savage-eyed, fierce-looking native wife, over whose shoulders fell long waves of black hair; and a child about five years old.

The second mate of the whaler, who was in charge of the boat, not liking the looks of the natives that swarmed around the newcomer, bade him a hurried farewell, and pushed away to the ship, which lay-to off the passage with her foreyard aback. Then the clamorous natives pressed more closely around Probyn and his wife, and assailed them with questions.

So far neither of them had spoken. Probyn, a tall, wiry, scanty-haired man, was standing with one foot on the tierce of tobacco and his hands in his pockets. His wife glared defiantly at some two or three score of reddish-brown women who crowded eagerly around her to stare into her face; holding to the sleeve of her dress was the child, paralysed into the silence of fright.

The deafening babble and frantic gesticulations were perfectly explicable to Probyn, and he apprehended no danger. The headman of the town had not yet appeared, and until he came this wild licence of behaviour would continue. At least the natives became silent and parted to the right and left as Tahori, the headman, his fat body shining with coconut oil, and carrying an ebonywood club, stood in front of the white man and eyed him up and down. The scrutiny seemed satisfactory. He stretched out his huge, naked arm and shook Probyn's hand uttering his one word of Samoan – *Talofa!** and then, in his own dialect, he asked: 'What is your name and what do you want?

'Sam,' replied Probyn. And then, in the Tokelau language, which the wild-eyed people around him fairly understood, 'I have come here to live with you and trade for oil' – and he pointed to the tierce of tobacco.

'Where are you from?'

'From the land called Nukunono, in the Tokelau.'

'Why come here?'

'Because I killed someone there.'

'Good!' grunted the fat man; 'there are no twists in your tongue; but why did the boat hasten away so quickly?'

'They were frightened because of the noise. He with the face like a fowl's talked too much' – and he pointed to a long, hatchet-visaged native who had been especially turbulent and vociferous.

'Ha!' and the fat, bearded face of Tahori turned from the white man to him of whom the white man had spoken – 'is it thee, Makoi? And so *thou* madest the strangers hasten away! That was wrong. Only for thee I had gone to the ship and gotten many things. Come here!'

Then he stooped and picked up one of Probyn's muskets, handed it to the white man, and silently indicated the tall native with a nod. The other natives fell back. Niābong, Probyn's wife, set her boy on his feet, put her hand in her

*Lit., 'My love to you', the Samoan salutation.

bosom and drew out a key with which she opened the chest. She threw back the
lid, fixed her black eyes on Probyn, and waited.

Probyn, holding the musket in his left hand, mused a moment. Then he
asked:

'Whose man is he?'

'Mine,' said Tahori; 'he is from Oaitupu, and my bondman.'

'Has he a wife?'

'No; he is poor and works in my *puraka** field.'

'Good,' said Probyn, and he motioned to his wife. She dived her hand into the
chest and handed him a tin of powder, then a bullet, a cap, and some scraps of
paper.

---

* A coarse species of taro (*arum esculentum*) growing on the low-lying atolls of the mid-Pacific.

Slowly he loaded the musket, and Tahori, seizing the bondman by his arm, led him out to the open, and stood by, club in hand, on the alert.

Probyn knew his reputation depended on the shot. The ball passed through the chest of Makoi. Then four men picked up the body and carried it into a house.

———

Probyn laid down the musket and motioned again to Niābong. She handed him a hatchet and blunt chisel. Tahori smiled pleasantly, and, drawing the little boy to him, patted his head.

Then, at a sign from him, a woman brough Niābong a shell of sweet toddy. The chief sat cross-legged and watched Probyn opening the tierce of tobacco. Niābong locked the box again and sat upon it.

'Who are you?' said Tahori, still caressing the boy.

'Niābong. But my tongue twists with your talk here. I am of Naura (Pleasant Island). By and by I will understand it.'

'True. He is a great man, thy man,' said the chief, nodding at Probyn.

'A great man, truly. There is not one thing in the world but he can do it.'

'*E moê,*'* said the fat man, approvingly: 'I can see it. Look you, he shall be as my brother, and thy child here shall eat of the best in the land.'

Probyn came over with his two hands filled with sticks of tobacco. 'Bring a basket,' he said.

A young native girl slid out from the coconuts at Tahori's bidding and stood behind him, holding a basket. Probyn counted out into it two hundred sticks.

'See, Tahori. I am a just man to thee because thou art a just man to me. Here is the price of him that thou gavest to me.'

Tahori rose and beckoned to the people to return. 'Look at this man. He is a great man. His heart groweth from his loins upwards to his throat. Bring food to my house quickly, that he and his wife and child may eat. And tomorrow shall every man cut wood for the house, a house that shall be in length six fathoms, and four in width. Such men as he come from the gods.'

*True.

THE CHOSEN VESSEL

BARBARA
BAYNTON
1857–1929

SHE laid the stick and her baby on the grass while she untied the rope that tethered the calf. The length of the rope separated them. The cow was near the calf, and both were lying down. Feed along the creek was plentiful, and every day she found a fresh place to tether it, since tether it she must, for if she did not it would stray with the cow out on the plain. She had plenty of time to go after it, but then there was baby; and if the cow turned on her out on the plain, and she with baby – she had been a town girl and was afraid of the cow, but she did not want the cow to know it. She used to run at first when it bellowed its protest against the penning up of its calf. This satisfied the cow, also the calf, but the woman's husband was angry, and called her – the noun was cur. It was he who forced her to run and meet the advancing cow, brandishing a stick, and uttering threatening words till the enemy turned and ran. 'That's the way!' the man said, laughing at her white face. In many things he was worse than the cow, and she wondered if the same rule would apply to the man, but she was not one to provoke skirmishes even with the cow.

It was early for the calf to go 'to bed' – nearly an hour earlier than usual; but she had felt so restless all day. Partly because it was Monday, and the end of the week that would bring her and baby the companionship of its father, was so far off. He was a shearer, and had gone to his shed before daylight that morning. Fifteen miles as the crow flies separated them.

There was a track in front of the house, for it had once been a wine shanty, and a few travellers passed along at intervals. She was not afraid of horsemen; but swagmen, going to, or worse, coming from the dismal, drunken little township, a day's journey beyond, terrified her. One had called at the house today, and asked for tucker.

Ah! that was why she had penned up the calf so early! She feared more from the look of his eyes, and the gleam of his teeth, as he watched her newly

awakened baby beat its impatient fists upon her covered breasts, than from the knife that was sheathed in the belt at his waist.

She had given him bread and meat. Her husband, she told him, was sick. She always said that when she was alone, and a swagman came, and she had gone in from the kitchen to the bedroom, and asked questions and replied to them in the best man's voice she could assume. Then he had asked to go into the kitchen to boil his billy, but she gave him tea, and he drank it on the wood-heap. He had walked round and round the house, and there were cracks in some places, and after the last time he had asked for tobacco. She had none to give him, and he had grinned, because there was a broken clay pipe near the wood-heap where he stood, and if there were a man inside, there ought to have been tobacco. Then he asked for money, but women in the bush never have money.

At last he had gone, and she, watching through the cracks saw him, when about a quarter of a mile away, turn and look back at the house. He had stood so for some moments with a pretence of fixing his swag, and then, apparently satisfied, moved to the left towards the creek. The creek made a bow round the house, and when he came to it she lost sight of him. Hours after, watching intently for signs of smoke, she saw the man's dog chasing some sheep that had gone to the creek for water, and saw it slink back suddenly, as if the man had called it.

More than once she thought of taking her baby and going to her husband. But in the past, when she had dared to speak of the dangers to which her loneliness exposed her, he had taunted and sneered at her. She need not flatter herself, he had coarsely told her, that anybody would want to run away with her.

Long before nightfall she placed food on the kitchen table, and beside it laid the big brooch that had been her mother's. It was the only thing of value that she had. And she left the kitchen door wide open.

The doors inside she securely fastened. Beside the bolt in the back one she drove in the steel and scissors; against it she piled the table and the stools. Underneath the lock of the front door she forced the handle of the spade, and the blade between the cracks in the flooring boards. Then the prop-stick, cut into lengths, held the top, as the spade held the middle. The windows were little more than port-holes; she had nothing to fear through them.

She ate a few mouthfuls of food and drank a cup of milk. But she lighted no fire, and when night came, no candle, but crept with her baby to bed.

What woke her? The wonder was that she had slept – she had not meant to. But she was young, very young. Perhaps the shrinking of the galvanised roof – yet hardly, since that was so usual. Something had set her heart beating wildly; but she lay quite still, only she put her arm over her baby. Then she had both round it, and she prayed, 'Little baby, little baby, don't wake!'

The moon's rays shone on the front of the house, and she saw one of the open cracks, quite close to where she lay, darken with a shadow. Then a protesting growl reached her; and she could fancy she heard the man turn hastily. She plainly heard the thud of something striking the dog's ribs, and the long flying strides of the animal as it howled and ran. Still watching, she saw the shadow darken every crack along the wall. She knew by the sounds that the man was

trying every standpoint that might help him to see in; but how much he saw she could not tell. She thought of many things she might do to deceive him into the idea that she was not alone. But the sound of her voice would wake baby, and she dreaded that as though it were the only danger that threatened her. So she prayed, 'Little baby, don't wake, don't cry!'

Stealthily the man crept about. She knew he had his boots off, because of the vibration that his feet caused as he walked along the veranda to gauge the width of the little window in her room, and the resistance of the front door.

Then he went to the other end, and the uncertainty of what he was doing became unendurable. She had felt safer, far safer, while he was close, and she could watch and listen. She felt she must watch, but the great fear of wakening baby again assailed her. She suddenly recalled that one of the slabs on that side of the house had shrunk in length as well as in width, and had once fallen out. It was held in position only by a wedge of wood underneath. What if he should discover that! The uncertainty increased her terror. She prayed as she gently raised herself with her little one in her arms, held tightly to her breast.

She thought of the knife, and shielded her child's body with her hands and arms. Even its little feet she covered with its white gown, and baby never murmured – it liked to be held so. Noiselessly she crossed to the other side, and stood where she could see and hear, but not be seen. He was trying every slab, and was very near to that with the wedge under it. Then she saw him find it; and heard the sound of the knife as bit by bit he began to cut away the wooden support.

She waited motionless, with her baby pressed tightly to her, though she knew that in another few minutes this man with the cruel eyes, lascivious mouth, and gleaming knife, would enter. One side of the slab tilted; he had only to cut away the remaining little end, when the slab, unless he held it, would fall outside.

She waited motionless, with her baby pressed tightly to her, though she knew that in another few minutes this man with the cruel eyes, lascivious mouth, and gleaming knife, would enter. One side of the slab tilted; he had only to cut away the remaining little end, when the slab, unless he held it, would fall outside.

She heard his jerked breathing as it kept time with the cuts of the knife, and the brush of his clothes as he rubbed the wall in his movements, for she was so still and quiet that she did not even tremble. She knew when he ceased, and wondered why. She stood well concealed; she knew he could not see her, and that he would not fear if he did, yet she heard him move cautiously away. Perhaps he expected the slab to fall. Still his motive puzzled her, and she moved even closer, and bent her body the better to listen. Ah! what sound was that? 'Listen! Listen!' she bade her heart – her heart that had kept so still, but now bounded with tumultuous throbs that dulled her ears. Nearer and nearer came the sounds, till the welcome thud of a horse's hoof rang out clearly.

'Oh, God! Oh, God! Oh, God!' she cried, for they were very close before she could make sure. She turned to the door, and with her baby in her arms tore frantically at its bolts and bars.

Out she darted at last, and running madly along, saw the horseman beyond her in the distance. She called to him in Christ's name, in her babe's name, still flying like the wind with the speed that deadly peril gives. But the distance grew

*'"LISTEN! Listen!"
she bade her heart –
her heart that had kept
so still, but now
bounded with tumul-
tuous throbs that
dulled her ears. Near-
er and nearer came the
sounds, till the wel-
come thud of a horse's
hoof rang out clearly.'*

greater and greater between them, and when she reached the creek her prayers turned to wild shrieks, for there crouched the man she feared, with outstretched arms that caught her as she fell. She knew he was offering terms if she ceased to struggle and cry for help, though louder and louder did she cry for it, but it was only when the man's hand gripped her throat, that the cry of 'Murder' came from her lips. And when she ceased, the startled curlews took up the awful sound, and flew shrieking over the horseman's head.

'By God!' said the boundary rider, 'it's been a dingo right enough! Eight killed up here, and there's more down in the creek – a ewe and a lamb, I'll bet; and the lamb's alive!' And he shut out the sky with his hand, and watched the crows that were circling round and round, nearing the earth one moment, and the next shooting skywards. By that he knew the lamb must be alive; even a dingo will spare a lamb sometimes.

Yes, the lamb was alive, and after the manner of lambs of its kind did not know its mother when the light came. It had sucked the still warm breasts, and laid its little head on her bosom, and slept till the morn. Then, when it looked at the swollen disfigured face, it wept and would have crept away, but for the hand that still clutched its little gown. Sleep was nodding its golden head and swaying its small body, and the crows were close, so close, to the mother's wide-open eyes, when the boundary rider galloped down.

'Jesus Christ!' he said, covering his eyes. He told afterwards how the little child held out its arms to him, and how he was forced to cut its gown that the dead hand held.

It was election time, and as usual the priest had selected a candidate. His choice was so obviously in the interests of the squatter, that Peter Hennessey's reason, for once in his life, had over-ridden superstition, and he had dared promise his vote to another. Yet he was uneasy, and every time he woke in the night (and it was often) he heard the murmur of his mother's voice. It came through the partition, or under the door. If through the partition he knew she was praying in her bed; but when the sounds came under the door, she was on her knees before the little altar in the corner that enshrined the statue of the Blessed Virgin and Child.

'Mary, Mother of Christ! save my son! Save him!' prayed she in the dairy as she strained and set the evening's milking. 'Sweet Mary! for the love of Christ, save him!' The grief in her old face made the morning meal so bitter, that to avoid her he came late to his dinner. It made him so cowardly, that he could not say goodbye to her, and when night fell on the eve of the election day, he rode off secretly.

He had thirty miles to ride to the township to record his vote. He cantered briskly along the great stretch of plain that had nothing but stunted cottonbush to play shadow to the full moon, which glorified a sky of earliest spring. The bruised incense of the flowering clover rose up to him, and the glory of the night appealed vaguely to his imagination, but he was preoccupied with his present act of revolt.

Vividly he saw his mother's agony when she would find him gone. At that moment, he felt sure, she was praying.

'Mary! Mother of Christ!' He repeated the invocation, half unconsciously. And suddenly, out of the stillness, came Christ's name to him – called loudly in despairing accents.

'For Christ's sake! Christ's sake! Christ's sake!' called the voice. Good Catholic that he had been, he crossed himself before he dared to look back. Gliding across a ghostly patch of pipe-clay, he saw a white-robed figure with a babe clasped to her bosom.

All the superstitious awe of his race and religion swayed his brain. The moonlight on the gleaming clay was a 'heavenly light' to him, and he knew the white figure not for flesh and blood, but for the Virgin and Child of his mother's prayers. Then, good Catholic that once more he was, he put spurs to his horse's sides and galloped madly away.

His mother's prayers were answered.

Hennessey was the first to record his vote – for the priest's candidate. Then he sought the priest at home, but found that he was out rallying the voters. Still, under the influence of his blessed vision, Hennessey would not go near the public-houses, but wandered about the outskirts of the town for hours, keeping apart from the townspeople, and fasting as penance. He was subdued and mildly ecstatic, feeling as a repentant chastened child, who awaits only the kiss of peace.

And at least, as he stood in the graveyard crossing himself with reverent awe, he heard in the gathering twilight the roar of many voices crying the name of the victor at the election. It was well with the priest.

Again Hennessey sought him. He sat at home, the housekeeper said, and led him into the dimly-lighted study. His seat was immediately opposite a large picture, and as the housekeeper turned up the lamp, once more the face of the Madonna and Child looked down on him, but this time silently, peacefully. The half-parted lips of the Virgin were smiling with compassionate tenderness; her eyes seemed to beam with the forgiveness of an earthly mother for her erring but beloved child.

He fell on his knees in adoration. Transfixed, the wondering priest stood, for, mingled with the adoration, 'My Lord and my God!' was the exaltation, 'And hast Thou chosen me?'

'What is it, Peter?' said the priest.

'Father,' he answered reverently, and with loosened tongue he poured forth the story of his vision.

'Great God!' shouted the priest, 'and you did not stop to save her! Have you not heard?'

Many miles further down the creek a man kept throwing an old cap into a waterhole. The dog would bring it out and lay it on the opposite side to where the man stood, but would not allow the man to catch him, though it was only to wash the blood of the sheep from his mouth and throat, for the sight of blood made the man tremble.

THE GOLDEN GRAVEYARD

HENRY LAWSON
1867–1922

MOTHER Middleton was an awful woman, an 'old hand' (transported convict) some said. The prefix 'mother' in Australia mostly means 'old hag', and is applied in that sense. In early boyhood we understood, from old diggers, that Mother Middleton – in common with most other old hands – had been sent out for 'knocking a donkey off a hen-roost'. We had never seen a donkey. She drank like a fish and swore like a trooper when the spirits moved her; she went on periodical sprees, and swore on most occasions. There was a fearsome yarn, which impressed us greatly as boys, to the effect that once, in her best (or worst) days, she had pulled a mounted policeman off his horse, and half killed him with a heavy pick-handle, which she used for poking down clothes in her boiler. She said that he had insulted her.

She could still knock down a tree and cut a load of firewood with any bushman; she was square and muscular, with arms like a navvy's; she had often worked shifts, below and on top, with her husband, when he'd be putting down a prospecting shaft without a mate, as he often had to do – because of her mainly. Old diggers said that it was lovely to see how she'd spin up a heavy greenhide bucket full of clay and tailings, and land and empty it with a twist of her wrist. Most men were afraid of her, and few diggers' wives were strong-minded enough to seek a second row with Mother Middleton. Her voice could be heard right across Golden Gully and Specimen Flat, whether raised in argument or is friendly greeting. She came to the old Pipeclay diggings with the 'rough crowd' (mostly Irish), and when the old and new Pipeclays were worked out, she went with the rush to Gulgong (about the last of the great alluvial or 'poor-man's' goldfields) and came back to Pipeclay when the Log Paddock goldfield 'broke out', adjacent to the old fields, and so helped prove the truth of the old diggers' saying, that no matter how thoroughly ground has been worked, there is always room for a new Ballarat.

Jimmy Middleton died at Log Paddock, and was buried, about the last, in the little old cemetery – appertaining to the old farming town on the river, about four miles away – which adjoined the district racecourse, in the bush, on the far edge of Specimen Flat. She conducted the funeral. Some said she made the coffin, and there were alleged jokes to the effect that her tongue had provided the corpse; but this, I think, was unfair and cruel, for she loved Jimmy Middleton in her awful way, and was, for all I ever heard to the contrary, a good wife to him. She then lived in a hut in Log Paddock, on a little money in the bank, and did sewing and washing for single diggers.

I remember hearing her one morning in neighbourly conversation, carried on across the gully, with a selector, Peter Olsen, who was hopelessly slaving to farm a dusty patch in the scrub.

'Why don't you chuck up that dust-hole and go up-country and settle on good

'SHE had pulled a mounted policeman off his horse, and half killed him with a heavy pick-handle, which she used for poking down clothes in her boiler. She said that he had insulted her.'

land, Peter Olsen? You're only slaving your stomach out here.' (She didn't say stomach.)

Peter Olsen (mild-whiskered little man, afraid of his wife): 'But then you know my wife is so delicate, Mrs Middleton. I wouldn't like to take her out in the bush.'

Mrs Middleton: 'Delicate be damned! She's only shamming!' (at her loudest). 'Why don't you kick her off the bed and the book out of her hand, and make her go to work? She's as delicate as I am. Are you a man, Peter Olsen, or a – ?'

This for the edification of the wife and of all within half a mile.

Log Paddock was 'petering'. There were a few claims still being worked down at the lowest end, where big, red-and-white waste-heaps of clay and gravel, rising above the blue-grey gum-bushes, advertised deep sinking; and little, yellow, clay-stained streams, running towards the creek over the drought-parched surface, told of trouble with the water below – time lost in bailing and extra expense in timbering. And diggers came up with their flannels and moleskins yellow and heavy, and dripping with wet mullock.

Most of the diggers had gone to other fields, but there were a few prospecting, in parties and singly, out on the flats and amongst the ridges round Pipeclay. Sinking holes in search of a new Ballarat.

Dave Regan – lanky, easy-going bush native; Jim Bently – a bit of a 'Flash Jack'; and Andy Page – a character like what Kit (in *The Old Curiosity Shop*) might have been after a voyage to Australia and some colonial experience. These three were mates from habit and not necessity, for it was all shallow sinking where they worked. They were poking down potholes in the scrub in the vicinity of the racecourse, where the sinking was from ten to fifteen feet.

Dave had theories – 'ideers' or 'notions' he called them; Jim Bently laid claim to none – he ran by sight, not scent, like a kangaroo-dog. Andy Page – by the way, great admirer and faithful retainer of Dave Regan – was simple and trusting, but on critical occasions he was apt to be obstinately, uncomfortably, exasperatingly truthful, honest, and he had reverence for higher things.

Dave thought hard all one quiet drowsy Sunday afternoon, and next morning he, as head of the party, started to sink a hole as close to the cemetery fence as he dared. It was a nice quiet spot in the thick scrub, about three panels along the fence from the farthest corner post from the road. They bottomed here at nine feet, and found encouraging indications. They drove (tunnelled) inwards at right angles to the fence, and at a point immediately beneath it they were 'making tucker'; a few feet farther and they were making wages. The old alluvial bottom sloped gently that way. The bottom here, by the way, was shelving, brownish, rotten rock.

Just inside the cemetery fence, and at right angles to Dave's drive, lay the shell containing all that was left of the late fiercely lamented James Middleton, with older graves close at each end. A grave was supposed to be six feet deep, and local gravediggers had been conscientious. The old alluvial bottom sloped from nine to fifteen feet here.

Dave worked the ground all round from the bottom of his shaft, timbering – i.e. putting in a sapling prop – here and there where he worked wide; but the payable dirt ran in under the cemetery, and in no other direction.

Dave, Jim, and Andy held a consultation in camp over their pipes after tea, as a result of which Andy next morning rolled up his swag, sorrowfully but firmly shook hands with Dave and Jim, and started to tramp outback to look for work on a sheep station.

This was Dave's theory – drawn from a little experience and many long yarns with old diggers:

He had bottomed on a slope to an old original watercourse, covered with clay and gravel from the hills by centuries of rains to the depth of from nine or ten to twenty feet; he had bottomed on a gutter running into the bed of the old buried creek, and carrying patches and streaks of 'wash' or gold-bearing dirt. If he went on he might strike it rich at any stroke of his pick; he might strike the rich lead which was supposed to exist round there. (There was always supposed to be a rich lead round there somewhere. 'There's gold in them ridges yet – if a man can only git at it,' says the toothless old relic of the Roaring Days.)

Dave might strike a ledge, pocket, or pothole holding wash rich with gold. He had prospected on the opposite side of the cemetery, found no gold, and the bottom sloping upwards towards the graveyard. He had prospected at the back of the cemetery, found a few colours, and the bottom sloping downwards towards the point under the cemetery towards which all indications were now leading him. He had sunk shafts across the road opposite the cemetery frontage and found the sinking twenty feet and not a colour of gold. Probably the whole of the ground under the cemetery was rich – maybe the richest in the district. The old gravediggers had not been gold-diggers – besides, the graves, being six feet, would, none of them, have touched the alluvial bottom. There was nothing strange in the fact that none of the crowd of experienced diggers who rushed the district had thought of the cemetery and racecourse. Old brick chimneys and houses, the clay for the bricks of which had been taken from sites of subsequent goldfields, had been put through the crushing-mill in subsequent years and had yielded payable gold. Fossicking Chinamen were said to have been the first to detect a case of this kind.

Dave reckoned to strike the lead,or a shelf or ledge with a good streak of wash lying along it, at a point about forty feet within the cemetery. But a theory in alluvial goldmining was much like a theory in gambling, in some respects. The theory might be right enough, but old volcanic disturbances – 'the shrinkage of the earth's surface', and that sort of old thing – upset everything. You might follow good gold along a ledge, just under the grass, till it suddenly broke off and the continuation might be a hundred feet or so under your nose.

Had the ground in the cemetery been 'open' Dave would have gone to the point under which he expected the gold to lie, sunk a shaft there, and worked the ground. It would have been the quickest and easiest way – it would have saved the labour and the time lost in dragging heavy buckets of dirt along a low lengthy drive to the shaft outside the fence. But it was very doubtful if the Government could have been moved to open the cemetery even on the strongest evidence of the existence of a rich goldfield under it, and backed by the influence of a number of diggers and their backers – which last was what Dave wished for least of all. He wanted, above all things, to keep the thing shady. Then, again, the old clannish local spirit of the old farming town, rooted in years way back of the goldfields, would have been too strong for the Government, or even a rush of wild diggers.

'We'll work this thing on the strict Q.T.,' said Dave.

He and Jim had a consultation by the campfire outside their tent. Jim grumbled, in conclusion: 'Well, then, best go under Jimmy Middleton. It's the shortest and straightest, and Jimmy's the freshest, anyway.'

Then there was another trouble. How were they to account for the size of the waste-heap of clay on the surface which would be the result of such an extraordinary length of drive or tunnel for shallow sinkings? Dave had an idea of carrying some of the dirt away by night and putting it down a deserted shaft close by; but that would double the labour, and might lead to detection sooner than anything else. There were boys possum hunting on those flats every night. Then Dave got an idea.

There was supposed to exist – and it has since been proved – another, a second gold-bearing alluvial bottom on that field, and several had tried for it. One, the town watchmaker, had sunk all his money in 'duffers', trying for the second bottom. It was supposed to exist at a depth of from eighty to a hundred feet – on solid rock, I suppose. This watchmaker, an Italian, would put men on to sink, and superintend in person, and whenever he came to a little colour –

showing shelf, or false bottom, thirty or forty feet down – he'd go rooting round and spoil the shaft, and then start to sink another. It was extraordinary that he hadn't the sense to sink straight down, thoroughly test the second bottom, and if he found no gold there, to fill the shaft up to the other bottoms, or build platforms at the proper level and then explore them. He was living in a lunatic asylum the last time I heard of him. And the last time I heard from that field, they were boring the ground like a sieve, with the latest machinery, to find the best place to put down a deep shaft, and finding gold from the second bottom on the bore. But I'm right off the line again.

Old Pinter, Ballarat digger – his theory on second and other bottoms ran as follows:

'Ye see *this* here grass surface – this here surface with trees an' grass on it, that we're livin' on, has got nothin' to do with us. This here bottom in the shaller sinkin's that we're workin' on is the slope to the bed of the *new* crick that was on the surface about the time that men was missin' links. The false bottoms, thirty or forty feet down, kin be said to have been on the surface about the time that men was monkeys. The *secon'* bottom – eighty or a hundred feet down – was on the surface about the time when men was frogs. Now –'

But it's with the missing-link surface we have to do, and had the friends of the local departed known what Dave and Jim were up to they would have regarded them as something lower than missing links.

'We'll give out we're tryin' for the second bottom,' said Dave Regan. 'We'll have to rig a fan for air, anyhow, and you don't want air in shallow sinkings.'

'And someone will come poking round, and look down the hole and see the bottom,' said Jim Bently.

'We must keep 'em away,' said Dave. 'Tar the bottom, or cover it with tarred canvas, to make it black. Then they won't see it. There's not many diggers left, and the rest are going; they're chucking up the claims in Log Paddock. Besides, I could get drunk and pick rows with the rest and they wouldn't come near me. The farmers ain't in love with us diggers, so they won't bother us. No man has a right to come poking round another man's claim: it ain't ettykit – I'll root up that old ettykit and stand to it – it's rather worn out now, but that's no matter. We'll shift the tent down near the claim and see that no one comes nosing round on Sunday. They'll think we're only some more second-bottom lunatics, like Francea [the mining watchmaker]. We're going to get our fortune out from under that old graveyard, Jim. You leave it all to me till you're born again with brains.'

Dave's schemes were always elaborate, and that was why they so often came to the ground. He logged up his windlass platform a little higher, bent about eighty feet of rope to the bole of the windlass, which was a new one, and thereafter, whenever a suspicious-looking party (that is to say, a digger) hove in sight, Dave would let down about forty feet of rope and then wind, with simulated exertion, until the slack was taken up and the rope lifted the bucket from the shallow bottom.

'It would look better to have a whip-pole and a horse, but we can't afford them just yet,' said Dave.

But I'm a little behind. They drove straight in under the cemetery, finding

'*no man has a right
to come poking round
another man's claim:
it ain't ettykit – I'll
root up that old ettykit
and stand to it – it's
rather worn out now,
but that's no matter.*'

good wash all the way. The edge of Jimmy Middleton's box appeared in the top corner of the 'face' (the working end) of the drive. They went under the butt-end of the grave. They shoved up the end of the shell with a prop, to prevent the possibility of an accident which might disturb the mound above; they puddled – i.e. rammed – stiff clay up round the edges to keep the loose earth from dribbling down; and having given the bottom of the coffin a good coat of tar, they got over, or rather under, and unpleasant matter.

Jim Bently smoked and burnt paper during his shift below, and grumbled a good deal. 'Blowed if I ever thought I'd be rooting for gold down among the blanky dead men,' he said. But the dirt panned out better every dish they washed, and Dave worked the 'wash' out right and left as they drove.

But, one fine morning, who should come along but the very last man whom Dave wished to see round there – Old Pinter (James Poynton), Californian and Victorian digger of the old school. He'd been prospecting down the creek, carried his pick over his shoulder – threaded through the eye in the heft of his big-bladed, short-handled shovel that hung behind – and his gold-dish under his arm.

''Ello, Dave!' said Pinter, after looking with mild surprise at the size of Dave's waste-heap. 'Tryin' for the second bottom?'

'Yes,' said Dave, guttural.

Pinter dropped his tools with a clatter at the foot of the waste-heap and scratched under his ear like an old cockatoo, which bird he resembled. Then he went to the windlass, and resting his hands on his knees, he peered down, while Dave stood by helpless and hopeless.

Pinter straightened himself, blinking like an owl, and looked carelessly over the graveyard.

'Tryin' for a secon' bottom,' he reflected absently. 'Eh, Dave?'

Dave only stood and looked black.

Pinter tilted back his head and scratched the roots of his chin-feathers, which stuck out all round like a dirty, ragged fan held horizontally.

'Kullers is safe,' reflected Pinter.

'All right,' snapped Dave. 'I suppose we must let him into it.'

Kullers was a big American buck nigger, and had been Pinter's mate for some time – Pinter was a man of odd mates; and what Pinter meant was that Kullers was safe to hold his tongue.

Next morning Pinter and his coloured mate appeared on the ground early, Pinter with some tools and the nigger with a windlass-bole on his shoulders. Pinter chose a spot about three panels or thirty feet along the other fence, the back fence of the cemetery, and started his hole. He lost no time for the sake of appearances; he sunk his shaft and started to drive straight for the point under the cemetery for which Dave was making; he gave out that he had bottomed on good 'indications' running in the other direction, and would work the ground outside the fence. Meanwhile Dave rigged a fan – partly for the sake of appearances, but mainly because his and Jim's lively imaginations made the air in the drive worse than it really was.

Dave was working the ground on each side as he went, when one morning a thought struck him that should have struck him the day Pinter went to work.

He felt mad that it hadn't struck him sooner.

Pinter and Kullers had also shifted their tent down into a nice quiet place in the bush close handy; so, early next Sunday morning, while Pinter and Kullers where asleep, Dave posted Jim Bently to watch their tent, and whistle an alarm if they stirred, and then dropped down into Pinter's hole and saw at a glance what he was up to.

After that Dave lost no time; he drove straight on, encouraged by the thuds of Pinter's and Kullers' picks drawing nearer. They would strike his tunnel at right angles. Both parties worked long hours, only knocking off to fry a bit of steak in the pan, boil the billy, and throw themselves dressed on their bunks to get a few hours' sleep. Pinter had practical experience and a line clear of graves, and he made good time. The two parties now found it more comfortable to be not on speaking terms. Individually they grew furtive, and began to feel criminal like – at least Dave and Jim did. They'd start if a horse stumbled through the bush, and expected to see a mounted policeman ride up at any moment and hear him ask questions. They had driven about thirty-five feet when, one Saturday afternoon, the strain became too great, and Dave and Jim got drunk. The spree lasted over Sunday, and on Monday morning they felt too shaky to come to work, and had more drink. On Monday afternoon, Kullers, whose shift it was below, struck his pick through the face of his drive into the wall of Dave's, about four feet from the end of it: the clay flaked away, leaving a hole as big as a wash-hand basin. They knocked off for the day and decided to let the other

party take the offensive.

Tuesday morning Dave and Jim came to work, still feeling shaky. Jim went below, crawled along the drive, lit his candle, and stuck it in the spiked iron socket and the spike in the wall of the drive, quite close to the hold, without noticing either the hole or the increased freshness of the air. He started picking away at the face and scraping the clay back from under his feet, and didn't hear Kullers come to work. Kullers came in softly and decided to try a bit of cheerful bluff. He stuck his great round black face through the hole, the whites of his eyes rolling horribly in the candlelight, and said, with a deep guffaw: ''Ullo! you dar'!'

No bandicoot ever went into his hole with the dogs after him quicker than Jim came out of his. He scrambled up the shaft by the foot-holes, and sat on the edge of the waste-heap, looking very pale.

'What's the matter?' asked Dave. 'Have you seen a ghost?'

'I've seen the – the devil!' gasped Jim. 'I'm – I'm done with this here ghoul business.'

The parties got on speaking terms again. Dave was very warm, but Jim's language was worse. Pinter scratched his chin-feathers reflectively till the other party cooled. There was no appealing to the commissioner for goldfields; they were outside all law, whether of the goldfields or otherwise – so they did the only thing possible and sensible, they joined forces and became 'Poynton, Regan & Party'. They agreed to work the ground from the separate shafts, and decided to go ahead, irrespective of appearances, and get as much dirt out and cradled as possible before the inevitable exposure came along. They found plenty of payable dirt, and soon the drive ended in a cluster of roomy chambers. They timbered up many coffins of various ages, burnt tarred canvas and brown paper, and kept the fan going. Outside they paid the storekeeper with difficulty and talked of hard times.

But one fine sunny morning, after about a week of partnership, they got a bad scare. Jim and Kullers were below, getting out dirt for all they were worth, and Pinter and Dave at their windlasses, when who should march down from the cemetery gate but Mother Middleton herself. She was a hard woman to look at. She still wore the old-fashioned crinoline and her hair in a greasy net; and on this as on most other sober occasions she wore the expression of a rough Irish navvy who has had just enough drink to make him nasty, and is looking out for an excuse for a row. She had a stride like a grenadier. A digger had once measured her step by her footprints in the mud where she had stepped across a gutter: it measured three feet from toe to heel.

She marched to the grave of Jimmy Middleton, laid a dingy bunch of flowers thereon, with the gesture of an angry man banging his fist down on the table, turned on her heel, and marched out. The diggers were dirt beneath her feet. Presently they heard her drive on in her spring-cart on her way into town, and they drew breaths of relief.

It was afternoon. Dave and Pinter were feeling tired, and were just deciding to knock off work for that day when they heard a scuffling in the direction of the different shafts, and both Jim and Kullers dropped down and bundled in a great hurry. Jim chuckled in a silly way, as if there was something funny, and Kullers

'THEY found plenty of payable dirt, and soon the drive ended in a cluster of roomy chambers. They timbered up many coffins of various ages, burnt tarred canvas and brown paper, and kept the fan going.'

guffawed in sympathy.

'What's up now?' demanded Dave apprehensively.

'Mother Middleton,' said Jim; 'she's blind mad drunk, and she's got a bottle in one hand and a new pitchfork in the other, that she's bringing out for someone.'

'How the hell did she drop to it?' exclaimed Pinter.

'Dunno,' said Jim. 'Anyway, she's coming for us. Listen to her!'

They didn't have to listen hard. The language which came down the shaft – they weren't sure which one – and along the drives was enough to scare up the dead and make them take to the bush.

'Why didn't you fools make off into the bush and give us a chance, instead of giving her a lead here?' asked Dave.

Jim and Kullers began to wish they had done so.

Mrs Middleton began to throw stones down the shaft – it was Pinter's – and they, even the oldest and most anxious, began to grin in spite of themselves, for they knew she couldn't hurt them from the surface, and that, though she had been a working digger herself, she couldn't fill both shafts before the fumes of liquor overtook her.

'I wonder which shaf' she'll come down,' asked Kullers in a tone befitting the place and occasion.

'You'd better go and watch your shaft, Pinter,' said Dave, 'and Jim and I'll watch mine.'

'I – I won't,' said Pinter hurriedly. 'I'm – I'm a modest man.'

Then they heard a clang in the direction of Pinter's shaft.

'She's thrown her bottle down,' said Dave.

Jim crawled along the drive a piece, urged by curiosity, and returned hurriedly.

'She's broke the pitchfork off short, to use in the drive, and I believe she's coming down.'

'Her crinoline'll handicap her,' said Pinter vacantly. 'That's a comfort.'

'She's took it off!' said Dave excitedly; and peering along Pinter's drive, they saw first an elastic-sided boot, then a red-striped stocking, then a section of a scarlet petticoat.

'Lemme out!' roared Pinter, lurching forward and making a swimming motion with this hands in the direction of Dave's drive. Kullers was already gone and Jim well on the way. Dave, lanky and awkward, scrambled up the shaft last. Mrs Middleton made good time, considering she had the darkness to face and didn't know the workings, and when Dave reached the top he had a tear in the leg of his moleskins, and the blood ran from a nasty scratch. But he didn't wait to argue over the price of a new pair of trousers. He made off through the bush in the direction of an encouraging whistle thrown back by Jim.

'She's too drunk to get her story listened to tonight,' said Dave. 'But tomorrow she'll bring the neighbourhood down on us.'

'And she's enough, without the neighbourhood,' reflected Pinter.

Some time after dark they returned cautiously, reconnoitred their camp, and after hiding in a hollow log such things as they couldn't carry, they rolled up their tents like the Arabs, and silently stole away.

CRANKY JACK

STEELE RUDD
1868–1935

I T was early in the day. Traveller after traveller was trudging by Shingle Hut. One who carried no swag halted at the rails and came in. He asked Dad for a job. 'I dunno,' Dad answered. 'What wages would you want?' The man said he wouldn't want any. Dad engaged him at once.

And *such* a man! Tall, bony, heavy-jawed, shaven with a reaping-hook, apparently. He had a thick crop of black hair, shaggy, unkempt, and full of grease, grass, and fragments of dry gum leaves. On his head were two old felt hats, one sewn inside the other. On his back a shirt made from a piece of blue blanket, with white cotton stitches striding up and down it like lines of fencing. His trousers were gloom itself; they were a problem, and bore reliable evidence of his industry. No ordinary person would consider himself out of work while in them. And the newcomer was no ordinary person. He seemed to have all the woe of the world upon him. He was as sad and weird-looking as a widow out in the wet.

In the yard was a large heap of firewood – remarkable truth! – which Dad told him to chop up. He began. And how he worked! The axe rang again – particularly when it left the handle – and pieces of wood scattered everywhere. Dad watched him chopping for a while, then went with Dave to pull corn.

For hours the man chopped away without once looking at the sun. Mother came out. Joy! She had never seen so much wood cut before. She was delighted. She made a cup of tea and took it to the man, and apologised for having no sugar to put in it. He paid no attention to her; he worked harder. Mother waited, holding the tea in her hand. A lump of wood nearly as big as a shingle flew up and shaved her left ear. She put the tea on the ground and went in search of eggs for dinner. (We were out of meat – the kangaroo-dog was lame. He had got ripped the last time we killed.)

The tea remained on the ground. Chips fell into it. The dog saw it. He limped towards it eagerly, and dipped the point of his nose in it. It burnt him. An aged rooster strutted along and looked sideways at it. *He* distrusted it and went away. It attracted the pig, a sow with nine young ones. She waddled up, and poked the cup over with her nose; then she sat down on it, while the family joyously gathered round the saucer. Still the man chopped on.

Mother returned – without any eggs. She rescued the crockery from the pigs and turned curiously to the man. She said, 'Why, you've let them take the tea!' No answer. She wondered.

Suddenly, and for the fiftieth time, the axe flew off. The man held the handle and stared at the woodheap. Mother watched him. He removed his hats, and looked inside them. He remained looking inside them.

Mother watched him more closely. His lips moved. He said, '*Listen to them! They're coming! I knew they'd follow!*'

'Who?' asked Mother, trembling slightly.

'*They're in the wood!*' he went on. 'Ha, ha! I've got them. They'll never get out, *never get out!*'

Mother fled, screaming. She ran inside and called the children. Sal assisted her. They trooped in like wallabies, all but Joe. He was away earning money. He was getting a shilling a week from Maloney for chasing cockatoos from the corn.

They closed and barricaded the doors, and Sal took down the gun, which Mother made her hide beneath the bed. They sat listening, anxiously and intently. The wind began to rise. A lump of soot fell from the chimney into the fireplace, where there was no fire. Mother shuddered. Some more fell. Mother jumped to her feet. So did Sal. They looked at each other in dismay. The children began to cry. The chain for hanging the kettle on started swinging to and fro. Mother's knees gave way. The chain continued swinging. A pair of bare legs came down into the fireplace. They were curled round the chain. Mother collapsed. Sal screamed, and ran to the door, but couldn't open it. The legs left the chain and dangled in the air. Sal called, 'Murder!'

Her cry was answered. It was Joe, who had been over at Maloney's making his fortune. He came to the rescue. He dropped out of the chimney and shook himself. Sal stared at him. He was calm and covered from head to foot with soot and dirt. He looked round and said, 'Thought yuz could keep me out, didn'y'?' Sal could only look at him. 'I saw yuz all run in,' he was saying, when Sal thought of Mother, and sprang to her. Sal shook her, and slapped her, and threw water on her till she sat up and stared about. Then Joe stared.

Dad came in for dinner, which, of course, wasn't ready. Mother began to cry, and asked him what he meant by keeping a madman on the place, and told him she *knew* he wanted to have them all murdered. Dad didn't understand. Sal explained. Then he went out and said to the man, 'Clear!'

The man simply said, 'No.'

'Go on, now!' Dad said, pointing to the rails. The man smiled at the woodheap as he worked. Dad waited. 'Aren't y' going?' he repeated.

'Leave me alone when I'm chopping wood for the missus,' the man answered, then smiled and muttered to himself. Dad left him alone and were inside wondering.

Next day Mother and Dad were talking at the barn. Mother, bare-headed, was holding some eggs in her apron. Dad was leaning on a hoe.

'I *am* afraid of him,' Mother said. 'It's not right you should keep him about the place. No one's safe with such a man. Some day he'll take it in his head to kill us all, and then –'

'Tut, tut, woman. Poor old Jack! He's harmless as a baby.'

'All right,' sullenly. 'You'll see!'

Dad laughed and went away with the hoe on his shoulder to cut burr.

Middle of summer. Dad and Dave in the paddock mowing lucerne. Jack sinking post-holes for a milking-yard close to the house. Joe at intervals stealing behind him to prick him with straws through a rent in the rear of his patched moleskins. Little Bill, in readiness to run, standing off, enjoying the sport.

Inside the house sat Mother and Sal, sewing and talking of Maloney's new baby.

'Dear me,' said Mother, 'it's the tiniest mite of a thing I ever saw. Why, bless me, any one of y' at its age would have made three of –'

'*Mind*, Mother!' Sal shrieked, jumping up on the sofa. Mother screamed and mounted the table. Both gasped for breath, and leaning cautiously over peeped down at a big black snake which had glided in at the front door. Then, pale and scared-looking, they stared across at each other.

The snake crawled over to the safe and drank up some milk which had been spilt on the floor. Mother saw its full length and groaned. The snake wriggled to the leg of the table.

'Look out!' cried Sal, gathering up her skirts and dancing about on the sofa.

Mother squealed hysterically.

Joe appeared. He laughed.

'You wretch!' Mother yelled. 'Run, *run*, and fetch your father!'

Joe went and brought Jack.

'Oh-h, my God!' Mother moaned, as Jack stood at the door staring strangely at her. 'Kill it! Why don't he *kill* it?'

Jack didn't move, but talked to himself. Mother shuddered.

The reptile crawled to the bedroom door. Then for the first time the man's eyes rested upon it. It glided into the bedroom, and Mother and Sal ran off for Dad.

Jack fixed his eyes on the snake and continued muttering to himself. Several times it made an attempt to mount the dressing-table. Finally it succeeded. Suddenly Jack's demeanour changed. He threw off his ragged hat and talked wildly. A fearful expression filled his ugly features. His voice altered.

'You're the Devil!' he said. 'The *Devil*! The DEVIL! The missus brought you – ah-h-h!'

The snake's head passed behind the looking-glass. Jack drew nearer, clenching his fists and gesticulating. As he did he came full before the looking-glass and saw, perhaps for the first time in his life, his own image. An unearthly howl came from him. '*Me father!*' he shouted, and bolted from the house.

Dad came in with the long-handled shovel, swung it about the room, and smashed pieces off the cradle, and tore the bed-curtains down, and made a great noise altogether. Finally, he killed the snake and put it on the fire, and Joe and the cat watched it wriggle on the hot coals.

Meanwhile, Jack, bare-headed, rushed across the yard. He ran over Little Bill, and tumbled through the wire fence on to the broad of his back. He roared like a wild beast, clutched at space, spat, and kicked his heels in the air.

'Let me up! *Ah-h-h!* Let go me throat!' he hissed.

The dog ran over and barked at him. He found his feet again, and, making off, ran through the wheat, glancing back over his shoulder as he tore along. He crossed into the grass paddock, and running to a big tree dodged round and round it. Then from tree to tree he went, and that evening at sundown, when Joe was bringing the cows home, Jack was still flying from his father.

After supper.

'I wonder now what the old fool saw in the snake to send him off his head like that?' Dad said, gazing wonderingly into the fire. 'He sees plenty of them, goodness knows.'

'That wasn't it. It wasn't the snake at all,' Mother said. 'There was madness in the man's eyes all the while. I saw it the moment he came to the door.' She appealed to Sal.

'Nonsense!' said Dad. '*Nonsense!*' And he tried to laugh.

'Oh, of course it's *nonsense*,' Mother went on. 'Everything I say is nonsense. It won't be nonsense when you come home some day and find us all on the floor with our throats cut.'

'Pshaw!' Dad answered. 'What's the use of talking like that?' Then to Dave, 'Go out and see if he's in the barn.'

Dave fidgeted. He didn't like the idea. Joe giggled.

'Surely you're not *frightened?*' Dad shouted.

Dave coloured up.

'No – don't think so,' he said, and, after a pause, '*You* go and see.'

It was Dad's turn to feel uneasy. He pretended to straighten the fire and coughed several times. 'Perhaps it's just as well,' he said, 'to let him be tonight.'

Of course Dad wasn't afraid. He *said* he wasn't. But he drove the pegs in the doors and windows before going to bed that night.

Next morning Dad said to Dave and Joe, 'Come 'long, and we'll see where he's got to.'

In a gully at the back of the grass-paddock they found him. He was ploughing – sitting astride the highest limb of a fallen tree – and, in a hoarse voice and strange, was calling out, 'Gee, Captain! Come here, Tidy! *Wa-ay!*'

'Blowed if I know,' Dad muttered, coming to a standstill. 'Wonder if he *is* clean mad?'

Dave was speechless, and Joe began to tremble.

They listened. And as the man's voice rang out in the quiet gully and the echoes rumbled round the ridge and the affrighted birds flew up the place felt eerie somehow.

'It's no use bein' afraid of him,' Dad went on. 'We must go and bounce him, that's all.' But there was a tremor in Dad's voice which Dave didn't like.

'See if he knows us, anyway.' And Dad shouted, '*Hey-y!*'

Jack looked up and immediately scrambled from the limb. That was enough for Dave. He turned and made tracks. So did Dad and Joe. They ran. No one could have run harder. Terror overcame Joe. He squealed and grabbed hold of Dad's shirt, which was ballooning in the wind.

'Let go!' Dad gasped. '*Damn* y', let me *go!*' – trying to shake him off. But Joe had great faith in his parent, and clung to him closely.

When they had covered a hundred yards or so, Dave glanced back, and, seeing that Jack wasn't pursuing them, stopped and chuckled at the others.

'Eh?' Dad said, completely winded. 'Eh?' Then to Dave, when he got some breath, 'Well, you *are* an ass of a fellow – *puff*. What the devil did *you* run f'?'

'What did *I* run f'? What did *you* run f'?'

'Bah!' And Dad boldly led the way back.

'Now look here' – turning fiercely upon Joe – 'don't you come catching hold of me again, or if y' *do* I'll knock y'r damned head off! Clear home altogether, and get under the bed if y're as frightened as *that*.'

Joe slunk behind.

But when Dad *did* approach Jack, which wasn't until he had talked a great deal to him across a big log, the latter didn't show any desire to take life, but allowed himself to be escorted home and locked in the barn quietly enough.

Dad kept Jack confined in the barn several days, and if anyone approached the door or the cracks he would ask, 'Is me father there yet?'

'Your father's dead and buried long ago, man,' Dad used to tell him.

'Yes,' he would say, 'but he's alive again. The missus keeps him in there' –

indicating the house.

And sometimes when Dad was not about Joe would put his mouth to a crack and say, 'Here's y'r *father*, Jack!'

Then, like a caged beast, the man would howl and tramp up and down, his eyes starting out of his head, while Joe would bolt inside and say to Mother, 'Jack's getting out', and nearly send her to her grave.

But one day Jack *did* get out, and while Mother and Sal were ironing came to the door with the axe on his shoulder.

They dropped the irons and shrank into a corner and cowered piteously – too scared even to cry out.

He took no notice of them, but, moving stealthily on tiptoes, approached the bedroom door and peeped in. He paused just a moment to grip the axe with both hands. Then with a howl and a bound he entered the room and shattered the looking-glass into fragments.

He bent down and looked closely at the pieces.

'He's dead now,' he said calmly, and walked out. Then he went to work at the post-holes again, just as though nothing had happened.

The man stayed on at Shingle Hut. He was the best horse Dad ever had. He slaved from daylight till dark, kept no Sunday, knew no companion, lived chiefly on meat and machine oil, domiciled in the barn, and never asked for a rise in his wages. His name we never knew. We called him 'Jack'. The neighbours called him '*Cranky* Jack'.

THE BATHE
A Grotesque

HENRY HANDEL
RICHARDSON
1870–1946

STRIPPED of her clothing, the child showed the lovely shape of a six-year-old. Just past the dimpled roundnesses of babyhood, the little body stood slim and straight, legs and knees closely met, the skin white as the sand into which the small feet dug, pink toe faultlessly matched to toe.

She was going to bathe.

The tide was out. The alarming, ferocious surf, which at flood came hurtling over the reef, swallowing up the beach, had withdrawn, baring the flat brown coral rocks: far off against their steep brown edges it sucked and gurgled lazily. In retreating, it had left many lovely pools in the reef, all clear as glass, some deep as rooms, grown round their sides with weeds that swam like drowned hair, and hid strange sea-things.

Not to these pools might the child go; nor did she need to prick her soles on the coral. Her bathing-place was a great sandy-bottomed pool that ran out from the beach, and as its deepest came no higher than her chin.

Naked to sun and air, she skipped and frolicked with the delight of the very young, to whom clothes are still an encumbrance. And one of her runs led her headlong into the sea. No toe-dipping tests were necessary here; this water met the skin like a veil of warm silk. In it she splashed and ducked and floated; her hair, which had been screwed into a tight little knob, loosening and floating with her like a nimbus. Tired of play, she came out, trickling and glistening, and lay down in the sand, which was hot to the touch, first on her stomach, then on her back, till she was coated with sand like a fish breadcrumbed for frying. This, for the sheer pleasure of plunging anew, and letting the silken water wash her clean.

At the sight, the two middle-aged women who sat looking on grew restless. And, the prank being repeated, the sand-caked little body vanishing in the limpid water to bob up shining like ivory, the tips of their tongues shot out and surreptitiously moistened their lips. These were dry, their throats were dry, their skins itched; their seats burnt from pressing the hot sand.

And suddenly eyes met and brows were lifted in a silent question. Shall we? Dare we risk it?

'Let's!'

For no living thing but themselves moved on the miles of desolate beach; not a neighbour was within cooee; their own shack lay hid behind a hill.

Straightway they fell to rolling up their work and stabbing it with their needles.

Then they, too, undressed.

Tight, high bodices of countless buttons went first, baring the massy arms and fat-creased necks of a plump maturity. Thereafter bunchy skirts were slid over hips and stepped out of. Several petticoats followed, the undermost of red flannel, with scalloped edges. Tight stiff corsets were next squeezed from their

moorings and cast aside: the linen beneath lay hot and damply crushed. Long white drawers unbound and, leg by leg, disengaged, voluminous calico chemises appeared, draped in which the pair sat down to take off their boots – buttoned boots – and stockings, their feet emerging red and tired-looking, the toes misshapen, and horny with callosities. Erect again, they yet coyly hesitated before the casting of the last veil, once more sweeping the distance for a possible spy. Nothing stirring, however, up went their arms, dragging the balloon-like garments with them; and, inch by inch, calves, thighs, trunks and breasts were bared to view.

At the prospect of getting water playmates, the child had clapped her hands, hopping up and down where she stood. But this was the first time she had watched a real grown-up undress; she was always in bed and asleep when they did it. Now, in broad daylight, she looked on unrebuked, wildly curious; and surprise soon damped her joy. So this was what was underneath! Skirts and petticoats down, she saw that laps were really legs; while the soft and cosy place you put your head on, when you were tired. . . .

And suddenly she turned tail and ran back to the pool. She didn't want to see.

But your face was the one bit of you you couldn't put under water. So she had to.

Two fat, stark-naked figures were coming down the beach.

They had joined hands, as if to sustain each other in their nudity ... or as if, in shedding their clothes, they had also shed a portion of their years. Gingerly, yet in haste to reach cover, they applied their soles to the tickly sand: a haste that caused unwieldy breasts to bob and swing, bellies and buttocks to wobble. Splay-legged they were, from the weight of these protuberances. Above their knees, garters had cut fierce red lines in the skin; their bodies were criss-crossed with red furrows, from the variety of strings and bones that had lashed them in. The calves of one showed purple-knotted with veins; across the other's abdomen ran a deep, longitudinal scar. One was patched with red hair, one with black.

In a kind of horrid fascination the child stood and stared ... as at two wild outlandish beasts. But before they reached her she again turned, and, heedless of the prickles, ran seawards, out on the reef.

This was forbidden. There were shrill cries of: 'Naughty girl! Come back!'

Draggingly the child obeyed.

They were waiting for her, and, blind to her hurt, took her between them and waded into the water. When this was up to their knees, they stooped to damp napes and crowns, and sluice their arms. Then they played. They splashed water at each other's great backsides; they lay down and, propped on their elbows, let their legs float; or, forming a ring, moved heavily round to the tune of: *Ring-a-ring-a-rosy, pop down a posy!* And down the child went, till she all but sat on the sand. Not so they. Even with the support of the water they could bend but a few inches; and wider than ever did their legs splay, to permit of their corpulences being lowered.

But the sun was nearing meridian in a cloudless sky. Its rays burnt and stung. The child was sent running up the beach to the clothes-heaps, and returned, not unlike a depressed Amor, bearing in each hand a wide, flower-trimmed, Dolly Varden hat, the ribbons of which trailed the sand.

These they perched on their heads, binding the ribbons under their chins; and thus attired waded out to the deep end of the pool. Here, where the water came a few inches above their waists, they stood to cool off, their breasts seeming to float on the surface like half-inflated toy balloons. And when the sand stirred up by their feet had subsided, their legs could be seen through the translucent water oddly foreshortened, with edges that frayed at each ripple.

But a line of foam had shown its teeth at the edge of the reef. The tide was on the turn; it was time to go.

Waddling up the beach they spread their petticoats, and on these stretched themselves out to dry. And as they lay there on their sides, with the supreme mass of hip and buttock arching in the air, their contours were those of seals – great mother-seals come lolloping out of the water to lie about on the sand.

The child had found a piece of dry cuttlefish, and sat pretending to play with it. But she wasn't really. Something had happened which made her not like any more to play. Something ugly. Oh, never ... never ... no, not ever now did she want to grow up. *She* would always stop a little girl.

TREASON

KATHARINE
SUSANNAH
PRICHARD
1883–1969

THERE was a couple of drovers used to come through our place, brothers, six feet both of them, great hairy fellows, strong as their own bullocks, and soft-hearted as children; but demons when they were drunk.

Nobody knew which was the elder, Ben or Bully. They might have been twins. We had been three years trying to grow wheat round Shallow Lakes when a woman came through with them.

A big-boned, hard-featured woman she was. The sun had bleached her hair to the colour of dry grass, her skin was wind-dried and tough; but her eyes fixed her in your mind. You would not forget her if you had seen her tailing the cattle; had stopped to speak to her, and she raised her eyes to your face. Clear grey, steady, far-seeing eyes they were, and gave you straight the sort of woman she was: just woman, downright and honest, and Bull Murty's mate.

She may not have looked like that always. She had been four or five months on the road when we saw her first, and the life of the road is a hard one. Few women could stand it. No woman I ever knew took to it as Mrs Murty did. She seemed to like it, and made no friends among women in the townships, when Ben and Bully were in to deliver a mob at saleyards.

She was always to be seen pottering about the horses, or the buckboard, in an empty paddock near the yard, if Ben or Bully were in Shallow Lakes. While they were under the weather at Tibby's, she drove the horses down to the tank in the evening, riding a good-looking old chestnut stock horse bareback, with one hand on his mane. As often as not she saw to reloading the carry-all, too. But whatever she was doing, whenever you saw her, she had a look of quiet content on her face. It was there when the buckboard jolted out of the town on a three-hundred-mile journey, north or west; and it was there when you saw her trudging behind the cart, and a mob of jaded cattle, into the town again.

Neither Ben nor Bully had much to say on the road. They scarcely spoke, except to curse the cattle or horses; but after the advent of Mrs Murty, Bully became quite communicative when he reached a homestead. With the air of a family man, he gave news of the weather, state of the country, births, deaths, and marriages, both likely and unlikely, in districts he had passed through. Ben had less than ever to say for himself or anybody.

People said Ben did not like Mrs Murty; he bore her a grudge for marrying Bully and going on the road with him. The brothers had been droving together for ten years when Mrs Murty joined them.

They had been nearly three months out, when we met them on the plains, bound for Shallow Lakes, one day at the end of the winter.

The mob, Ben and Bully on their rusty horses, the buckboard and Mrs Murty trailing behind the cattle, were the only creatures moving under the bare, blue sky, except ourselves, our horses, and a couple of crows flecking the sky in the distance.

'CLEAR grey, steady, far-seeing eyes they were, and gave you straight the sort of, woman she was: just woman, downright and honest, and Bull Murty's mate.'

I had often seen Mrs Murty walking like that behind the cattle, as they moved slowly, feeding – if there was anything to feed on by the stock routes – or following just behind, if the cattle were crawling in a cloud of dust, her eyes on the far horizon of the plains, northward, or on the dim outline of low hills to the south. But this day, when she smiled by way of greeting, her eyes were shining; there was a smiling in them like light in the sky at dawn.

When Ben and Bully came into Shallow Lakes with a mob of five hundred store bullocks, a few months later, Mrs Murty was sitting in the buckboard with a baby in her arms.

That night Ben and Bully went on a spree in the township. It was a record even in the annals of their sprees. You could hear them yelling and singing in Tibby's bar from any of the score of tin-roofed huts and stores which composed Shallow Lakes' hamlet. Their great laughter, and the noise of their voices, reached Mrs Murty where she sat in the back of the cart in a paddock near the saleyards, nursing her baby, and looking over the dark earth and the star-flung sweep of night sky; but it did not disturb her.

Ben and Bully's celebration disturbed no one in Shallow Lakes except Mr John Wiley, and he was new to the district. Almost every able-bodied male drank with Ben and Bully, and those who did not drink sympathised with them.

Mr Wiley had, perhaps, an exalted idea of his importance as preserver of law and order in Shallow Lakes. It was said that he had come from a down-south, quiet, suburban district for the good of his health, and Shallow Lakes believed it.

At any rate, after Bully broke a window at Tibby's, and Ben had sent a couple of bottles and three or four glasses through the gap to test his marksmanship, the pair of them were brawling pleasantly about the result on the road outside the pub, when Mr Wiley stalked up to Bull Murty and put his hand on the sleeve of Bully's shirt.

'You come along with me,' he said.

Bully overlooked him. Wiley was a sharp-faced little man, with plenty of courage, and some opinion of the moral effect of his uniform. Bully's arm swung out. He felled the policeman with a blow, and stood over him, six foot of drunken, swaying giant.

'Here, Ben,' he called, thickly, 'lend us your pocket-knife while I ear-mark this cow, so's we'll know him again.'

Next morning, when Wiley recovered consciousness, and his wounds and vanity were smarting, Pat Rusden, the saddler, who lived next door to Wiley's, asked the policeman what on earth he had said, or done, to rile Bully Murty, and bring that mighty left of Bull's upon him.

'I was arresting him,' John Wiley began, indignantly, 'and ...'

'Arresting Bull Murty?' the saddler gasped. 'What for, in the name-er-blazes, were you doin' that?'

'He was drunk and ...'

'Drunk and disorderly,' Pat scoffed. 'He was wettin' his baby's head, man. That's what he was doin'. He's got a son, and if that's not something for Bully to go on the bust over, I'd like to know what is.'

He was a son to go on the bust over, too, Bully's kid, as it turned out. You wondered how such a child came to two ordinary, plain people like Bull Murty and his wife. When he could walk, you would see William Ben trotting beside his mother behind the cattle on the plains, or playing near her round the buckboard, when the drovers were halted at a station or in town.

He had a mop of curly hair, William Ben; all the fire from his mother's hair seemed to have drifted into his. It was bright, as the gold in creek sand, and his eyes were brown like Bully's, and Ben's. The blood bloomed under his clear skin, soon as tanned as his mother's; his lips were fresh and red. It was not often an up-country child had so much colour. That was why, perhaps, people talked so much about him.

Bully was proud of his son. Mrs Murty looked at him much as a lioness does her cub, her eyes licking him over with maternal tenderness. But Ben, you never saw anything like the worship and reverence in his eyes for that youngster. Yet he was so dumb and undemonstrative about it that some of the countryside busybodies declared Ben regarded Bully's kid as just another of Mrs Murty's offences against the old partnership.

Their ability to travel cattle with any men in the north-west, and the years they had been at the game, brought Ben and Bully all the business they wanted. It was said they were doing so well that presently they would be buying a crib for Mrs Murty and the kid; but in the meantime there was the buckboard. Mrs Murty and William Ben went wherever Ben and Bully were droving.

'The road's good enough for me,' Mrs Murty said. 'And it'll be good enough for William Ben.'

Everywhere they went, the talk was of Bully's kid: what a fine little chap he was, and how quickly he grew. When strangers said anything to Bully about his son, his pride would swell and utter itself, always in the same words:

'Got shoulders on him like a bullocky!'

It was when they were taking a big mob to the Hill for Baird's that the kid got sick. At first Bully and Mrs Murty did not take much notice of his ailing. They thought he had eaten something wrong, as he had done once or twice before, that was all. But Ben did not like this sickness. He watched William Ben when he did not eat, and listened anxiously beside him as he cried in his sleep. After three days, William Ben no longer trotted along beside his mother; but lay on the floor of the buckboard, limp and fretful, and a panic took Ben. They were a hundred miles from Shallow Lakes when he beat back to the doctor.

Ben returned with the doctor. There was a dazed expression on the faces of Bully and Mrs Murty. Ben did not speak to them. He could not ask what had happened. He had been away two nights and the better part of two days. He followed Bully's and Mrs Murty's eyes, saw their track in the sand; and went along the creek bank to where they had heaped the sand over William Ben.

We did not see anything of the Murtys for a long time after that. Once or twice I caught a glimpse of them, across the plains in the distance, the two men on their horses, the slowly-moving cattle, and the woman trudging along behind the buckboard. Wherever they went, the talk was still of the bright-haired youngster, who no longer wandered over the country with them. Everybody missed William Ben. Ben and Bully still went on sprees in the townships they passed through; and Mrs Murty, refusing all well-meaning and neighbourly overtures, stayed with the buckboard in the saleyard paddocks.

It was a couple of years later that I met Ben and Bully in the Hill. Their faces were mahogany coloured after a night at Mick Fisher's, where they had put away whisky enough for ten men, it was said.

After the usual greetings I inquired for Mrs Murty.

Bully beamed.

'She's fine,' he said. 'Come and see!'

He led the way to a stretch of open ground outside the town where, near some thorn bushes with yellow blossom, the buckboard stood. And there, sitting in the back of the cart, looking out to a dim green sky on which the first stars were glittering, sat Mrs Murty with a baby in her arms.

We went across to her, Bully as happy as a schoolboy, Ben slouching along silently. Mrs Murty and I talked over the baby. There was the same bare, animal satisfaction in her eyes, the same pride and joy in Bully's eyes that there had been for their first-born. I looked at Ben. His face was dull and sullen; his gaze smouldered on Mrs Murty with all the old resentment.

Was he thinking of William Ben, I wondered, and of the way sand blows along the dry creek beds up north, silting high under the trees and covering all tracks and landmarks on the banks?

Bully took the baby from his mother's arms.

'Got shoulders on him like a bullocky,' he said.

Ben's hand went out in a gesture of rage, blind and desperate. He stumbled away into the gathering darkness.

THE RAINBOW BIRD

VANCE PALMER
1885–1959

ALL afternoon as she bent over her slate, Maggie's mind had been filled with a vision of the bird. Blue-green shot with gold, its tail an arrow. Her hair fell over her intense, grape-dark eyes; she hardly knew what she was writing. It was the same every day now. The hands crawled down the cracked face of the clock with aggravating slowness; the teacher's voice droned on and on like a blowfly against the windowpane; the other children squirmed in their seats and folded paper darts to throw across the room. But all she lived for was the moment when she would again see the coloured shape skim from its cavern in the earth, making her catch her breath as if its wings had brushed across her heart.

As soon as school was out she flashed a look at Don, racing down to the bottom fence and along through the bushes that covered the side of the hill. Don was a little behind, limping because of his sore toe; flushed and breathless Maggie had reached the bottom of the gully before he emerged from the undergrowth. One stocking had fallen over her ankle and her hat was at the back of her neck, held by the elastic around her throat, but she cared for nothing but getting away.

From the bottom of the playground she could hear the other girls calling her.

'Wait on, Maggie! We're coming, too.'

She tried to shut their voices from her ears. None of them must find out her secret. She hated their empty faces, their coldly mocking eyes; they made fun of her because she carried beetles' wings and cowries about in her matchbox to stare at under the desk.

'Come on, Don,' she called back impatiently, 'they'll all be on us soon.'

He growled as he caught up with her.

'It's all right for you – you got boots on. This prickly grass hurts like blazes. Why didn't you go down the road?'

'This is nearly half a mile shorter. . . . Come on.'

They panted up the other hill and across a cleared paddock that lay between them and the beach. Before the eyes of both of them was the deep cleft left by the store truck when it was bogged months before, and the little round hole with a heap of sand in front of it. Such a tiny tunnel in the side of the rut that no one would notice unless he saw the bird fly out. They had come on it together when they were looking for mushrooms; there had been a sudden burr of wings almost beneath their feet, a shimmer of opal in the sunbright air, and then a stillness as the bird settled on the she-oak thirty yards away, making their hearts turn over with the sheer beauty of its bronze and luminous green.

A rainbow bird! And it had come from that rounded tunnel in the sandy earth where the couch grass was growing over the old rut. Don had wanted to put his hand in and feel if there were any young ones, but Maggie had caught his arm, her eyes desperate.

'No, don't! She's watching. She'll go away and never come back – never.'

She wanted just to stand and let her eyes have their fill. That stretch of cropped turf, with the she-oak on a sandy rise above the beach and the miraculous bird shining out of the greeny-grey branches! It was only rarely they surprised her in the nest, for she usually seemed to feel the pattering vibration of their feet along the ground and slip out unobserved. But they never had to look far for her. There in the she-oak she shone, flame-bright and radiant, as if she had just dropped from the blue sky. And sometimes they saw her mate skimming through the air after flies, taking long, sweeping curves and pausing at the top of the curve, a skater on wings, a maker of jewelled patterns, body light as thistledown, every feather blazing with fire and colour. The vision came back to Maggie each night before she closed her eyes in sleep. It belonged to a different world from the school, the dusty road, the yard behind the store that was filled with rusty tins and broken cases.

'That girl!' her mother said, hearing her mutter on the pillow. 'It's a bird now.'

They hurried across the road, past the spindle-legged house with no fence around it, past the red-roofed cottage where there were bathing-suits hung out to dry. Surely this afternoon the little birds would be out in front of the nest! The day before when they had lain with their ears close to the ground they had heard something thin but distinct, a cheeping and twittering. It had come to them through the warm earth, thrilling them with intense life. Those bits of living colour down there in the dark – how wonderful it would be when they came out into the light!

Maggie pulled up suddenly in the final run, clutching at Don's arm.

'Wait! … Someone's there.… Don't go on yet.'

Breathing hard, Don stood staring at the big, dark figure on the slope overlooking the sea.

'It's Peter Riley watching if the mullet are coming in.'

'No, it isn't. It's Cafferty. I know his hat.'

'Cafferty?'

'Yes, Cafferty the Honey Man.'

The man was standing almost on the nest, looking down into the she-oak by the beach, his body still as a wooden stump, his eyes intent as their own. He moved slightly to the right; they saw he had a gun at his side. Horror laid an icy hand on the girl's heart. What was he doing with a gun there?

Suddenly she started to run.

'Come on! I believe he's found the nest. I believe.…'

Her slim legs twinkled like beams of light over the turf, her print frock blew up over her heated face, and Don found it hard to keep up with her. She was out of breath when she reached Cafferty and her eyes were points of fire. He was too occupied to notice her; he was shifting the gun in his hands and watching the she-oak tree. She saw a lump in the pocket of his shirt, a stain of blood.

Words came thickly from her throat.

'What're you doing with that gun?'

'Eh?' he said, hardly looking round.

'You – you've been shooting something.… What's that in your pocket?'

Cafferty let his eyes rest on her stolidly, a slow grin parting his lips.

'Guess.'

'It's not.… It's a bird.'

'Right. Right, first shot. Most people'd have thought it was a rabbit.… Ever see one of those coloured bee-eaters, little girl? Her mate's somewhere about. I'll get him, too, before long.'

He took the crumpled bird from his pocket and dangled it before her proudly. Through a blur she saw the ruffled bronze and emerald of its plumage, the film over its eyes, the drop of blood oozing from its beak. Then she threw herself on the turf.

'Beast! That's what you are.... A b-beast.'

Cafferty looked from her small, sobbing figure to that of the boy, a sheepish bewilderment in his eyes. He was a hulking, slow-witted fellow, who lived in a humpy on the other side of the creek, surrounded by his hives and a thick growth of tea-tree.

'What's the trouble?' he asked. 'That bird, is it?'

Don had no reply. He was confused, half ashamed of his sister.

'Lord, you don't want to worry about vermin like that,' said Cafferty. 'Death on bees, them things are – hanging round the hives and licking 'em up as they come out. And they're not satisfied with robbing you like that, the little devils; they'll go through a flying swarm and take out the queen. It's a fact. Dinkum ... I'd like to wipe the lot of 'em off the face of the earth.'

He went over to the tiny opening of the tunnel and bruised the soft earth down over the face of it with his heavy boot. There was a dull passion in his absorbed eyes, a sense of warring against evil.

'No, you don't want to trouble about the likes of them. Unless it's to go after them with a shanghai. There's sixpence a head waiting for any you fetch me. Tell the other youngsters that – a tanner a head. I'm going to clear the lot of 'em out this winter.'

Shouldering his gun he moved off down the beach, a lumbering heaviness in his gait. Maggie was still stretched prone on the turf, her face in her arms, and Don watched her awhile, awkward and ill-at-ease. But the superiority of one who has not given himself away was slowly asserting itself. Picking up the dead bird that Cafferty had thrown on the grass he fingered it clumsily, wondering if there were any bees in its crop. It was still warm, but its plumage was ruffled and streaky, and it didn't look nearly so wonderful as when it had shot into the air, the light on its wings. Death on bees, the Honey Man had said. He began to feel a contempt for it.

'Come on, Mag! He's gone now. And the other kids'll be coming along soon.'

She rose from the grass, tossing back her hair and looking at the bird with reddened eyes.

'Chuck it away.'

'Why? I'm going to take it home and skin it.'

'Chuck it away!' she stormed.

He hesitated a moment, and then obeyed her. They trailed over the grass toward the store, Don swinging his bag and whistling to show he didn't care. There must be a lot of rainbow birds about, and if the Honey Man kept his promise.... Sixpence a head! He could go out with the other boys on Saturday mornings, looking all along the sandy banks. But he wouldn't use a shanghai – no fear! His new Bayard was three times as good.

Maggie took no more notice of him than if he were merely a shadow behind her. Their father was standing waiting for them at the bowser outside the store, and Don had to go for orders on his pony. Maggie trudged upstairs to the room over the shop and flung herself down on the bed. Darkness had fallen over her life. Whenever she closed her eyes she could see the Honey Man's evil face, the broken, tobacco-stained teeth revealed in a grin through the ragged growth of beard. Hatred welled up in her as she thought of him squatting among the tea-tree on the other side of the creek, his gun between his knees, his eyes watching the leaves above. Devil! Grinning devil! If only forked lightning would leap out of the sky and char him to ashes.

When the evening meal was over she went upstairs again without waiting to do her homework. Her mother's voice followed at a distance, dying behind the closed door:

'What's the matter with Maggie now?... The way that girl lets herself get worked up.'

Lying awake, Maggie tried to imagine herself running down the slope and stopping suddenly to see the rainbow bird whirling round over three spots of colour on the grass. But no! She could only see the soft earth around the nest, squashed by the Honey Man's boot, and the dead bird lying on the grass with a drop of blood on its beak. Wonder and magic – they had gone out of everything! And Don was swaggering round, pretending he didn't care.

A light rain had begun to fall, making hardly any sound upon the roof, dropping with a faint insistent tinkle into the tanks. There were people coming and going in the store below. Between broken drifts of sleep she heard voices running on and on, the telephone's muffled burring, the occasional hoot of a car. But all noises were muted, coming through a pad of distance, of woolly darkness. A funeral, she thought vaguely. They were burying the rainbow bird.

Near morning, or so it seemed, she heard someone come upstairs, and there was a blare of light in her eyes. Her mother was bending over her with a candle.

'Not asleep yet, dear? Have those people kept you awake?'

The drowsy aftermath of feeling made Maggie's voice thick.

'N-no; it wasn't that. It was because.... Why do they all come here now?'

Her mother tucked an end of the quilt in.

'They brought Mr Cafferty to the shop to wait for the ambulance. He had a little accident and had to be taken in to the hospital.... Go to sleep now.'

Maggie's eyes were wide open.

'He's dead?'

'Good gracious, no! Nothing to worry about. He must have been dragging the gun after him as he climbed through the wire fence across the creek, but they found him soon after it happened. Only in the thigh the wound was.'

Through Maggie's mind flashed a sudden conviction.

'He will die. I know he will.... Serve him right, too.'

'You don't understand what you're talking about, child,' said her mother in a formal, shocked voice. 'Everyone's fond of the Honey Man and hopes he'll be all right soon.... You've been lying awake too long. Go to sleep now.'

She faded away, leaving Maggie to stare up at the ceiling in the dark. But the vision of a world oppressed by a heavy, brutal heel had vanished. Her mind was lit up again; everything had come right. She could see the cropped slope by the sea, the overgrown wheel-rut, the small, round tunnel with the heap of sand in front of it. And it was the man with the gun who was lying crumpled on the grass. Above him sailed the rainbow bird, lustrous, triumphant, her opal body poised at the top of a curve, shimmering in the sun-bright air.

'A light rain had begun to fall, making hardly any sound upon the roof, dropping with a faint insistent tinkle into the tanks.'

GANT AND HIS HORSES

BRIAN JAMES
1892–1972

J ACK and Tom got old Gant to run over the new field with the heavy harrow – an ominous-looking wooden triangle with shocking iron spikes in it.

Morris Gant was reckoned the most successful man in the district, and was hated, if possible, more than anyone else. You can't grow better passion-fruit and citrus and get a lot more for them and draw big money for early potatoes and late tomatoes without incurring much envy and hate. People remembered, too, how mean Gant was, and how he wouldn't take advice – unless it suited him – and how he had been as poor as a church mouse when he came to the district; 'not a penny to bless himself with' when he took on that piece of scrub.

The women pitied his wife and daughters – 'fine girls if they only had a chance, but he works them like horses' – and recalled the scandal, long since passed into local history, that old Gant had got the local blacksmith to make special hoes for the girls, with six tines on the fork, so that they would cover more ground. 'Six tines!' That's what he was like. If other girls had to work in the orchards at all they used only five tines.

Also, old Gant didn't really belong. He was an Englishman, not a 'pommy', mind you. It seemed he hadn't even reached to that dignity. He was just an Englishman who had farmed in England. And had ideas – and you couldn't shift them. 'Not a bit like us,' they all said. Grab every penny he could; let his girls dig in the orchard or chip round the passion vines while he went out working. Not for nothing, neither. He knew how to charge; always a bit extra, because he had bigger and better horses than anyone else. Give him that; he had good horses, and he treated them well. A darned sight better than he treated his girls or would treat his old woman – only she wouldn't stand for it. Boys! The whole three of them cleared out – couldn't stand it. The youngest went when he was sixteen.

Gant appeared at eight, *punctually* on eight. He was very precise in such matters; start at eight sharp and stop at five to the tick. And charge twenty-five bob for it; ten shillings for the horses and fifteen for himself. He didn't boast, but he let it be understood that he and the horses were worth it. And if you didn't believe it you could have Bill Bray with *his* scraggy team and *his* light harrows; hardly heavy enough for orchard work, much less lumpy new ground.

The harrow weighed the best part of a ton, it seemed, and Jack gave a hand to get it off the dray while Tom and old Gant eased it down on to the ground. Old Gant reckoned if you let it down suddenly it might break, and there wasn't another harrow like it in the district. Then the horses dragged the harrow – on its back, of course – from the headland to the furrows, where Tom and old Gant heaved it over.

Old Gant was really quite a pleasant old chap to talk to, though his appearance wasn't particularly prepossessing. His big round face was blotchy in spite of the tanning from the weather, and he sprouted large quantities of hair from his ears and nostrils. He had bushy eyebrows and a moustache that looked like a hay rake. He was powerfully built, but he had a stomach and a craw. These were easily accounted for – *secret drinking*. Everyone knew, to the thimbleful almost, how many gallons of plonk old Gant got through each week. Kept it in this shed in big wicker jars, he did, and never a taste of it to anyone else.

The harrow, heavy as it was, bumped and heaved over the rough ground. It was a bit too dry to fine properly, so a big bloodwood post was tied on top of the harrow to keep it down. The horses grunted and sweated at the pull. A hidden root caught a tooth and bent it right back, but old Gant took the mishap philosophically – 'sort of thing that can happen any time.' He didn't even swear; in fact, he and Sam Henderson were the only two men in the district who didn't swear. Both of them were Englishmen, though Sam had the additional excuse of being a lay preacher and a JP. There was Enoch Rath, too, of course; he didn't swear; but then, no one counted *him* as a man.

Old Gant hadn't much begun the job when Wiseman from next door came down among his lemons to work.

The lemons adjoined the new land and the harrowing. It mightn't have been strictly necessary to work over them just now, but then, again, it might have been. Anyway, Wiseman started to snip the dead wood out of the trees. At the same time he could keep an eye on the harrowing. Wiseman was always filled with neighbourly interest. Also, he felt it necessary to see that Jack and Tom weren't taken down by anyone.

Morning tea was at ten. Wiseman happened over – casually. He and Grant greeted each other in proper terms.

No, Wiseman wouldn't have a bite; had some tea an hour ago.

After a long pause, 'Ever think of a rotary?' he asked Jack quite innocently. Jack hadn't.

Old Gant had a rotary hoe, an early, clumsy affair, horse-drawn and de-signed for chewing up rough ground.

'You'd break a rotary on ground like that,' said Gant thoughtfully. 'Never get through the roots and rocks.'

'I thought you used it on the patch where you've got the beans now.' Wise-man winked at Jack as an intimation that he was scoring heavily. But old Gant took a noisy swill of tea through his hay-rake moustache and said no more.

'Got any die-back in the lemons?' Wiseman wanted to know, as if the in-formation was vitally important.

Old Gant hadn't. Reckoned if you green-manured and worked a place prop-erly you didn't get die-back.

But Wiseman did these things by his lemons, and *he* had die-back. There must be other reasons. And he drained, too, so it couldn't be that either. Had no end of work cutting out dead stuff. He flicked his pruning shears back and forth. He carried the shears attached to his belt by a steel loop, and they hung down on the side of his leg. He prided himself on the arrangement, as it left his hands free, and he always had the shears with him. He now complained that cutting dead wood made the blade dull and he had to carry a small black-stone and 'a drop or two of oil' with him.

Gant was mildly interested. 'But you don't cut dead wood, do you?' he asked.

Wiseman stole another sly wink – to Tom this time – and declared with mild emphasis, 'Always!'

'Then the dead part keeps going back further still,' said Gant.

'Not if you cut in the right place. The green wood grows over the end and there's no weeping.' Wiseman gave this in the kindly fashion of a benevolent old gentleman with a small boy who was in grievous error.

Gant couldn't quite see it, however, and Wiseman, with sundry looks, preened himself on a second victory. Later, with trimmings, he would relate how he had a row with 'that Gant'. And showed him 'where he got off'. In the present process it certainly didn't look like a row at all, but then, Wiseman had his own peculiar methods of waging war.

Gant prepared to go back to the horses.

'By the way,' Wiseman asked in good-neighbourly tones, 'how is Colin get-ting on?' Colin was Gant's second boy.

Gant answered vaguely, 'Haven't heard from him for some time', and went straight to the harrow.

It was a mean victory that, because Wiseman knew how Colin was getting on. So did everyone else almost, and it was impossible that old Gant wouldn't know, too.

Then Wiseman told Jack and Tom that 'that there Colin is in trouble again; made a proper mess of it *this* time'. There followed an account of Colin's crime, related with all the detail of an observant eyewitness, combined with the artistry of a born storyteller. Some of the details were really revolting, but Wiseman didn't seem to mind at all, and lingered over them. He ended with, 'Of course, the jury will find him guilty. Couldn't do anything else. And it's a hanging matter. But, of course, they won't hang him. Not with this crowd in power.'

Wiseman spoke bitterly of 'this crowd'. Their sparing of Colin was not the least of their ways of ruining the country. 'Of course,' he summed up in a humanly-speaking tone, 'of course, it's hard on the family. But you can't be sorry for Gant – not the way he treats those girls. And I'll say this, if he had been a bit decent to the boys this wouldn't have happened either. It's the girls I'm sorry for. He thinks more of those horses than he thinks of his girls. He's a mean cow.'

'THE horses were plodding heavily and stolidly along the opposite edge of the clearing, when wild and sudden commotion broke forth, so quickly that one could only realise it in the retrospect.'

The big harrow jiggled and jolted over the ploughland. Wiseman went back to his lemons. Jack and Tom started to carry off the biggest of the roots and stones to the headland.

The horses were plodding heavily and stolidly along the opposite edge of the clearing, when wild and sudden commotion broke forth, so quickly that one could only realise it in the retrospect. The horses slewed out of the ploughed ground into the straggling stringybarks, and from a dull walk leapt into a reckless and mad gallop, and that in spite of the heavy harrow.

It was too quick for the eye to take in, with the brain trying to catch up in a confused way with a reason for it all. Jack, at the moment, happened to be watching the team, and his impression was that of something quite inanimate bursting in the fraction of a second into mad life and activity. He stood gaping, and later had the clearer picture of old Gant rushing towards the heads of his horses. He never got there.

Tom was turned the other way at the time, struggling with a large floater, and he missed the first act of the swift drama. By the time he gathered that something was happening the horses were disappearing into the scrub, with old Gant careering after them.

There was a confusion of sounds – snapping of underbrush, jangle of chains and the inarticulate cries of old Gant. Wiseman, at the edge of his lemons, was just standing and gaping. Then there was a crash in the timber, and the voice of Gant exhorting and whoaing. It sounded like a sob.

Wiseman was the first to move. 'Must be a snake!' he yelled. He dropped his shears (later he took hours to find them, and blamed Gant for losing them) and ran towards the scrub. Jack and Tom did the same. At the edge of the clearing the cause of the team's mad bolting was revealed – the white box under a stringy, and many bees flying round in wide and buzzing circles. It was a swarm that Tom had boxed a month or two before as the beginnings of an apiary he was going to establish one day.

They veered to the left to avoid the bees and ran through the timber. As Wiseman said later, 'Bees in that frame of mind would do anything. The old fool should have known better than to go near a hive with sweaty horses.' Soon they came to the harrow, smashed and caught between a bloodwood and a big stump. Broken swinglebars and bits of chain were scattered round, and a back-band from one of the horses.

The ground sloped down fairly steeply, and broken bushes and small saplings showed the way. There were no further sounds to guide them. Where the slope ended was a wall of sandstone – dropping in a small cliff to the lower level eight or ten feet down. It was a pretty spot, with soft bracken, maidenhair and scattered bottlebrushes growing on the damp, sandy soil. Beneath the wall, in a huddled heap lay the big bay horses – very still. Old Gant was standing near them – very still, too.

Wiseman, Jack and Tom stood and looked down. It was plain enough what had happened – the horses had gone over the cliff and broken their necks. Jack asked Gant if he were hurt.

Gant didn't answer the question. He only said, very softly, 'They're gone!' Then he just sobbed.

There is something inexpressibly pathetic in the sight of a man in tears. But there is something comic, too, in a fat man blubbering. Poor old Gant was a fit subject for anyone's pity; but his heaving shoulders and quivering, quaking sides were absurdly incongruous. And all the while the fine bay draughts looked like a waste of Nature's gifts. Their heads were twisted and half obscured beneath their shoulders. A hind leg of one of the horses was broken, obviously, unmistakably broken. As if fascinated, Gant gazed at this broken leg as if it were the sole proof of life departed. And every time he looked the heaving sobs started more violently.

The three above looked down. There was nothing they could do, nothing they could say. Wiseman hadn't even the heart to wink – not now. Jack thought of offering to get the remains of the harness, but he didn't know how to offer. At last he beckoned the others to depart. There was nothing else to do, it seemed.

The three walked up the slope, each touched in his own way by the tragedy. Wiseman at last rolled a cigarette very deliberately, and then found it wouldn't draw. He unrolled it and put the tobacco back in the tin, and let the crumpled, punctured paper float off in the breeze. Then he said, 'Well, I will say this much for Gant, he has a fine pair of horses.'

Tom and Jack, rather badly shaken, said nothing. They walked back to the broken harrow, as if that would help in some way or other.

'Still,' went on Wiseman, 'he thinks more of them horses than he does of his girls.'

He used the present tense.

And a week later Wiseman was relating the story with trimmings.

'His own fault, really ... sweaty horses near a beehive ... looking for trouble, really ... blubbered just like a kid. Too right, he did! ... Them poor girls with six-pronged hoes ... bloody mean cow, that's what I say....'

A WOMAN KIND TO MEN

MYRA MORRIS
1893–1966

THE farm, sprawling untidily over the flat, was held in a wide, silver loop of the river. From a distance it had an appearance of prosperity due to the thick, all-over growth of the lush green grass that remained green even in summer. The cows waded through the rippled swathes of colour that overflowed into the orchard, and splashed a dim, subaqueous green among the quince-trees and the apples and the plums.

Close at hand you saw that the fruit trees were untended, crusted with lichen, and trailing branches like creepers. You saw also that the sheds about the farm were dilapidated, the cow-bails broken, the pigsties just holding together.

The general air of neglect persisted right up to the doors of the house, a low-roofed weatherboard with a bricked veranda and ant-eaten posts. The garden was untidy, with screwy arches over which tumbled cascades of jasmine and pink tecoma, and weedy paths that provided promenades for white leghorns walking with flopping scarlet combs, or an occasional perambulating pig. The bushes round the back door were hung perpetually with greasy rags and drying, ill-washed clothes. The whole farm was obviously a man's place, showing no sign of a woman's presence anywhere.

Lew Davies, the owner of Applecross, would have scoffed at the bare mention of a woman about the place. And anyhow, the hunchback was as good as a woman. He had picked him half-drunk out of the roadside bushes one winter's evening, taken him back to the farm, and looked after him. Out of work, unattached, at war with life as he had known it, he had stayed on at the farm, finding his niche there, expressing himself in his devotion to Lew and Lew's interests. He had been in his time shearers' cook, circus hand, and rouseabout. Ageless, with grizzled curly hair, malicious green eyes, and long, ape-like arms, he shuffled about the house sideways like a crab, doing the inside jobs to the best of his ability, while Lew, a big fair giant of a man with an endearing look of boyish simplicity, attended to the outside work – the ploughing, the planting and digging of potatoes, the milking, and care of the cows and pigs.

The association after five years was a satisfying one, more in the nature of a friendship than a relationship between master and man. It was complete in itself and admitted no outside influence. The two men lived exclusively alone, Curly the hunchback leaving the farm rarely, and Lew only when he drove into the township of Musk Valley, a few miles distant, to bring household necessities or to go on a periodic jag at the pub. These jags were becoming less and less frequent now, but were dreaded by the hunchback, heralded as they were by an unfamiliar sulkiness and restlessness on Lew's part, and followed by a period of intense melancholy.

Now, the hunchback, moving about the farm kitchen like a fussy woman, was waiting for Lew to return from Musk Valley. This time he had been gone for

more than two days, and the hunchback knew exactly how he would appear –
with a shamed air and evasive, red-rimmed eyes and a dejected droop to his
great shoulders.

'Mustn't ask him how he feels,' the hunchback thought cunningly. 'That
always riles him.... And plenty of coffee on. That's it – plenty of coffee.'

He stirred the coffee in the long, dinted pot and went to the window, where he
stood looking across the valley, tracing in his mind the way that Lew would take
– Lew slumped down in the gig and the little red horse flecked with lather, his
ears laid back. Past the spindly groups of peppermint-gums they would go,

past the river flats where the cloudy, pollarded willows bunched themselves under an evening mist that was the purplish-white of bloomy grapes, past the hop gardens in the hollow, where the vines swung in their alleys like long green curtains, past Smither's farm on the bracken-covered ridge.

Again Curly hung over the bubbling pot on the stove, his long face held sideways – the face of an anxious, loving mother, the face almost of Lew's old mother, who had cooked and done for him at Applecross till death had come.

The hunchback steadied himself against the sounds of Lew's arrival. There was a clatter of wheels in the yard, the barking of a dog, voices. Feet were coming up the bricked path. Two pairs of feet. The door was flung open. There stood Lew in the dimness of the kitchen with a woman close beside him, and a big, shaggy suitcase in his hand. The hunchback stared. Something inside him grew cold and heavy, and he knew in that moment that his secret fears had taken shape at last. Law Davies had brought a woman home.

If it had been a girl – one of the smart pieces with painted nails and lips who came to Musk Valley for the hop-picking – it would not have been so astonishing. But a woman! A decent body, middle-aged, with wide hips and an ample bosom thrusting over ridgy corsets. She wore a dark, patterned frock and a straight-brimmed hat that revealed a swathe of coarse, greying hair. Her skin was clear, her eyes, an odd three-cornered shape, were bright and very blue. She looked respectable, matronly, but in her face, lurking behind her eyes, there was a spark of fun, of devilry that threatened any moment to break through.

'Mrs Biggins – Stacey,' said Lew with a nervous laugh. He set the suitcase down carefully. 'She was at the pub at a loose end. I brought her home.'

'Pleased to meet you, I'm sure,' said the woman, smiling.

Curly made a grimace, drawing his lips back from his long, yellowish teeth. His little misshapen body shuddered, and his hands hung at his sides simply like a pair of dirty, shapeless gloves. Jealousy burned in him until his whole body felt on fire. Three in the house now and there was only room for two. Only room for him and Lew. He'd be the unwanted one now – thrust outside. He watched the woman walk across the room on her silly high-heeled shoes, her heavy tread making the china on the dresser rattle. She stopped over the dinted pot on the stove.

'You don't want to let coffee boil,' she said in a playful voice. 'Only simmer – at the edge, like.'

'Stacey's been a cook,' said Lew in a would-be jovial way.

'I been a cook too,' said the hunchback. 'Cook and rouseabout and char and nurse and all.'

'I know,' said Lew looking downcast. 'You've been all those, Curly.' He took up the case and pushed the woman gently down the passage. 'In there, Stacey,' he murmured. 'The room at the end. You don't want to take any notice of Curly. He'll get over it.'

He went back to the kitchen, and the hunchback, throwing knives and forks and spoons on to a blue expanse of tablecloth, gave him a malevolent look. 'What you done now?' he asked viciously. 'What you done now, Lew Davies?'

In the bedroom the woman took off her hat and sat on the edge of the bed. The bed had a honeycomb quilt with a tattered fringe, and looked as if it had not been slept in for a long while. Everything in the room was clean though shabby, and a smell of dust lay faintly under the smell of mothballs and varnish. Through the small-paned window there was a look-out over a strip of orchard where the white leghorns, bluish in the dusk, were pecking away among the end-of-summer grasses.

Stacey smiled contentedly. She liked the room. It had an air of permanency. She felt that she had come home, though often before she had had that feeling of homecoming for no reason at all, and had learnt to distrust it a little. She had been a servant all her life, used to a succession of strange bedrooms. Poky rooms at the backs of decent houses, rooms looking on to gutters that stank like over-ripe bananas, rooms furnished with sticks of broken furniture and little cakes of cracked yellow soap. She had come to the pub at Musk Valley in the Otways in answer to a newspaper advertisement, and had found the position already filled when she arrived. Lounging around the pub, talkative with no one to talk to, she had run across Lew Davies, and summed up the situation at once with a practised eye. There was something about the big, fair man, some look of helplessness that appealed to her. He was the type that needed to be mothered. She got him out of the hot little pub bedroom down on to the cool bank of the tiny river that ran through the township. Here with her fund of stories and her high, rather cackling laughter she had kept him amused, and had finally led him into talking of himself. Men were babies – boys who never grew up. They had their faults, but they were as the good God made them. When they were miserable they needed comfort, and who better than she knew how to give it? She had always given generously of herself, of everything she had. When Lew, bemused a little, clinging to her as a drowning man clings to a support, suggested that she should accompany him to the farm, she had fallen in with his idea. She was tired of chopping and changing round. Housekeeper ... mistress ... wife. One slid imperceptibly into the other sometimes, though she had never yet succeeded in bringing any one of her 'gentlemen' to the point of making an honest woman of her. Fur coats, trinkets, tips for the races, yes. But never marriage.

Smoothing her hips and humming softly under her breath, Stacey went down the passage into the kitchen, where the lamp had been lit and the two men waited in silence with something furtive in their looks.

'Well, least said, soonest mended,' she said cheerfully. 'If you want a hair of the dog, don't mind *me*. I'm always used to having one with the boys.'

‘STACEY smiled contentedly. She liked the room. It had an air of permanency.’

———

There was a woman in the house now, and Curly chewed the cud of his bitterness as he watched her. She was always whisking briskly about the place, singing as she worked, trailing a pair of hideous red slippers at the ends of her bare white legs, which were patterned with a delicate tracery of varicose veins. Curly hated her. He hadn't a chance. She made all his efforts in the house look silly. Her scones, whisked up in a moment, were light as froth. She had a 'hand' with pastry. Her rich plum cake that Lew loved to get his teeth into was made with a minimum of labour and expense.

Her presence in the house filled Lew with delight. It was a delight that seemed to start with Stacey and spread out like a ripple in sunny water, gilding the edge of everything it touched. Stacey had done something to him. He had never got over a jag so quickly, so easily before. He told himself that he would never go on a blind again. It was a mug's game.... And there was her gaiety. He had never laughed so much before. Of a night, when they sat in the kitchen with the hunchback biting his nails in the corner, Stacey, sitting with her knees wide apart, her odd, three-cornered eyes full of merriment, would tell them stories of

'places' she had had, of gentlemen she had cooked and done for. Old man Borham, bald as an egg and sensitive because of his baldness, wearing his hat even to the bathroom.

'And into the bath, like as not!' Stacey's laughter was infectious. 'And then there was Mr Dearden. A real gentleman if ever there was one! Always stood up when I entered a room and opened the door for me. Lent him ten pounds I did, and never saw a skerrick of it again. Not but what we didn't have our fun. That time at the races with me in a new little crepe shrunk up past me knees in the rain! "We'll stick be you, Stacey, you're a good sort," they'd say, but they always got off with the young ones in the end, and who'd blame them? Not me – the poor lambs.'

'You're a caution, Stacey,' Lew would roar, his smooth, boyish face creased with delight, and wonder how long it would be before he drifted into becoming one of Stacey's 'gentlemen', with Stacey more mistress than housekeeper – finally, perhaps, more wife than mistress. The prospect alarmed him a little, because he realised his growing dependence on her, and his warm feeling for her that had sprung in the first instance out of gratitude. He had been shy with women before – apt to compare them unfavourably with his mother, a tall, white-haired woman who had presided over the household with dignity. Stacey was comfortable, easy to talk to, and undemanding. It was like having his mother grown youngish and gay back in the kitchen.

'She'll end by marrying you,' the hunchback told him slyly. It was a cold windless day at the beginning of autumn, and the frail pink trumpets of the tecoma flowers lay fallen on the wet garden path. The hunchback ground the flowers into the mud. 'She's that kind of woman, Lew. Designing.'

Lew stared at the hunchback, despising him, hating his crooked body and the long furrowed face that he seemed to be seeing plainly for the first time.

'I don't know what'll come out of it, Curly,' he said honestly. 'But I like her. She's a good woman. And it's like having my own mother back in the kitchen. She cooks like my mother used to cook.'

The hunchback said nothing, but he walked off pondering. From that day his tactics changed. He fawned on Stacey, flattered her, begged her to teach him how to cook properly.

'I never had a chance,' he told her humbly. 'I was brought up rough.'

She was generous and full of patience, for the hunchback was unbelievably awkward. With his long face bent over the mixing-bowl, he would mix his ingredients with a deadly sort of absorption that made Stacey laugh.

'You're not a bad sort, Curly. You didn't like me at first.'

'I like you now fine, Stacey,' he would say, breathing heavily.

Outside and in, the farm was changed. Stacey had turned on Lew.

'I won't have those fowls messing about in the garden,' she had said with a smiling firmness. 'Nor pigs either. Each is all right in its own God-appointed place, but outside that – no! And those poor misguided fruit-trees! However –'

'All right, Stacey,' said Lew peaceably.

He mended the fences, put a new floor in the milking-shed, knocked the broken sties together. In the orchard he hacked out the diseased trees and lopped and pruned and sprayed. It was a new Applecross.

Lew looked on his handiwork at the end of the first month, and was grateful in a bewildered way. It was Stacey who had done it all. Stacey at him in a nice, merry way – no bullying – Stacey at it herself – sweeping, cleaning, raking the paths, putting new curtains at the small-paned windows.

It was Stacey's energy that turned on her. She was chopping little slivers of wood for a sweet-pea fence when the tomahawk slipped and got her foot. The sharp blade bit deep into the flesh, and when Lew came running she was floundering about in a pool of blood, the whiteness of her face showing a patterning of tiny red veins.

'It's bad, Lew,' she told him calmly. 'You better do something.'

He made her a bandage clumsily and got her into the gig. But the gig was too slow. At Smither's farm he changed the gig for a rattly car and drove to the hospital at Inva, the market town.

The pain hurt Stacey, going up her leg in burning tremors and covering her whole body. But the look of Lew's face was compensation and his words as he left her in the hands of the brisk country doctor.

'You've got to get right soon, Stacey love. I couldn't do without you now at Applecross. You're a fine, good woman, Stacey.'

'He was near crying,' Stacey thought happily in her pain. 'A simple boy and only a few years younger than me. He wants a woman to mother him. I shouldn't wonder if we make a do of it yet, him and me.'

Stacey was at the hospital a month. It was an inconceivable time. Her face grew a little sharper as she lay there thinking of the farm and Lew. Once Lew came to see her, shy and lumbering and inarticulate. Twice he wrote to her without telling her anything at all. He paid her hospital fees and sent her fruit and vegetables and bunches of tall, pink-belled heath picked from the dripping forest.

Stacey waited, counting the moments until she could leave, trying out her foot with the help of a good, stout stick, laughing at the doctor's counsel of patience.

The day of her release came swiftly at the end. She could hobble about quite well now, and the doctor was going through to Apollo Bay in his car. He was passing Applecross. He could drop her at the very door of the farmhouse. Stacey began to cry weakly when she knew. It was because she was going *home*. For the first time since girlhood she was really *going home*.

The doctor, crazy with hurry, dropped her at the gate, and she walked up to the house herself. She walked slowly, savouring the moment, savouring the smell of the place, the rich look of the long, drowned grass, the chrysanthemums sprawling drunkenly across the beds. Her eyes were bright with expectation, her mouth eager. Lew didn't know that she was coming home. They would run out, the two of them, when they heard her.

She walked round the side to the orchard. In the late lilac afternoon the white leghorns were picking and scratching along the paths. They were scratching right up to the kitchen door. Stacey shooed them away with a weak anger. Those horrid fowls again. It was too bad. And after all her trouble. Near the veranda steps a pig moved, grunting as it walked. The gate had been left open. Stacey looked, frowning. The gate was broken again; broken and no one had mended it.

With her pleasure dulled she walked towards the kitchen. Everything there looked dirty and cold and neglected at first sight, and the hunchback was standing over the stove just as he had stood on that late summer afternoon of her arrival.

She hobbled in, tapping her stick, and the hunchback turned round startled, his green eyes shining.

'Well, you're back, Stacey!' His rasping voice had no enthusiasm. 'Lew's down with the cows.'

Stacey sat down breathing gustily. The kitchen was certainly dirty as in the old days, but there was a lovely smell of cooking.

'Scones,' said the hunchback, 'the way *you* taught me to make them. As good as yours now. And the plum cake too! Smell it! His mother used to make one like that. Lew liked having you around, Stacey, because you cooked like his mother. It was like having his mother around, he said, having you in the kitchen.'

'Oh, he said that, did he?' asked Stacey heavily.

She was silent waiting for Lew to come.

When he came he was not quite quick enough to wipe out his look of concern and embarrassment in time.

'Yes, we're all anyhow, Stacey,' he said nervously. 'If we had known you were coming –'

'Sort of slipped back into the old way, haven't you?' Stacey's voice was dry.

'Oh, we've got along all right,' said Lew smiling all over his big, simple face. 'We've got along.' He bent down and began to unlace his muddied boots, and the hunchback sidled close to him.

Stacey looked at the two men, measuring them, looked at the rough table set for two. She knew in a moment. They had been happy there without her. At first they had missed her, but gradually they had slid back into their old slack ways, and now they would never want to take a pull up again. She was an intruder. An intruder in her own kitchen. They were full and satisfied without her. Comfortable too. That was the trouble. Lew could have his hungry stomach filled in the way he liked it to be filled. And she, *she* had taught the hunchback how to cook! Cooked like Lew's old mother, did she? And now the hunchback cooked the same....

Lew was looking at her uncertainly.

'Come along, Stacey,' he said kindly. 'I'll help you –'

'I'll get along all right,' said Stacey, with a rough good nature, and she pushed past him into the passage.

Sitting on the edge of the bed she opened her shabby black handbag. Tucked inside was a small newspaper cutting that she strangely enough cut out of a paper only the day before. She began to read it in a matter-of-fact, purposeful way.

'Wanted by elderly gent, a good working housekeeper. No washing. Every comfort. Suburbs. Apply –'

'Well, I never stay where I'm not needed,' Stacey told herself cheerfully, and felt with the stub of her shoe for the suitcase under the bed.

'SHE was an intruder. An intruder in her own kitchen.'

THE GOOD HERDSMAN

FRANK DALBY
DAVISON
1893–1970

I T was early morning. In his camp Old Isaac Burgess was sharpening his scalping knife before setting out for the line of wallaby snares in the belah scrub at the back of his selection. He was an odd little man, shrunken with years, but spry, clad in dungarees and blue flannel, earth-stained and faded. His knotty arms and his face were dark with something more than sun-tan and there was a depth in the darkness of his brown eyes that seemed to belong very much to the bush. Ordinarily he was unreflective and closely intent upon whatever he was doing; but just now his face was heavy with thought, and the hand that slid the bright little blade along the whetstone moved slowly. Ordinarily he was eager for the day's activity, but this morning he seemed to lift a weight with every movement.

Last night, stumbling home in the dark from a visit to the store, he had passed his friend, young Bert Gifford, whose selection adjoined his at one end.

'That you, Isaac?'

'That's me, Bert.'

''Bout time you sold those heifers, Isaac!'

Isaac had long known that the day when it would be time to sell the heifers was approaching, but the thought was unpleasant and he had avoided it. Because he knew Bert's remark to be friendlily intended it made him jump.

'Yes, I'll sell 'em soon, Bert.' His voice sounded reedy in his own ears. He was unable to avoid letting it seem as if Bert's remark was a command, and his reply a promise to obey.

Bert, his disinterested words flung out in passing, went unconcernedly on his way. Isaac stood staring into the darkness into which Bert had disappeared; then he hurried back to his camp, his composure much disturbed. He thought to escape in sleep, but recollection was waiting for him when he wakened; and as he dressed and made his breakfast the incident kept re-enacting itself unpleasantly in his imagination.

He didn't want to sell those heifers. He liked having them in his paddock. They were good sorts, those heifers of his, finely bred, good colours, red, white and roan; well-grown beasts, most of them standing almost as high as his shoulder. He had bought them a couple of years ago, a mob of twenty-four skinny little milkers' poddies, about as big as sheep, swollen-bellied, razor-backed, harsh of coat and poverty-struck. But they had their breeding to recommend them, and neighbours had turned knowing eyes into his poddock. They had suggested then, and from time to time since, that he would want to sell them some day. His neighbours were family men, building up dairy herds; he was a local oddity, an old bachelor bushman, planning to live only by grazing in a small way.

At first he had encouraged talk of the day when he might sell; sunning himself a little in the warmth of other men's covetousness. Yes, they would be for sale

'FROM their young strength there seemed to come a glow that he could feel through his old body. Here was life, and in some mysterious way he was both part of it and it was his.'

some day; but now, when they had grown to early maturity, and it would be the part of good business to listen to offers, he fought shy of the thought.

In the two years since he had bought them, while they grew, he had come to like them just for themselves. He liked having them in his paddock, enjoying his bounty, under his protection. They and he and a couple of quiet old horses were the sole inhabitants of the small compact world in which he lived behind his boundary fences. When he went away, as he must from time to time to earn a little ready money, it was to hold that small world together; and when he returned his first and happiest duty was to go down the paddock to renew acquaintance with its creatures, and learn from loving observation how they had fared in his absence. He had bought the poddies with a view to turning them into cash when grown, but somehow life seemed to have carried him away from his intentions. Bert's friendly remark was an unpleasant reminder that his neighbours were interested in his affairs, probably making them a matter for discussion.

Recollection that the heifers were in calf – on their natural way to mother-hood and the milking bails – stilled the hand that wielded the scalping knife. Cutlack, another neighbour, had a fence-jumping bull that had seen to that, a fact about which Cutlack had reminded him with noisy bawdry each time he came to recover the bull. Memory of Cutlack's raucous shouting, linked to memory of last night's incident, was suddenly too much for thought to bear. As he had hoped last night to escape in sleep, so now he fled to activity. Along the snare line the night's catch would be waiting. It was time he got a move on. He sheathed the knife, put the whetstone aside, and in a few minutes was on his way down the paddock, his feelings disposed to return to his difficulty, but his thoughts fixed resolutely upon his errand.

The morning was bright and fresh, the ground striped with long shadows from the newly risen sun.

Isaac met his heifers grazing up the slope from the creek. At sight of them his small secure world closed round him, and his mood changed with the facility of a child's. A pretty sight the cattle made – the red, the roan and the white – as they came feeding along under the bare twiggy branches of timber he had ring-barked the year before. Heads down to the good grass; twenty-four of them, in the bloom of young life, at one with the morning.

Reaching them the old man lingered, hobbling from one to another, rubbing this one behind her ears and patting that one on her flank, delighting in the touch of their warm silken hides. The skinny little poddies of a couple of years ago were now but a scarcely credible recollection. All the beauty of young maturity was with them. Their smooth hair felt nice under his fingers. Their breath was fragrant with health and the sweetness of good pasture. From their young strength there seemed to come a glow that he could feel through his old body. Here was life, and in some mysterious way he was both part of it and it was his.

Eager in his care for them, he passed with caressing hand around a red-coated beast to free the silvery tail-tuft of a roan from a small trailing branch that had got caught up in it. And as he cast the branch away he took advantage of his change of position to examine a small wound on another. She had staked herself, but he had dressed the cut and tarred it to keep the flies off, and it seemed to be healing well.

As he moved among them he talked to them. 'And how's the littlest one gettin' on, hey?' He asked the question with a chuckle to himself. Or, as he put a hand on one that was the least trustful of them all, 'You feelin' quiet this mornin'?' One might lift a dewy muzzle from the feed and blink at him for a moment with large liquid eyes, but that was the only way any of them showed awareness of his presence. They would have walked off quite smartly if a real stranger had tried to move about among them; but they thought he was one of themselves, almost. The sound of their cropping, soft explosions moving in and out of the sound of their blown breaths, was like words with music to Isaac. A strawberry roan came up beside him, taking the grass with swift strokes of her elegant head. He put out his hand to enjoy contact with a bright warm hide just once more before going on his way.

'Makin' love to 'em, are you?' The words, in a shout of derision, came from behind Isaac.

He turned as if he had been shot at, his mouth falling open. He saw Cutlack, big noisy Cutlack, standing about a hundred and fifty yards away, at one of the posts of the fence that divided their selections from each other. His arms were folded on top of the post, his pipe was in one hand, a foot rested on the bottom wire of the fence. He had evidently been an interested, amused – and probably chagrined – observer of Isaac making much of his cattle.

'First time I seen a bloke kissin' his cows good mornin'!' There was a note of satisfaction in Cutlack's jeer.

Isaac made no reply. He wasn't capable of any. He had thought himself secure – and here was one of those neighbours who wanted to tear his treasure from him. His mouth closed, but the corners of it twitched uncontrollably. A moment before, as he pottered happily among his livestock, he had appeared a reasonably vigorous old man; but now his frailty, his defencelessness, was to the fore. He blinked, and the hand that rested on the strawberry roan trembled. He was a picture of badgered weakness.

''Bout time they was in somebody's milkin' bails, ain't it, earnin' their keep?'

Still no word from Isaac. He swallowed once or twice but no sound came from his throat. The roan moved on, following the others as they grazed away from him up the paddock. His arm fell to his side like the arm of an effigy, and he stood staring toward Cutlack as if transfixed until the other chose to release him.

Cutlack slid his foot from the wire and turned away with a grunt; then Isaac, after a glance back at the heifers and another towards Cutlack's retreating form, hurried on his way, stumbling occasionally as if he were not in complete control of his limbs.

He crossed the creek and toiled up the slope whose top was marked with the dark selvage of the belah scrub; but not directly toward the beginning of his snare line. He had suffered spiritual assault, and in his distress and blind preoccupation with the wound to his feelings his feet led him astray. He had almost reached the top of the rise before he became aware of his loss of direction. He stopped then and looked back toward where the disturbing incident had taken place. His lips moved as if he were addressing some image held before his inner vision; then he turned and tramped on.

Arrived within the margin of the scrub he was in no condition to work along the snare line. He sat down on a log behind a thin screen of stunted belahs that fringed the giant scrub behind, and felt for his pipe. He was breathing heavily; his eyes were over-bright; his movements jerky and fumbling. His gnarly old fingers had difficulty in extracting a match from the box, and the hand that held the lighted match above the bowl of his pipe trembled.

He sat for a while, his lips tight on his pipestem, forgetting to draw smoke, peering through the scant belah needles. At a distance, and some way below him, he could see a few of the roofs of his neighbours' homesteads embedded in the timber. He looked from one to another as if each offered him a threat. There was a weak defiance in his posture, but a hunted look in his eyes.

The hardness of his breathing died down and his body relaxed a little. He looked about him, at the scrubby belahs, at the leaves of the turkey-bush twinkling in the cool shadows of the tall scrub behind him. He was like a beast escaped into hiding from a driven herd, but which doesn't know what it will do next, and fears a return of the drovers.

His eyes turned again to the distant rooftops, and he seemed to feel himself shrink in stature. He took his pipe from his mouth, and a great weariness and misery settled on him, a coldness even of the flesh. For the first time in his life he felt very old, lost and inadequate. His neighbours wanted him to sell his heifers; they wanted themselves to possess them. It was time the heifers were sold, and his neighbours were offended at his perversity. He was an object of ridicule. He had bought the heifers with a view to trade. He would profit well from them. Change and gain! He had intended – and greatly looked forward to – investing his profit in other cattle from which further profit would come. While the heifers were still poddies he had even imagined exactly the kind of stock – the much better stock! – which would eventually take their place.

To solace himself he tried now to recall the cattle he had had in mind. He failed, for two reasons. Somehow, in the time he had had the heifers growing in his paddock his plan for their replacement had come to lack imaginative validity. Change and gain held no attraction for him now. He couldn't think happily of his paddock empty of its present inhabitants. He failed, in the second place, to bring clearly before his inner vision the herd which would replace the heifers, because the effort involved a disloyalty to creatures he had come to love.

Isaac didn't know that he had been caught between a feeble business sense and a large capacity for personally identifying himself with whatever living thing came to the care of his hands. He was conscious only of being torn between reason and feeling, of a shaken belief in himself.

In search of some consolatory image of himself his mind reached back to the time – between three and four years ago – when he had first settled on his selection. Men had said to him, 'You're a game old bloke to be taking up land at your time of life!' He had mildly resented their suggestion that the infirmity of years was upon him. He'd show them that he had plenty left in him. In that image of himself he recalled a man who vigour yet to spend.

He had fenced his selection, built a good permanent camp for himself, built

his stockyard, ringbarked a lot of his timber. Men, looking at the work of his hands, had said, 'Well, you do a good job, Isaac!' He had been a little contemptuous of their praise, nettled at their patronage. What were they used to? All his life he had done a good job.

And now he was on the wrong side of life. He had planned to live by change and gain; he who now discovered that he wanted only what he already had. Change and gain were after him now, like dogs snapping at his fetlocks.

An hour passed before Isaac moved; an hour of troubled thoughts, of alternately living in the deep contentment of his past two years, and trying unavailingly to reconcile himself to what must follow. With bodily rest his thoughts at length came back to the immediate present, finding temporary relief in the thought of duty waiting. If he didn't get a move on the ants would be at the catch. He got up from the log and turned into the head-high wilga under the tall belahs, thoughts of work comforting him like a fresh dressing on a wound.

There was a good deal to do that morning. Old snares to be taken up, repaired when necessary, fresh wallaby pads sought out, a place on the fresh pad selected where the old snare could be newly set to best advantage, and the looped snare bent above the pad craftily so that the quarry, coming along on his affairs at late evening or early morning, would be firmly caught by the neck and not brush the snare aside in passing. Then there was the night's catch to be skinned as he came upon them. Four were waiting for him; four furry bodies, prone and still in the depths of the scrub, each lying in a circle of torn and scratched earth, witness of its struggles to get free.

It was almost noon – later than usual – when Isaac came to the end of his snare line and, with the four pelts dangling over his shoulder, headed for home. Absorption in work had freed his mind in greater part and cleared his face, but as he emerged from the scrub into the open grazing country thought of his trouble was waiting for him, just as his snares had waited for the wallabies. Animation departed from his features, and he plodded towards his camp with set look, inwardly intent, he who ordinarily was aware of even the smallest happening within range of ear or eye.

'Good morning, Mr Burgess!' The words came in tones that were crisp, clear and pleasant.

The earth itself might have spoken behind him, so sharply did Isaac stop and turn. Peering, he saw, through the saplings that edged the side road, that the voice came from a man seated in a buckboard. The vehicle was at a standstill. He recognised the voice at the moment of seeing the man. It was Morrison, from over on Breakfast Creek, a very politely-spoken chap.

Isaac attempted a reply to his greeting, but could manage only a croak of surprise and alarm, until he should learn what the other wanted of him.

Morrison saw Isaac's mouth open. He heard no sound, but, as the breeze was against Isaac, concluded that his reply had been carried away.

'I was just noticing your heifers as I came along the road,' he said, raising his own voice a little and speaking with a backward motion of his hand toward the direction from which he had come. 'A very choice little lot! And pretty well ready for sale now, eh? You should do quite well out of them!'

The mood of rising happiness in which he had scrambled across the creek fell completely away from Isaac, leaving him spiritually naked. The heifers were close to calving, and by that as close to their natural destiny, the milking sheds of his neighbours. That white heifer, the one with her tail lying across her back, was springing; it wouldn't be more than a few days before she calved. That large red one – the pick of them all – she was coming along fast. Soon they'd all be young mothers, with calves running at foot. The image touched his heart. It also reproached him.

For the first time since he had watched them, as forlorn little poddies, straggling uncertainly up the ridge to a night camp at the close of their first day in his paddock, Isaac felt himself outside their circle. Looking at them now, trying without avail to enter into his usual intimate delight in their docility and animal perfection, he realised that although he had given his care and labour for their well-being, they had grown and waxed beautiful, not to please him, but to fulfil their own lives. They would rest as contentedly in any other man's paddock. They belonged to themselves.

Isaac turned and went on his way, more slowly and even more thoughtfully than he had since rising from his bed.

The hill rose sharply beyond the flat, and among the trees on the crown of the first little hummock he turned and looked back. The heifers were grouped now within the compass of a single glance, about a hundred yards away and a little below him, camped in the shade, across the sunlit flat, framed between the dark trunks of the trees that grew close beside him. As pretty as paint, they looked. He felt no surprise that he had come to care for them so much, only amazement that it should have brought him pain.

The moment was one to be seized. After a little time – after a moment of struggle – Isaac's face lifted, and lit with the look of a man who has brought himself to meet the challenge of life. His lips moved, although no sound came from them. Late this afternoon, when the sun was just above the treetops, he would go out to the front sliprails. He would speak to the children on their way home from school. He would say to young Madigan, the cattle dealer's boy, 'Tell your father, sonny, that I'm ready to make a deal with him about them heifers of mine.'

The light died from Isaac's face, and he turned away. He would do as he had resolved; but as he made with slow steps toward his camp, the only moving thing on the hillside, his catch of pelts dangling from his shoulder, he looked very small and forlorn.

Isaac Burgess had no word for the act of renunciation, but he knew its pangs.

There was a pause during which nothing was said. In so far as he was acquainted with him, Isaac had a quite friendly regard for the man on the road, but faced with his talk about the heifers, just at their moment, he could achieve nothing in the way of a little amiable intercourse. He just stared.

The other stared back, somewhat at a loss to account for the old man's silence; then he decided to bring the rather lame interview to as pleasant a termination as possible.

'Yes, you certainly bought very wisely. I wish I were in a position to make you an offer myself. Well, good morning, Mr Burgess!' He gathered up his reins and, with a friendly waggle of his whip, drove on.

'. . . HE realised that although he had given his care and labour for their well-being, they had grown and waxed beautiful, not to please him, but to fulfil their own lives.'

Isaac managed a movement of his hand which he thought and hoped passed muster as a farewell salute, and then turned on his way. He was doubly stricken now, with that friendly, disinterested voice echoing in his ears. The very skies seemed to be talking about his heifers, the saplings whispering about them.

Halfway down the slope toward the creek he halted beside a felled tree, dead this twelve months, the axe marks on its butt already weathering. It had a meaning for him, which came back to him gradually as he stood beside it. He had cut that tree down for a bees' nest. For two days he had worked, busy and contented. It was toward the close of gum-blossom time and the hive was well-stocked. He had carried the comb to his camp in a kerosene tin and there carefully refined it. He had got a great lot of honey. Some of it he had given to young Bert Gifford and his wife and the rest he had traded at Linklater's store for a new flannel. Linklater had thrown in a plug of tobacco. He had kept both for Sunday. He remembered sitting, that Sunday, on a box in the shade outside his camp, wearing the new flannel and cutting a pipeful from the plug – a strong happy man, at peace with himself and the world.

He went on down the slope comparing his condition then and now. He caught sight of his heifers, distantly. They had gone down to the creek for a drink and were making their midday camp in the shade of some apple-box trees near the waterhole. Ordinarily he would have turned at once to pass close by them and enjoy for a moment close observation of their placid routine. Today his face set at sight of them and for some distance he tramped straight on in a direct line for his camp; then resolution faltered, heart and face softened together, and he turned toward them.

The heifers, full-bellied with food and water, were camped to chew their cuds and drowse away the warm noontide hours. They had chosen a tiny enclosed flat, where the creek made a horseshoe bend under its bower of apple-box trees. Isaac's footsteps quickened as he caught sight, at short distance, of their backs between the branches. Here, at least, was a friendly and sympathetic atmosphere, a little island of temporary forgetfulness, however ringed about with trouble. He scrambled down and up the creek banks, and stood looking at his cattle. He had hoped to recapture, even if only for a little while, the happy mood in which he had moved among them in the early morning. Standing there, he waited for it to come to him, but it eluded him.

The heifers were camped under the leaning arms of the trees, on earth splashed with shadow and shine. A few were standing, the rest lying down, all were cud-chewing, contentment was with them. It was deep noon, bright and warm, and the somnolence of the hour seemed to absorb the monotone of their swinging jaws. Above them, sky and foliage were the green and cobalt of a parrot's wing. The air was faintly scented with the smell of apples, with the leaves of the trees, and heavily scented with cattle breath. The occasional sound of a deeply blown sigh and the intermittent chirring of a lone cicada sounded loud in stillness. Some of the heifers – at Isaac's sudden appearance – turned large dark eyes on him; bland bovine eyes, disinterested, ruminative, self-absorbed.

THE PELICAN

CECIL MANN
1896–1967

I T used to be one of the familiar sights to see Mr Grigg (as he then was; he has moved up socially since) taking his regular Sunday stroll along the Twelve-mile Beach. A sight the inhabitants viewed with feelings between amusement and contempt.

The weather made no difference to Mr Grigg. On bright and sunny Sundays he dressed what there was of him in cream flannel trousers, black blazer with white pipings, panama hat and white pipeclayed shoes. Not sandshoes. Good leather. And stiff-collared white shirt, and black necktie.

Or else he would give his dark-blue serge, bowler and black shoes an airing. A high-cut white vest. A small black bow tie. Long-linked gold watchchain. Large gold ring on a left finger. Cane.

When rain came it fell at the Beach in a prodigious waste. It drove down in a heavy mass for days, sometimes weeks on end. A thousandth part of it would have been more than ample for the few straggling pumpkin vines, the occasional pie-melons and chokos that constituted the inhabitants' gardens. It belted loudly on the red iron roofs scattered through the tea-trees and banksias. It came in from the open sea between the headlands at either end of the long curved beach like an advancing grey wall. It flogged the sea flat, belted the sloping sand smooth, filled the tea-tree swamp, swelled the weed- and swamp-stained acre of lake till sometimes it broke through the sand-silted block and emptied its brown wine-like water and its landlocked fish for a while into the sea.

Then Mr Grigg took his Sunday stroll in rubber kneeboots, black oilskin, black sou'wester. He leant his meagre frame against the gale, trudging the hardened sand. Hands in the oilskin pockets. Hunched like a black pigmy. The lumps of rain struck him. They bumped from his shoulders up under his neck and trickled down his chestbone. For all his protective covering, he returned to his shop wet. He did so again the next Sunday, if it was raining twice as hard.

Mr Grigg never fished on Sundays. That there was no church at the Beach made him all the more meticulous in keeping the Sabbath, in his fashion, holy. He compensated his soul with the thought that you could commune there in the Almighty's own vast cathedral, though its roof did leak rather badly at times. As you went along communing, you might, without desecration, spot out holes and channels in the breakers that would be likely places for jewfish and bream. Next night, the Sabbath over, you could be off down the track through the tea-trees and she-oaks and along the beach to cast out at the prospected spot, marked by the gibbet silhouette of a banksia up on the sand ridge.

It was a local legend of Mr Grigg that one Saturday night he hooked a tremendous jewy. He had out a brand new 200 yards of No. 12. The jewy made him use the lot of it. It drew him out into the surf up to his waist. Not so good a fisherman, stones heavier than Mr Grigg, would have had no chance with it. As it was, the struggle in the night took him four miles along the beach. With the

whole of the taut line out, the fight lasted for over two hours. Then, not having landed it by midnight, Mr Grigg threw the log-like cork after it and let it go. Rather than desecrate the Sabbath. Anyway, that's how the tale went.

It wasn't that many of the others fished, or felt any desire to fish, on Sundays. To them, fishing was something you did if you happened to want fish to eat or, seasonally, when the big black-nose whiting or bream were in. Only an occasional one or two, apart from Mr Grigg, even went out when the huge jewfish were known to be patrolling at night close in in the breakers. Mostly, indeed practically unanimously, they just preferred not to fish. But if there was any one day of the week when they might abandon their preference, or habitual laziness, it was Sunday. Then, perhaps with some visitors down from town, a few of them might wet a line.

They called Mr Grigg Mr Grigg. Friendly enough folk, they could have accepted Mr Grigg going to church on Sundays, and some of the women might have gone, too, and the children been forced to go. It was just that Mr Grigg's Sabbath abstinence set him apart. It made him superior. And the gap was not lessened by the fact that if there was one thing above all others positive about Mr Grigg, it was that he was a regular crank on fishing.

Great red-shouldered jewfish that he could hardly lift. Bronzed-silver whiting; bream and tarwhine; and brown-backed, white-bellied sand flathead by the dozen. Caught and pulled, turning and leaping through the green-and-white swirl of breakers along the Beach by Mr Grigg, and by Mr Grigg given away gratis to any of the inhabitants who would eat fish, or sent by the mail-car up to THE PELICAN

gratis to any of the inhabitants who would eat fish, or sent by the mail-car up to town, to the hospital. With Mr Grigg's compliments.

To Mr Grigg, his discovery of fishing was practically a discovery of life itself. Two other discoveries went along with it.

One was that there were seven days in the week, instead of only one. Monday, Tuesday, Wednesday, Thursday, Friday, Saturday, Sunday – seven. Then start all over again: Monday, Tuesday – each a whole day, a whole twenty-four hours. Not a rush into the city inside the hot, screaming cylinder of an electric train. Bacon department. Put on the white apron. Sharpen the knife. Get busy. 'Thank you, madam.' 'A beautiful cut, madam.' 'A nice piece for boiling? Yes, madam. Let me see now.' Take off the apron. Join the crushing exodus. Rush home again. Read the evening paper. Eat sausages. Put out the light in the single room. Open the window. Sleep.

No. Complete days. Composed of time; of aged hours; of early morning, later morning, noon, afternoon, evening, night. Days and nights. Some wet, some windy, some sunny, some hot; pitch black, moon-flooded, starlit. Curve of open beach sweeping its twelve miles from headland to headland. Gulls winging over the whitecaps. Surf breaking on the sand. Sun-haze dancing on the horizon. Pelicans floating on the acre of swamp lake. Breaths of loose sand puffed by the wind along the crests of the sandhills. Fish.

Something to discover from the bacon department.

The other discovery had gall in it for Mr Grigg. He read the advertisement, made the great decision, bought the grocery-and-residence shop (three unlined weatherboard rooms in all) at the Beach. The previous owner had amassed wealth there. Enough of it to go to the south that Mr Grigg came from and buy a pub in salubrious surroundings. Paddington.

Mr Grigg did not do so well. He made less than his bacon department wages. The inhabitants did not do anything so incredible as ostracising Mr Grigg. By no means. They did not feel that way about him at all. He could have dressed in purple tights and painted his face ultramarine. He could even have built a church. That would have been his affair. The inhabitants would have been surprised, perhaps, but would shortly have got used to it, and accepted it.

There was only the one shop, anyway. Grigg's; formerly McCarthy's.

The reason for Mr Grigg's failure was the reason for McCarthy's wealth. It was not what was in the tins and jars on the sandy shelves. It was in what McCarthy kept under the counter. It was twenty-five miles up river to the town. The male inhabitants relied on McCarthy to make that immaterial to them. So did those who came down and lived in tents at Christmas and Easter.

It was a felon blow to Mr Grigg. It led him to fishing. Fanatically. From then on – in old cabbage-tree hat, old coat, trousers rolled to the knees, bare-footed – he lived fish, talked fish and fished. Except on Sundays.

Some, perhaps – the dilettanti who wet a line about once a year, when on holidays, and wouldn't know a sergeant baker from a morwong – might not appreciate what that meant to Mr Grigg. They wouldn't know the wild joy of standing or squatting alone at night on a windy beach, wet to the thighs from getting the heavy jew line well out over the breakers. They would be routed in one black engagement by the driven sand and salt peppering into their eyes and mouths and down their necks. They would shiver in the chill wet winter nights, and be tormented by blazing hearth-fires, warm beds and steaming food. They wouldn't know the obliteration from a line jerked suddenly taut by a terrific strength; the sizzling of it cutting through the fingers, the whishing of it through the water. Obliteration for anything up to an hour or more till the fifty-pounder was there, phosphorescent, thumping and leaping up on the beach.

What could they, the inhabitants or anyone else, know of what went on in the mind of Mr Grigg, taking his Sabbath stroll? If there is not one already, there should be a Saint Alfred in the exclusive hierarchy. Or there should have been. At least let it stand to his glory in the past tense. Let it stand to his glory, Lord, when he and they and the creatures of Thy making, yea even unto the mis-shapen, the toad-fish in the shallows, the pelicans on the beach, come up for the judgment.

The pelican Mr Grigg saw on his Sabbath stroll squatted on the sand away ahead of him. As he approached, Sunday-neat in cream flannels, black blazer, panama, Mr Grigg focused on the old fellow squatting there, great yellow beak pointed out to sea like a signpost. It surprised him, drawing nearer, that the big bird did not get up and float at first awkwardly, then superbly, away. Instead, with a display of confidence that at once touched Mr Grigg, the old fellow got up on his short legs and came towards him. The big feet scarcely marked the sand; but a dragging wing-tip cut a thin line in it. A yard away, half-straightening the thick S-neck, the bird opened up his vast cavern of beak. In his throat he made a raucous, squawking sound. He spread out and flapped his good wing; clattered the long yellow slats of bill together like pieces of board.

Mr Grigg looked down on the grotesque white body, fawn and brown down the wing-edges and over the abrupt square tail. The big bird squatted on his yellow webbed feet, looking up expectantly at Mr Grigg with watery brown eyes.

'Hullo,' Mr Grigg cried sympathetically. 'What's the matter with you now? Eh? Broke your wing, is that it? Somebody shot you, eh?'

The bird affirmed Mr Grigg's deductions. He squawked more, flapped his good wing. Mr Grigg put a friendly hand out to stroke him, but jerked it back as the hook on the end of the long beak nearly caught it. The bird shied off, snapping, backing away, half-falling over the dragging wing. The short white feathers on his neck came up like a dog's hackle.

It distressed Mr Grigg. Kindliness rebuffed, he turned and began walking back along the beach. After him the pelican waddled, flapping the good wing to try to keep up, with the other drawing a crooked furrow over the damp sand.

The distance between Mr Grigg and the waddling grotesque widened out. Mr Grigg's brows puckered thoughtfully. Gradually, a thought, a turn of mind, an inspiration; fighting at first thinly, then strongly, for acceptance.

Mr Grigg stopped, turned about, waited for the old fellow to catch up with him. The pelican came on awkwardly to within a few feet. The good wing flapped; cavernous beak opening and shutting.

'Yes, that's it,' said Mr Grigg loudly. 'That's it, isn't it, eh? You're hungry, aren't you? You want a feed, don't you? Fish? Fish, eh? Fish,' shouted Mr Grigg. 'Fish! *Fish*!'

Opening and clapping his beak, flapping his wing, the grotesque leered at him. It sat back on its hooked spurs watching him. The watery brown eyes glared malevolently. Mr Grigg looked down on it in an ecstacy. He turned again on his heel and went in short, quickened steps along the beach, up the track through the tea-trees and she-oaks, into the shop.

In old trousers and grey flannel shirt, old cabbage-tree hat, bootless, he emerged again. A small gut line rolled round an empty bottle in one hand. In the other a lidless jam-tin half-filled with sand and seaworms. Bait.

A quiet Sunday afternoon. The breakers falling lazily in slow crashes. Mr Grigg with the surf washing round his shins. The light gut line over the shelf of sand. On the beach the old pelican a squatted, grotesque monument of Patience.

The thin line in Mr Grigg's fingers jerked slightly. At the next jerk he hooked it. Trousers in a wet roll at his knees, barefoot, he backed through the shallow to the sand, pulling it in as he went.

The silver streak of whiting came skipping, gleaming through the water. The old bird, flapping and squawking down, nearly beat him to it. Mr Grigg took the silver streak from the hook. He held it out to the bird, as if he was showing a bone to a dog. The flapping and guttural squawks taken as gratitude, he tossed the fish to the open beak.

The bird caught it deftly in the air. Juggled the still flipping fish between the

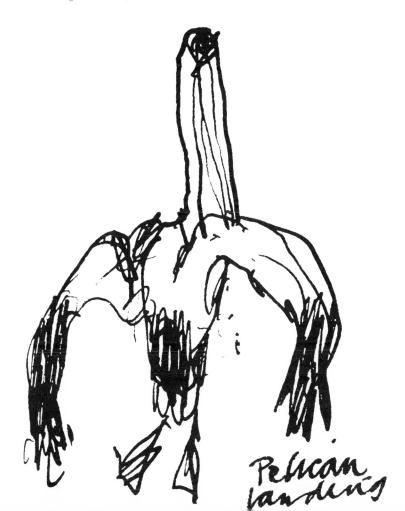

Pelican
landing

slats of his bill so that it would pass down his throat head first, without the fins obstructing. Mr Grigg watched entranced. He saw the moving length passing down and swelling out the old bird's throat.

He saw half-a-dozen more go the same way. Unawares, oblivious, Mr Grigg had joined the company of the damned.

Alf Grigg, as they speak of him; Alf, as they speak to him; Old Featherlegs, as they not unkindly refer to him – that is, Mr Grigg that was – has moved up all that way socially. He fishes on Sunday, like any other heathen. He fishes on any of the entire seven. The pelican follows him like a feathered dog. Lives with him; camps on the veranda of the shop. Squawks at strangers.

Often they sit there on the veranda together, thinking about fish. Otherwise the shop isn't much different from when it changed hands. There's still the same bell without a tongue standing on the counter. On the four sandy shelves a row of biscuit tins, jars of lollies, half-pounds of tea, packets of self-raising flour, tins of camp-pie, boxes of hooks and lines and sinkers.

If the door's shut, it's no use knocking. They will be out along the beach, fishing. There's nothing for it, if you want, say, a drop of overproof rum to warm the cockles of your heart, or a bottle of beer to quench your thrist, but just sit down and wait till they come back.

THE PERSIMMON TREE

MARJORIE
BARNARD
1897–

I saw the spring come once and I won't forget it. Only once. I had been ill all the winter and I was recovering. There was no more pain, no more treatments or visits to the doctor. The face that looked back at me from my old silver mirror was the face of a woman who had escaped. I had only to build up my strength. For that I wanted to be alone, an old and natural impulse. I had been out of things for quite a long time and the effort of returning was still too great. My mind was transparent and as tender as new skin. Everything that happened, even the commonest things, seemed to be happening for the first time, and had a delicate hollow ring like music played in an empty auditorium.

I took a flat in a quiet, blind street, lined with English trees. It was one large room, high ceilinged with pale walls, chaste as a cell in a honeycomb, and furnished with the passionless, standardised grace of a fashionable interior decorator. It had the afternoon sun which I prefer because I like my mornings shadowy and cool, the relaxed end of the night prolonged as far as possible. When I arrived the trees were bare and still against the lilac dusk. There was a block of flats opposite, discreet, well tended, with a wide entrance. At night it lifted its oblongs of rose and golden light far up into the sky. One of its windows was immediately opposite mine. I noticed that it was always shut against the air. The street was wide but because it was so quiet the window seemed near. I was glad to see it always shut because I spend a good deal of time at my window and it was the only one that might have overlooked me and flawed my privacy.

I liked the room from the first. It was a shell that fitted without touching me. The afternoon sun threw the shadow of a tree on my light wall and it was in the shadow that I first noticed that the bare twigs were beginning to swell with buds. A watercolour, pretty and innocuous, hung on that wall. One day I asked the silent woman who serviced me to take it down. After that the shadow of the tree had the wall to itself and I felt cleared and tranquil as if I had expelled the last fragment of grit from my mind.

I grew familiar with all the people in the street. They came and went with a surprising regularity and they all, somehow, seemed to be cut to a very correct pattern. They were part of the mise en scene, hardly real at all and I never felt the faintest desire to become acquainted with any of them. There was one woman I noticed, about my own age. She lived over the way. She had been beautiful I thought, and was still handsome with a fine tall figure. She always wore dark clothes, tailor made, and there was reserve in her every movement. Coming and going she was always alone, but you felt that that was by her own choice, that everything she did was by her own steady choice. She walked up the steps so firmly, and vanished so resolutely into the discreet muteness of the building opposite, that I felt a faint, a very faint, envy of anyone who appeared to have her life so perfectly under control.

There was a day much warmer than anything we had had, a still, warm, milky day. I saw as soon as I got up that the window opposite was open a few inches, 'Spring comes even to the careful heart,' I thought. And the next morning not only was the window open but there was a row of persimmons set out carefully and precisely on the sill, to ripen in the sun. Shaped like a young woman's breasts, their deep, rich, golden-orange colour seemed just the highlight that the morning's spring tranquillity needed. It was almost a shock to me to see them there. I remembered at home when I was a child there was a grove of persimmon trees down one side of the house. In the autumn they had blazed deep red, taking your breath away. They cast a rosy light into rooms on that side of the house as if a fire were burning outside. Then the leaves fell and left the pointed dark gold fruit clinging to the bare branches. They never lost their strangeness – magical, Hesperidean trees. When I saw the Fire Bird danced my heart moved painfully because I remembered the persimmon trees in the early morning against the dark windbreak of the loquats. Why did I always think of autumn in springtime?

Persimmons belong to autumn and this was spring. I went to the window to look again. Yes, they were there, they were real. I had not imagined them, autumn fruit warming to a ripe transparencyin the spring sunshine. They must have come, expensively packed in sawdust, from California or have lain all winter in storage. Fruit out of season.

It was later in the day when the sun had left the sill that I saw the window opened and a hand come out to gather the persimmons. I saw a woman's figure against the curtains. *She* lived there. It was her window opposite mine.

Often now the window was open. That in itself was like the breaking of a bud. A bowl of thick cream pottery, shaped like a boat, appeared on the sill. It was planted, I think, with bulbs. She used to water it with one of those tiny, long-spouted, hand-painted cans that you use for refilling vases, and I saw her gingerly loosening the earth with a silver table fork. She didn't look up or across the street. Not once.

Sometimes on my leisurely walks I passed her in the street. I knew her quite well now, the texture of her skin, her hands, the set of her clothes, her movements. The way you know people when you are sure you will never be put to the test of speaking to them.I could have found out her name quite easily. I had only to walk into the vestibule of her block and read it in the list of tenants, or consult the visiting card on her door. I never did.

She was a lonely woman and so was I. That was a barrier, not a link. Lonely women have something to guard. I was not exactly lonely. I had stood my life on a shelf, that was all. I could have had a dozen friends round me all day long. But there wasn't a friend that I loved and trusted above all the others, no lover, secret or declared. She had, I suppose, some nutrient hinterland on which she drew.

The bulbs in her bowl were shooting. I could see the pale new-green spears standing out of the dark loam.I was quite interested in them, wondered what they would be. I expected tulips,I don't know why. Her widow was open all day long now, very fine thin curtains hung in front of it and these were never parted. Sometimes they moved but it was only in the breeze.

The trees in the street showed green now, thick with budded leaves. The shadow pattern on my wall was intricate and rich. It was no longer an austere winter pattern as it had been at first. Even the movement of the branches in the wind seemed different. I used to lie looking at the shadow when I rested in the afternoon. I was always tired then and so more permeable to impressions. I'd think about the buds, how pale and tender they were, but how implacable. The way an unborn child is implacable. If man's world were in ashes the spring would still come. I watched the moving pattern and my heart stirred with it in frail, half-sweet melancholy.

One afternoon I looked out instead of in. It was growing late and the sun would soon be gone, but it was warm. There was gold dust in the air, the sunlight had thickened. The shadows of trees and buildings fell, as they sometimes do on a fortunate day, with dramatic grace. *She* was standing there just behind the curtains, in a long dark wrap, as if she had come from her bath and was going to dress, early, for the evening. She stood so long and so still, staring out – at the budding trees, I thought – that tension began to accumulate in my

mind. My blood ticked like a clock. Very slowly she raised her arms and the gown fell from her. She stood there naked, behind the veil of the curtains, the scarcely distinguishable but unmistakeable form of a woman whose face was in shadow.

I turned away. The shadow of the burgeoning bough was on the white wall. I thought my heart would break.

MY BIRD

ALAN MARSHALL
1902–1984

IT was not a silent darkness. Away out over the flat swamp water came rustles, splashes, quacks and the quick flap of wings being stretched and folded again.

Swans cried out and were answered, and plovers, flying low over the water, called to birds standing on the sandhills that divided the swamp from the bay.

The smell of water weeds and reeds and thrusting roots hung over the swamp and the tall marram grass growing on the bank.

It was just after midnight, the morning of the opening of the duck season. The day before, Dan Lucey, an inspector of the Fisheries and Game Department, had arrived at Werribee in a utility truck. He had gone into the swamp lands during the afternoon and carried out an inspection before preparing for the arrival of the shooters that night.

The swamp lands were divided into two areas, one of which was a sanctuary for native birds.

Shooters were forbidden to enter the sanctuary, and here the water birds were allowed to breed and live in peace.

What was left of the swamp lands was known as the Main Swamp. This section was thrown open to shooters for three months of the year, a period known to sportsmen as 'The Duck Season'.

The main swamp was divided from the sanctuary by a levee. During the open season, shooters could roam the main swamp as they pleased but beyond the levee they must not go. This wall of earth was a boundary between two countries, one of which was given to war and the other to peace.

It was Dan Lucey's task, on this opening day, to keep shooters off the sanctuary and to prevent the slaughter of protected birds. During the close season all ducks were protected but when, by official proclamation from the Office of the Director of Fisheries and Game, the duck season opened, those birds that were losing the struggle to survive were still forbidden game and men who shot them were open to fines and the confiscation of their guns.

Dan Lucey stood beside his truck watching the headlights of cars coming in to the turn-around beside the swamp where shooting was allowed.

For almost a year he had guarded these ducks against men with guns.

He had patrolled the swamp lands on moonlight nights, listening and watching, sometimes running in a crouch from shadow to shadow towards the report of a forbidden gun.

He had waded waist-deep through tangled places where the nests were, had drawn aside the reeds and seen the eggs warm from birds he had startled. He had watched the wild ducks leading flotillas of quick-paddling ducklings across smooth patches of water and had seen their first heavy, ungainly flight.

'It's good to look at ducks flying,' he had once said. 'I like to see them coming in to land at sunset.

'It's great to hear the whistle of their wings then look up and see them swerve away from the movement of you. Ducks are good, you get to love them.'

Dan Lucey had been born on the Murrumbidgee and here, where the slow river flowed between high clay banks, and gnarled red gums leant over the water, he had spent his childhood. As a man he was tall with a blackfellow's grace of movement and a face that was at peace with the bush, but, as a child, barefooted and brown, he had not yet come to terms with his surroundings. He had been restless and questioning and pursued some illusive revelation, some answer, some final discovery that he felt awaited him around each river bend, behind each tree or beyond each rise.

He was a searcher, lifting pieces of dry bark where centipedes shrank back from the light, thrusting his hand into hollow limbs where possums slept or parrots nested and wading through lignum swamps, parting branches and peering or standing silent with his face turned to the sky where the whistle of a driving wing still lingered.

Had there been, in his home, books in which poets sang the truth of things, or great writers wrote inspiringly, he would have sat cross-legged beneath the belah tree in his backyard, and the book upon his knee would have been as wings to him.

But there were no books, and in the flight of birds his need of beauty found its answer, in the strength and power of scarred red gum trunks, deep-rooted in the earth, he felt the lift of spirit that comes to the man of books when he reads great literature. The drama and poetry he knew passed through no interpretative pen before enchanting him; it came to him from its source, pure and clear like a bullock bell.

He knew the river birds well. He had gazed on the egg, the splintering shell, the powder-puff young ones, the fat squeakers still unable to fly. He had watched the close-plumaged, grown ducks coming down wind with the long sun of evening upon them. They had come in with swerve and bank and flash of jewel and he had held his breath to the singing within him.

Yet, he had, with other boys, fired shanghai stones at resting birds, but his shots were wide. It was the twang of rubber and the soaring stone that delighted him.

Later, proud with the responsibilities of a new manhood, he had carried his birthday-present gun through the swamps, and had slain ducks as he went. He had tied the necks of bleeding birds to his belt and had come home with tales of marvellous shots he had made.

But he couldn't kill without a feeling of shame. With a draggled bundle of dead ducks at his belt the flight of those still living was always a withdrawal from him. He was left earthbound and solitary, weighed down by his betrayal.

He had put away his gun, only taking it out to clean it or to feel the satisfaction of squinting down its gleaming barrel before returning it to its brackets on the wall.

When he finally came to the city looking for work he went straight to the Fisheries and Game Department, where he was engaged as an inspector. He was eager and enthusiastic, inspired by a vision.

Now he stood in the darkness thinking of these things, his vision gone.

The drone of engines, like a requiem, moved with the cars that stretched in a broken line from Werribee to Melbourne. The cars thrust out feelers of light towards those ahead of them. They lurched over ruts of swamplands, and the dust-laden beams shot up and fell again, illuminating tussocks of grass and striking glitters from the chromium bumpers of vehicles rocking ahead.

On a circular area flattened in the grass on the bank of the swamp, they came to rest. They crowded together in dark clusters divided by passageways along which those arriving nosed their way with whining gears, searching for a space in which to park. They moved into these places then stopped, their blazing eyes flicked out, their engines became silent.

More came, and more. Men carrying torches or hurricane lanterns jumped back and stood aside while groups moved past. In all those hours of darkness the sound of engines never ceased. A thousand cars came in that night, three thousand shooters stepped from them and moved off into the dark, their gun barrels gleaming in the headlights of the cars still seeking a resting place.

Legs moved in the light of swinging lanterns, passing and re-passing each other while their shadows made frantic sweeps over the grass. Silhouetted men swore softly, called to companions, asked questions, proffered information.

'Where's Jack? ... Have you got my gun? ... I've been here before; we'll go this way.... Where's the best place?'

They stepped high over tussocks, they walked with bent heads, watching the uneven ground, they stooped and pushed their way through brush.

'Over here. This way. I can hear them quacking.'

Men hurried for positions of vantage. The swamp was ringed wih men. They were shoulder to shoulder on spits of land where the ducks swept low for a landing. They stood side by side on the hillocks. They crouched like waiting soldiers in the hollows.

'We start at six.'

'We're into them at six.'

'We'll let them have it at six.'

The uneasy birds on the dark water moved towards the centre of the swamp. There was a pale sky in the east.

Shells were thumbed from belts, locks clicked and snapped. Guns were shouldered and lowered, swept round and back, tested and thumbed and gripped.

'Don't swing over my area.'

'I never swing over any man's area.'

Dan Lucey drove the utility truck along the swamp bank and into the sanctuary. He left the truck near a patch of scrub and walked to the swamp's edge from where the water lay stretched beneath the dark in a pale light of its own.

He paced the bank, restless, feeling, in all that was around him, the existence of an intense awareness, an emotion of his own creating. The very air was listening, the trees were expectant and still.

He waited while the sky grew lighter and the darkness retreated to the shelter of the banks. Patches of darkness lay netted in grass and hollows where the tea-tree grew, but birds could be faintly seen on the water.

Dan slowly rolled a cigarette.

That teal with the one leg. A cod had probably taken the other one when she was a duckling. Or maybe a trap. Some men set rabbit traps on sandbanks to catch ducks, spread wheat around them. By hell, she was tame! Maybe she won't leave the water when they start. She'll be safe in the sanctuary. But the noise will start the lot off. If she's with a flock she'll go but she might be in the reeds. No, she'll take off with the rest. She'll rise with them. Having one leg won't affect her flying, anyway. You never know, though.

She may not be able to swerve as quickly. But she'll go high. They always do. She might get above it.

He looked up at the paling sky, seeing, in his imagination, the sanctuary it seemed to offer streaked with screaming pellets. He turned away.

It was half past five when the first gun was fired. In the stricken moment that followed, men's voices shouting a protest came from different parts of the swamp. A double report drowned their cries. Rosebuds of flame quivered above clumps of reed. Single reports followed each other rapidly. They made a staccato of sound that merged and grew till it became a thunderous volume of sound that pressed on Dan like a weight.

The air above the swamp, torn apart by the explosive roar, eddied across the still water, leaving a quivering surface and the smell of smoke behind it.

There were no gaps of silence in the sound. It was continuous and violent and controlled. Yet, within it and apart from it, could be heard the thrash of wings, the splash of falling bodies, quick, terrified quacks and the whish of speeding flocks hurtling by like companies of projectiles.

The thin, whispering whistle of shot, torn out of shape by pitted barrels, threaded the din and sent speeding birds into swerves and dives of terror.

Piercing the rumble in stabs of sharper sound, two hollow cracks came at intervals from the far side of the swamp.

Dan raised his head and listened.

Homemade cartridges? There they go again! No. Poley chokes on their guns. That American idea for greater range. They'll get the high ones.

One more ... Two ... Three ... Struth! That finiishes the high ones. That pulls them down. No hope up on top now.

He suddenly took off his hat and shook some pellets of shot from the crown.

They must be as thick as rain up there.

When the firing began in the swamp, a panic swept across the birds on the waters of the sanctuary. Some swam swiftly to and fro while others took to the air in a flurry of wings. Those leaving infected the undecided ones with fear and in a moment they were all leaving the water, some in silence, others with quick cries of alarm.

Black duck, the first to leave, rose sharply, shooting upwards, their wings drumming. They held their wings low down, flying with short, swift chops, straining for speed. They banked in a sweeping turn at the sanctuary's edge and came round over the head of the watching man, the whistle of their speed trailing just behind them.

Dan's head jerked round to follow them.

By the hell, they're hiking! They'll circle twice before they beat it.

The flock swung off the sanctuary at the second spiral and the guns reached up for them in a bay of sound that rose above the steady roar of the continuous shooting.

They're for it. Dan drew a deep breath.

A hail of shot broke the formation and scattered the ducks like leaves in the wind. One bird, a broken wing raised above it like a sail, came down in a tight spin, its uninjured wing thrashing desperately. It struck the levee bank between the sanctuary and the open swamp with a thud. A dozen men rushed towards it yelling. 'My bird!'

A flock of grey teal, flying in line, followed the black duck up from the water then shot out over the open swamp on their first circle. A blast from a group of shooters broke their line into two groups, the centre birds tumbling from the sky like stones.

Pelicans and swans circled in a slow climb. The pelicans beat their giant wings with slow, deliberate strokes, their heads tucked back, their heavy bills resting on curved necks. With them were cranes, herons and avocets.

Ducks rising from the water passed through and over this layer of heavy birds, circling on a different level before shooting out over the bay to safety.

Shot, whistling upwards to the high ducks, sometimes struck the heavy birds screening those above them, and they faltered in their slow climb, because agitated, called to each other or plummeted earthwards in silence.

The protected widgeon, slower than the grey teal or black duck, circled the sanctuary in jerky, uneasy flight, swerving unnecessarily when the gunfire from the swamp suddenly sharpened. They chattered as they flew, their voices like

'THE pelicans beat their giant wings with slow, deliberate strokes, their heads tucked back, their heavy bills resting on curved necks.'

the sound of rusty hinges, continuing even when, in sweeps over the open swamp, they fell singly and in twos to the guns of men out to kill every bird that passed.

Dan swore in a sudden anger.

Half these bastards don't know their birds. They don't know a widgeon from a black duck. I'll pick them up. I'll get them on their way out.

'You damn fools,' he shouted.

He watched each flock as it passed and when, against the dawn sky, he saw the wide shovel-bills, the heavy heads, the set-back wings of the widgeon as they banked and turned for the open swamp, he cupped his hand to his mouth and yelled 'Widgeon!' across the water to where the first line of shooters were blazing at all that went over.

Some lowered their guns at the yell, others went on shooting.

A pair of grey teal came hurtling across the open swamp making for the sanctuary. A wave of sound followed them, its peak just beneath them as they moved. They were flying high and fast but a crack shot blasted the rear bird sideways in its flight and it began to drop. Five shots struck its falling body before it reached the water where it floated without movement.

The leader faltered in its flight when its mate was hit. Then it gathered itself and flew on till the sanctuary lay beneath it.

It came in as if to land but rose again and returned for its mate.

Dan gestured hopelessly. He's gonner. He'll cop the lot. He's finished.

When the shot struck it, it didn't fold up and fall uncontrolled from the sky. It came down in a swift, steep glide, its body still in the position of normal flight. When it struck the ground it bounced and rolled like a football.

The last birds to leave the water of the sanctuary were eight wood duck. They had been sheltering in some rushes, but fear drove them out and they took off in a ragged group, their wings almost touching. As they gained height a drake moved forward and took the lead. The others fell naturally into the V formation behind him.

He led them down the water of the sanctuary, their necks undulating as they put power into their climb. They circled over the far end of the reserve then came back, their speed increasing with every chop of their wings. They banked above Dan Lucey, their mottled breasts bright in the dawn light, then turned for another round.

When they again reached the limits of the sanctuary, the drake, leading them in a steep climb, banked and lost height in a short, steep dive, then flattened out and brought them back towards where Dan was standing. Dan saw the man-oeuvre and was puzzled.

Hell! he came down. Must be a heavy wind on top. No. He's building up speed. That's the stuff! Give it all you've got! Into it!

The drake, as if seeking a gap of silence through which to pass, kept turning his head from side to side as he flew.

Dan suddenly saw him as a symbol. The things that he stood for and in which he believed made a continued preoccupation with the killing around him in-tolerable. This bird lived and was free. A strong heart beat within him and blood flowed through his veins. His survival became important to Dan. If he lived, a thousand slaughtered ducks lived on in him, if he died there was nothing but death upon the swamp.

'Round again, round again,' Dan muttered aloud as he watched him. 'Bring them around again, damn you!'

But the drake had made his decision: he led them on towards the open swamp. They passed over Dan's head at ninety feet or so, their wings whistling.

They're for it now, he thought. There they go – the suicide squad.

He watched them, standing in a slight crouch, his hands clenched. He *must* make it. He *must*. He *must*. He took a deep breath and stood still.

The ducks crossed the first line of shooters into the open swamp in a perfect V. The crest of a roaring sound-wave leapt up towards them as they went over and the drake led the group in a swerve as it struck them.

Now with the light of the morning full on them, the eight wood duck were a target for every gun. Barrels like black reeds fringed the open water along which they flew, reeds that exploded then jerked down in the recoil.

Dan, watching the birds, stood in a crouching attitude as if he were facing enemies.

One gone!

The duck to the left, and just behind the drake, changed from something firm and hard and full of power to a soft and shapeless bundle of feathers that fell without resistance towards the water.

Dan was up there with them now. He swung and lifted to their wings. He made each downward plunge to earth.

The V closed up and the gap was filled. The drake led the remaining six in quick swerves and dives. Every turn and twist he made, each violent, evasive movement was followed by the six ducks behind him.

Their every action was born of his, they had no mind but his.

The whisper of shot drove him to more desperate turns and his followers repeated them. But, in the centre of the swamp, one of the rear ducks suddenly lost height. It fluttered, fell, then flew again. It followed the V at a lower height for a few yards then its wings went limp and it fell loosely to the water.

'My bird!' cried splashing men holding guns aloft.

A third bird was plucked from the formation before they reached the last line of shooters beyond which was safety.

The drake, leading his four companions across this last barrier where the shooters were side by side, suddenly banked steeply as shot whistled past them. He flew a moment in indecision then, as another duck fell, he brought the remnant of his flock round and made down the swamp once more.

Dan, watching him through his field glasses, cursed softly.

A shout rose from the shooters as the ducks turned. Again the wave of sound moved beneath the birds.

The drake dropped all evasive tastics now. He was dazed with noise.

He flew straight ahead with the remaining three birds in line behind him.

He led them down in a shallow dive to increase their speed but rose steeply as two of his companions fell together, a puff of feathers left floating behind them.

There was only one duck following him now. With a quick chop of her wings she closed up, moving a little to one side till her head was level with his body. But she began to flag and he drew away from her.

The shot that hit her threw her violently upwards and she turned over on her back before crashing at the feet of the shooters on the levee.

The drake was alone now. He swept out over the sanctuary to a last burst of sound then turned and made out over the bay.

To the man this speeding bird, like some winged vessel, bore in its seed the life wrenched from a thousand slaughtered ducks upon the swamp. He felt the lift of victory, the faith, the elation. As, against bright clouds, the drake rose to an upward swing of air, twinkled and was gone, he flung his arms up in an acclaiming gesture, then turned and faced the shooters on the levee.

'*My* bird!' he yelled. '*My* bird, damn you! *My* bird!'

THE MILK RUN

CHRISTINA
STEAD
1902–1983

LYDHAM Hill was the name of the knoll and of the cottage, too; it was painted on the stone pillars where the iron carriage gates closed the now unused drive. The cottage stood on the crest of a high ridge overlooking Botany Bay, some eight miles distant and was built four-square, east-west, so that they could look from the veranda straight between the headlands, Cape Banks and Cape Solander, to the Pacific.

They could see from the attic windows the obelisk standing where Captain Cook first landed with his botanists, Banks and Solander, and they could see on stormy days the little launch they called *The Peanut* tossing between the heads as it went towards Kurnell. The cottage was built of rough-hewn sandstone blocks cut in the quarry down the hill and hauled up in the old days. The trees round the house, Norfolk Island and other pines, pittosporum, camphor laurel, were seventy and more years old and the pines had seeded in the old neglected orchard where the seedings grew higher every year, faster than the children. The knoll itself was ironstone capped and penetrated by heavy, thick and almost pure clay, gamboge yellow, stained red where the ironstone stuck out its nodules.

It was almost country still; few houses, large pastures, unpaved streets of sand or clay, foul and grassy gutters. The short street Lydham Avenue, which went over the hump before the house, westward, was a hazard, almost impassable in wet weather. Cartwheels, horseshoes, boots, umbrella ferrules were sucked in by the clay. In the hot sun the clay soon turned to dough and then to pottery. A messenger boy, the young postman, the women and children of Lydham Hill, had to cross the clay to get to the tram or the shops and might lose a handkerchief, a parasol, a shoe, a parcel; and after poking at it gingerly, afraid to fall in the muck, would abandon it and struggle to the clay bank and look back just as if the thing had been carried out to sea. The postman's prints, first of a sandshoe which he lost as he crossed to Lydham and then of his naked foot, and a copy of the *St George Call*, which he had dropped while trying to get his shoe back, remained week after week. The footprints and tracks remained and even at the next big rain they did not disappear, but only formed little foot-shaped puddles and long canals.

The Council occasionally sent men with a cart and shovels to scrape off the surface; and with it they gleaned the lost articles and went away with the cart, leaving behind an identical clay surface, but with the banks higher now, until the people in Lydham Hill had to cut steps in the bank, yellow clay steps.

It was warm, October, summer just beginning. October is the month of the roof-raising equinoctial gales, which, shouting, bring down trees and capsise sheds. It was a Saturday. The day and night before there had been gales; rain in the morning – in the evening, a sunset the colour of the saffron tea-rose at the gate. Matthew, going for milk on Friday, had lost a sandshoe. 'Clumsy ape,'

IT was almost country still; few houses, large pastures, unpaved streets of sand or clay, foul and grassy gutters.'

91

said his father goodnaturedly, flipping his cheek with the nails of his left hand and at the same time explaining that he and Matthew were lefthanded; and he went on to explain how very difficult this made things for his neighbours, a lady, say, at public dinners; and that Matthew, later on, would find it awkward, too. Matthew was seven. Then his father, going barefoot, had squelched happily out into the mud and got the shoe back. It needed soaking and cleaning. Said his father, 'From now on you go to Dappeto barefooted; it's good for the feet anyway.' Dappeto was his grandfather's place, where he got the milk.

All the week, in the evenings, his father with his elder brother Jimmy-James, had been lopping the lower boughs off the Norfolk pines down the horse-paddock side. They called it the horse paddock because it was rented to a brown horse for one pound a week, a lonely horse that could be seen streets away on their slope and which people thought was their horse; but they were not allowed to speak to it.

With the cut branches the three of them built a gunyah, an Aboriginal shelter, placing the tall boughs against a good-sized trunk, lacing them together with small branches. It made an odorous half-tent, green, dark, with a floor of old brown pine needles, nine inches to a foot thick, so that even now it was dry and warm, on the slope.

Matthew had dragged some of the other boughs to the bottom of the white paddock, a pony's paddock, so called because it had a white railing. In it they kept two full-grown emus named Dinawan (a native word for emu) and Dibiyu, (a native word for the whistling duck because this emu whistled). Dinawan and Dibiyu had come to them newly hatched chicks, striped and about the size of fowls. Beyond this fence at the bottom Matt had built this gunyah to share with his friend Lyall Lowrie, also seven years old, a boy who lived in one of the new brick cottages downhill. There was building all around them, fascinating for the boys.

Matt and Lyall were sitting in the gunyah close together, talking in low interested voices. It was quite warm, though the sun was striking higher at the trees as it westered. Matt, though he did not say so, was hiding from the house. The boys had torn away the rough pine needles and were poking in the soft blackish felted earth. They had found some small red ants.

'That's the beginning of an ants' street,' said Matthew.

'I know, one street on top of the other,' said Lyall.

'Like a city of the future,' said Matthew.

A whistling began. Matthew peered through the pine branches. A woman's voice came down the hill. Matthew said, 'I have to go for the milk. Do you want to come?'

'Where is it? The dairy?'

'It's my grandmother's place: about a mile.'

But Lyall had to go home. He climbed a branch, reached out for the fencetop, dropped down, shouted, 'I'll see you tomorrow.'

'If I don't have to work,' said Matthew.

Matthew toiled up the orchard path, made of pebbles stuck in clay. At the south end of the house was a lattice, with one panel sagging from the gale. His father was repairing it. A tall strong fair man, burnt red by the sun, he stood in

the opening leading to the brick yard, a courtyard almost entirely enclosed by domestic buildings in sandstone, a shelter from the hilltop wind.

'Milk-oh!' said his father.

'I made a gunyah,' said Matthew.

'Good-oh. And now skedaddle.'

Matthew was a fair sturdy boy who closely resembled his father. His sun-bleached hair was whiter; he had a thick down over his temples joining his pale eyebrows, and it ran over the sides of his cheeks where his beard would be.

As soon as he came in sight of his father, his eyes became fixed on the man's face, he smiled with an unconscious faint rapture and, his head turning, his glances followed his father, a restless, energetic man, never still.

'Do you love your Dad?' said his father, smiling with coquettish cunning at the child.

The boy burst out laughing, 'Yes, Dad!'

His worship of his father was a family joke, a public joke and something that irritated his mother. They talked about him when they thought he was not listening. He was always listening idly, his head turned away, while he played with ants, bees, wasps; and mooned, as they said. The ants, bees, wasps did not sting him; they would hang resting on his hand. His idling, playing was not a ruse. In his dreamy pastimes, he liked to be a part of what he heard, the snatches and inconsequence of their talk, part of the wasps, the rush of wind, an entire life, vague but delicious. He could sit in the sun watching the ant trails for hours; he never hurt the ants. His father told him they were ant-engineers, ant-architects, ant-soldiers, ant-nurses, ant-scouts; but he scarcely thought of it. 'Perhaps another Darwin,' said his father; and he said the same when it turned out that Matthew was slow in school. Darwin was slow in school. But at other times, Matthew galloped about shouting; no one knew what he shouted.

His father was pretending to block the way. Matthew could get very angry. His father was curious about it and teased him. With a rough push, the boy got past and went to the kitchen. The milkcan stood on the table, a workman's billycan of grey flecked enamel with a tin top that served as a cup. He set off. His feet were bare. They were solid well-formed feet, with the skin grown thick and horny on the soles and blackened underneath, dark grey with dirt you could not get out, yellow-splashed at the sides, with deep cracks on the soles right down to the red flesh. He was used to having sore feet and dug deep into the soft mud, soothed.

He went down the grass slope outside the iron gates, where they were now laying the foundations to build. The men had gone and he picked up a few bright nails from between the floor joists for his father. The men liked him and let him take nails anyway.

At Wollongong Road he scanned the dairy farm opposite. Then he crossed the road and walked along by the two-rail fence. The farm buildings of whitewashed planks lay slightly below the swell of the meadow, towards Stoney Creek gully. Matt trotted down the deeply rutted tussocky footway. He had not gone far before the boy he feared came out from the brick wall of the old house where he had been waiting, with a mad scowl, his features jumping as if on red and black wires, his teeth showing. He rushed to the fence and swung his greenhide throng on to Matthew's shoulder and face. He did not say a word but with a fierce grin of hatred jerked and swung.

'Don't,' said Matthew. He hurried along, the milkcan swinging wildly on its wire handle. His enemy followed him to the next panel and the next, but did not get through the fence on to the footway. The greenhide bat, about fifteen inches long and three or four inches wide, slapped down on Matthew's left side. He started to cry and ran along the ruts, the milkcan insensately hopping up and down and doing somersaults. But the boy, having caused terror, ceased after a few more panels and walked diagonally toward the milking-sheds, turning round to make a face. The cows were coming up from the gullyside and gathering at the door of the shed. The milkman's son was a thin muscular boy of about ten, with dark hair and regular features; but when Matthew saw him he was always snarling, scowling, grinning in fury.

Matthew reached the next block, all small red-roofed houses; but it was some time before he saw the ochre-coloured picket fence of Dappeto. Until a fortnight before, it had been his sister Emily, a clumsy girl of eleven, always in the wars, as they said, who had gone for the milk to Dappeto, every evening after school. Then one day, almost home, she fell in the clay and sent the can flying. She came home dirty, her long fair hair wet and dark-streaked over her red cheeks, with no milk for the baby and the story, 'a boy beat me'. 'What boy?' 'I don't know.' Though Matthew knew the boy, their unbelief made him think it was a lie, too.

Now, though they did not believe her and he was smaller, it had become his job to go for the milk. Even his mother had made no protest.

Here was his grandfather's house, Dappeto. Inside the fence grew all kinds of trees, camphor laurel, pittosporum, swamp box, eucalypts, wattles. He went down the lane to the side where was a big gate for the buggy. He dug his toes into the asphalt softened by the day's sun. There was the old camphor laurel with the broad low arms good for climbing and hiding, there the giant *Araucaria bidwillii*, with shining dark green stabbing leaves. There was the man Tom Grove, called The Man, in the cow paddock at the salt-lick. Matthew went in under the archway where were the feed bins and up into the second kitchen. No one was there. Up a step into the kitchen. Mary the maid sat at the window knitting.

'I saw you coming. How's your mother?'

'All right.'

'What dirty feet! Where are your shoes?'

'I lost one.'

He went up another step, on to the veranda, turned right; there was the double pantry: preserves beyond in a dark room; here on the shelf three large shallow pans of milk for skimming. Mary came and poured milk into his can.

The parrot sitting on his perch on the veranda put down his head engagingly, said, 'Cocky want a bit of bread and sugar?' Mary dipped a crust in milk and sugar and gave it to the boy.

'Give it to Joe.'

'No, no,' he said, flushing. The parrot had a cunning eye and heavy beak.

'Emus have bigger beaks,' said Mary. She was a country woman from Hay ('Hay, Hell and Booligal,' he knew) and saw no sense in keeping emus.

'Emus don't bite,' said Matt.

Mary, in her long flowing skirt, stepped along the veranda and handed the parrot his crust. He was a handsome Mexican said to be forty years old, as old as Mary herself.

'Go and see your grandmother; I'll get some butter for your mother.'

Up another slate step into the house, where right beside the door there was a little room called the housekeeper's room, where his grandmother liked to sit.

'Is that you, Mattie?' called a voice very like the parrot's voice.

A large solid neat old woman, with white hair strained back into a little bun, in a black dress with white trimmings, a housekeeper's dress, sat in an armchair stuck between the table and the wall. She could look out through two windows in the angle, one towards Wollongong Road, one towards the greenhouses. She smiled fondly but did not stop revolving her thumbs in her clasped bloated hands.

'Look at the dirty feet! Doesn't your mother give you shoes to wear?'

'I have sandshoes.'

'Where are they?'

'HERE was his grand-father's house, Dap-peto. Inside the fence grew all kinds of trees, camphor laurel, pittosporum, swamp box, eucalypts, wat-tles.'

'It's healthy to go without shoes.'

'Come and kiss Old Mum. How's your brother?'

'Jamstealer is all right. He's playing football this afternoon.'

The grandmother said suddenly, 'Jamstealer is not a nice name to call your brother.'

'It doesn't mean jamstealer: it's a name. Daddy calls him that.'

'It's not a nice name for your father to call his son.'

Matthew frowned. The old woman rose and took his hand.

'Come and I'll get you some flowers for your mother. How is she?'

'Mother's lying down.'

She plucked flowers from the beds along the cracked asphalt drive. Her flat monk's shoes slid off the grassy verge.

'I nearly fell down on my bum,' she said, began to laugh, opening her mouth wide in her creased floury face. She kept her eyes on the little boy. 'What would your father say to that?' Matthew was shocked but said nothing. 'Milking, we had a stool called a bumstool,' she said. She had come from a dairying family on the South Coast. He eyed her straight. They came back to the kitchen.

'Tell your mother to come and see her mother one of these days.'

Mary handed him the butter in a bag and the flowers and the milk.

'Scratch Cocky,' said the parrot. He lowered his head and ruffled the feathers, showing grey skin.

'Beat the gong,' begged Matthew.

Mary picked up the chamois-headed stick which hung on the gong beside the back door. Joey shifted his feet in a slow respectable dance. Mary hit the gong twice: Joey screeched:

'Stephen! Walter! Edward! Anthony! John! Arthur! Matthew! Robert! Frederick! Albert! William! Leah! Rachel! Pitti!'

It was a country woman's screech.

No air-thin boys and girls came gambolling from the paddocks and orchard, from the gardens and bowling-green, hungry for dinner; though in years long gone they had come racing, in flesh and blood. Those were his uncles and aunts and Pitti was his mother, the youngest, 'Pretty'.

Matthew went back up the asphalt drive, the homemade butter in one hand, the flowers and the quart milkcan jostling in the other. When he came back to the dairy on Wollongong Road, he hesitated. He could cross towards Forest Road, heading round a triangle of land just being fenced in and invisible to the dairy boy. But he was a little afraid of the new route. He crossed and came along the other side of the Wollongong Road, along a tall apricot-coloured fence of new hairy boards. At the farther point of that triangular plot, too, was an interesting wooden post, very old and grey and eaten inside by termites. It had been smouldering for weeks, set alight by the sun, not extinguished by the rain. The sun was on the horizon. Shafts of red touched him across the dairy. He reached the end of the new fence and Lydham Hill could be seen with its great head of trees. He stumbled on a big tussock and fell. Though he kept hold of the things, the milk spilled. He got up quickly and righted the can, but there was very little milk left. He tried with the lid to catch some milk from the ground, but it had soaked away into the sand, leaving a light stain. Just a

'THE sun was on the horizon. Shafts of red touched him across the dairy.'

few of the grass blades held a dew of milk. When he shook them, the dew fell. He did not know what to do. He was too tired to go back to Dappeto. At home, they might beat him, worse, shout and deplore. As he still poked stupidly about looking for milk, he saw a gold coin, a sovereign, under the tussock. He knew it, for his father brought home his pay on Saturdays, spread the coins on the table, gold sovereigns and half sovereigns, silver, and let them finger it. He was proud of it, what he earned.

Matthew picked up the gold coin and hurried home up the yellow clay, past the saffron tea-rose, the 'Chinaman's Finger Tree', a tree with yellow bell flowers, so called because they put the flowers on their fingers and rushed at each other, shrieking, 'I'm a Chinaman.'

He had his statement ready, 'I fell over the grass and spilled the milk.'

His mother was in the kitchen in her grey silk dressing-gown, with the silver and gold dragons on it, at the bottom gold water-waves and a gold tower. She had a baby's white shawl round her head, a sign of neuralgia.

'I was tired,' he complained.

'Barely a cupful,' she said contemptuously. 'Open the condensed milk, Eva. What's that?'

'Butter and some flowers and Old Mum says to go and see her.'

'I'll go and see Mother tomorrow. I wish I could leave this darn windy barn. And the emus walked in this evening and ate your father's cat's-eye waistcoat buttons that were lying on the kitchen windowsill.'

'I found this,' said Matthew, 'it's a sovereign.'

Until he had shown it, he had not been quite sure about it. Was it really there?

The two women came close. 'Yes, so it is,' said his mother; 'some poor brute of a workman lost his wages and is getting a tongue-banging this minute, I know.'

'Can I keep it, Mother?'

'I don't suppose so. We'll ask your father.'

But his father said, 'It's no use crying over spilt milk', and he said Matthew could keep the sovereign. 'You can start a savings account at school on Monday.'

Matthew turned up his fair flushed face, radiant, and looked at his father's face: it seemed to him all pure love. He exclaimed, 'Tommy Small whaled me; with a greenhide bat.'

They drew back, inspecting him curiously.

'Where?'

He pulled up his sleeve and there, to his surprise, there really was a broad bruise. He now expected his father to break into shouts of indignation. His mother stood in doubt; his father also stood away with a strange expression, a queasy, almost greedy expression, yet shy and frightened, too. Matthew felt that they would do nothing about it.

'It's a dirty dairy,' said his father.

'Must I go for the milk tomorrow?'

'Of course, gee-up, milk-oh!'

His mother said, 'You must be a man, my son.'

They did not believe him. They thought he was copying Emily. He did not go further. Muteness crowded his mouth: his throat closed. He saw they had abandoned him, and expected nothing. On Sunday he went with his mother for the milk. 'It isn't half a mile,' she said. After that he never saw Tommy Small again. This too was something he did not comprehend; he began to feel that perhaps he was a liar, like Emily. But then the gold coin was inexplicable; and what astonished him most, in secret, was that it was he who had found it. He knew he was not clever or lucky. A thought grew inside him, evolving out of doubt and fluff, 'Perhaps later I will have just one big piece of luck'; and the gold coin remained shining in the soft animal darkness of his mind.

When the new houses were finished and he could no longer go there for nails for his father, people came to live and presently a new dairy sent round a cart. He would rush out when the milkman came, glorying in the spurting foaming quarts that they took in, in two big jugs they had bought. He stood on the brick landing outside the kitchen and watched, his tongue at his teeth. 'Two quarts, please,' his mother always said, standing in her long pink dressing-gown, her black hair fluffed out. Oh, the milk! The flowing milk.

LENA

JOHN MORRISON
1904–

'Tins, Joe!'

Half past three, and the usual note of irritation has crept into Lena's voice. Without getting up from my knees, I reach backwards, seize a couple of buckets, and push them through under the drooping leaves of the vines. Before I can release them they are grabbled and pulled violently away from me. Between the top leaves, and only fifteen inches away, I get a glimpse of a freckled little face, keen eyes leaping from bunch to bunch of the clustering grapes, always a spilt second in front of the darting fingers and slashing knife. I hear the thump of tumbling fruit, and get up wearily. No use trying to feed her with tins as we go – she's too quick, too experienced, too enthusiastic. Or is it just that I am too old and too slow?

Empty tins are thrown only into alternate rows, leaving the other rows clear for the passing of the tractor that takes away the gathered fruit. Right from the start of the picking it has fallen to me, no doubt as gentleman's privilege, to work that side of the vines where the empties are. As Lena and I make equal division of the day's earnings, I try to keep up with her, but every now and then forget to keep her supplied with tins.

'You should let me know before you cut right out, Lena,' I say gently as I push the first ones through just ahead of her.

She doesn't answer, which means that she's lost patience with me. I, too, am irritated. Irritated by this tally anxiety that seizes her every day about this time. But I remind myself that at tea tonight, with the day's work over, she will forget everything, wait on me like a devoted daughter, chatter brightly about the circus we're all going to in Redcliffs, ask me if I have anything for the wash tomorrow. So I go about twenty yards down the row, pushing through a couple of tins every few feet, and say nothing until I get back.

It is a relief to bend my aching legs again, to press my knees into the warm red earth, to get my head out of the sun and stare into the cool recesses of the vine leaves. Off the first bunch of grapes I pull a handful, stuff it into my mouth, swallow the juice, and spit out the residue. While I've been away Lena has conscientiously picked right through to my side, leaving only one or two clusters she couldn't reach, so that in only a few minutes I'm up with her again. I can't see her, but the violence with which she is banging the buckets tells me that she is still sulking.

'Angry with me?' I ask.

No answer. I wait a few seconds, then bang a bucket myself just to let her see that I too can be provoked.

'You never have much to say this time of day, do you?' I venture.

'You can't talk and work.'

'You can in the mornings. You were telling me all about your dad before lunch.'

'That's why we're behind. We only got two hundred and ten buckets this morning.'

'Only! Isn't that good?'

'We should have got two hundred and fifty. We'll be going flat out to get four hundred and fifty today.'

'Do we *have* to get four hundred and fifty?'

'Yes!' Very emphatically.

To that I give no reply. Everything I could say has already been said, more than once. I can, at the moment, think of no new lead in an argument which has become wearisome. To Lena, piecework is the road to riches – 'The harder you work, the more you get.' She's too young to know anything of the days when armies of unemployed converged on the irrigation belt to struggle for a chance to pick grapes at 5 shillings per hundred tins. We're due for a visit from a union organiser; I keep wondering what she'll say when he asks her to take a ticket.

I'm working on, not saying a word, but she takes my silence as a sign of weakness and presses the attack herself.

'It's all right for you. I need the money.'

'We all need money, Lena.'

'You'll get plenty when you get back to the wharves. And get it easier too, I bet!'

'Sometimes. It depends on what the cargo is. But we never get paid by the ton!'

'Wharfies wouldn't work, anyway.'

Hitting below the belt. She must be quite upset to say a thing like that. I let it go, though, because it would be a preposterous thing to fall out with her. We're both Australians, but in a way that has nothing to do with geography I know that we come from different countries. She's a big, lovable child, inherently forthright and generous, and usually quite merry, but her philosophy is a bit frightening to a man brought up on the waterfront of a great city. She comes from a poor little grazing property deep in the mallee scrub over the New South Wales border. One of a family of eleven. For forty-six weeks in the year she works sheep and helps to bring up nine younger brothers and sisters. The six weeks' grape-picking is the annual light of her drab little life: money of her own, appetising food, the companionship of other people's sons and daughters, above all the fabulous Saturday morning shopping excursions into Mildura. After the picture of home that she painted for me this morning I can understand all this, but I'd give something to open her innocent young eyes to the world I know. Her conception of fighting for one's rights extends no further than keeping a wary eye on the number of filled buckets. 'You've got to watch these blockies,' she tells me every day. It would never occur to her that there are robbers higher up, that hard working Bill McSeveney also may not been getting what he deserves. That is why at night-time here, looking out through the fly-wired window of the men's hut, I'm conscious of a darkness deeper than the heavy shadows that lie between the long drying-racks and over the garden of the sleeping house.

And it seems to me that this obsession of Lena with piecework is where the darkness begins. There was the twilight of it just a minute ago when she passed

that unpleasant remark about wharfies.

We pick on in silence for perhaps a quarter of an hour.

I'd always imagined that there was a fair amount of noise associated with grape-picking. Perhaps there is on some blocks. On this one it is always quiet. The rows are unusually long, and between the visits of the tractor to replenish the supply of empty tins and take away the full ones, we hear nothing except the occasional voices of the two boys picking several rows away, and the carolling of magpies in the belars along the road. The sun is beginning to go down at last, but it's been a particularly hot day – a hundred and ten in the shade at noon – and I'll be glad when five o'clock comes, whatever the tally. That is always the best part of the day, when we trudge up to the house and throw ourselves on to the cool buffalo grass under the jacarandas, and Bill, the boss, cuts up a big sugar-melon, and hands out pink juicy slices that we can hardly open our jaws on. It would be better still, though, if they would talk of something else then besides the day's work. Smoky, the house cat, usually joins us, and I can never contemplate his great lazy blue hide without reflecting, O, You wise old brute! Even as I went out to work this morning you were lying in the coolest spot under the water tank, and every hour of the day you've followed the shifting shadows. While I –

The hum of the approaching tractor gives promise of some relief, and as the crash of falling buckets sounds far off down the row I say to Lena, 'Here they come. How many have we got?'

'If you were such a good union man you'd be counting them yourself.'

True, no doubt, but coming from Lena it's quite meaningless. She doesn't know what a trade union is. Instinctively I cast a glance up the row to see if our long-expected visitor, the 'Rep' is coming.

'Aren't you going to tell me the tally?'

'All I know is we're behind. We only had three hundred and thirty at smoko, and this is the shortest run.'

'That patch of mildew kept us back early in the afternoon.'

'It wasn't that.'

'Was it through me not keeping you up in buckets?'

She doesn't answer that. Whether she knows it or not, she's angry with me not for what I do or don't do, but for the things I say. I work hard, but I've said some harsh things about piecework, ridiculed her persistent argument that 'the only way to get money is to work for it'. It would be a good world indeed if that were true. She knows I don't approve of competing with the boys for big tallies, but she can't see that, out of principle, I must try to keep up with her because I get half of our combined earnings.

The tractor pulls up, and I crawl through to Lena's side and go for the water-bag hanging from the canopy. The grimy faces of Bill McSeveney and Peter, the rackman, smile down at me. They call me 'Sponge-guts' because of the vast amount of water I drink without getting pains.

'How's your mate, Joe?' asks Peter.

'She's got the sulks again. She thinks I'm sitting up on her.'

Bill, in the driving-seat, gives Lena a friendly wink. Naturally they're his grapes. He's a good employer, even as employers go these days, but I'd be interested to see his form if pickers were easier to get. He and his wife think the world of Lena. She's an expert picker, but she's also a nice change in the home of a couple who've raised three sons and no daughters.

He's observing her now with all the detached benevolence of a bachelor uncle.

'Get your five hundred today, kid?'

She steals a cautious sidelong glance at me, pouts, and shakes her head. She makes a charming picture of bush youth, standing stiff and straight in the narrow space between the tractor wheel and the vines. She wears old canvas shoes, a pair of jodhpurs several sizes too big for her, a man's work-shirt with the sleeves cut off, and a limp-brimmed sun-bonnet that throws a shadow over half of her cherubic face. The fingers of the hand nearest me fidget ceaselessly with the knife. Usually she's full of talk, particularly with Bill, but at the moment she only wants to work. And she can't even kneel down with the tractor standing where it is. Her restless eyes leap from me to Peter, and from Peter to Bill.

'Come on,' she says, 'load up. We've got over a hundred buckets to pick yet.'

'All right, Boss!' Bill releases the clutch, and as the tractor moves on I swing the first bucketful up to Peter.

Slowly we move along the row. Sixty full buckets, about twenty pounds of fruit to the bucket – 'Fill 'em up to water-level!' They get heavy towards the end; one has to work fast to keep up even with the snail-crawl of the tractor. I come back to Lena sweating afresh, and blowing a bit.

She hears me, and without stopping, or looking at me, demands peremptorily, 'How many?'

'Sixty on the load, and twenty-five left.'

'That makes three hundred and ninety. We've got fifty minutes to get sixty more.'

'Who says so?'

'I do.'

'Suppose we don't get them?'

'We've got to get them.'

It's on again, but before the usual evening dispute can get properly started a man I haven't seen before ducks through from the next row and confronts me. I give him good-day. Lena takes a long curious look at him, then goes on working. Middle-aged, and wearing a blue suit with an open-necked sports-shirt, he carries a couple of small books in one hand, and in the other a handkerchief with which he wipes his moist forehead. He'd have made a better first impression if he'd kept those books in his pocket a few minutes longer.

'Sorry I've been so long gettng around,' he says affably. 'I'm the union rep, Australian Workers' Union.'

'I'm glad to see you.'

We've been picking here for four weeks, and the AWU is the wealthiest trade union in Australia. Something of what I'm thinking must be showing in my face, for his manner becomes a trifle apologetic.

'I've been going flat out like a lizard since eight o'clock this morning. My God, it's hot, ain't it? How're you for tickets here?' He just can't get to the point soon enough. 'I've seen the boys through there; they're all right.'

'I've been waiting for you,' I tell him, bringing out a ten shilling note.

He opens one of the little books, takes a pencil from his breast pocket. 'Good on you, mate! How about the girl?'

'I'm one of the family,' replies Lena, with a promptness that shows not only that she has been listening, but that she has been well-schooled. McSeveney has no time for trade unions.

The organiser gives me a conspiratorial smile, which I do not return.

'You could still join if you wanted to, girlie.'

Lena doesn't answer that. She hasn't stopped picking for an instant. She's already a few feet away along the row, slashing and bucket-banging in a way that tells both of us not to be too long about it.

I watch him write in the date.

'I wish they'd all come in as quick as you,' he says in a lowered voice. 'You've got no idea the song some of the bastards make about it. I can give you a full ticket if you like? Cost you thirty bob.'

My gorge rises. What does he think he's selling? The great Australian trade unions weren't built by men like him.

'No thanks – just a season ticket. I'm already in a union. You don't cover me in my usual job.'

He begins to write. 'Okay. What are you in?' Just making conversation; he doesn't really care.

'Waterside Workers' Federation.' And for the life of me I can't keep a note of superiority out of my voice. I get the very devil of a kick out of it.

He goes on writing, without looking at me, but I can fairly see the guard coming up. 'That's a pretty good union. You'd make better money on the wharf than up here, wouldn't you?'

'Yes. We're well organised.'

A deliberate challenge, but he pretends not to see it.

'Up here for a bit of a change?'

'I was ill. Told to get out of Melbourne for a few weeks. A family man has to keep working, though.' I wouldn't tell him even that much, only I don't want him to think I came here for the 'big money'. Seventeen and six per hundred tins! – and fill 'em up to water-level....

I'm tempted to ask him if he's been to the next block, where the pickers are working all hours and living like animals, but he's too easy to read. He isn't an organiser; he's a collector. If he were doing his job he would talk to Lena, as I've talked to her. I watch him tramp away through the dust quite pleased with himself. He's got my ten shillings. He didn't ask if I am getting the prescribed wages, where I sleep at night, what hours I work, or what the food is like here.

It's a relief to get back to Lena. At least she's honest. She'd fight all right if she thought anybody was trying to put something over her. She just doesn't understand, that's all.

For minutes after I catch up with her we work without speaking. She's picking furiously, savagely, and by and by I find that I, too, am clapping on the pace. I've seen it elsewhere, the instinct to do one's bit, to keep up with one's mate. Piecework isn't an incentive, it's a device. But there's something else fermenting in me. A longing to please her, to win her respect, to get her to listen to me, to chase out of her eager young head some of the lies and nonsense that have been stuffed into it. Only last night I put in a hectic hour at the dining table trying to explain to her – and others – that it isn't wharfies and railwaymen who gum up the works on the man on the land. Not wharfies and railwaymen....

The falling bunches go plump-plump into the buckets. I know that she, too, is thinking. She wants to say something. Every time I catch sight of her bobbing head through the leaves I observe that she is peeping, as if trying to gauge what kind of humour I'm in.

By and by it comes, a non-committal, uncompromising little voice that nevertheless sends a thrill through me:

'Joe.'

'Hullo there.'

'What *is* a trade union, anyway?'

Lena, Lena, where am I to begin...?

THE GARDEN OF DREAMS

E. D. SCHLUNKE
1906–1960

For two hundred miles of travelling, always westerly, always into more sparsely settled and arid country – through the familiar box and pine trees of the wheat-farming lands, into the vast grazing land of the grey-green, drooping wilga trees and ephemeral western grasses – we had been thinking with pleasurable anticipation of the big riverside town ahead of us. For the last twenty miles the road had approached and retreated from the river, giving us glimpses of the immense serpent of green formed by the rows of rivergums, dense along both banks; there were patches of private irrigation, small areas of bright green sorghum, or ambitious projects, almost as far as the eye could see over the flat plains, which must have cost tens of thousands of pounds to establish and had produced a paradisaical richness of growth that seemed incredible and miraculous in that kind of country. It made the river appear to be an exciting and almost magical thing; and the town, which I had never seen before, would be worthy of the river, I felt sure.

'We shall be entertained royally in this place,' my friend Robert Stevens said to me. 'A man called Sampson has been writing to me off and on for years, urging me to come and visit Nangotta.' Then he went on to give me quite a biography of the man. Stevens is a member of parliament, and talking about everything comes easily to him.

'Sampson is one of those born with a silver spoon in his mouth. Son of a big grazier; sent to a Great Public School and Sydney University, though I imagine that what he chiefly learnt there was the first steps in becoming a man of the world: a big place of his own as soon as he reached his majority, and a beautiful woman for his wife. He gets around a great deal; he is well known in Sydney and Melbourne, as well as all over the country.'

'He certainly seems to have been lucky.' I said, recalling the stories of hardship and struggle we had been listening to in the last few days.

'Well, not entirely. His wife's people are family friends of mine, close enough to get me involved in her affairs. I was shocked recently to have a letter from her saying that she thought she would have to leave him. But, as I said before, he's going to see that we have a wonderful time in this town.'

That sounded promising to me. We couldn't exactly say that we'd had wonderful times in the towns we'd been calling at in the past few days. Towns in the marginal farming areas; towns planned optimistically in the boom days after the first world war, when it was thought that all that was needed to turn the dry areas into prosperous wheat farms were railway lines and closer settlement, but which had never revived after the setback received in the depression of the nineteen thirties. Towns where there was no electricity, and no water supply except the minimum quantity of rainwater that each householder collected off his galvanised-iron roof; hence there were no gardens and no lawns, and a parched, dried-out, and dusty aspect wherever one looked. Places in which it was the oddest sight to see how the first keen businessmen had made their choice of corner sites to build their shops, garages, or hotels in the new and coming towns, and now, thirty years later, still to see no buildings between the original ones. Unless you could visualise the surveyor's pegs and the markings of the proposed streets, you might think that the citizens hated each other so much that they couldn't endure to be near each other. Sometimes this seemed to be actually the case; someone would be waiting for us, hot with his all-consuming grievance against another inhabitant, usually one vested in a little authority in the comically farflung, skeletal, footpathless village.

My friend's secretary had sent telegrams ahead of us, saying: 'Mr Stevens will be at————on Tuesday afternoon', or whatever the anticipated time might be; and it was always a matter of interest to discover what response the telegram had evoked. His tour was both official and informal; a forestalling of the possible complaint. 'He never comes to visit *our* town.' Always we were entertained in the public bar of a hotel – *the* hotel, in the smaller places – normally a tolerable enough way of being entertained, but when it started at ten in the morning at Aramah, and ended at ten at night in Zandibingal, the beer was as hard to get down as if it were dishwater, while whisky or gin merely had a scarifying effect on the stomach, without the slightest exhilaration accompanying it.

The character of the towns, and of our receptions, seemed to depend to quite a degree on the size of the population, which we always calculated by the number of hotels. In one-hotel towns our coming was an important event. Here the chairman of the local branch of our political organisation would be on the look-out, with his telegram in his pocket, to tell us how many hours he had been waiting. He was usually an aggressive type of farmer who ran all the public bodies (and the smallest towns seemed to have as many as the largest) – the Parents' and Citizens', the Show society, the recreation ground, the public hall and the cemetery trusts; sometimes even a progress association in towns which seemed to have made no progress in thirty years.

The first concern of the local man would usually be some vital and secretive matter: some shortcoming he'd discovered in the local postmaster, or some check he'd received from a government department in connection with his public responsibilities, which it would give him enormous satisfaction to circumvent by making use of the powerful intervention of the local Federal member. All these requests, no matter how fantastically puerile some of them might be, Stevens recorded in a little brown notebook, to take up conscientiously with the proper authority in due time.

Then the local gentleman, having set the world to rights, would rush around the village and collect everyone who was at a loose end at the moment. A mixed lot, composed of the indolent aged and the idle youth, a few impatient farmers waiting for broken parts of their tractors to be repaired at the garage; always an entirely masculine audience, unless there happened to be a barmaid at that hotel, who would watch the goings-on with a blandly indifferent curiosity.

There was some reward for Stevens in the awe and respect with which he was treated in these places; ejaculations of amazement followed his pronouncements, and the most obliging laughter greeted every sally. It was relatively easy

'THE character of the towns, and of our receptions, seemed to depend to quite a degree on the size of the population, which we always calculated by the number of hotels.'

to get away from a one-hotel town. The audience was likely to start breaking up fairly soon; terrifically important things had to be done in those little unheard-of villages, which the presence of even their parliamentary member must not be allowed to delay. It ended with Stevens thanking the chairman cordially for what he had done.

'You know,' he'd say to me after we'd got going again, 'I've got to admire a man like that; doing all that onerous voluntary work in a little, thankless place, which very few men would think was worth their while.'

Two-hotel towns were likely to pay us less public attention, but the people we met generally had a little more sophistication. There was the same deplorable lack of water, though usually a local electricity supply, generated by an enterprising garage-owner with a big diesel engine. The gaps between the houses were filled in a little more, they had pavements of a kind in certain sections, and they invariably had a big Greek or Italian cafe, gleaming with lacquer, chromium, and glass, reminding one of Russell Drysdale's paintings, such as 'Joe's Garden of Dreams', picturing the owner and his shop set against a background of hot, dry, treeless plains.

In these cafes my parliamentary friend was always immediately recognised and made much of by the proprietors. At first I put it down to a surprising political awareness on the part of the Greeks or Italians, but Stevens told me that it was due to the fact that these people were always applying to him to get them landing permits for relatives whom they wanted to bring out to Australia. In two-hotel towns the party officials did not wait expectantly for our arrival. They were likely to be storekeepers or bank officers, busy at their jobs, but willing to neglect their duties while they took us to the better of the hotels, where an audience of a kind accumulated gradually, with the usual requests to be written down in Stevens's little notebook. It took us a bit longer to get away.

'I have to be grateful for what is done for me there,' Stevens always said. 'It's a grim and tedious job keeping an organisation like ours going between elections.'

But now at our beautiful river town, where the inhabitants splashed and sprayed the abundant water extravagantly on parks and gardens as if impelled to create a verdant oasis that would compensate for the millions of arid acres surrounding them, we had the promise of the man Sampson that our reception would be worthy of a parliamentary representative and his friend.

Naturally, we couldn't expect to be welcomed immediately on arrival, as in the small towns where nothing could happen without everyone knowing about it; so, since we'd had no lunch and it was already three o'clock in the afternoon, we went to one of the characteristic chromium, glass, and lacquer cafes. This was owned by an elderly Italian who, as I might have expected, was one of Stevens's far-flung acquaintances. He had a lined and ravaged face that was not without a certain dignity, and an air of immense and perpetual seriousness. He was proud of having fresh fish on the menu for us, something rare and inviting so far inland – perch and yellow-belly, taken that morning from the river which flowed close past the back of his shop. He invited us to have a look at his river view while our meal was being prepared.

There at the back of the cafe, we discovered, he had tried to recreate a little of

old Italy with a fountain, fishponds full of little golden fishes, garden seats and flower beds, even some broken columns made of cement, though all on so small and economical a scale that beside the broad river and the endless plains that stretched beyond it rather failed in its effect. Yet we gave him credit for it, and commended him. Undoubtedly it was his Garden of Dreams, and represented the investment of a considerable sum of money from which there would be no hope of a return – always a matter of serious concern to an Italian cafe proprietor.

The fish was really good, done with loving care, tender and palatable, though having the slightly flat flavour of inland river fish. Our host watched over us solicitously, or stood silently and unmoving behind his counter (it being the quiet time of the afternoon for cafes), with his sad and ravaged face composed, while he watched his young assistants bustling about the shop, tidying and cleaning in the tireless, efficient way of Italians.

'That man has quite a story,' Stevens said to me. 'He came out here about thirty years ago with nothing, and worked prodigiously hard for many years, until he was able to buy this cafe. Then he arranged, in the way that the Italians do, for a girl to be sent out for a wife. She was a lovely young woman and the marriage turned out to be remarkably successful, as these arranged marriages among Greeks and Italians so frequently do (don't ask me why). They were idyllically happy, had three beautiful children, but then a terrible thing happened. She was taking the children on a visit to some cafe people in a neighbouring town, in a car they'd recently bought, and, through some mishap or lack of experience, she stalled it on a level crossing, right in front of an oncoming train. They were all killed.'

I looked at the man's face and could see the story written there.

'Some people have the most dreadful misfortune,' was all I could think of to say.

'Oh, that's not all,' said Stevens. 'For years he seemed to suffer appallingly. He kept the cafe going in an automatic and half-heedless manner, mainly because of the excellent assistance he got from these two young fellows; then finally he got the idea that he hadn't much longer to live, and that he ought to do something about the pretty good inheritance there would be for someone when he died. He started writing letters to Italy, and at last it was decided that his youngest sister, with her husband and family of five, were to come to Australia at his expense. That would mean a big outlay for him, but it was the only way, because his sister's family was extremely poor. This was the stage at which I became involved in his affairs. They had trouble about getting landing permits, and I was asked to look into the matter.

'The confidential department explanation I got was that the husband's state of health was the obstacle; he was a bad case of TB. That started another spate of correspondence with the relatives. At first they denied that there was anything wrong with the husband's health; they said he'd never had a day off work in his life, which might have been quite true too. But presently the tone changed; the man was desperately ill, and the wife and children destitute. By this time Pelagio had come to feel responsible for the family, and so a lot of money which had been set aside for the fares went to maintain them.

'After a cruelly long period of suffering, the husband died. That seemed to be the chance to get the family out, but there were more delays; the sister was terrified of bringing out the children on her own, and our medical authorities were apparently cautious about giving a clean bill of health for the family without a precautionary interval. All this, let me tell you, took years to happen. Now, at last, everything is cleared up, and the family is on the way over.'

At this point Pelagio, who had been watching us at intervals, and who was, I had no doubt, well aware in his supersensitive Latin way that he was being talked about, took some letters off a shelf, and after sorting through them came over to our table in a hesitating manner with some photographs in his hand.

'Excuse me,' he said, in his sad, old, guttural voice, 'this is my sister with her children. Quite big children they is now.'

They looked very much like the photos one sees in newspapers or on the newsreels of Italian peasants dressed in drab clothing, with round, dark faces and big, apprehensive eyes. It brought home to one with a shock just what pangs the decision to emigrate must have cost them; and just how forlorn and fearful they would feel when they arrived in this country.

'Yes, nice big children,' Stevens agreed. Then he added with a great amount of circumspect kindness in his manner, 'They must be about the same age as yours would have been.'

Pelagio gave a great, heartfelt sigh. 'Oh, yes,' he said, without apparently taking the point that they would be a recompense for him, 'soon they will be here, and at last the end of the great expense.'

'It will be wonderful for you,' said Stevens, who was never willing to see anything but the best in people, 'to see your sister again.'

'Yes, yes,' Pelagio agreed, without cheering up to any great degree, 'but she knows no word of English to work in the shop.'

'The children will learn quickly enough, and they'll soon be able to help you.'

'Yes, yes,' Pelagio said, still a little doubtfully. Then he went back to the counter to serve a customer with cigarettes.

'These Italians,' I said, 'have a very keen appreciation of the value of money. He's worried that he won't get enough back in assistance to justify the expense the family has been to him.'

'You do him an injustice,' Stevens rebuked me. 'He has the profoundest affection for that family; but he's so sure he's going to die soon that he's worried about the prospects of getting them familiar with running the business before they're left without him.'

'Your sentiments do you great credit, Rob,' I said.

Just then a man came swinging into the cafe who looked as if he owned all the town and the surrounding country within a fifty-mile radius – one of those substantial grazier types, short, solid and robust of physique, somewhat ruddy in the face, dressed a bit carelessly in the very best kind of sports-coat and slacks, the characteristic wide-brimmed, flat-crowned felt hat, a silk shirt, and a woollen tie to show his faithfulness to the interests of his industry.

'Hey, Pelagio,' he called out, regardless of the fact that the proprietor was serving a customer, 'have you seen any distinguished visitors in the town? I'm expecting a Very Important Person.'

'Oh yes, Mr Sampson, he is here.' He made a delighted gesture towards our table. 'There he is – Mr Stevens.'

The man came charging across, scattering the afternoon-tea people who were beginning to fill the place.

'Rob, old boy, I'm delighted to see you here. Sorry I didn't find you in time to take you to lunch, but I've been shockingly busy.'

He sat down as if he was suddenly exhausted, pulling off his hat as he did so. Close up he looked both younger and more dissipated, and not so impressive as when he'd appeared at the door. He had obviously been drinking. He greeted me with polite cordiality, but he had an air of being on his guard in the presence of a stranger; a little uneasy that he wouldn't make just quite as good an impact as he would like to. Pelagio came fussing over to him.

'Mr Sampson, you like some nice fresh fish, too? Perch or yellow-belly? You ask these gentlemen; very nice.'

'No thanks, Pelagio, this is one of my fast days.'

Pelagio looked at him, greatly concerned. 'To eat, a very good idea.'

Sampson turned to us. 'Good old Pelagio; great friend of mine; always trying to mother me.' He waved him away and turned to us urgently. 'Say, if you're finished here, what about coming where we can be comfortable and have a good

'*JUST* then a man
came swinging into
the cafe who looked as
if he owned all the
town and the sur-
rounding country
within a fifty-mile
radius.'

talk?' He led the way briskly to the nearest hotel.

'I didn't think,' Stevens said, looking a bit surprised, 'that you'd patronise *this* place; I remember it as rather seedy and run-down.'

'As a matter of fact,' Sampson said, continuing with his headlong stride, 'it still is seedy and run-down. But it's near, and that's something.' He gave us a speculative grin. 'In fact, it's a hell of a lot.' He grabbed a shirt-sleeved cigarette-sucking individual by the arm and said 'Scotch' with the same kind of fervour and reverence that you see in the whisky advertisements in the expensive American magazines. He led the way to what was obviously a hastily improvised beer garden, done out after ten o'clock closing had been introduced. It had a floor of rough, unevenly worn bricks, and garden furniture of hard wooden slats. Knowing country hotels, I immediately realised from the steady through traffic in both directions that it had previously been, and still actually was, the passage from the public bar to the lavatory, now covered with a bleak galvanised-iron roof, and sprinkled with potted palms.

'We're coming on,' I said. 'It's the first time we haven't been entertained in the public bar.'

'The only civilised way to drink,' Sampson said, dropping into one of the hard seats with a resounding clatter. But he soon bounded out again to hurry the drinks.

'That man,' Stevens said, 'has a beautiful, charming, and cultured wife, three delightful children, and a magnificent home, but he seems to prefer to spend his time in places like this.'

Soon Sampson was back with an enormous tray full of drinks, and an assorted company of gentlemen at his heels. They looked much more sophisticated than the men we'd been meeting in the smaller towns, and I soon discovered them to be stock and station agents, owners of considerable businesses, professional men, and landowners of substance. Some of them knew Stevens, and all the rest of them were soon calling him by his first name. The majority of them looked the definitely hard-drinking type. They surrounded us and submerged us in a dense, high-pressure area of volatile fumes and cigarette smoke, while beating upon our ears with a battery of high-spirited conversation. Here there was no awed waiting upon the oracle. Stevens was allowed to speak, if he was quick enough to seize the opportunity, and out of some concern for him the subject of politics cropped up now and then, but most of the time it seemed to me that everyone was talking at once, and anyone who lacked a listener immediately bustled away to the service hatch to order another tray of drinks, thrusting it upon us with a fervid cordiality that could not be denied.

The only admittedly legitimate way of getting a little temporary relief from the flood was to join in the ever-increasing procession that went through the beer garden to the lavatory. However, that respite could be only brief, partly because the place was so nauseating, but mainly because one of the party would soon turn up, take one by the arm urgently and say, 'Come on, we'd better hurry back, or we'll be missing a round.' Then the chairs and the tables and the suffering drinkers hurrying out, swirled and eddied around us, and the uneven floor harassed our feet, till it seemed to be something achieved to be safely seated again.

'THAT man, has a beautiful, charming, and cultured wife, three delightful children, and a magnificent home, but he seems to prefer to spend his time in places like this.'

I shouted to make myself heard above the noise, 'Rob, we'd better get out and see more of the townspeople before the shops close!'

But Sampson overheard and cut in. 'Don't worry,' he said, his speech now slower and more deliberate, 'you'll see everybody without moving. I've had the word passed around, "Rob Stevens is at the Royal". If you go away now, you'll be missing people who want to see you.'

Then he looked at his watch and with difficulty focused attention. 'Four o'clock, by hell! I had a terrifically important appointment with my solicitor at three twenty, to fix something up for my wife. Got to hurry like damnation. Now, don't move from here. I'll be back quite soon to look after you some more.'

He charged off, leaning forward in his eagerness, with a bemused look n his face, getting into traffic difficulties when he had to dodge around people, and as he was going through the door. But that didn't lessen the pressure on us. New people, just as Sampson had promised, kept turning up, each eager to buy a drink for his parliamentary representative, and each obliging him, by the inviolable law of the liquor trade, to return the compliment; each, of course, included the entire party that waxed and waned about us, and started another cycle that had to be worked to its conclusion.

'Have to go now, Rob,' I said, 'or we'll miss dinner at our hotel.'

But then two men came in with outstretched hands, and as soon as they had been accommodated there were others. Even on his several walks out to the back, Stevens would be tagged by men seizing the chance for an urgent request to get them out of their troubles with the taxation department, and these men, on returning, expressed their gratitude by speeding up the tempo of the rounds. It seemed that the town was too large and Stevens's fame too great for the party ever to come to an end naturally. An hour went by, with no notice taken of the compulsory six-thirty break, while the liquor-logged participants leant blurrily upon the whisky-spattered table, or lurched out over the beer-soaked floor.

'Your ulcer, Rob,' I said, becoming inventive as a last resort. 'If you don't get some bland food wrapped round it you'll be a cot-case tomorrow.'

That made an impact on the dazed wits about us. 'Ulcer!' they said, perturbed.

'Yes, I've got to look after him.'

'My word, yes. We'll never get another member like him.'

Stevens rose – gratefully, I'm sure – and we hurried out before someone else could come in and start the cycle off again.

On the way out through the public bar we were surprised to find Sampson, deeply immersed in another party.

'Did you fix your business with your solicitor?' I chipped him.

He looked at me as if he could vaguely remember seeing me somewhere before; then recognition came slowly. He put out a hand as he laboured for words. 'Matter of fact, I telephoned him when I found I'd missed my appointment. Made another appointment for five fifteen.'

'You'll have to hurry, then,' Stevens admonished him. 'It's after seven now.'

Sampson looked at Stevens as if he had difficulty in identifying him, too, then laboriously at his watch.

'Ah, damnation! Have to phone him again.' He started off, but at the door his host's responsibilities overtook him.

'Where are you going now? I'm going to take you to dinner at the best hotel. Don't forget that.'

We reminded him of the time, and that there was nothing for it but Pelagio's.

'Meet me there. Meet me there in ten or fifteen minutes. Remember, it's on me.' We saw him walking down the street quite jauntily, though when people nodded to him he seemed to have difficulty in recalling who they were.

Pelagio welcomed us. He overlooked our sodden condition, and urged hot soup, coffee, and other restoratives upon us. 'Mr Sampson,' he said anxiously, 'he not with you?'

'He's gone to his solicitor's,' I said, not meaning to give him away, 'has to sign an important document.'

But Pelagio was quick to reach his conclusion. 'Oh, poor Mr Sampson. Too much whisky, too many times. And he with the beautiful wife and the beautiful children. Why in the name of God should he drink so much?'

'Oh, he's a nice fellow,' Rob said to redeem my slip.

'Oh, yes, yes, he is a very nice man. He is my friend for a long time. Always speaks to me and makes me laugh.'

This gave me a new light on both of them. I hadn't thought it possible for anyone to make Pelagio laugh. We ate our food and drank our coffee, feeling distinctly better; taking our time and, for my part, at least, hoping that we'd seen the last of our eager host Sampson. But just as we were about to leave and get some rest at our hotel, he arrived.

'I must apologise. Terribly sorry. Couldn't get on to my solicitor anywhere. Rang all the places I could think of, then I started a round of the pubs to see if he was in any of them.'

It wasn't really necessary for him to tell us the latter part. Sampson was now very close to the state when he could no longer be respected. When he lurched, Pelagio held him up by the arm and looked most distressed.

'You sit down here, Mr Sampson, eat some nice hot soup, drink some strong coffee. I get you some quick.'

'No, no, Pelagio. I'm all right. I'm not hungry today. Besides, I've got social obligations. I've promised a lot of fellows to take Mr Stevens round to the club, so they can buy him a drink or two.'

Pelagio did not presume to say anything, but he looked at us as if he had a vast amount of compassion for people whose social eminence obliged them to consume great quantities of liquor. He made a covert sign to one of his assistants, and presently took a cup of coffee from his hands. He offered this to Sampson.

'Very hot, very sweet,' he said, as if this had occurred a considerable number of times before.

Sampson took him by the arm and shook it. 'I'm drunk, am I?' he demanded.

'Oh, no, no!'

Sampson's face broken into a slow smile, the stiffened facial muscles of the alcoholic responding tardily to the impulses from his muddled brain. 'You're a good friend of mine, Pelagio,' he said. 'I'll drink your coffee, even if it kills me.'

'Coffee will never kill you.' It was the nearest Pelagio went to a reproach. He watched Sampson drinking the coffee, with a touching look of sympathy on his face. Sampson put down his cup. He looked at us, and it took him so long to formulate his thoughts that for a while I wondered whether he was going to say anything or not.

'Pelagio is getting his sister and her five children out from Italy. That will be a great thing for him, won't it?'

We agreed. Then suddenly we were all alarmed. A dreadful greeny-yellow colour had suffused Sampson's face; perspiration stood out in drops on his forehead. He rose giddily to his feet. Immediately Pelagio had him by the arm and supported him out the back door. Stevens looked very upset. 'There's no hope for a man like that,' he said regretfully. 'He has to go on being a dreadful worry to his wife and an increasing embarrassment to his children until he dies.'

Presently Sampson returned, trying to look as if there was nothing wrong with him. 'Now to the club,' he said, with a courageous attempt at jauntiness.

'Look here,' said Stevens, 'let's drop the club. We need some rest. We've had a hard day, and I have phone calls to make and letters to write.'

Sampson was perturbed. 'A promise is a promise. A lot of fine fellows are expecting me to bring you around. If I don't bring you, I'll have to spend the rest of the night explaining and apologising and consoling them with drinks.'

We got up to go. There was nothing else to be done.

At the club we met some of the people who had been entertaining us in the afternoon, and a lot more like them. For a while Stevens contrived to maintain a lively political discussion, with the attention off the drinking, but it soon turned into the usual cyclic bout, and the man most responsible for speeding up the intake was Sampson.

When the club at last closed down, I thought we had reached the end of our orgy, but Sampson had other ideas. He had got an invitation to a friend's place, a doctor who apparently rated highly in the social life of the town. It was round eleven, and Stevens and I were full of misgivings that the invitation had really been for a more suitable hour. But Sampson was adamant and in such a state of mind that he would have been deeply offended and most difficult if we had refused to go with him. The hosts had obviously given us up, after expending any pleasurable anticipations they might have had while they waited; now they were deadly weary.

We spent an embarrassing hour there; it was much worse than in the hotel or the club, because in a bar-room crowd at least there is a sort of individual indistinguishability, but in the tired doctor's house whatever anyone did stood out in bold relief. We flogged along a dreary, inanimate conversation; we tried to cover up poor Sampson's deplorable condition; we made many resolute efforts to move him, but did not succeed until there was not a drop of liquor left in the house.

The only thing to do with him, we decided, was to take him to our hotel and see if we could find a place for him to sleep – a not very hopeful prospect, with all the staff undoubtedly in bed. But he was determined to drive his twenty miles home.

'Get a drink of coffee from Pelagio, and I'll be right.'

'*PELAGIO is getting his sister and her five children out from Italy. That will be a great thing for him, won't it?*'

Pelagio's was closed, but he opened the door after a lot of knocking, and quite uncomplainingly made coffee for all of us. And that wasn't all he was prepared to do. He got into the car with Sampson to see him safely out of the town, through the difficult creek-crossing where the bridge was unsafe, and on to his long, straight road home. We made a rather half-hearted offer to drive out with them and bring Pelagio back, but Sampson was quite outraged at the suggestion; he was our host, and it would be unpardonable of him to cause us any inconvenience.

We went to bed thankfully, and slept as well as the conflict between our drugged brains and our outraged stomachs would allow us. We were late for breakfast in the morning, and the injured waitresses declined to talk to us, though we suspected, from the excited way they were going on among each other, that something extraordinary had happened.

'We'll go and say goodbye to Pelagio before we leave.'

But at the cafe the young assistants told us, with dramatic voices and anguished faces, that Pelagio was dead. Sampson too. The car had been wrecked at the damaged bridge, and both men had been killed instantly.

We went back to the hotel and had a drink of our own volition.

'Well, that's that,' Stevens said. 'One could have expected it for Sampson. But Pelagio – that was a real tragedy.' He got out his little brown notebook. 'We'll have to send wreaths to both the funerals, and a condolatory letter to Sampson's widow.' Then he looked at me with troubled eyes. 'But what am I going to do about that poor unfortunate sister of Pelagio's? Arriving in Sydney next week, and not one person in the whole wide continent that she knows.'

We left our drinks unfinished, finding them unbearably distasteful.

Then he said, 'Come on, my boy; off to the next town. See what's waiting for us there.'

FRANCIS SILVER

HAL PORTER
1911–1984

O NE grows relievedly older and less an amateur: the high noon of middle age is free of the eccentricities of the innocent, one's senses are correctly disposed, one does not permit oneself the pleasure of discreditable actions; altogether, reality has no frayed ends. One can, at worst, fortify oneself with memories. Nevertheless, there is one disconcerting, even disenchanting, thing: what one oneself remembers is not what others remember. In this, women as annalists are terrifying. One expects them to get their recollections as exact as the amount of salt in Scotch Broth. Beyond the practical area, of course, one has no illusions: if a woman talks about democracy or eternal peace or disarmament one sees instantly and with the most telling clarity that these things are pure nonsense. One does not, however, expect a handful of salt or no salt at all in either Scotch Broth or memories, but what one expects, and what one gets – oh, dear. Take my mother for example.

'SHE sang all the time, particularly, I think I remember, on ironing day.'

As eldest son of a family of seven I got the best of her memories, partly because mothers of that period had time to make their special offerings to first-born sons, partly because her enthusiasm and salesmanship were fresh. Among her recollections the most recurrent were of Francis Silver.

Right here, I must indicate that mother was multiloquous, gay and romantic. Whatever else a large family tore from her, it was not her vivacity. She sang all the time, particularly, I think I remember, on ironing day. The pattern of this day was that of a holy day; there was an inevitability, a feeling of religious ritual. It was always Tuesday, always Shepherd's Pie day. To mother's heightened singing the kitchen-range was stoked with red-gum until a mirage almost formed above its black-leaded surface on which the flat-irons had been clashed down. The piled-up clothes-baskets and the kauri clothes-horse were brought into the kitchen; the beeswax in its piece of scorched cloth was placed ready. These preparations over, and while the irons were heating, a tranquil overture began. Mother and the washerwoman took each bed-sheet separately and, one gripping the bottom edge, one the top, retreated backwards, straining the sheet taut in a domestic tug-o'-war, inclining their heads to scan it for signs of wear then, this done, advancing towards each other with uplifted arms to begin the folding. These retreatings, advancings, inclinations and deft gestures, repeated sheet after sheet, had the air of an endless figure of a pavane in which, sometimes, I attempted to represent the absent washerwoman. It was while thus engaged, and later, while mother was ironing, and between her ironing-songs which were more poignantly yearning than, say, her friskier carpet-sweeping or cake-mixing songs, that I recall hearing much about Francis Silver.

As a young woman mother lived in a middle-class seaside suburb of Melbourne. Plane trees lined the three-chain-wide streets from which cast-iron railings and gates, and paths of encaustic tiles of Pompeian design, separated two-storeyed brick houses overtopped by Norfolk Island pines exuding sap like

candle grease. These houses had such names as *Grevillea, Emmaville, Dagmar* and *Buckingham*. Stucco faces of gravely Grecian cast stared in the direction of the beach on to which oranges thrown from P and O liners rolled in with sea-lettuce, bladderwrack and mussel shells. A bathing enclosure advertised HOT SEA BATHS and TOWELS AND BATHING DRESS FOR HIRE. Mother strolled the Esplanade, tamarisk by tamarisk, or sipped Lemon Squash Spiders in the Jubilee Cafe with the apparently numerous young men who were courting her. Of these beaux, two young men, one from the country, one from another suburb, were favoured most. In marrying the country wooer, my father, and darning his socks and bearing his children and darning their socks, mother left the suburb for a country town set smack-flat on the wind-combed plains of Gippsland. She also left behind Francis Silver, whom she never saw again, at least not physically. He lived on, remarkably visible, in a special display case of her memories.

Since the time of mother's young womanhood was pre-Great War there had been a conventional and profuse to-and-fro of postcards. She had garnered several bulging albums of them. The most elaborate cards, in an album of their own, were from Francis Silver. These had a sacred quality. In my eyes they belonged to Sunday. My parents were pagan enough to regard the church merely as a setting for wedding, baptism and funeral services, but, largely for us children, I suspect, though also because of what had been dyed into the texture of their late-Victorian childhoods, they were firm about the sanctity of Sunday. On this day mother played on the piano, or sang, hymns only. We were forbidden to whistle or go barefoot. Reading was restricted to *The Child's Bible, Sunday at Home* or *Christie's Old Organ.* Apart from meals of great size and gorgeousness the only permissible secular pleasures were to look through the stereoscope at Boer War photographs or at Francis Silver's postcards.

Hypocritically careful, we resisted licking our fingers to turn the interleaves of tissue paper because mother hovered wrestling with herself. Invariably, at last, she could resist herself no longer. Perhaps a postcards of stiffened lace, *moiré* rosettes and spangles would set her off. Her eyes and her voice would detach themselves in focus and tone from the present.

'Yes,' she would say in this unique, entranced voice, 'Francis Silver sent me that after we'd had a tiny tiff near the Williamstown Time-ball Tower. We had gone for a stroll to St Kilda to listen to the German Band. When we got there the ferry-boat to Williamstown was at the pier – the dear old *Rosny*. It was such a perfect day we decided to go across to Williamstown. There was a little man on board playing a concertina. I had on–oh, I remember it so well – a white *broderie anglaise* dress, and a hat with enormous peach-coloured silk roses on it. And a parasol of the same peach with a picot-edged triple flounce. I'd made Francis Silver a buttonhole of Cecile Brunner roses. And when we were on our way back, he threw it from the *Rosny* into Port Phillip Bay because I wouldn't talk to him. It was all because I refused to give him my lace handkerchief as a keepsake. How silly it all was! I'd have given him the hanky if he didn't said he

was going to sleep with it under his pillow. And the next day he sent me this card. But I was quite firm, and didn't send the hanky. It was mean of me, I suppose, but I was terribly well-brought-up.'

All mother's memories of Francis Silver were of this vague, passionless kind. The time seemed eternally three o'clock in the afternoon of a deliciously sunny day, band-music drifted cloudily in the background, no one hurried or raised voices, there were no inflamed rages or cutting malices. It was a delicate game of teasing played in Sunday clothes and while wearing mignonette. It had its fragile rules no one would be untamed enough to break. As people walking on the fresh boards of a new floor soil it in gingerly and gentle fashion, so did mother and Francis Silver serenely walk the floor of their affection.

From accounts as lame as this, of incidents as small, flat and pointless as this, it amazes me, now, that so vivid and important an image of Francis Silver became mine.

As I saw it, Francis Silver was extraordinary handsome in a certain way. He had a shortish, straight nose, a little black moustache with curled-up ends, lips clearly cut as a statue's, white teeth, small ears with lobes, definite but not untidy eyebrows, tightly packed black wavy hair, and an olive skin. His hands were hairless and supple; the half-moons showed even at the roots of his little fingernails. He had a light tenor voice he exhibited in such songs as *Only a Leaf*, *After the Ball*, *'Neath the Shade of the Old Apple Tree*, and *She Lives in a Mansion of Aching Hearts* – songs laced with misunderstanding, regret and tears. He was a picture-framer go-ahead enough to have his own business. In the sense of handling Christmas supplement oleographs and 'art photographs' of Grecian-robed women holding waterlilies or bunches of grapes he was artistic and sensitive. He smoked Turkish cigarettes, did not drink, was popular with other sensitive young men, wore a gold ring with a ruby in it, was very proud of his small feet, and loved the theatre.

Throughout the years, mother had provided these and many more details, partly by anecdote, partly by a system of odious comparisons ('Mr Willough-by's eyebrows are much untidier than Francis Silver's'), partly by setting a standard we fell far short of ('You must press back the quicks of your fingernails each time you dry your hands: the half-moons on Francis Silver's nails, even on the little fingers, showed clearly'). It was incredible what we children knew of him: he disliked mushrooms, tomatoes and ripe apricots, he had cut his hand at a Fern Tree Gully picnic, lost his father's gold watch in Flinders Lane, had four sisters, used Wright's Coal Tar Soap, and was double-jointed.

During all the years of talk not once did mother call him anything else but Francis Silver, never Mr Silver, and certainly never Francis, despite the fact that, seemingly to us, she had given him every consideration as a possible husband. This possibility was never directly expressed. We presumed from constant obliquities. At one stage of my early adolescence, when I was sullenly inclined to regard father as the malice-riddled offspring of parents like Simon Legree and the Witch of Endor, I yearned to be the son of a merrier, more handsome and talented father. I knew exactly whom, and spent much time practising in various ornate handwritings names I greatly preferred to my own ... Hereward Silver, Montmorency Silver, Shem Silver, Fluellen Silver.

My placid actual father (it was his placidity I regarded as a sinister malice) was as aware as he was of anything of mother's indestructible interest in Francis Silver. It was a sort of joke with him which, as children, we loved: Francis Silver was so often a bore.

'Woman, dear,' father would, for example, say, seeing mother and some of us off at the railway station when we were going for a few days to Melbourne, 'if you are not back by Friday, I'll assume you've put the children in a comfortable orphanage, and have run off with Francis Silver. I shall, therefore, set up house with Mrs Tinsley.' This, to us, was hilariously funny: Mrs Tinsley was a gushing woman who irritated father so much that he went and talked to the pigs when she appeared. If mother displayed herself in a new hat or dress, badgering father for an opinion, he would say, 'Now, woman, dear, you know you look very nice. You must have a photograph taken for Francis Silver.'

'Jealous beast,' mother would say.

This light-hearted chyacking about Francis Silver made him appear for ever twenty-four, for ever dashing, for ever harmless. He was the legendary Gentleman first to his feet when Ladies entered; he daily cleaned his shoes, and the *backs* of his shoes.

Once only did this image of him take on sootier colours, and throw a disturbing shadow. This happened the one time I ever heard my parents really quarrel. What the quarrel was about I shall never know. To my alarm I was trapped in its orbit without the nous to consider flight let alone perform the fact of flight. There mother and father were, upbraiding each other ferociously, in the glare of kitchen daylight, she songless and shrill and stripped of her vivacity, he loud-mouthed and stripped of his dry-tongued placidity. At the height of heat mother dashed a colander of French beans to the linoleum and, crying out, 'I wish I'd married Francis Silver!' rushed from her kitchen, slamming its door, then the vestibule door, next her bedroom door. Horrified as I was at the quarrel itself which seemed the disreputable sort of thing poor people, common people or drunk people did, I was more horrified at this vision of Francis Silver as a mother-stealer. I had the impression father was startled; the framework of his being somehow showed; he seemed much less a father, nuder of face, younger, like nothing so much as a bewildered man. I began to pick up the beans so as not to look at him directly, but I absorbed him foxily. He was, as it were, reassembling himself and dressing his face again, when the kitchen door opened quietly. The slam of the bedroom had scarcely died but mother had done something neatening to her hair.

'I have,' she said, 'just caught a glimpse of myself in the glass.' It was a girl's voice. She tried a smile. It was too weighed out of balance with uncertainty and rising tears to succeed. 'I was quite hideous with temper. I'm sorry, Henry. Of course I didn't mean ... honestly....'

'Woman, dear,' said father, 'Francis Silver would have been a lucky man if you had married him. Out to play, boy, out to play,' he said, crossing to mother who began to cry. I knew he was going to sit her on his knee. That night we had festive jelly with bananas and a dash of port wine in for pudding: a sure indication that, although he wasn't mentioned, Francis Silver was still in the house. Nevertheless, it was several months before I forgot him as a peril and could see him again as the eternal charmer.

When mother died at the age of forty-one I was eighteen.

Several hours before she died, her singing forgone for ever, her gaiety tampered with by the demands of dying, I was alone with her for a while. After saying what, I suppose, all dying mothers say to eldest sons, most of it trite, she asked me to take Francis Silver the album of postcards he'd sent her twenty-odd years ago.

'I know what the girls are like,' she said of my sisters. 'They'll marry and have children, and let the children tear them up. I'm sure he'd like to have them. He's still alive, and still in the same place, I think. I've looked in the obituary notices every day for years.'

I began to cry.

'Stop that,' she said, as though I were breaking some deathbed rule, 'and listen. There's something else. In my little handkerchief drawer there's a pink envelope with his name on it. It's got a lock of my hair in it. Before I married your father I was going to give it to Francis Silver. But I decided against it. Burn it, throw it away, anything. Don't tell your father. About the album doesn't matter. Not about the envelope. Be a good boy, and promise.'

In agony I promised.

It was not until several months after the funeral that I told father of mother's wish about the postcards.

'Yes,' he said, 'your mother told me she'd spoken to you. Women,' he said, giving me that two-coloured look which at one and the same time questioned my knowledge and informed my ignorance, 'are strange, strange mortals, and this is a strange gesture. He was very devoted to your mother, and may like to have them as a memento.'

'Would *you* like to take them? It might be better if you took them – more – more suitable.' I was trying a man-to-man briskness.

Father looked me over, and came to his decision about what I was up to.

'Why?' he said. 'Why on earth would it be more suitable? I've never met Francis Silver in my life. Anyway, you promised your mother, didn't you? Which issue are you trying to avoid?'

That my father did not know Francis Silver astonished me. Reading between the lines of mother's tales I had pictured Francis Silver and father, stiff-collared, in pointed button boots, carrying heart-shaped boxes of chocolates in their hands, and arriving (often) at the same moment on the basalt doorstep of mother's front door.

'I'm not avoiding anything,' I lied. 'Are you sure ... are you absolutely sure you've never met him?'

'I am absolutely sure.' He looked me over again. 'I'll be looking forward to hearing about him. And, although I've never met him, I think, in the circumstances, it could not be considered too much if you conveyed my kind regards.'

Despite my death-bed promise, I had had hopes of finding father willing to return the postcards to Francis Silver. I'd justified these hopes by telling myself that Francis Silver would be more touched by receiving the album from his widower rival than from the son of the woman he had hoped to marry, from the son he might have had himself. My father's defection meant I should have to

'As though preparing to meet God or have an accident, I had a shower, and cleaned my teeth, for the second time that day, put on all my best clothes, my new shoes and tie, and took much trouble with my hair.'

keep my promise. About this I was not really happy. At eighteen I conceived myself cynical; disillusionment was daily bread.

That next time I travelled to Melbourne the album went with me. As well, I took the pink envelope which I had not destroyed – there had been no moral pause, no sense of treachery in the betrayal. On her deathbed, I told myself, mother had tangled her values, her judgment had been marred. I ... *I* ... considered that the anguished man I would be meeting would be doubly consoled by this more personal memento.

I had no sooner arrived at the Coffee Palace in which I was staying in the city than it became imperative to set about handing over the album and the envelope: mother had been dead for four months; the cards with their velveteen forget-me-nots, their sequins, and intricately folded and embossed layers, the envelope scented from its long secret life in the handkerchief drawer, were too precious and unfitting to lie about for even an hour on the public furniture of a room that had been occupied by unknown, impermanent, maybe sinful people. As though preparing to meet God or have an accident, I had a shower, and cleaned my teeth, for the second time that day, put on all my best clothes, my new shoes and tie, and took much trouble with my hair. With the envelope in a pocket, and carrying the album as though it were frangible time, and dreams of finest glass, I set out for Francis Silver's.

Since all this happened before World War II and post-war vandalism, the picture-framing shop had not been contemporarised: it was still turn-of-the-century elegant in a slightly abraded way. Three etchings with the enormously wide creamy mounts and narrow black frames fashionable at the period were disposed behind the plate-glass on which, in Gothic gold-leaf, was the name I had heard all my life, the name in my mother's handwriting on the pink envelope containing the piece of her hair she'd called a lock. I went into the shop. There was no one behind the counter. The sound of elfin-cobbler hammering came from behind plush curtains, black, on which were appliquéd pale gold lyres, and which obviously concealed a workroom. When I rang the small brass bell attached to the counter by a chain the tiny tap-tapping continued for a few moments, and then ceased. I heard no footsteps, but the curtains were parted. A short, fat man stood behind the counter.

'And what,' he said in light and somehow wheedling voice, 'can I do for *you?*' His small eyes (beady, I said to myself) stitched over me in an assessing way. He was the most strikingly clean-looking man I had ever seen, composed of the blackest black (his suit and tie and eyes and semi-circular eyebrows) and the whitest white (his shirt, the handkerchief protruding from one sleeve, the white slices of hair curving back from his temples).

'I should like to speak to Fr ... to Mr Francis Silver, please.'

He lowered his lids while pretending to pick something languidly from his sleeve, and to flick delicately with fingertips at the spot nothing had been picked from.

'You are,' he said, interested in the fact, 'thpeaking to that very perthon.'

I was not prepared for this, a disillusion not cut to my template. My face must have run empty.

'I athure you,' he said, 'I *am* Franthith Thilver. Have I been recommended?

You *mutht* tell me by whom. You want thomething framed?'

'My ... my mother ...' I said, and placed the album on the counter. 'My mother sent this. Postcards.'

'To be framed?'

He opened the album.

He turned over several pages. 'My dear,' he said. 'My dear, how thcrumptious!'

I saw on his hand the ring with the ruby mother had told us about. I saw the fingernails with each half-moon, even on the little fingers, unmistakably revealed.

'Jutht look! I've been nothing like thethe for ...' He pushed out his lips in a depreciating smile, '... for more yearth than I care to thtate publicly. I uthed to have a pothitive mania for them.'

'They are yours,' I said. 'They *were* yours. You sent them to my mother. Years ago,' I finished uncertainly.

'I did? Gay, reckleth boy I wath! May one have little lookieth?' He took one of the cards and examined its back. 'Tho I did! My handwriting hathn't changed a bit. How ekthordinary, how very ekthordinary! And now they are to be framed?'

'No,' I said. 'No, not framed. Mother thought you'd like to have them back.'

I knew I was expressing mother's wish very badly, but could do nothing else: the situation had become bewildering not only to me but also to Francis Silver who said, 'Oh!' There was, moreover, something beyond the bewilderment of a clumsy social situation; there was something wrong. Francis Silver had not asked me who had sent the postcards. Some film clogging natural curiosity, even polite inquiry, some flaw in his humanity, made him seem careless and carelessly cruel.

I did not want to say it but I said it: I told him my mother's maiden name.

He became fretful: the past was not for him. Nevertheless he acted good manners of a sort. 'Now, let me thee,' he said, and he put the tip of his forefinger on his forehead in an absurd thinking posture. He pouted.

'My dear,' he presently said, 'the mind ith blank. Abtholutely! Nothing thtirs in my little addled brain. I'm very, very naughty. But you muthtn't tell your mother. I thhould be *tho* humiliated. You mutht tell her I loved *theeing* them but I couldn't *deprive* her of them. It'th a wonderful collection and in *faultleth* condition. Oh, if only my friend Rekth were here ... he *adorth* pothcardiana, if I may coin a phrathe, abtholutely *adorth*.'

Scraps of the past were blowing about my brain like the litter at the end of a perfect picnic.

'And you don't remember my mother?'

He could have smacked me.

He tossed his eyes heavenwards but not too high.

'Be reathonable, *pleathe*! More than twenty yearth! One would adore to remember, of courthe. But too much water under the bridge. There've been too many people, too many, many people. I *thaid* I wath terribly humiliated. I couldn't akthept them now, could I? You take them back. And thank your mother very, very much.' He smiled a conspirator's smile, grasped my wrist and squeezed it boldly yet furtively. 'I know you'll keep my ghathtly thecret, just *know*. You've got a nithe kind father, haven't you? But there've really been too many people. I'm thure your mother ith ath charming ath you. But I don't remember her at all.'

I detached myself. Without a word I left the shop.

The album of cards remained with whom I'd promised to give it.

By the time I had returned to the Coffee Palace through the sort of exquisite day I used to imagine a pretty mother and a jaunty Francis Silver flirting through along the seafront, I had made up an outline of lies to satisfy and comfort my father for whom I felt the truth, as I saw it, to be of the wrong shape. By the time, days later, I was home with him, I hoped to have filled in that outline with unassailable detail: I dared not shock him. As my first adult chore, my initiation task, I would make a fitting Francis Silver for him, one that matched the Francis Silver of mother's recollections. In the room at the Coffee Palace I looked at the pink envelope older than I. For one weak moment I felt like making a film-actor's gesture and kissing it. I remembered in time it was not mine to kiss. It was no one's. In that room with its Gideon Bible on the glass-topped bedside cabinet, its ecru net curtains, its oatmeal wallpaper and petty frieze of autumn Virginia Creeper, I burnt the envelope. In its first resistance to flame it gave up its ingrained scent. It twisted, fighting the flame and itself. It emitted a stench of burning hair. It writhed and writhed in an agony I could not bear to watch.

YOU CALL ME BY MY PROPER NAME

DAL STIVENS
1911–

THE car had no muffler and as it went down the mountain road it made a noise like a motor boat. It was early morning and during the night there had been a frost. The car was a 1934 Dodge open tourer. The girl in the front seat was hunched up under a coat and she had thrust her hands, Chinese-fashion, into its sleeves. The boy who was driving didn't seem to mind the cold. He sang, out of tune:

> *My name is Sammy Hall, Sammy Hall,*
> *My name is Sammy Hall, Sammy Hall,*
> *My name is Sammy Hall,*
> *Here's my curse upon you all, God damn your eyes!*
>
> *I killed a man 'tis said, so 'tis said,*
> *I killed a man 'tis said, so 'tis said,*
> *I hit him on the head,*
> *With a bloody lump of lead,*
> *And I laid the bastard dead. God damn his eyes!*

He sang it right through and then he repeated it twice. He had been drinking and he drove a little wildly. This morning he had not shaved and there was a blue-black growth on his face. He had a narrow chin and small eyes.

Starting the song for the fourth time, he turned to the girl and said:

'Why don't you sing? There ain't hardly been a chirp out of you since we left Melbourne.'

'I feel cold,' she said. 'I'm doing a freeze.'

'You sing too, Vera. It'll make you feel warm.'

'No. You sing all you want to.'

She shuffled on the seat and drew her legs up under her. She was blonde and wore her hair like Veronica Lake. Her eyelids were heavy, her eyebrows had been plucked to a thin line, and her big pouting lips were letterbox red and greasy with lipstick.

'You ain't never been so quiet before, Blondy.'

'That ain't my name,' she said. 'I don't like it. You call me by my proper name.'

The boy turned to look at her. The car went close to a wall of rock and she yelled at him.

'You keep your eyes on the road, Joe.'

They drove on for four minutes after that without speaking. Their breath rose in little clouds and as the sun got warmer and higher steam began to rise off the road. They passed a farmhouse and Joe waved to two children. The road ran into the bed of a valley and he stopped the car and lifted out a suitcase from the back seat. He shook the bottle of port wine, poured out a glass, and passed it to the girl.

'No,' she said. 'No, you drink it.'

'It'll make you feel warmer, Vera.'

'No. I don't want any. You drink it.'

'You've got something on your mind,' he said. He put the glass and bottle down on the floor, slid over the seat and put his left arm around her shoulders.

'You've worrying about your old man,' he said.

'Him!'

'Something's on your mind. I ain't never seen you this way before.'

The girl didn't answer, but when he went to kiss her she turned away. She pushed at his face with her hands.

'No,' she said. 'Don't kiss me. I don't want you to kiss me.'

'Well, slit my throat!' He said loudly. 'Slit my throat.' He said the words with a sharp exhalation of breath.

'What the hell's biting you? You weren't like that two nights ago.' He mimicked her: 'Kiss me, Joe. Kiss me. Kiss me. Joe, I love you.'

The girl put her right thumb to her mouth. She bit it, once, twice, thrice. She breathed through her teeth as she did so. Her elbows pressed into her sides and her eyes grew smaller.

'I hate you,' she said. 'I hate you. I hate you.'

'Hell!' Joe said.

'I could slap your face,' she said. 'I hate you.'

'Go on,' Joe said. He thrust his face close to her. 'Go on. Slap me. Slap my face.'

Vera threw up her right arm, slapped him loudly across the cheek. Joe went pale. Tears of pain came into his eyes.

'You bitch,' he said. 'You bitch.' He put his hand to his face and sat looking at the road. Then he bent down, corked the bottle, and emptied the glass on to the road. He put his foot on the self-starter and started the car noisily. He jammed his gears loudly. He drove, looking at the road and holding the wheel tightly.

The car began to climb. The sound of the engine was loud and hollow. The

sun came into their eyes. A dew-heavy shrub brushed against the front right mudguard and threw water on the windscreen.

The girl began to cry, softly at first and then loudly. Joe slowed the car down and turned his head a little. She saw him turn and put a hand on his arm.

'I'm sorry, Joe,' she said. 'I'm sorry I hit you. Honest, I am. I don't know what got into me.'

'Forget it.'

'You say you forgive me. I'm sorry. Honest.'

'I forgive you.'

He stopped the car on top of a rise and she put up her lips for him to kiss.

'I don't know what got into me,' she said.

'I shouldn't have told you to have a crack at me.' He pushed his hat on to the back of his head and ran his fingers through his hair.

'I ain't never seen you this way before.'

He kissed her again.

'My old man says all women have moods,' he said. 'You're not sorry about the last two nights?'

'They were lovely, Joe. You know I loved them.'

'Don't let's go back today. Let's go back tomorrow. Your old man can't get any madder.'

'I don't care about him. I can manage him.'

A green and white bus came up the hill. The driver had to slow down to a crawl and edge past their car. He yelled out:

'What the hell are you doing there? You ought to give a man more room.'

'You go and take a jump at yourself,' Joe told him.

He and the girl laughed loudly. The bus driver leant out, shook his fist, yelled something they couldn't hear.

'You'd think he owned all the road,' Joe said.

'You're a scream,' Vera said.

'That's the way I like you. I ain't never seen you the other way before—not in two years.'

'Three years.'

'Three years. Did you miss me when I was in Geelong?'

'I thought about you.'

'Your old man will be mad when he knows we've picked up again.'

'Let him get mad,' Vera said. 'That's all he ever does. You could have knocked me over with a feather when you called up for me on Friday. Why didn't you write?'

'You asked me that before,' he said. 'You known I ain't much of a letter writer.'

'Maybe I mightn't have got it. My old man has asked me a hundred times if I heard from you.'

'He can go to hell.'

'Yes,' she said. She toyed with the brooch on her right coat lapel. The brooch was of imitation diamonds set in the shape of a swallow.

'Another day won't do him any harm,' she said. 'I ain't seen you for six months until now. Darling, say you forgive me.'

'I forgive you.'
'Joe, I love you. I'm going to keep on loving you. Joe, Joe.'

———

At Ringwood next morning they stopped the car and Joe went into the hotel for a drink. Vera didn't want a drink and she sat alone in the car. At the station a bus set down passengers for a train. A man came out of the station carrying a suitcase and got into a hire car. In front of the grocery shop a boy wearing a white apron laid the dust with a watering can. Three schoolchildren walked past the car, waved and smiled when they saw Vera.

The grocer's assistant saw her, put down the watering can, and came across.
'Hullo, Blondy,' he called out.
'My name ain't Blondy,' she said.
'Getting all hoity-toity, uh?'
'You call me Vera.'
'Giving yourself airs, eh Blondy?'
'My name's Vera,' she said. 'You remember that, Freddy Welsh.'

'Your old man will give you Vera.'

'What do you mean?'

'You'll see, Blondy,' Freddy said. 'You'll see.'

'You tell me what you mean, Freddy Welsh,' she said loudly. 'You tell me what you mean.'

'Been tearing the town upside down, your old man. He's had the police out looking for you. He'll give you Vera, Gorgeous.'

'You shut your trap. I'm not frightened of him.'

'Where have you been? He says you haven't been seen since Friday.'

'Where I've been is my business.'

'Putting on airs again, Blondy.'

Joe came out of the hotel and began to walk towards the car. Freddy saw him and started off back across the road.

'I get it,' he said. 'You've picked up with that Joe Kennedy again. I get it.'

'You go to hell,' Vera said.

'You're forgetting to be a lady, Blondy.'

Joe said, 'What's going on here? I'll give you a hit under the ear, Freddy, if you're giving lip.'

'You and who else?' Feddy said.

Joe started off across the street.

'Joe!' Vera said. 'No, not here. Let's go home.'

'He could do with a good kick in the tail.'

'Let him alone. You drive me home, Joe.'

'He could do with a kick in the goat,' Joe said. He got in the car and started the engine.

'Well, it's back to the cactus,' he said. The car moved off. Joe took his hat off and threw it into the back. The engine was still cold and the car went sluggishly.

'What was Freddy Welsh cheeking you about?'

'Nothing,' Vera said. This morning she wore shoes with open toes and, stamping her feet, she said:

'I'm cold. What's the time?'

Joe stretched his left hand forward out of the sleeve and looked at his watch.

'Nine o'clock.'

The car began to climb a little. A rabbit bounced across the road and Joe jammed down on the accelerator. The rabbit reached the side and Joe laughed.

'Missed the cow,' he said.

A milk cart came towards them and Joe waved; the driver waved back and whacked the horse on the rump with the reins.

'Hoy, Vera,' he called. 'Hullo, Joe.'

The cart fell behind and Joe said, 'Bill Fisher. I ain't seen him for months. I ain't seen him –'

He broke off and pointed up the road with his left hand.

'Do you see what I see, Vera? It's old bug-a-lugs.'

The green and white bus was coming towards them. As they passed, Joe leant out and called, 'Do you want all the bloody road?'

The bus driver sat straight up suddenly.

'Why you – you little squirt, he yelled.

Joe leant out and thumbed his nose. The bus dropped behind. Joe laughed.

'Old bug-a-lugs got made,' he said. He shook with laughter; then he nudged the girl in the ribs. She smiled but didn't say anything.

Ten minutes later they took a side road and the girl sat up and began to watch the road. The car ran across three little bridges and then past a wooden gate.

'Here we are,' Joe said. He drove on a little way and turned the car off under a clump of gum trees.

'Home, sweet home,' he said, switching off the engine.

The engine died with a choking cough. Joe leant back and pulled out a packet of cigarettes. He passed it to Vera. She shook her head. He lit a cigarette, blew smoke out through his nose, held the cigarette between right thumb and forefinger, then slid his left arm round the girl.

'You slip home with your case and come back,' he said.

'No,' she said. 'I better go in.' He went to kiss her but she had her face down. He passed his right hand across, holding cigarette, lifted her face up and kissed her. She kissed him back. Then she looked down at the floor. Her right hand played with the swallow brooch.

She said, her eyes half-closed:

'Joe!'

'Yes?'

'Joe, I ain't – I ain't going to see you again.'

'You what?'

'This has to stop. I ain't going to see you again.'

'You don't meant that,' he said. 'You can't mean that.'

'This has to stop. I mean it, Joe.'

He said slowly:

'You're having a joke.'

'No, Joe. It ain't no joke and I mean it.'

'You take your port up and come back to the car.'

'I ain't coming back, Joe. Honest, I ain't.'

She got out of the car, stretched her legs, tugged at the seat of her dress. Then she reached into the back seat and lifted out a suitcase. She set off across the road.

'You're crazy, Vera.'

She stopped and said, 'Maybe I am. I don't want to see you again.'

She put the case down and shook a lock of hair out of her face.

Joe laughed. He said, 'The last two days you've been as touchy as a bulldog ant. What's got into you?'

He walked over and put his hand on hers.

'Don't you try to stop me or I'll scream,' she said.

Joe didn't say anything. Then he gave a short laugh and said sharply:

'I got it. You got another bloke.'

'You men,' she said. 'You're all the same. You always reckon it must be another fellow when a girl says she don't want to see you any more. You're all the same, the lot of you. You only want one

'It ain't like you to talk this way.'

'SHE kissed him back. Then she looked down at the floor. Her right hand played with the swallow brooch.'

'What the hell do you know about me?' Vera said loudly. 'All you men only want one thing from a girl.'

'You like it,' he said.

The girl's face went red and her head went down. Her hair fell over her face and she said softly:

'It's all right for men. It's different for girls.'

'Who's been getting at you, Vera?'

'No one,' she said. She bent down and picked up the case. 'You get on my nerves with your "you-ain't-been-this-way-before-Veras" and "who's-been-getting-at-you-Veras". You get on my works. I'm going to scream.'

She walked across the road and through the gate.

'I'll wait for you,' Joe said. 'You come back or I'll hang round here all day.'

'You better not. You ain't popular round here.'

'I'll be seeing you,' Joe said.

'You better get. We have a gun up there now.'

Joe walked back to the car, sat down on the footboard and lit a cigarette. The girl went up the patch to the house. She found her sister ironing in the kitchen. She looked up and said:

'Where have you been, Vera? You're in for it.'

'Nowhere.'

'You look pale,' her sister said. 'You look as though you've seen a ghost.'

'Perhaps I have,' Vera said.

You say the queerest things at times. What are you looking for?'

'I'm looking Bill's gun. Where is it, Kath?'

'What do you want it for?' Kath asked.

'Joe Kennedy is at the gate. I want to give him a fright. He says he is going to hang around all day.'

'You be careful what you do with that gun,' Kath said. 'It's in the laundry. It ain't loaded but you be careful.'

Vera went into the laundry and picked up the gun. She walked down the path. Joe saw her coming and walked up the path to meet her.

'Now, go on. You get,' Vera said. 'I don't want to see you no more.'

Joe laughed.

'You ain't scaring me,' he said.

She lifted the rifle up and pointed it at him. The barrel was about three feet from Joe's chest.

'I ain't joking,' Vera said loudly, biting her lip. She shook the rifle and put her finger on the trigger. Joe laughed. There was a sharp explosion. Joe seemed to shake. His face looked puzzled. He fell in a half-sitting position and then went over on his back.

'You've shot me, Vera.'

'No, no, Joe. No.'

She stood there. Smoke came out of the barrel and coiled and swung in the air. Then she ran forward and bent over him.

'Joe,' she said. 'Joe!'

She began to shake him, softly at first and later roughly, gripping him with both her arms.

MAKING A LIVING

ANOTHER journey. But this time we went on holidays. Well, not exactly holidays, but something near enough.

It was the summer after I had my thirteenth birthday and Father said, 'If we don't get out of the city for a while we'll starve like dogs in an orphanage.'

Father's affairs were going badly again; bottle dealing was worse than bad, nobody bought bottles and no one had any to sell. Times were hard.

So Father had become a horse-dealer. He bought a few horses and all the would-be buyers yawned, scratched themselves, looked sideways and said, 'Things are bad. We'll do with the horses we've got.'

And those buyers who could afford more horses as soon as they set eyes on Father's decided to go in for motor cars instead. When Father took up horse-dealing motor cars were becoming popular. Honestly, evil fortune followed Father like a faithful hound.

Father sat about the house for days and puzzled the whole matter out. He had an idea. He would take several of his horses to the outskirts to the city and

JUDAH WATEN
1911–1985

let them loose – they would finish up in a municipal pound. But his two best-looking horses could still be put to some use. He would take them to a holiday resort where he would hire them out as riding hacks to timid holiday-makers.

The more Father thought of his plan the more intoxicated he became with it and he was convinced that the timid holiday-makers were waiting for just these two horses. And of course there were many other things Father could do at the holiday resort.

Thus was born a second idea to Father. He would drive his cart round the hills buying rabbit skins and hides and tallow and whatnot, while I would be responsible for the two horses, hiring them out at the guesthouses, the hotels, and in the street. After all, why shouldn't I help in making a living for the

family? I was no longer a child. I had a tongue and a pair of hands. What harm would it do my mind? Father asked with passion.

Without looking at him Mother replied, 'I always said our son would have to struggle here just as I did back home. I knew it from the first day we landed in this golden kingdom.'

But despite Mother's words I was elated that it fell to me to help the family in such hard times. I could see no reason for her unhappy reflections. I felt like the other boys in the street and all of them had to do something for their families. Some of them had begun to work years ago.

Father's plan mapped out, every detail well cared for, off we went to Berrigullen, the fashionable holiday place in the hills. In such a resort Father said even if we only ate dry bread it would still be a holiday for all of us. Why, even the air in Berrigullen was noted for its wonders – it was said that the old became young, the sick healthy, and more besides. That was why so many important people in our community were beginning to go there for their holidays.

We locked up our house and loaded the spring-cart with blankets, pots and pans, saddles, spare sets of harness, three black hens, a white rooster, and a part fox terrier that, property speaking, belonged to the whole street. The two horses that for a change were going to help feed us were tied by halters to the back of the cart.

The street turned out to see us off. Friends, acquaintances, neighbours came out of their houses as though to watch a funeral or a brawl. Some of them stood on their verandas and waved to us. And as there were many men out of work at the time a large crowd of people of all ages stood round the cart, laughing, gossiping, giving friendly advice, and wishing us good fortune.

It was a warm send-off, but Father was filled with gloom and his pale-blue eyes were dull and sad as though with pain. He had hardly spoken a word. He nodded his head absent-mindedly and stared unseeingly at the neighbourly men and women and barefooted children.

'Ah, these accursed journeys,' he suddenly whispered to me, 'and for what?'

His voice was filled with such sorrow that it seemed to me Father had suddenly seen through all his dreams and schemes and his heart had emptied at the prospect before him at the end of this new journey. I understood then how much Father had always hated moving.

I felt with him and I was fretful at leaving the neighbourhood. As we drove off and I waved to my companions I envied each and every one of them. There were Tom and Joe and Benny, and I thought of everything they would do this day – the stories they would tell each other, the games they would play, the walks through city lanes and streets.

My peevishness grew as we jogged through miles and miles of suburbs. Everywhere bystanders gazed in our direction. What was it they were looking at? Was it that the harness on the chestnut drawing our cart was thread-bare and held together with wire and string, and that tufts of yellow straw stuck out of the collar? Or was it because one wheel of the cart wobbled

I knew it was neither. The people were looking at us. Th   ing new, for we were frequently stared at when we drove throug   .ets. But now it was different. Everything affronted me – th   ·ctable houses, the broad clean streets, the complacent, healthy faces of the people so different from those we had left behind. My irritation grew into anger when a group of men and women looked at us a little too long. There was something ironical about their gaze and one woman pointed with amusement to the two horses jogging resignedly behind the cart.

'What are you staring at?' I shouted at them. Then I picked up an empty bottle from the floor of the cart and I threw it at the group where it crashed into splinters at their feet.

Mother, startled out of her reverie, glanced in the direction of the people gesticulating at us. Then she looked at me angrily.

'Why did you behave like a hooligan?' she demanded.

I was stubbornly silent and she repeated her question. I refused to speak, it would have been impossible to explain why I had thrown the bottle. If I could have done so she might have understood and perhaps she would have ceased her bitter and ironical musings.

She said, 'You remain silent. I think I understand why. We hardly speak a common language any more. You belong to one world, I belong to another. With your new ways you have almost become a stranger to me.' And then she asked in her gentlest voice, 'Please tell me one thing – where did you acquire the cultured habit of throwing bottles at strangers?'

She went on and on but Father said nothing. He was absorbed in his own thoughts, but for some reason I felt that he secretly understood my behaviour. Perhaps I had in some way expressed his feelings, too.

We were all silent when we drove into the main street of Berrigullen. We were all too moody and far away to take in the beauty of the surroundings. The township was like a garden with its rows of poplars and elms and the fruit trees that hung over fences and hedges. On all sides in the distance tier upon tier of hills rent the fading blue sky and walled in Berrigullen.

It was not in the main street or on the heights that we lived. We had a furnished cottage in a hollow below the township where seldom any traffic passed; the sound of voices in that neighbourhood almost created a sensation.

There was an unfriendly look about our new house and at night the paper pasted over the chinks of the windows sounded in the breeze like the patter of frightened feet. It was the last cottage on the road and the bush came right up to the side fence and the backyard was overgrown with bracken. Half a mile down the road a row of cottages similar to ours stood close to each other. There were no holiday-makers in those dwellings. There lived old-age pensioners, rabbit trappers, and fruit pickers.

I had no time to explore round the houses on our road, I had work to do. The day after we arrived in Berrigullen I was to take the two horses into the township, stand near the hotel or one of the guesthouses, preferably the biggest and best, and get clients, the timid holiday-makers who were waiting for our two mounts. Father explained everything, what I was to say and how I was to say it. Apparently satisfied that I should be successful, he drove away into the hills.

Saddled and ready to be ridden, the horses ambled behind me up the steep track towards the main street. From a distance some boys called to me but I

ignored them. How were they to know that I was on a most important mission? It was the first time I had taken any part in the making of a living for the family and nothing would divert me. I dreamt of the money I would bring home. In my mind I counted my earnings over and over again. I could see the coins stacked on the kitchen table so that even Mother would have to admit that she was wrong and that Father was not foolish in sending me to hire out the horses. I was filled with pride and everything round me quickened my elated feelings – the summer morning, the sweet scent of gums, the hum of insects, the cries of birds, the hot, still air. How wonderful everything seemed just then!

But as soon as I was in the main street my elation began to ebb and I saw my task in a more sombre light. Slyly fear and shame had crept into me. Where would I start? I looked round at the large houses with trees and flower bushes hiding from sight the doors and windows, and I wondered if they were the guesthouses from which I should get my customers. To make matters worse, all the words Father had carefully impressed on me vanished from my mind. I had forgotten what to say and what to do.

In despair I walked the horses up the street and then back again. The two steeds were resigned to their fate and their heads drooped in philosophical contemplation, like wise parrots in a cage.

I stopped when children's voices floated towards me from the lawn of a long, rambling house that I rightly believed must be a fashionable guesthouse. In a

moment I made up my mind, walked over to the gate and tied the horses to a telegraph post. Behind the low fence boys and girls played, while well-dressed men and women sat on garden benches under trees, some reading, others just chatting.

I scanned the faces of the men and women and I recognised Mr Frumkin and his wife. They were well known to me, particularly Mr Frumkin, with whom Father had for so long dealt. He was now the leading dealer in the bottle business while his wife was a notable in various ladies' societies in our community. They sat stiffly and silently and neither of them smiled or waved back to me when I shouted cheerfully, 'Hullo, Mr and Mrs Frumkin!'

And, imagining that they might be interested in my doings, I called again, 'I've got two horses here I want to hire out.'

They shifted their gaze and stared down at their feet.

'For a moment I was bewildered, but the snub from the Frumkins in some unexpected way gave me strength and entirely restored my faded confidence. I thought of how I could increase their discomfiture and then I remembered the purpose for which I was outside the gate of the guesthouse.

Swaggering slightly I called to the guests on the garden seats, 'Who wants to hire a good horse? Only a bob an hour.'

Nobody rose from his seat. Here and there an amused smile, a haughty stare; even the children went on with their playing. Several boys made as though to come over to me but they were stopped by the grown-ups.

I continued to call my wares as though at the market. Even there one had to shout and shout to attract customers – sooner or later someone must come over.

Without a glance in my direction the Frumkin couple left their seats and made for the veranda of the guesthouse. I called insolently to Mr Frumkin. 'What about you, Mr Frumkin? The horse's back is wide enough for your behind.'

There were a few sniggers and, needing little encouragement, I continued to shout at the Frumkin couple until they disappeared into the house. Then I went on again with my business cries. Soon a man came up to the gate and he stared at me severely.

I looked him up and down and said, 'You can have your pick. Only a bob an hour.'

His face went crimson.

'Clear out,' he said angrily. 'Nobody wants your horses. Get!' he added furiously.

I edged back slowly towards the horses.

'What if I don't get?' I said.

'I'll see that you do,' he said menacingly.

'Well, I'm not going for you, anyway,' I said and turned to the guests, who had risen from their seats at the commotion.

'Who wants to hire a good horse? Only a bob an hour!' I shouted at them and out of the corner of my eye I watched the menacing gentleman.

He made as though to open the gate, and with a sudden onrush of rage I stooped down and picked up a handful of stones. I held them in my clenched first, ready to throw the lot at him should he but go past the gate. He stared

intently at me as though to judge how serious my intentions were. He must have been quite satisfied, for he turned abruptly on his heels and walked back to the guests who were strolling towards the gate. He said something to them as he passed and they, like sheep, followed him until they all disappeared. Only a few boys remained on the lawn playing with a bat and ball.

I put my thumb to my nose and shouted derisively at them. Then, with exaggerated slowness I took the horses down the road again. There and then I decided I would have nothing more to do with guesthouses. As I passed one after another it seemed to me they were all the same, with their stiff lines and their hard, suspicious exteriors. Perhaps I attributed to the buildings something that rightly belonged to the people sitting on the well-kept lawns.

The horses stopped to drink from a trough near the hotel. The air was hot and still in the broad, sleepy road. Across the way a store rested drowsily in the shade of two poplars and the creek behind murmured gently. Overhead green and red and yellow rosellas flew with a faint hissing noise from tree to tree.

I tethered the horses to posts and walked to the veranda of the hotel. Under the open windows of the bar-room two old men sat without speaking to each other. They looked as if they were part of the wooden bench and from their ancient, shiny serge suits I guessed they were natives of the township and not holiday-makers.

One of them was idly drawing his stick over the floor and both looked up at me with expectant eyes, as though glad of any diversion.

'Do you think anyone in the hotel wants to hire a horse – cheap?' I asked.

'Well, I don't know, sonny,' one of them said. 'There's a riding school here and besides, the hotel's got a few hacks.'

'My horses would be as good as the others,' I said.

'I wouldn't know,' the old man replied and winked slyly at his companion.

He, with a faint grin wrinkling his face, screwed up his eyes and with the air of an expert gazed at the two horses.

'They look good horses to me,' he said. 'Not as young as they used to be and a bit short of wind, but I can see they've been good workers.'

I walked with firm steps into the bar, believing my horses vouched for by two old men, and I spoke with a full heart to the men standing at the damp, glistening counter.

'I've got the best two horses in Berrigullen for hire. Wonderful to ride and only a bob an hour.'

The drinkers turned around slowly and looked at me with lazy eyes. One of them said, 'We've got no time for riding.'

There was laughter at his words and another man said, 'Come and have a drink, lad. Lemonade, eh?'

I stood up against the counter and, imitating the men, I held my glass of lemonade as jauntily as they held their beer. I pushed my cap back and sipped my drink slowly as I looked around the bar. On the walls and above the shelves laden with bottles there were framed pictures of horses, boxers, and footballers. Some of them were familiar to me, others were heroes of before my time.

I could make neither head nor tail of the conversation that continued around me. There were jokes about a party that had been held in the hotel the night

'I put my thumb to my nose and shouted de-risively at them. Then, with exaggerated slowness I took the horses down the road again.'

'SILENCE lay over the township and the sun shone down on the rust-red gravel with a fiery brilliance.'

before. And there was talk about hang-overs and how they should be cured. I was afraid to finish my lemonade, thinking of finding at least one customer.

I turned to the man who had bought me the lemonade.

I said, 'Wouldn't you like a ride on one of the horses?'

He looked at me humorously and then put a shilling in my hand. Without a word he joined in the conversation again.

I gazed sheepishly at the shilling until the barman leant over and, tapping me on the shoulder, pointed his thumb at the door. I hastily gulped the rest of my drink and walked out into the sunlight, my face red with the knowledge that the barman had thought I was a beggar. I was ashamed to look the two old men in the face.

'No luck?' one of them asked sympathetically.

The other said, 'These blokes in there never ride horses. They spend all their time drinking. You went to the wrong place, sonny.'

'You'll never make anything out of those blokes,' the first old man said. 'They're takers, not givers.'

I suppose the old men knew all about the holiday-makers in the hotel, for they sat on the wooden bench all day. But it didn't console me and my heart was heavy when I went back to the horses and led them across the road so that they could nibble at the tufts of grass under the trees.

I blindly reproached myself with my failure and I felt guilty about my behaviour at the guesthouse. I had one shilling to show for all my effort and I clutched it as if afraid that even it might fly away. Sitting on the edge of the road I stared disconsolately ahead. Only the two old men were to be seen and they looked at me with faraway eyes as if constantly turning over their memories. Silence lay over the township and the sun shone down on the rust-red gravel with a fiery brilliance.

I rose from the ground to take my charges back home. The two sleepy, timid horses were stuck to me like a tail and they were my responsibility until I could return them to Father.

The main street, the guesthouses, the hotel, disappeared from my sight as we descended the steep track. Nothing could now elate me. Around me was just lonely bush, grey trees and blackberry-bushes encroaching on both sides of the track. Behind the horses dust rose in tiny clouds and rolled away towards the trees. I felt my face. It was covered with dust and my fingers were black and sticky.

When I reached the bottom of the hill near our house I stopped by a tree and watched the horses nibble happily at the dry brown leaves on the ground. I couldn't face my mother just yet. I had suddenly become afraid of her intent searching eyes, her bitter words. Something had happened to me this day that would want thinking out. For the first time I had stepped out into the world and I had touched with my own hands the hard kernel of life, getting a living.

THE LETTERS

PATRICK WHITE
1912–

MRS Polkinghorn remembered she ought to write a letter of sympathy to Maud. Any illness tended to irritate her, but dear funny old Maud Bles, so loyal, if so colourless, she must really say someting about Maud's blood pressure. Or was that Sibyl Farnsworth? No, Sibyl's sounded far more technical.

Mrs Polkinghorn still *enjoyed* sitting down at her marquetry desk in the morning room, and dashing off a few letters, many of them unnecessary, after her pretence of a breakfast. It seemed, in these days, to uphold her status. She was lucky in having Harriet, who would not last for ever, though.

Mrs Polkinghorn's breath caught.

'Charles?' she called, not for any particular reason.

No answer.

She chose a sheet of the second-best writing paper – the lettering was nicely engraved, however:

Then Mrs Polkinghorn was ready.

> *WISHFORT,*
>
> *SARSAPARILLA,*
>
> *nsw.*

Dearest Maud [she wrote, in what had been referred to as her bold hand],

I can think of nothing more tiresome than to be told to 'go slow'! You can imagine how distressed we, too, shall be, since it will deprive us of your little annual visit. The blossom at 'Wishfort' promises to be particularly fine this year, and you do so love it. Still, we must bear our crosses.

I broke the news to Charles, who received it in silence. But I know he will sadly miss the company of his beloved Auntie Maud on the important occasion. *I did have hopes of coaxing him out to our matinée this year, especially as this will be his fiftieth birthday. I cannot believe it! Though of course there is every evidence. Indeed, at times Charles acts so old he makes his poor mother feel positively young!*

Here Mrs Polkinghorn was unable to resist a glance. Her eyes could still ravish the glass.

Maud dear, it is not my habit, as you know, to load others with my troubles, but your godson has been worrying me more than usual. There is nothing one can put one's finger on . . .

For a moment she wondered whether that looked vulgar. She was sorry she had underlined it.

But . . . [she continued bravely] *. . . the complications do increase. Since his 'withdrawal', you will remember I have taken pains to devise little routine occupations to give him an interest in life. My efforts, however, have not always been successful. My plan for him to mow the grass was perhaps an understandable failure. Charles is not mechancial, and grass*

is so tedious. The grass-mowing did not last for long (Norman had to resume; he is now so deaf and rude, but we are lucky, I expect, to have him). A comparatively recent 'brain-wave' on my part was to persuade Charles to walk up to Sarsaparilla and fetch the letters. I rented one of those amusing little private boxes, and Mrs Sugden, the postmistress, is such a decent soul – I knew Charles to have a particular affection for her. All went well for several months, until last week my darling, tiresome son announced he was unable to continue fetching the letters! So now, if you please, the mail is once more delivered at our gate, and I must think of something fresh for Charles.

    I do not doubt all this will sound trivial to anyone so far distant as Melbourne. Of course, it is something that concerns me, and I would not breathe it to another person, unless to his

godmother, and you do seem to have some influence over him, Maud dear. I have always been
so grateful....

Here Mrs Polkinghorn paused again. Funny how dowdy, simple Maud had
known unexpectedly what to do in many a situation. Was it humility? Oh, but
Mrs Polkinghorn had *prayed* for humility. She was frowning hard now, and the
glass had grown unkind.

Relax.

Mrs Polkinghorn began to smile, but slackly, but spiritually, as she had
learnt it.

One last wish for your restored health, dear Maud, and I am sure we shall both *be*
thinking of you with deepest affection as we stroll amongst the blossom at 'Wishfort', before
Harriet summons us to the birthday luncheon.

My very best love –
URSULA

PS. *If you should write to him, please do not mention any of these matters.*

When she had sealed the envelope, which tasted rather nasty, Mrs Polkinghorn went in search.

Charles was sitting in the dining room, in that big leather armchair, so
hideous, but it had belonged to Dickie. Charles was reading something, or so it
appeared. She could see the back of his head, the careful, straw-coloured hair,
which he would arrange to cover as much as possible of that fragile dome.
Sometimes the mother almost expected to see a pulse still beating in her child's
head.

'Charles,' she said, gently, going round, 'you are reading.'

He was, and continued.

'What,' she asked, 'are you reading, Charles?'

'*Rearing of Fowls on the Free Range System.*'

His small moustache, straw-coloured once, had been dirtied by the shadow of
grey.

'But we have no fowls,' she said. 'They smell.'

He continued reading.

'Or perhaps you would like me to buy you some,' she considered. 'Half-a-
dozen chickens,' she begged. 'The grown-up kind. Those little day-old things
are such a trouble, and you'd be sure to catch a cold.'

Charles said:

'No.'

He continued reading.

Mrs Polkinghorn could not endure the creaking of that huge leather
armchair. She was glad of Norman's lawn-mower. With only a little collaboration from her mind, the blast from the machine could destroy almost all other
noises, sensations, presences.

'Well,' she sighed.

She rearranged her hat. It was the big old straw she wore for the garden, but
like all large floppy hats, it suited and pleased Mrs Polkinghorn. The big droopy
ones created an atmosphere of weddings.

'Did you go,' she remembered, 'to the gate, to see whether the postman has brought our letters?'

'No,' he answered.

His cheek did twitch just a little. Or was it another of those infinitesimal wrinkles opening in the skin?

'But *why*, darling?'

He was reading, and reading.

Mrs Polkinghorn could not control her irritated breath.

'Then I shall have to fetch them myself. Harriet is busy, and Norman so rude, one hardly dares suggest any longer.'

She went out, into the garden she had planned herself, though that landscape creature had claimed the credit. The house, with its little seemly lozenges of leaded panes, set in the Tudor sprawl of shaggy brick, was by now far too big, but when Dickie died she had determined she would make the effort to keep it up. Now she walked along the path, touching the roses of which she was proud. Somewhere jasmine whipped her cheek. You could not say it was a sob that burst from her mouth, but refractory jasmine did recall the contrariety of life.

Nothing but bills, of course. At best, receipts. Two of the more sumptuous circulars for Charles, and the Firm's report from Cousin Ken.

After Charles's 'withdrawal', Mrs Polkinghorn had arranged – in confidence – with Cousin Ken and Mr Beddoes that the Firm's reports be forwarded regularly to her son. *To keep him in the picture*, she said. It pleased Mrs Polkinghorn to collect the idiom of those decades to which she had never succeeded in belonging. Her theft of such phrases made her feel she had entered into conspiracy.

But this morning events seemed to be conspiring against her. She almost tripped near the steps, by slipping her foot into a noose of the couch grass Norman could never be persuaded to uproot.

She went on, clutching her bills.

Dickie would have attended to bills. Dickie Polkinghorn, a large man, though mild, whom almost everyone had forgotten. Even his widow was sometimes surprised on catching sight of Dickie's face in one of the many silver frames which contained all that was left of him.

But I did, did love darling Dickie.

Thus assured, Mrs Polkinghorn returned to the dining room with the letters. She did not wish to. It was her duty, however.

'Here are your letters, Charles,' she offered.

He took them.

'Are you not going to open them, and see?'

He had put down the pamphlet. He had put his hand to his mouth for a moment. Unlike his father, his bones were fragile.

'There might be something exciting,' she coaxed.

'Yes.'

But he got up, and shut them in the lacquered box which dominated the mantelpiece.

Mrs Polkinghorn was helpless. If only Maud, now.

'I have just written,' she announced, 'to Auntie Maud. About her trouble.

Who knows when my letter will get posted, though. Norman will refuse to leave the mowing.'

When Charles Polkinghorn made a most remarkable offer.

'Give me the letter,' he said. 'I shall take it to Sarsaparilla.'

His mother hardly knew whether to feel gratified or pained. She always experienced a little pang to discover afresh that the wells of human nature were deeper than she was able to plumb.

She gave up the letter, however, and Charles went out with the light, nervous steps of brittle bones, so unlike his father, whose movements had always been attended by a squelch.

Alone with the photograph of Dickie, she remembered those other men whose company she had enjoyed. English tweed went to her head, and the gloss on the toe-cap of a well-shod foot. She would glance at a man's wrist while fanning his vanity with what he supposed to be her attention. She was very expert. The lips of many congested, jolly, tweedy men would still droop open at the recollection of Ursula Polkinghorn's smile.

Now she walked through her house – it was unmistakably *her* walk – trailing the garments which clothed her spirit, while in fact wearing some she did not particularly care for. Ursula Polkinghorn (one of the Annesley Russells of Toorak) had always favoured the trailing dresses, weeping sleeves, stoles tipped with feather, to throw casually round her throat. That throat! Whenever she had made her entrance, at weddings, for instance, smoothing the long kid gloves, or hand barely passing through the faint effulgence of her pale hair, everybody forgot the bride. Yet her eyes hardly encouraged them, for of course she had never trifled with *any*body's affections. She had *adored* her Dickie. Though her mouth would smile for someone she might never confess.

Involved in a kind of composite of all the weddings at which she had assisted,

Mrs Polkinghorn made for the pantry, where she still did the flowers, every morning, after the ritual of her desk. Harriet had found the scissors, so easily lost, and stood a wrong selection of vases.

For Mrs Polkinghorn to preside.

'Lovely, lovely roses!'

But this morning something was eating the roses.

Her rings clashed. She never took off her rings by day, unless to demonstrate to Harriet the number of folds for rough puff. Which Harriet secretly knew.

But today the rings were brutal.

Nor could she resist one quick look out of the window – she always took the greatest precautions – before treading smoothly back, into the dining room. It was empty. Breathless. Presences still lingered there. She almost expected Dickie's leather armchair to creak.

Mrs Polkinghorn opened the lacquered box. There was quite a bundle of letters inside. All unopened. Several days of them.

At that point she began to dread something she might not be capable of understanding.

―――――

The first moment after stepping outside into the brilliant, fleshy garden, Charles Russell Polkinghorn had sidled rather. The light blinded his sandy eyes. He held on to the letter, though.

The morning had grown silent in which old Norman squatted, to fiddle with the mowing machine.

Charles paused, because one did.

'What is it, Norman?' he asked. 'A cog?'

Norman never looked up for Charles.

'Cog! It's the bloody maggy!'

Charles Polkinghorn might have been relieved.

'Patch it up!' Norman complained. 'Patch up the bloody maggy!'

Because, she had said, I shall spend nothing further on the mower. Horrid thing. If it had been something attractive.

Charles Polkinghorn continued on through what his mother was pleased to call the Great Eastern Shrubbery. He was picking at the sliver of dry skin which grew alongside one of his nails. As a little golden boy he had begun to take an interest in those pieces of dead-seeming skin, often fraying them till he bled. He would stand beside the woodshed, or slip inside the shrubberies, to pick.

'Don't you find them interesting, Auntie Maud? The corners of skin. Except you sometimes pick too hard.'

To Maud Bles her godson was a most fanciful little boy.

'Yes,' she said.

And touched his hair.

Married to a poor clergyman of acceptable family she had failed to reproduce.

Charles Polkinghorn walked up the road to Sarsaparilla. It was *his* road, though nobody knew. Although his shoulders were narrow, and his waist thin, in the black pin-stripe he was wearing out he walked purposefully now. Nor did he turn his head, though suspecting faces. There were, too. Ladies would pause, in their dusting or conversation, to observe 'that Mr Polkinghorn'.

Who arrived at last. And skirted round. To slip the letter, quietly, deftly, into the box.

As soon as done, he escaped. Not even the postmistress had seen: Mrs Sugden, of straight, upstanding hair, for whom he had the affection.

Not a bad lot this morning, a pretty respectable bunch, Mrs Sugden used to remark in the days when Charles fetched the letters from their private box.

Charles Russell Polkinghorn was returning jauntier than he had come.

He had been to the circus with his Auntie Maud. The clowns began to terrify, especially the one who broke his neck. Poor, poor Charles, she comforted; now you may look, it was nothing, only horseplay. Horseplay? There hadn't been any horses, only terrifying clowns. Just a lot of silly nonsense, she reassured. He raised his head slowly from her breast. She smelled of nothing, he was surprised to find. But kindness. Her hand, chafing his skin, looked so natural, he continued staring at it after the clowns and his terror had vanished.

It wasn't real, she explained; it wasn't meant.

Charles Russell Polkinghorn had often wondered what is meant. Now he whimpered a little going down the hill.

'Good morning, Mr Polkinghorn,' said old Miss Langlands.

'Good morning, Miss Langlands. You are looking well.'

Could it be that she liked him?

Entered for the right school, Polkinghorn had acquired manners. That he distinguished himself scholastically, people had forgotten. His mother would sit below the dais, waiting for afterwards, waiting for him to heap the prizes in her arms.

They sent him over to Cambridge, too. Dad had agreed. Polkinghorn trod warily at first. In his second year he had invited two or three men to tea and crumpets. They had not come again. But Charles was immersed in all that he had discovered. He took a degree, with honours. Only a second, it must be admitted. If that hour of amnesia hadn't occurred in the course of his final paper, his tutor considered he might have managed a first. Charles was quietly crushed. He had cherished the prospect of a prolonged affair with the Romance languages in some academic backwater. Curiously enough, languages enabled him to communicate – discreetly, though – with other people.

But all that would have been impossible, of course. For other reasons.

His mother had written:

... did not cable, because I understand the greater shock cables can give. You will be happy at least to know, dear, that Dad died painlessly, in his sleep. Only the suddenness of it! I expect it will take me quite a time to recover, but I shall throw myself into as much as I can. There is always the Firm to consider. Cousin Ken and Mr Beddoes are, mercifully, towers of strength. Dad had the greatest confidence in them, but Charles, darling, it was always his dearest wish that his son....

Charles returned.

She was not at the boat to meet him, preferring to stage their reunion away from the hurly-burly, in the setting they both loved.

'HIS mother would sit below the dais, waiting for afterwards, waiting for him to heap the prizes in her arms.'

She had come down the steps towards him, offering her face which tears had tightened. Her eyes astonished by their blueness. She patted his arm, lingering on it for a moment to enjoy the texture of English tweed.

Charles Polkinghorn at that stage was what is called a dapper little man, with his small, evenly-divided moustache, discretion in his clothes and cufflinks. In those days he could still tell a story. Cigarette smoke acted as a screen. The music had not begun to throb. One or two girls had even looked him over at dances.

'Tell me,' his mother asked, offering her face, 'there must be someone.'

'Someone? Who?'

'Why,' she laughed, 'you silly old boy! Some charming girl!'

Charles Polkinghorn was thunderstruck.

'But,' he said, 'I thought I had done everything that was required of me.'

On leaving the room he mopped his forehead with a handkerchief.

His mother had to wet her lips. And to return on frequent occasions to the inquisition. Her eyes were at their bluest then.

'Surely,' she said, 'I cannot believe there isn't some lovely girl. Otherwise it just isn't natural.'

She watched his mouth as it tried out shapes.

'There is no one,' he said.

And stuck to it.

Considered from certain angles the situation was unfortunate, Mrs Polkinghorn told Miss Langlands. But she and Charles were very happy together. They had so many interests in common.

In those days Charles Russell Polkinghorn was scrupulously observant once he had made up his mind to a thing. Caught the train every morning to the works. Cousin Ken had explained the plant. The men acted hearty, while they thought it was expected of them. Charles was given an office, not the one which had been his father's – Cousin Ken had taken over that – but a smaller, no less airy, well-equipped room. At intervals during the day, secretaries placed papers in his tray. Miss Gregson smelled of Ashes-of-Roses. Charles Russell Polkinghorn would take the papers out of his tray, and examine them gravely.

It was the noise which began to worry him. Sometimes Miss Gregson's lips would move without sound. It was the machinery, at which he never learnt to look without wanting to avert his face.

There was the annual dinner and dance, at which his mother put in an appearance. Mr Beddoes would hand her through the waltzes. His wristwatch was far too small for him.

'Do you care for Greta Garbo, Mr Polkinghorn?' Miss Gregson inquired.

'Enjoying yourself, darling?' his mother asked.

She, at least, never failed in her performance.

After the first year or two, somebody hit on the idea of introducing paper caps and streamers. To make the dance jollier like.

Charles Polkinghorn suspected a private joke, the point of which he would never see.

Yet, there was his mother, dancing with the toolmakers, too.

He began, worse, to suspect the machinery. How it belted, as he sat examining Miss Gregson's papers. Voices did not carry. That had a certain advantage. Or most voices would not.

There was that Badgery, though, of Thompson Johnson constructions.

'Everything running smoothly, Ken?'

Throwing his gravel into the machines.

'Smoothly? Couldn't be smoother. Even with our extra cog!'

The bits almost flew off then, the oily fragments, into Charles Polkinghorn's office. He put Miss Gregson's papers into the wrong tray.

On returning home that evening, Polkinghorn stayed away for a week.

'I must tell you, Ken, in confidence, though,' his mother rang up the office, 'Charles is suffering from a slight breakdown.... Yes, rest is what he needs.... I shall keep in touch.... Thank you, Ken, dear. You're a brick....'

But Charles returned at the end of the week. He would sit it out.

They allowed him to keep his office. He continued to go there to read the *Herald*, until finally, as Mrs Polkinghorn herself put it, Charles 'withdrew'.

At 'Wishfort' the years turned over quite as regularly as the most merciless machine; the difference was they were oiled with silence. Although he had given up reading, excepting the pamphlets and the circulars, there were lines that troubled Charles Polkinghorn still. *De l'amour j'ai toutes les fureurs* ... might sound its muffled trumpet. He would slip out into the shrubberies, there to pick at his more placid thoughts, or the skin that had died at the sides of his nails. Sometimes the knots in his throat would almost soften into words of wonder, images almost crystallise somewhere at the back of his eyes.

Sometimes his mother would call to him, but he only answered when it suited.

On the morning of his fiftieth birthday Charles Polkinghorn woke early, aware that something had to be done. It could have been the presents; presents still gave him a thrill, though he was clever at finding out in advance.

His mother came, bringing the half-dozen Swiss voile shirts embroidered with his monogram. In all the house, she always rose the earliest. She kissed him. Her cheek, of legendary complexion, had the taste of icy water.

'Many happy returns, dear Charles!' she said, so brightly, she could have been speaking through falling water.

'Aren't they lovely?' she prompted. 'Feel.'

'Yes,' he said.

He looked at them.

Presently she went down into the garden into the dew and spider-webs. She liked to visit it before the heat, to sever the heads of roses. Thorns would tear at her silken wings, of a rose colour too, but she always won in the end.

The day was already promising a blue blaze, in which the new, feverish leaves would do little to allay apprehensions. Still, Charles was prepared for it: the tufts of blossom blowing brown in a withering wind. This year Auntie Maud would not be there to share his distress. In other details the program promised to be much the same: roast chicken, and chocolate mousse; Harriet had iced a cake – Harriet, whose wizened face was one of those perennial loyalties he

'*PRESENTLY she went down into the garden into the dew and spider-webs. She liked to visit it before the heat, to sever the heads of roses.*'

dared not look directly in the eye.

Charles went down. After breakfast, which his mother's figure did not allow her to share, he knew for certain there was something. Thumping. At times, his heart would sound like a man approaching in crêpe-rubber soles along a linoleum corridor.

He realised then; sleep perhaps had planted in him the necessity for correcting a mistake. It was the boxful of unopened letters. The lacquered box on the mantelpiece.

Could it be that the sealed letters might breed the dangers he thought to escape, secrets stirring, gases expanding, poisons maturing? His rubbery heart was maddening him. And towards nine, the postman would arrive with more.

At nine, precisely, he did. Clocks accompanied the event. Charles, who was watching, noticed the peak of a cap glinting through the cotoneasters.

Inspiration drove him down the path. To liberate. The flaps of his hacking-jacket flew.

There was something this morning disguised as a bill. Something more innocent-dangerous. And – might he thank Heaven? – a letter from Auntie Maud.

Charles Polkinghorn returned quickly to the dining room, to decide, but not quickly enough, which letters to open first. To repair. To avert. The box tumbled the whole collection out on the table, into the marmalade, amongst the crumbs.

Then he opened. One.

... this machine will cut closer, wear better than any other on the market. It will demolish

the worst growth of Paddy's lucerne, Paterson's Curse, paspalum, or that most stubborn invader of the home lot, Kikuyu grass.

The rotator's cut....

Charles Polkinghorn recoiled. Almost mown by the wind the machine made in passing, he kept his balance with difficulty. Once, he remembered to have read, a blade had become detached and embedded itself in a human eye.

But a certain minutia of evil had been dispersed simply by the opening of an envelope. His hands faltered in search of increased relief. To do his duty. If it was not – for he could not claim to be noble – to save his own skin.

He had opened, again, at last.

... otherwise [the next threat ran] *your supply may be disconnected without further warning....*

So that his neck was straining, his eyes grew polypous, his veins shrank until it seemed they might fail altogether to convey the flow.

Then Charles Polkinghorn remembered his godmother. Auntie Maud, he was convinced, must save. If his swollen tongue had not choked him before he tore the envelope.

My dear Charles,   [it was herself speaking]

This is just a note to wish you the happiest of birthdays. I am truly disappointed not to be with you on the occasion. But the doctor forbids me to attempt it since my 'turn'.

Dear Charles, I want you to know what very great happiness you have given me, almost as though you were my own son. I have been an unsatisfactory godmother, I admit, what with the actual distance that has always separated us – and, well, just my own inadequacy. My only consolation is a belief that it is not possible to discuss things of the spirit without their losing something of their purity. Will you, too, my dear, console yourself in realising this? I have always liked to think we have brought each other comfort of a kind.

Now, Charles, I must take you into my confidence – that is to say: I do not wish to upset your mother – but there is every possibility that I may not last so very much longer. The truth is always a risk, but at some points one has to risk it. I asked, and I was told. In the meantime, I shall pray that I remain with you, always, always, *in the spirit.*

I am sending you a little package for your birthday. If it should arrive beforehand, I ask you to keep it until the day for which it is intended.

Your loving godmother –
MAUD BLES

Then Charles Polkinghorn had to cry out. *Blessés!* The two – or was it the three of them?

But was not Auntie Maud aware that packages contain the worst of dangers, threatening the lives of politicians, diplomats, film stars, all people of importance? At least the package had not arrived. Or had they put it away, and forgotten it was thriving and throbbing in the dark of some unvisited cupboard?

He began to go round the room. The windows were open. Through them he suddenly heard the approach of animals above the gibbering of Norman's mower. The soft, but insidious animals. Or rain? It was the first enormous drops of rain padding through the mulberry leaves. None the less, he closed the windows.

But could not shut out his own heart.

'What is it?' his mother asked very quickly on coming in. 'Ah, you have opened the letters! I am so glad! Did you find anything of interest?'

Did he!

Mrs Polkinghorn saw that it had happened.

'Charles,' she said, 'we must not give way.'

She was trembling, though.

As for Charles Polkinghorn, the walls had started screeching.

When she bore down on him, her face had become a circular saw, teeth whirling, eyes blurred into the steel disc.

He screamed back.

'Darling,' she cried, 'what has been done to us? We must, we *must* be *strong*!'

After that, they were seated on the sofa, their knees trembling in the same piece. He, no longer so very frightened. Crying, though, because he had forgotten how to stop. By now she had compressed her face into a lump of the marshmallow he used to love, and even now he might have popped it into his mouth, if the white mass had not been smeared so palpably with blood.

He continued crying for all they had forfeited, or never found.

'Strong, *strong*!' Mrs Polkinghorn commanded.

Was this her son? This bunch of twigs she held in her hands? She could almost have snapped the brittle stuff.

But caught sight: the old, slanting teeth set in the remnants of her own face.

'Remember, remember,' she uttered, fainter, 'I shall always be at your side.'

It did not stop him.

Though he did, at least, remember. She was standing at the foot of the stairs. In white satin. *Remember*, she said, *Charles*, as he slowly descended, paying out the smooth rail through his hand, *remember you are of an age where you must not open letters. Other people's affairs are their own. Besides, she added, you might discover something to hurt you. Always remember that.*

Remumber. Oh, Mum, Mum, Mum, oh, Mummy!

'I shall help you,' his mother was saying, 'if you will let, if you will trust me.'

She was holding his head against her brooch. Sapphires were threatening to gouge his eye.

'Oh, yes! Yes, yes!' he cried, or mumbled.

Descending still farther on the spiral, into the remoter, satiny depths, he stooped to pick up her voice, its shell. *Isn't he an angel? Look, Dickie! A cherub off a palace ceiling! He is mine! My angel!* Oh, delicious persuasions! And when she touched, flooding him with satin.

'Charles! *Charles*!' Ursula Polkinghorn had begun to rattle.

'Oh, God help us!' she called.

If Charles had been less involved, he might have heard the pennies drop. But must push past, ever deeper, past the sapphires and the wrinkles, in search of darkness.

'Oh, horrible! Oh, Charles!'

As soon as he began to nuzzle at her, Mrs Polkinghorn threw him off. How did she deserve? Ever! Her beastly, her unnatural child!

DUEGARA

*Yeah we'll talk about this *bugawamba* you know -
*bugawamba** that's that stone we show you -

all right -
now -
this is old Duegara --
you know that's Duegara that's a true man you know -
he's a true person -
this time I seen 'im too -
old man he's a king -
Duegara -
he's a king --
he had his wife too -
married tribal way you know -
his wife -
so --
this 'nother young fella come along he -
young man come along he pinch his woman -
you know take 'im away from 'im steal 'im -
run away with 'im -
took 'im 'way -
he took 'im riight up to -
Beagle Bay --
Lombadina -
aall round that country he bin round there ooh nearly one year I think round
    that place -
and then he -
all these people come back now he thought this old fella forget about this fella
    you know, well he had to come back to -
to make himself clear you know --
they must have a fight -
in tribal way --
to make it square whether he can give 'im this -
if they have a fight well he can let him have this woman --
if the old fella beat 'im well -
beat the young fella well old man will have to bring that woman back -
but if the young fella can beat him well he can take the woman -
it's that way -

PADDY ROE
(*with Stephen Muecke*)
circa 1912–

*Meaning 'bad man' and referring to a phallus-shaped stone at Fisherman's Bend.

so they all come back -
all the way from Beagle Bay -
they started from Beagle Bay they went back to Broome now on the beach you
    know all the way -
when they all come back -
he only went far as -
oh Barred Creek -
Quondong Barred Creek and Willie Creek -
Willie Creek -
now that Willie Creek you know I showed you that rock? that time -
that cave -
that's their camping ground if any rain -
but no rain they don't camp in the cave -
they camp outside --
all right -
somebody went into Broome -
from that place -
they told this old man -
'Well old man' they said 'we bring this man back he's in Willie Creek now' they
    tell-im you know they tell old Duegara -
'Oh he come back?' -
'Yeah' -
'Woman and man come back' -
'Yeah' -
'And what he say?' -
'Well we come up to pick you up -
bring you back to Willie Creek to pick up your missus -
you know your woman' --
'Oh good -
well' he say 'I won't go -
they can stop there -
in Willie Creek, I'm not going -
I don't want to pick 'im up -
if he want to come back there well let 'im come right back here but if he don't
    want to come back well let 'im stop there I won't go' -
'Oh', so this man went back he tell these fellas -
'Oh we bin want to bring old man so you can clear -
make everything clear you know fight out here -
but the old man won't come' -
'Oh' -
'So I think you better go' -
'No I won't go' say -
this man and woman said 'No we won't go -
let 'im come here' -
'Ah' -
so this man went back again -
ah -

back to Broome -
he tell 'im 'No they got goin' to come' -
'Oh well leave them -
I don't want 'im' say -
'I don't want the woman' he say
'Let 'im have 'im -
he can have the woman' -
'Oh good' -
so this fella come back again -
he tell these fellas -
'All right that old man said no more he -
he don't want any trouble -
no fight no nothing -
so you keep the woman' -
'Aah all right' he say -
but this man know too -

so one day -
they went out in the cloudy day too but it's rain time you know this is the rain
    time --
that's why I show you that -
cave you know where that's their place where they -

PADDY ROE

go in -
from rain you know -
no rain time this is different *manggala** -
manggala manggala rain time -
dis is *manggala* -
all right -
four there was about -
five man -
five man and five woman -
they, camping in that ground -
so these five man went looking for fish -
they go through the creek -
come out other side -
they went other side gettin' fish -
oh long way you know you seen that creek -
where he run they went that way -
and these womans all sit down home -
in that little island now -
langunguru we call 'im -- [Stephen: Mm mm]
[Soft, breathy voice] they siddown -
all riight -
oh big rain you know cloud coming up -

*One of the five seasons, as indicated in the Nyigina language.

biig cloud -
biig cloud -
soon as he come close you know ooh lightnings everywhere -
biig lightning -
strike everywhere -
'Oh we better rush back' these fellas said -
big rain comin' they had lotta fish too -
they all run back this five man -
and five woman there too --

all right when these womans seen all these, whatname comin' you know the
    rain -
oh they pick up all their -
blankets and tucker whatever they had you know put 'im aall inside -
and the cave is like that -- [Draws]
you know that's where they go in from -
the cave is more like that you know -
that's the place they go in -
this is their door -
to go in -
and this is all rock you know on top --
that's the island like --
that's the island runs right around you know everywhere --
that's their place camping ground --
proper too from *bugaregara** you know -
long time -
well that's their camping ground in that island [Fade] -

[High] all right -
oh the rain start now straight away -
so they all went in -
that woman was here in the middle they put 'im -
he got four womans here -
see four woman oh they got dogs too -
they had some dogs inside -
four woman -
there's one woman -
'nother woman 'nother woman 'nother woman and here him in the middle --
they put 'im in the middle --
ooh they know lightning everywhere --
biig lightning, everywhere strike -
these man comin' ooh still long way from creek --
very hard --
they come they had big load too fish -
so this lightning now -

*This place is charted in the 'dreaming' stories.

PADDY ROE   rain rain rain rain rain jus' pouring -
now ONE LIGHTNING COME -
he strike -
he strike right underneath this woman -
you know ah -
lift 'im up -
chuck 'im outside -
pieces and guts head -
oh liver heart everything -
aall pieces everywhere -
and this woman was in the middle -
this two --
four woman here you see they put 'im in the middle -
but the lightning come from right underneath him -
lift 'im up just chuck 'im through the door in pieces and finish -
and aall this other four woman -
two fall down here inside you know - [Laughs]
and 'nother two here too they only laydown just outside here -
only one woman he lift him out from the -
from that cave chuck 'im right out pieces -
dogs [Laugh] -
all layin' down --

[Soft] all the man come -
[Soft growl] hellooo 'Hello might be something wrong' that man said -
that lightning strike right there -
they couldn't see too -
lightning you know -

so they all come up they look -
hello they see two woman layin' down outside and 'nother one is all pieces -
hello which one -
they look round 'nother two woman layin' down here inside -
'nother two here -
and this fella he just -
he lift 'im from there chuck him outside pieces -[Laugh]
aall in little pieces -
leg hand head liver everything [Laugh] pieces -
'Mm-mm' --
dogs all big sleep -
all come up there look oh they start to cry now -
they know straight away -
'Oh my woman bin get killed' -
'Yeah' -
'My woman get killed' -
'Yeah' --
all cry now all them man, ah these fellas don't know -

they crying crying crying crying -
one woman get up --
one woman -
'What's wrong?' he say -
'What yupella crying for?'
'Oh lightning bin hit you fellas -
yeah' -
'Oh -
yes?'
'Yes' -
'And what yupella crying for' --
'One woman -
finish' --
he look -
aah [Laugh] pieces -
'nother woman get up again, 'nother one inside -
they all get up one by one you know --
all get up finish --
they come out right dogs all get up too [Laughs] -
all the dogs not one dog got killed -
or them other four woman nothing -
only from shock I s'pose eh
the lightning -
yeah jus' fall down -
but only one he only wanted one woman -
couldn't get 'im from any other way so the lightning come out from under-
    neath -
to lift 'im out - [Laugh]
now this is the magic belongs to black man - [Laugh]
that's Duegara -
mm --
that's why he said to this man we don't, I don't want that woman he can stop
    there that man can have 'im -
but he know he wouldn't have 'im too long --
that's his thing there now that *bugawamba* --
same man, he went in his dream -
he make that fella into lightning -
kill that woman [Laugh] -
that's him -
that fella now -
that's him that's his spirit --
sometime when we go past 'Hello' -
don't go there that's old man there they say you know, [Laugh] womans -
we know Duegara --
so we only bin show you stone you know -
soo --
that's how powerful that thing is

THE WATER LUBRA AND THE LOTUS BIRD*

ROLAND
ROBINSON
1912–

A GIRL called Wirreitman came out of the water of the river Kimmul. She put on a man's hairbelt and she bound up her long hair. She took a spear and a wommera and she went out hunting for wallaby. The girl went hunting through the bush and she could use the spear. She speared Ngalmungo, a hill kangaroo. She made two firesticks and made fire, and she cooked the kangaroo in a ground oven.

A man called Nogamin had been out hunting. He was carrying a wallaby up on his shoulders. He looked out and saw smoke rising beyond the trees. He started to walk up to the camp of the girl.

Wirreitman the girl looked out from her camp and saw him coming. The spear and the wommera she put to one side. Then she lay face down in the dust with her arms folded in front of her, waiting for the man to come up.

The man Nogamin came up carrying the wallaby. 'Ai! What is the matter?' he asked.

'Ah, I am no good,' said the girl. 'My stomach is no good.'

'What is the matter that you do not get up?' said Nogamin. 'You want to get up and open up that kangaroo.'

'You, old man,' said the girl, 'you can take that kangaroo out for me. You can leave me the arms and legs.'

'Well,' said Nogamin, 'you want to get up.'

'No,' said the girl, 'I am sick in my stomach. I will get up by and by. You take that kangaroo and leave me the arms and legs.'

Nogamin took the kangaroo out of the ground oven. He cut and broke away the arms and legs. He picked up the body of the kangaroo and left the camp. 'Battai ya,' he called to the girl.

When Nogamin was gone the girl got up quickly. She picked up the parts of the kangaroo, the spear, and the wommera and ran away.

As the man Nogamin walked along he thought about Wirreitman lying down in the camp. He thought of the way she was lying down and the way she hid her eyes when she spoke. 'It might be that one is a girl,' thought Nogamin. Nogamin stopped in his tracks. 'It might be,' he thought. 'I must go back and find out.'

He put down the wallaby and the kangaroo and went back. The camp was empty. Nogamin came up and looked at the place where Wirreitman had lain. In the dust he saw the imprint of her body. He saw the imprints of her thighs and folded arms and there, deep in the dust, were the two hollows her breasts had made.

---

*As related to the author by Kianoo Tjeemairee of the Murinbata tribe.

Nogamin found the girl's tracks going out of the camp. He followed them, running, stopping to pick them up again, then running on. He called out to her, he stopped to find her tracks, then ran on again.

The girl had climbed up into a bottle tree. Nogamin came up running. He looked and saw the girl sitting in the thrust-out branches of the bottle tree. It was a big tree. He did not see how he could climb up its smooth round, bottle-shaped trunk. Nogamin breathed hard. Then he called softly to the girl. 'O, come down to me, girl. You and I are good friends.'

The girl in the bottle tree laughed down at Nogamin. 'Ah, no,' she said. 'This is my bottle tree. I like sitting up here. But you,' she mocked at him, 'you come up to me.'

Nogamin tried to climb the tree. As he did so the girl in the branches sang the tree and the bottle tree began to get bigger and bigger and grow up more and more. And the girl mocked Nogamin as he tried to climb. She showed herself to him to make him mad. She sat this way in the branches and that way in the branches and she leant out and down to him, stretching her arms.

Nogamin could not climb the tree. He could find no hold on the big, rounded trunk. He sat down under the tree and cried for the girl. He cried, 'O, you sit over there.' He looked up at her. He cried to her, 'O, come on, come on! You've got to come down to me!' Nogamin was out of his mind for that girl.

It was a little bit dark. Nogamin slept. He woke up and cried to that girl sitting in the branches of the tree. He slept and woke at the foot of the tree. And then, at last, when Nogamin was asleep, the girl slipped down out of the tree and ran away.

Laughing, the girl ran back to the river Kimmul. There, lying on the sand near the young paperbark trees with the river glittering past them, were all her sisters, the Murinbungo, the water lubras.

Nogamin woke up. It was little-bit daylight. He looked up and saw the arms of the bottle tree bare against the stars. As soon as he could see, Nogamin began to follow the girl's tracks. All those girls lying along the river heard Nogamin coming. Weirk the white cockatoo rose screaming out of the high paper-bark-trees. 'Ah,' the girls cried, 'it might be that it is that man now who is frightening Weirk.'

Nogamin came running. He saw all those girls lying out in the sun on the river sand. When the girls saw him coming they got up and dived in the water from all along the river bank. Nogamin was running down the bank to dive in after them when he saw their father, the Rainbow Snake Kunmann-gur, rear up out of the water. In deep mud near the river bank Nogamin came to a stop. He cried out in a strange voice, 'Keir, keir, ngeir!'

He had changed into the lotus bird who runs over the broad floating leaves of the lilies crying out and looking for its food.[*]

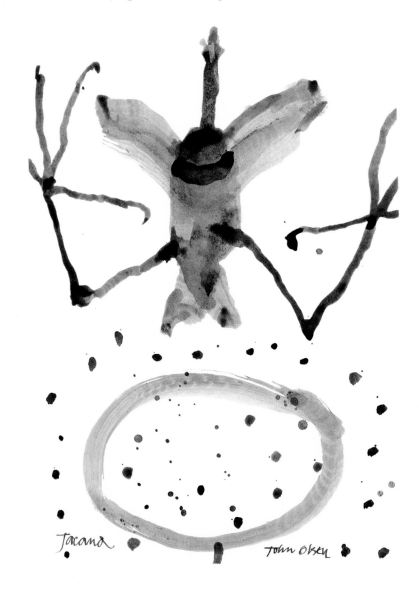

[*]And the place where Nogamin tried to jump in the water is called Kiyerr, on the Fitzmaurice River. A stone is the dreaming of that man Nogamin whose spirit is now a bird. The wommera belonging to Wirreitman is the cypress pine growing there, called Lakomin; the wommera of Nogamin is the Leichhardt pine, Pitji. The spear belonging to the girl is Woolgooboo, and the spear of Nogamin is Oonjirri the jungle tree.

THE FENCE

PETER COWAN
1914–

THERE was a high dark-trunked blackbutt by the gate, and to the left of it an enclosure that might at one time have been a small orchard but was now covered by thick fern. The shapes of some old almond trees pushed above the fern, one of them in leaf. To the right the green and brown fern gave way to trodden dusty earth, and there were sheds and a milking-yard. Perhaps a hundred yards from the sheds was the house.

Max got out of the utility and dragged the gate back. He drove through into the yard, closed the gate, and leaving the utility walked across to the house. There was a wire-netting house fence around it, and over part of the fence and along a sagging trellis to the house where it spread over one wall was a creeper whose leaves were a deep green. Inside the house fence there was a vegetable garden, and near the low back veranda some rose bushes had been planted. They looked neglected and the soil about them was brown and hard.

He went across the veranda and knocked, and from inside he heard someone move hastily as though he had disturbed them, and then he heard footsteps tap on the boards. The door had been half closed. It was pulled in and a girl stood in the doorway. She looked at him quickly, as though startled. She kept one hand on the door.

He said: 'Can you tell me where I can find Mr Butler. Frank Butler.'

'He's not here,' she said. 'He's – over at his father's place. He's been working there –'

'Oh, I thought he'd be back,' Max said. 'Anderson's my name. Max Anderson. I'm doin' some fencing here. I was talking to his father about it in town, I been working for him last couple a weeks –'

'Yes,' the girl said. 'I know about the fencing. But we didn't know when you'd be coming –'

'Wasn't sure m'self,' he said. The girl was looking down, as though her eyes took in the lower part of the strong hewn upright of the door and the worn threshold. Her hand that held the door moved it slightly, but as though she were unaware of the movement. She wore a short, white dress that was too small for her thin figure. Her hair was dark and straight, and now untidy. She felt him looking at her and she moved uneasily, though still not looking at him.

'Well, I may as well go on down and find a place to camp,' he said. 'I suppose you don't know when Frank'll be back?'

'No,' she said.

'I got a fair idea where the piece is, but if you could just put me right for the gates and that –?'

'If you go down just past the old orchard up at the top,' she said, 'there's a gate there. There's a track goes out through that long paddock, and Frank's put a new gate in the far corner. You can't miss it.'

'Righto,' he said. 'Thanks.'

'THE shapes of some old almond trees pushed above the fern, one of them in leaf.'

'All right,' she said.

He heard the door close as he turned and stepped off the veranda. He went back to the truck and drove down past the old fern-encroached orchard. He found the way easily to the uncleared part where he was to fence. He had been told where the creek ran, and he walked from the new gate to where it was. He found a part where there were peppermint trees and little undergrowth. If I can get the old bus down here, he thought, it should make a nice camp. Might be a few Joe Blakes; still, they're anywhere. He picked a way through the timber, driving slowly, and left the truck in the shade of one of the big peppermints. He cut some straight poles and began to put the tent up. He worked without hurry, liking the cool and the shade of the peppermints. It was about four when he had the camp fixed and he went along the creek to see if there was a place to bathe. Some distance up, nearer the house, though the timber screened it from view, he found a wide pool. The bank was worn and there was a track leading into the timber in the direction of the house. He had not meant to bathe, not having worked that day and having cleaned up when leaving old Butler's place to go into town and then out here, but the look of the still clear water and the broad patch of sun that cut across it made him want to go in. He looked in the direction that the house would be. He thought it's not likely she'd come down here by herself. He had not brought his towel and could not be bothered going back for it. With the sun there was no need.

He stripped off and went in. The water was cold, but he swam a few strokes and splashed about. The bottom was clear of snags and pebbly under his feet. When he began to feel the cold he climbed out and squatted on the bank in the broad patch of sun. He made a cigarette and smoked and looked at the karries on the ridge that went up steeply along the back of the creek. This might be quite a fair job, he thought. The sun dried him quickly and he got into his clothes and went back to the camp. He dragged some boughs from the timber and broke wood for a fire. There was very little wind and the fire burnt evenly and quickly in the fireplace he had made. He put on his billy and some potatoes in an old can and sat on a log near the fireplace smoking and watching the fire. The bush was getting slowly darker so that the fire took on a deepening colour and he could hear now and again the wood snap. After a time he got up and from the box mounted on legs which he used as a safe he took some steak he had brought from town. He put it in the frying pan and moved the potatoes over to make room on the fire. He ate sitting on the log, keeping the fire burning for light. It gleamed on the low, hanging leaves of the peppermints and their grooved dark trunks, and on the white of the tent. When he had finished he put the plate and cup and knife and fork in a quarter kerosene tin and poured hot water over them. He washed them and threw the water in the tin out, hearing it slap hollowly on the dry earth. From the fire he lit his lantern and put it on the box at the head of his stretcher. Lying in bed he read for a time a paper he had brought from town. Little of what he read seemed to have much concern for him, camped in the stillness under the peppermint trees. He was not much interested. He read till he felt tired, then dropped the paper and blew the lamp out, first lighting a cigarette from it. While he smoked he thought of the work in the morning.

In the morning he found, as old Butler had told him, that the fence line was marked, and in part there were a few chains of an old post-and-rail fence. Clearing that away took him all the morning. It was not work he liked, and he worked on past his usual lunch hour to get it done and make a start with the fencing after lunch. When he had eaten he thought that he would go up to the house and get some meat so that he would not have to knock off early in the evening. He went along the boundary fence and cut across one of the paddocks, a shorter way than by the track. As he came across the veranda he heard the girl in the kitchen. She came to the door.

'Oh, hullo,' she said quickly.

He smiled. 'Afternoon.'

'Frank hasn't come back yet. I think he'll be back any time now, though.'

'I've got a start down there now,' he said. 'All quite clear, so there's no hurry. I can see him when he's not busy. I was wondering if I could get some meat. I don't want to go in, except weekends. So if you could let me have it –'

'Yes,' she said. 'There's some there. I'll get you some.'

She went into the kitchen and got the knife and went down the veranda to the small dark storeroom. She cut the meat and weighed it. When she gave it to him she said:

'You could have milk if you like. We've plenty, if you want it.'

'Thanks,' he said. 'Only thing is, coming across for it, y'u see.'

'Yes, of course,' she said. 'Well, any time you do want it you can get it.'

'Yes, thanks.'

She looked at the wrapped parcel of meat in his hands. He saw that she wore the same short, tight white dress that was too small for her. It had no sleeves, and her arms were thin and white, but as though possessed of a kind of quick strength. They moved nervously, nakedly, as she twisted her hands together.

'It's hot, isn't it?'

'Yes,' he said. 'Late season.'

'Yes.'

'I don't mind it. Doesn't make the post-holes any easier to dig, though. The ground's very hard.'

'It's so dry.'

'Yes.'

'Last year,' she said, 'it was a late season.'

He nodded. 'Not much winter.'

'No.'

'Well,' he said. 'Better get back on the job.'

'As he passed the creeper he saw the girl still standing on the veranda, her arm against the post and her head on her arm.'

She looked past him to the high timber along the ridge. He stepped down from the veranda. She nodded and put one hand on the veranda post, leaning her weight to it. He went along the path past the high green creeper whose leaves seemed to deride the heat. When he reached the house gate he paused suddenly, not opening the gate, and then turned and went back. As he passed the creeper he saw the girl still standing on the veranda, her arm against the post and her head on her arm. She was looking down as though at the sharp stain of shadow from the veranda on the hard brown earth. Her short dark hair was fallen forward across her cheek. She heard him and looked up suddenly, twisting upright away from the post.

He said: 'I forgot to tell you – I asked Robinson if he'd bring my bread out with your things – it'll be with them – I'll come across and get it.'

'Oh – yes,' she said. 'All right. Yes.'

He went down to the fence and across the paddock. It's not my business, he thought. It's nothing to do with me. It might be there's no one there and she's been left on her own. It might be anything. I don't know. You can see all sorts of things working for people. But then we can all make a pretty decent mess of things. The thing is, keep out of it, you get no thanks not minding your own business. No. He got back to the camp and hung the meat up in the meat bag and went through the peppermints into the timber to his work. He cut posts until after a time he realised he had left his waterbag at the tent. He left the axe against a tree and went down to the creek. The undergrowth was heavy, but he found a clear space, and kneeling down drank from the clear water that looked brownish from the brown coarse sand and stones of the bottom. As he was going back he stopped to listen, and he heard a car or light truck from the direction of the road, close to the farm. He supposed it was Frank come back.

In the morning Frank came over to where he was working, and they discussed the job. He looked older than his sister; he was short, slightly built, though wiry. He had the same dark hair as his sister, and there was a resemblance in the small regular features.

'I'm finishing off a job with the old man,' he said. 'But I'll be back here at night. Anything you want, I'll be up at the house there.'

'I'll be right,' Max said.

'I'm going into town Sat'dy afternoon, if you want to come in. But I s'pose you've got your own bus here.'

'Yes. Don't know whether I'll go in, Sat'dy. Might work and go in Sunday all day.'

'Yair. Well, anything you want –'

'Right,' Max said.

In the afternoon while he was working he thought he saw something move up the slope of the ridge. He thought it might be a roo, and he stopped, staying still, looking up through the undergrowth and the ferns. He saw the movement again, a light colour that was not like anything he could recognise, and then he saw that it was the girl. It occurred to him that he had seen a track going up along the right from the swimming pool, and she was on that. She could not have moved through that under-growth without him hearing her. He lifted the axe and the sound of it went through the timber again. He lost sight of the girl. He worked till dusk, when he went back to the camp, where it seemed darker under the low peppermints.

Next morning about midday when he knocked off work for lunch he went up to the house to get his bread, which should have been brought out by Robinson, who delivered mail, and would bring out bread and small parcels. He went through the house gate and along past the creeper. He stepped across the veranda and knocked. There was no answer, though he thought he heard someone move inside. He looked about the veranda and saw on one of the boxes by the door a parcel that was obviously bread. He looked and saw his own name on it. He picked it up and went back across the paddocks to the camp, where he

boiled the billy and had lunch.

It was about the middle of the afternoon when he heard something move among the ferns behind and a little to one side of him. He turned and saw the girl. She was only a few yards from him. She came towards him. With one hand she twisted a bit from the wide green ferns, breaking it up in her hand so that the green became mixed with the brown underleaf.

For a moment he could think of nothing to say, and because of what it looked like he felt a sudden unsought elation, a puffing out of himself, and then that went quickly and left him puzzled and rather uneasy, and he said, because he saw she was unhappy and did not know what to say herself:

'Pretty warm, isn't it?'

She nodded. 'I was just – going for a walk.'

'It's a – good place about here. Nice where the peppermints are and that.'

'Yes, I like the peppermints.'

'I got my camp under there. Makes a bonza camp.'

She looked at the posts he was cutting. He lopped some branches. He did not like to look directly at her. He worked awkwardly. She wore a pale blue-coloured dress. It fitted her properly, not like the one he had seen her in at the house, and dressed like that it seemed to set her away from him, so that he was more awkward than when he had talked to her before. She had no hat and her short dark hair was done neatly.

'I – saw your camp,' she said. 'I went past there.'

'Yes?' he said. 'Makes a good camp there. Creek handy and that.'

He put the post with some others. He thought most likely she is tired of being by herself, she might be lonely, scared or something. But I don't know. There's something there. He had enough posts cut, and he thought if he were to go and dig post-holes he would have to go further down the line and she might go. He said:

'I got to dig a few post-holes down there now.' He shouldered his axe.

She looked at the posts spread on the ground.

'Just down there,' he said.

'Could I – come?'

'Eh? Yes. Yes, if you want to. Nothin' to see, though. I mean –'

'It might be better than being by myself,' she said.

They walked down to where he had his bar and post-hole shovel. He picked up the bar and began to drive at the hard dry earth.

'Better when the ground's wet,' he said. 'Some places y'u can't fence in the dry season at all. Got to wait for the rain.'

She had leant against the clean part of a big black and white log whose scarred length arched up above the fern.

'Y'know,' she said suddenly. 'Some ways I think you're lucky.'

'You do? It's news to me.' He grinned. 'How d'y'u make that out?'

'Well, I don't know. I mean you've got your camp there, it's a lovely place, and camping like that must be wonderful, and then you can go where you like and work. I mean, you can get something to do anywhere.'

'Can't always get paid what you'd like for it, though,' he said. 'Still, there's that side to it. There's the good and bad. Can't grumble.'

He shovelled the loosened earth and used the bar again and he said:
'D'y'u – get tired being in the one place?'

She nodded, but he felt she had not thought about what he said. She put her hands behind her on the log and gave a jump so that she was sitting on the log, her feet off the ground. The thin skirt pulled up above her knees. He had watched her when she moved, and he was aware of the whiteness of her legs and thighs exposed in movement and then partly left bare when she settled herself by the tight updrawn skirt.

He barred at the hard earth, seeing it loosen in the small round hole, and he knew it was not what it looked, she was not like that. How do y'u know? he thought. How d'y'u know? They're all the same, don't they reckon? You can't tell. No, he said, no, there's something not right. I'm not getting mixed up in anything. But the image of her white soft thighs was there and he had only to look up and it was swept into the reality of her flesh, her bare legs and the strip of spreading flesh white below the blue of her tight-drawn skirt. He wished she would go, and yet he did not want to think of her getting off the log and going, and him in the empty afternoon.

She said suddenly: 'Don't you ever – mind being all the time by yourself?'

'Well, I'm not all the time,' he said. 'Sometimes I might be working with a gang, sometimes another feller. I do a job by m'self now and then. Just depends what's offering. I rather like it on my own for a bit.'

'But – oh, I don't know.' She laughed.

He laughed with her. 'You find you get a bit tired of it when you're on your own?' he said.

'Well, sometimes,' she said. Then she said quickly: 'And sometimes I'd rather be by myself – right alone – than anything – anything. I hate it, people, everything.'

He made no answer. He could not answer lightly, and he had no other. The dry, loose earth from the hole was piled up round the edge and the hole deep enough. He picked up the bar and moved down to where he was to dig the next hole. He worked methodically, as though his whole concentration was on the heavy bar and the dry earth.

She got down from the log and looked at the line of post-holes and came towards him, and what had seemed to be there was gone, as though he might have completely imagined it. She said:

'Well, I'll have to get back.' She grimaced. 'Work to do. I don't know why we're always working.'

'Got to do something, I s'pose,' he said.

She went up the rise towards the track where he was sure he had seen her yesterday, and then he could not see her for the high undergrowth. He knew he had not imagined it, and it puzzled him, for it was something outside his experience, until he gave it up. Man's here to get this block fenced, he said, and his voice sounded strange in the silence. Leave it alone. But in the round of his thoughts it came back to him as he lay in bed after tea, smoking. There were patterns of shadow on the ground and he could hear the close leaves of the peppermints in the light wind. He put the cigarette out and pulled the blanket up and rolled over impatiently.

'THE heat beat down on the dry earth, and where he was working there was little shade.'

In the afternoon early after lunch he heard the car go from the farm. The heat beat down on the dry earth, and where he was working there was little shade. He went to the creek for a drink, and he thought that he would knock off a bit early and go up to the pool. Then in the morning he could go in to town early. There was still plenty of light when he decided to finish and went across to the camp. He got the towel and soap and went up the creek to the pool. Though there was still plenty of heat in the air, or in the sun if he stood in the direct rays, the water was biting cold and he did not stay in any longer than to swim the length of the pool, soap up, and swim back. But out on the bank and dry he felt good, clean, hungry for tea, the week's work behind him. He whistled as he went back to his camp. He got wood and made the fire, and put on the billy and a tin of meat in a can of water to heat up. He put on a couple of potatoes in an old black billy without a handle. His tobacco was in the tent, and he went in and rolled a cigarette and went back to sit on the log and watch the fire. The billy boiled and he pushed it and the can with the meat to one side. When the potatoes were done he brought out his plate and mug, and sitting on the log began his meal. He had finished and was drinking his tea and smoking the cigarette with which he followed his meals when he looked up suddenly and saw something move in the darkness under the peppermints. The light from the fire made it hard for him to see. The figure seemed to be moving away. He knew then it was not an animal. He got up and stepped quickly out of the light of the fire towards it. He saw then it was the girl. She looked round and he thought she was going to run, but he came up to her and she stood still, her head turned sideways so that he could not see her face. He put his hand on her bare cold arm. He said:

'Thought – didn't know what it was – here –'

He felt her tremble, and he thought she was going to twist away. He said:

'Come over by the fire.'

She followed him and sat on the log and he sat by her. His foot kicked against the empty plate. Abruptly she said:

'Oh – I should be dead – I –'

He could see she was crying, and with a queer hopelessness and bitterness. He put his hand out, but he was afraid to touch her.

'Don't,' he said. 'Can I – is there something I c'd do – don't do that –'

She beat her hands on her knees. 'Don't take any notice of me –'

He put his hand on her arm, hesitatingly, and then as she made no resistance put his arm round her shoulder.

'I mightn't be much good at it – but I'd like to help. You shouldn't be like that –'

'It's no good.'

'If you like to tell me – p'raps it might help if you talked a bit. Is it you're by yourself?'

'No,' she said. 'No.'

'I thought you'd have gone into town with your brother.'

'I could have. No,' she said, 'perhaps it is that I'm by myself. But it's not what you think – I know what you think –'

'I don't think,' he said. 'I don't know. I feel like I might wake up and find I'd

'HE wondered if he should follow her. It does queer things, he thought, the bush, loneliness.'

dreamed this.'

'Listen,' she said, 'when I came here just now I – it was partly what you must have thought – but I thought I'd make you – oh no. No. I'm crazy.' She tried to get up but he held her, frightened for her if she should go.

'It wasn't much that,' he said. 'I'm not that much of a fool.'

'Well –'

'I don't know why you came,' he said. He said gently, 'D'you?'

'Yes. Yes. And you won't because you can't hate yourself and know there's no way out of it and do anything to get away from it like it's made me now –'

He did not say anything.

She said: 'I must go. I'm all right. Please. Oh, if I hadn't let you see me – I'm all right –'

'If you like,' he said, 'I'll come over. Anything I can –'

'No. I'm sorry – about this. You'll think I'm mad. I'm sorry. But I'm all right. I'll go.'

He stood up. She moved away and he heard her going through the ferns in the darkness. He wondered if he should follow her. It does queer things, he thought, the bush, loneliness. I don't know. But he turned back to the fire that was almost out. For a time he stared at it. It's not a dream, he thought. God knows. What can I do? He saw the plate and mug on the ground and picked them up and put them in the quarter kerosene tin and poured cold water over them to keep the ants from them. He kicked the embers of the fire out and went to his tent.

In the morning he had made breakfast and had got the truck ready when he saw Frank coming through the timber. He did not at once see Max, and stood looking about the camp. When he saw him he came over. Max looked at him and thought, so it's last night.

Frank put his hand in his pocket. He pulled out a small diary and took a slip of paper out.

'Here's y'u cheque,' he said. 'You can finish up.'

'What's wrong?' Max said.

'You can finish up and get the hell off my place.'

'Something wrong with the work?'

'Never mind the work.'

'Look,' Max said. 'I'm not breakin m' neck to stay on your place. But you come at me like this you can tell a man what's wrong. What's the strong of it?'

'Y'u can finish up. Here's y'u money.'

'You can stick the money.' He looked at the white face. 'If you think – ' he said slowly.

'I'm not arguin' with you. You pack up and get off the block –'

'If you're thinking –'

His voice rose. 'I'm not talkin – I tell you the job's off. You can go.'

Max saw the dark inflamed eyes. It began suddenly to come together in his mind. 'By Christ,' he said. Then: 'A man ought to take a crack at you –'

Frank moved to one side and then he turned and went off under the peppermint trees into the timber towards the paddock. The coloured piece of paper he had held lay on the ground.

COME ON, BILLY

I

DAVID CAMPBELL
1915–1979

WHEN horses gallop at night, the sound is mysterious. There was Billy, frowzy with sleep, ambling through silence downhill on a drooping night-horse. The frost, after a week of rain, had sharpened the hoof-falls. The horse's paunch creaked, and Billy was aware of the silence. He was aware of the cemetery on the dark ridge where the owls moped.

Riding through star-shade, his mind tasted honey. That grandmother witch of a gaunt gum had a wild-bees' hive in its branches. And the boy was assured until a filly whinnied. The pace of the night-horse quickened, and he rode rigid. And to his heartbeats the horses were suddenly galloping. They crossed the fearful landscape of an earlier dawn. Billy whooped to his courage, and his whip sang in the frost.

Up the hard road he chased his phantoms, neck and neck with fear. But the old mare was a stayer, and on the hill-crest day was breaking. Serpent-heads tossed in the first light; a breakaway gelding bucked, exploding, down the skyline; but the mob came in to the whip. In the heavy stockyard the horses stood steaming, hock-deep in mud.

Billy's flat hand clapped the mare's withers. Hobbled, she browsed a stubble of frost. The rabbiting pack yelled, leaping like lions up the wire net of their yard. And slowly the morning came over Bald Hill, whistling a tune of gold. The great clatter sent the ghosts packing, and here were the stockmen to daunt them.

'Morning, Billy. Morning, Billy.'

Billy, shy and proud, stood astride like his father, glad to be part of the morning bustle. Dogs snuffed for rats between the slabs of the stall; horses were led out from the yard and saddled up; in twos and threes the men rode off to work between the misty gum trees. The smell of their tobacco-smoke remained. And, to forget a sudden sadness, Billy turned and ran a hard race down the rutted road to the homestead.

II

'And I wasn't frightened, neither.'

Lined with porridge and cream and the fat meat of chops, Billy could taunt his sister and any old ghost.

'It was easy,' he said. 'While Len's sick, I'll get the horses in every morning. You're only a girl.'

'I'm older than you are.'

'That doesn't count.'

But Janet only smiled. Her blue eyes were in their corners and she looked far away. Her indifference was elaborate, her smile mocked in secret.

'Let's go to dad's office and squash flies,' she said.

The office was a dark high room in the old part of the house. A giant roll-top desk stood open in the light from the one window, where dead fingers of vine gripped the gauze. A few early blowflies staggered up the panes. They were easy to catch, and made a fine mess when slammed in a ledger.

The fair heads touched. And 'Ach!' said Billy, twisting his neck and screwing up his face, eyeing the open page obliquely with the pleasure of disgust. 'Just look at that one, Jan.'

The fly had spread out like a blot over the neat figures: 3000 weather weaners at 16s. 1od. made one broad stain.

Janet puckered a sweet angel's nose, and her eyes were wide and bright. But she turned to trace a signature cut sharply in the glass pane.

'A. G. Wise,' she spelt out at length. 'Know who he was?'

'Of course.' Billy was busy.

'He went mad and cut his name in the pane with a diamond ring.'

'I know,' said Billy, loud with impatience. 'I know.'

'Look, Billy, feel it. Give me your finger. He died and he's buried over in the cemetery. He must have been a silly old man, don't you think?'

'I know all that,' Billy said. 'I knew all that before you did. He buried his fortune at the front gate.'

'He must have been a silly old man.' And then, in joyous fright, 'Look out, here comes the colonel!'

Janet slipped like a slim wind over the sill and under the swinging gauze. Her head bobbed once, gold, and was gone, leaving Billy in panic in the dim office, holding the ledger.

Clop, clop, clop!

Colonel Graham's steady footsteps rang on the veranda. So Billy walked when he thought of it, firmly, in meditation, aping the big man he feared. But this was no time for laughter; he was trapped. He ran to the window, papers blew about him in the draught. He grabbed at them, listened, and dived to crouch, pale, in the knee-cavity of the desk.

Clop! and the window banged down. He could see his father's tan boots amongst the papers, and, hugging the tell-tale ledger, he prayed, 'Please, God!' But God would not listen to him, for he had been killing flies. This was what came of it. And he thought of those yellow blots with shame and hatred.

A large red hand was picking up the papers. The backs of the fingers were tufted with brown hair. Billy watched, fascinated. And then from still eyes,

like a cornered animal, he stared into his father's wind-veined face. His own cheeks flushed. How absurd he must look!

'Come out of it! What are you doing there?'

Billy could not explain, but laid the ledger on the desk.

'I wasn't reading it,' he said. 'I promise.'

He could have bitten his tongue out for this remark, and his neck burnt. He felt his father's remote eyes looking down on him, and the glassy sneers of the deer-heads round the walls.

'You know I won't have you children making a bear-garden of the office!'

But the big man was suddenly embarrassed, feeling the gulf between himself and his son. And he made excuses. He was a busy man, without time to reach their immature minds. At any rate, one was enough. And he shrugged. His wife seemed to give up her whole time to them. But he was troubled by the thought of two locked doors facing one another at the end of a passageway.

'All right, old chap,' he said, fumbling. 'No trouble with the horses this morning? That's the boy. Game for tomorrow? Good.'

And he nodded his head, winking, manly, buffeting Billy with restraint on the chest.

'All right, old chap. Run along now.'

Billy ran along. His feet beat fiercely on the veranda. And, hearing them, his father sat perplexed. He shook his head. Must see more of the children. But what the devil was his son doing under the desk? He liked a boy to stand up for himself. And he squared his shoulders and opened the ledger.

'Billy!'

But Billy was chasing Janet through the orchard, stumbling over the furrows between the pink cherries and the clouded pears.

'I'll kill you!' he cried. 'It was your fault. I'll murder you when I catch you.'

And he ran panting, with a pain in his chest, fiercely forgetting, after long-legged Janet with her short flying skirt and bobbing hair, who slipped through the fence and was away like the wind over the green paddocks.

'You can't catch me,' sang Janet, looking back through fair hair. And, 'Ha ha!' she mocked from the graveyard. Then she was lost, swallowed up. And the great pines sighed.

'Ah!' said the black pines, leaning over. Brier-roots clutched the stone. Their tangled arms had torn the netting from the fence, and the gate hung loose on one hinge.

'Jan-et!'

Billy searched amongst the tombstones, peering here, peering there, through the bare briers in the shadow of the pines.

'Janet! Come out, I know you're here.'

But he was alone.

'Janet' – almost sobbing – 'come out, Jan. Where are you? I won't touch you. I give in. Promise.'

Lost amongst the grave gravestones.

'Please, Jan.'

And there she was, balancing, with one leg out and arms wide, on a leaning tombstone, smiling her secret smile. She stood still in sunlight on the stone, flushed from her run and victory, and daffodils were bright below her.

'What did he say?' she said.

'Not much.' Billy turned away, diffident, indifferent.

'Go on, tell me, Billy.'

'He didn't say anything.' And Billy scowled.

'I'll bet he said, "Keep out of the office!"' And Janet began to chant, 'Keep out of the office! Keep out of the office!' till Billy, cheered, joined in.

'Well, old chap,' he said in a deep voice. 'Any trouble with the horses, old chap?'

Their pealing laughter rang through the graveyard. Billy strode, clop, clop.

'No trouble, eh? That's the chap.'

'Oh!' Janet was giggling. 'Oh!' merrily mocking. They were both happy with the intimacy of this secret between them. And, coming down from her tombstone, she walked with him arm-in-arm across the graves. The daffodils shook in the wind, and the hips of the briers danced, glinting.

'Here's old Wise's grave,' said Janet, and she lifted a pincushion of moss from the rotting granite. '"The loving husband of Phillipa Sarah." Phillipa! Oh! Phillipa Sarah!'

The young heads touched beneath the pines, and their laughter was mingled.

'Silly old Wise,' Janet said, and she stamped up and down the grave. Death, what was death on a fine morning? A fraud like Santa Claus. And she mocked the pious faces and don'ts and hush, claiming a victory over that strange world of grown-ups where death had a meaning.

Billy stamped, too. And, to outdo his sister, who was only a girl, he had a good idea. The thin stream played on the tombstone. So much for old Wise. Happily the children straggled back through the sharp sunlight to the house for lunch.

III

Clamour!

The alarm clock was crowing in the children's sleepout to the dark morning. Billy leapt from bed and was half dressed when his teeth began to chatter. He looked out fearfully through the wire gauze. The stars were high and pale, and the far pines stood darkly, like fists, against the coming light. A terrible dread ran its fingers up Billy's spine.

'I'm sorry, God. I'm sorry, truly, God.'

Through the wall, he could hear his father's steady breathing.

'Jan, are you awake?'

A whisper, 'Yes, Billy.'

'It's terribly dark, isn't it? I wish....'

And he sat down on Janet's bed. She could feel him shiver, and suddenly she clutched him to protect him, thrilling at the same time with the panicky joy of fear.

'Oh, Billy,' she cried, half laughing, half awestruck, 'there's something outside. Don't go, Billy!'

But, as Billy struggled with her, he forgot momentarily the thing outside and the remote lifting of his father's eyes. He was conscious only of a desperate need to break free.

'THE daffodils shook in the wind, and the hips of the briers danced, glinting.'

THE VINEYARD WOMAN

JUDITH WRIGHT
1915-

L ADRONES was scaled like a lizard with rust and flaking iron; her decks were black with diesel oil, her holds were sloppy with old, old water, dark and thick as soup. They were never covered now, since all she carried was timber – logs for the big mill at the town, brought from the forestry settlement on Cedar Head.

It was only a six-mile run; sometimes Luke managed it in a day, setting out in the grey of dawn to the loading creek, back in the afternoon, slow as the river water itself. But more often, on the way back, *Ladrones* was caught on a mud bank, for the banks were always shifting with the tides, and unless it was high water the old hulk, narrow in the beam and deep-draughted, often scraped across them or grounded. Then Luke would stop the engine on the little launch tied to *Ladrones's* side, which pushed her up and down river now that her engines were gone, and play patience on the oil-black table in the old galley where he ate and slept, until the tide was high again.

If the mud bank happened to be near Lemon Tree Point, Luke sometimes sat on deck and watched the house and the vineyard beside it. Except from the river, he knew nothing of the place; he had never been there, though he had often thought vaguely, sluggishly, of untying the dinghy that rocked at *Ladrones's* counter and rowing across – just rowing across, to see. For in the house lived the Vineyard Woman. Sometimes he saw her hanging out the washing in the garden, and he knew from what was on the line whether she was alone there or whether the man was at home.

Seldom, nowadays, was the man at home, it seemed; Luke had heard somewhere that he 'worked away'. The washing was meagre in his absence – a sheet or two, a towel or two, a few bright-coloured dresses and what Luke called 'bits of things'. He liked the look of her bare arms curved above her head as she pegged and unpegged; and of the shape of her shoulders as she worked between the rows of vines in the little vineyard. Sometimes she had waved to him, seeing him out on deck; but Luke was slow-thinking and slow to move, and hesitated

so long before answering that now she waved seldom, only turning briefly to look at *Ladrones* as she passed, ugly and mud-stained, shoved along by the busy, batting engine of the diesel launch.

Luke had been on the Cedar Head run for ten years; and, like *Ladrones*, he was getting old. The work of loading and unloading, when he had to handle the winch and manoeuvre the logs into the holds and out again, was getting too difficult. The bare-chested, bare-armed young men on the Forestry wharf or up at the mill disconcerted him by moving too fast, being too impatient, shouting at him when the winch hovered uncertainly or made a false move. Once one of them, bold and black-haired, had even called him 'Pop' and asked when he was going on the pension.

Luke had begun to shake and turn red; even now he had not got over his youthful habit of blushing when he was angry and embarrassed. That night he lay awake a long time in the hard narrow bunk in *Ladrones*' galley, and thought of the young man and of his words. 'Just a bit of a kid,' he said to the darkness in the oily room; 'a bloody kid. He needs his nose wiped. And by the Lord I'd do it, only....'

After that, he began to think of finding someone to help on *Ladrones*. It was too much work, there was no doubt about it; he had to start the diesel engine on the little launch, *Seabird* she was called, then climb aboard *Ladrones* (the two boats pitching and bumping together in rough or windy weather), and go up to the bridge where the wheel was, moving fast before *Ladrones* swung to the engine's shoving.

There he would stay for the rest of the trip, watching for the channel that was always changing position. And then, getting into the wharf – that was a nightmare nowadays, for there was all that running up and down the companion and into *Seabird*'s cabin to the engine; and though he had his own ingenious system of lashing the wheel, and knew his work to the fraction of an inch, he was not as fast on his feet now as he had been, and twice he had bumped the wharf and bored off a plank or two, while the young blokes watching cursed and laughed.

Luke had been proud of his handling of the job, but now he wasn't; it was a bit too much, a bit over the odds. He would have liked to find an older man to give a hand; someone he could yarn with, someone who would play cards, who moved at his own pace. But there was no one who would take on the job, except Leo.

He knew Leo well enough, a kid from his own street at the river's edge. 'Just left school and still needs his nose wiped,' Luke grumbled to his wife, though Leo was nearly eighteen now.

Leo was tall and moved well, a good-looking boy; he played an accordion and was popular with girls – the little girls who crowded in the corner milk bar on Luke's street and worked in the factory up the town. But he was what they called a bit of a lair; he couldn't keep a job and had run through three already, loose-lipped and not much caring.

Engines, though, were Leo's gift. He went aboard *Seabird* and straightaway knew all that Luke knew about the little diesel, and some more as well. He tightened this and cleaned that and had her running sweet as a daisy. He even rigged up a shower in the disused cabin, with a pipe for hot water from the diesel and a tap over the old basin Luke used for washing dishes, clothes and hands alike.

He wouldn't come at tea, however, which Luke always drank; he brought aboard bottles of soft drink, which Luke himself termed lolly-water, or made coffee, black and synthetic, from a tin. He brought queer food aboard, too, doughnuts from the milk bar and delicatessen sausage. But, though he didn't join Luke in a game of cards, preferring to sit on his bunk and play the accordion, at least he didn't interrupt Luke's games, and he was swift and handy with the logs. For a few days Luke thought grudgingly that he might do all right.

Indeed, Leo liked the life. It was free and easy enough, with Luke in charge and long lazy times with nothing to do but tinker with the engine, play the accordion and cook himself little messes on the primus while he waited for *Ladrones* to reach the wharf. He brought aboard an old canvas deckchair begged from his mother, and fixed up a kind of awning made from hessian, where he sat in the shade on deck while *Ladrones* crept along the channel under Luke's guiding hand, and played tunes or read comics or watched the banks of the river gliding by – mangroves, pasture, and dairy cows, a house or two, kids on their way to school. It was quiet, it was easy; better, he thought, than the stoking job at the factory or the mill work or the job of yardman at the pub, which he had tried already and found too much trouble.

One day, leaning back in the canvas chair, while *Ladrones* nosed down river, he noticed the house on Lemon Tree Point. Luke was watching it, too, through the broken glass on the bridge, while he handled the worn old wheel.

The Vineyard Woman was out in the vineyard picking grapes. She straightened her back and watched *Ladrones* going past, interested evidently by the awning and the deckchair and Leo's long handsome brown legs stretched out in the sun. Suddenly Luke saw her wave, a thing she had not done for months past, but which he was always uneasily, secretly, pleasantly expecting her to do.

With his usual few seconds of hesitation, he leant out and waved back; but then he saw that Leo, below him, was waving too. It took him suddenly aback, like striking an unexpected mud bank. It was as though Leo had intruded on something personal, his own and nobody else's – had pushed him aside and claimed the thing for his own. It was as though Leo had shoved him away from the wheel of *Ladrones* and taken over Luke's reason for existing.

Luke turned very red and looked away from the Vineyard Woman, who was still waving pleasantly; he went on steering *Ladrones* meticulously between the crowding mud banks. But he said to himself some time later, having meanwhile almost forgotten the reason for it, 'Me and that boy won't get on unless he changes his ways.'

At midday, when *Ladrones* was tied to the wharf at Cedar Head and the loading was half done, he met Leo again in the galley, where the bent and greasy knives and forks were set on the table, with the corned meat and bread and tea for Luke's meal on one side, and Leo's doughnuts and hamburger and coffee on the other. For the first time Luke felt the need to comment on Leo's eating habits.

'Damn useless things you eat, son. That milk-bar stuff isn't no good to a man. Why don't youse try a bit of honest meat and tea? Do you more good than that rot. You'll be bringing ice-cream and lollies aboard next.'

Leo looked at him with slight surprise, raised his eyebrows and whistled a hit-parade tune to himself.

But he made no answer, eating busily until his side of the table was cleared.

'Gee,' he said after a while, leaning back and lighting a cigarette, 'that woman at the grape orchard don't look so bad. 'Jever go ashore and try for a piece of her, Luke? They tell me she's real easy.'

Luke stopped eating, but found nothing to say and after a moment started eating again. 'A kid – a kid with his nose wet.' He stood up at last, looking at Leo with real dislike, then went out to the winch and pretended to be oiling and readjusting it. He was glad when the two young Forestry loaders came out of their tin huts at the wharf and lounged down to start work again.

The tide had been going down; it was not long on the make when *Ladrones* started upriver again. There was a new mud bank forming close to Lemon Tree Point, and Luke watched for it anxiously, though he could not clarify in his mind any special reason for his wish to get through this afternoon, more than other afternoons. Usually he rather welcomed the leisure of his sojourns in the galley with the patience cards, waiting for the tide to float *Ladrones* off again. But he swore this afternoon when, trying a sharp turn round the tail of the bank to keep in the narrow channel, he ran *Ladrones* aground so firmly that it was clear *Seabird* could not get her off.

Nevertheless, Luke tried every manoeuvre he could think of, driving Leo down to the engine for half an hour's hard work, until Leo protested.

'We ain't got a chance of getting her off, Luke, and you know it. You're just wasting time and money. I'm going to lay off on deck till there's more water; I've had this.'

Luke gave in. He tried to entice Leo into the galley for a game of cards, but it was no use. Leo had been watching the house on the point, he knew, and sure enough after a few minutes of sitting on deck he came into the galley.

'I'm going off in the dinghy for a bit of a row round, Luke. Be back when the tide's higher.'

Luke made no answer. But after a time he went out and leant on the rail, watching Leo and the dinghy making for Lemon Tree Point. The Vineyard Woman was on the veranda, shading her eyes from the afternoon glare as she watched Leo tie the boat to a branch at the foot of the orchard.

Luke saw them meet when Leo went up to the house, watched them talking together until they walked round the veranda out of sight, and went inside again to his game. He looked at the legless alarm clock propped on a shelf.

Tide was rising; say an hour and a half or two hours to wait. But he couldn't settle down to the cards again; he wandered restlessly up to the bridge and back, leant overside awhile and watched the mud-brown ripple at *Ladrones*'s side, fiddled with this and that, and now and then stole a glance at the house as though someone there were watching for just such a betraying sign.

All was quiet, all was motionless in the silver glare of an afternoon too large for the landscape; except that ripple, and a black shag perched near by on a dead driftwood branch in the mud bank, which now and then plunged soundlessly and came out with something in its beak or bulging its black-and-white throat. The rows of vines on the point were green and still in the windless afternoon; the brown river crept past the hulk, and her old nose parted it into a widening wedge that lost itself over the mud banks far away.

Luke watched the clock intensely. An hour; an hour and a half, and now *Ladrones* was beginning just to answer the tide, not in a movement but in a promise of movement. Ten minutes more, Luke thought, straining his eyes ashore where the dinghy still lay under the tree and the house was as still as before. Now they had passed; now he would try.

He ran along the deck by the hold piled high with logs, and ducked down into *Seabird*'s cabin as though he did not want to be seen. He poured out the spirit from the bottle feverishly, lit it, and waited in the blue glare until he could get the engine going, then dashed up again to the bridge.

The battering of the engine startled the silver reach of the river, and the old shag flew off heavily downstream. Looking across at Lemon Tree Point, Luke saw Leo running down the garden to the dinghy. He spun the wheel methodically, feeling for the shape of the bank under *Ladrones*'s foot. Would she move or not?

Leo was rowing over now, his long brown arms pushing the oars till they moved as fast and smoothly as the legs of an insect scudding over a pool's surface. He could row, that boy, Luke said to himself; but *Ladrones* was feeling the engine's shove now, her nose moving round towards the current, the mud

'ALL was quiet, all was motionless in the silver glare of an afternoon too large for the landscape.'

giving way slowly with a live feeling through the ship's timbers, like the arms of a sea-anemone that drag at the withdrawn finger.

Now Luke could see Leo's eyes as he turned his head, amazed and shocked, over his shoulder at *Ladrones*'s movement. Luke chuckled at his look of a child distressed by something not understood and outraged at the world's unpredictability.

Slowly *Ladrones* made her way into the current and swung her head upstream. She was clear now, and gathering way, but Leo was close under her counter, and Luke remembered the rope trailing there.

He felt as he did when he listened on the radio to a race on which he had a bet. 'Teach the little so-and-so,' he muttered. 'He'll find out he can't have everything his own way.'

He could hear Leo shouting, incredulous but with a pleading note, but he could no longer see him. Still, he wouldn't get that rope now; he was in the full current of the river. And sure enough his voice faded slowly back, behind the beat of *Seabird*'s engine, into a half-distinguishable succession of curses.

Straight ahead now for a bit. Luke lashed the wheel and ran down to the stern. There was the dinghy, dropping back farther and farther, Leo's straining back wet with sweat that marked the gay shirt at which Luke had mocked inwardly. Now he was giving it up, turning back towards the Point. As his face came into view, Luke waved once, and went back to the bridge, filled with the swelling delight of victory in the race.

'Teach him something,' he muttered again, and set himself to the accustomed task of bringing *Ladrones* upriver to the mill wharf again.

He had a job to berth her; the river was running strongly. When at last he had the ropes across, and the mill official came aboard, he was more tired than he had ever been. He went to the galley and sat limply down at the table, where his unfinished game still lay.

The mill official came in with his books, surprised at Luke's not greeting him as usual.

'Lo, Joe,' Luke said heavily. ''Ere we are at last.'

'Lorst your dinghy?' said Joe.

'Yair; she'll be somewhere around Lemon Tree, I reckon.'

'What about Leo? Thought you had him aboard this trip.'

'So I did, but it'll be the last time. Can't get on with that kid anyways.'

'Bit of a lair, eh? Where'd you manage to lose him? His ma'll be off her head if she knows he ain't on board.'

'He's old enough to look after himself, I reckon. Went ashore down Lemon Tree in the dinghy; there yet, I s'pose. Wasn't much use to me anyways. But it don't matter; I'm selling out next trip. Too old for the game, Joe. Youse can find some other bloke to run your logs in.'

'What you going to do with yourself, then?' asked Joe with interest. 'Taking the pension or something?'

'Yair,' Luke said, gathering up the patience cards. 'That's right; I'm taking the pension.'

THE VOYAGE NORTH

NANCY CATO
1917–

THE sheep came on at Fremantle, and at once it was apparent that they were of more importance than the human passengers. There were two thousand of them, and only eight of us. They cluttered the foredeck and the afterdeck, they filled the holds; and their smell permeated the whole ship. After two days of a following breeze we could even taste sheep with our dinner.

When somebody ventured a protest to the Captain over coffee (he was a tall, broad Swede), he replied unconcernedly, 'But it is very healthy! You have coontry air at vun end of the ship, und sea air at the other. Vot more could you vant?'

The sheep had just been shorn, for their own comfort, for they were travelling to the tropics. The first night they were silent, jammed so closely together that they couldn't move; but as we drew away from the coast they began an uneasy crying.

Then it began to rain: cold, heavy rain. The sheep raised their heads to it – here was something familiar, remembered from the land. Gradually they became soaked. They stood hock-deep in swilling water and dung.

Next morning the rain had gone, the sea calm, the air motionless. Flying fish flipped out of the bow-waves and skittered away in flashes of silver.

As the sun came out it turned the Indian Ocean to an incredible deep rich blue, like best fountain-pen ink. By midday, with the sun almost directly overhead and no awning or protection of any kind, the deck sheep were visibly distressed. They panted, with hollowed flanks and heads hanging.

The English passenger and his wife now became indignant and vocal.

'It wouldn't be allowed in England, I'm damn sure of that,' said he, polishing his red, sunburnt pate with a white silk handkerchief. 'Damn' shame, really. These fellers don't give a rap for the sufferin' of animals, y'know! Means nothing to them.'

'If I were at home I'd write to the RSPCA at once,' said his wife. 'Poor, dumb creatures! I saw one of the seamen kicking one today to make it stand up; grinning all over his face, too.'

'Yes, the Chinese are cruel beggars. Got no feelin's.'

The Australian returning to the islands gave the opinion that the sheep were in pretty good condition, and most of them should survive the journey if it didn't get too rough. The two wealthy Malayan merchants showed no interest; their money was not involved.

The elderly woman, widow of an Indian Army officer, who was going to join her son at Port Swettenham, was not indignant for the sheep but for herself. She didn't like sheep cluttering the decks, dirtying the ship, polluting the atmosphere and baa-ing all night outside her cabin.

'In Indiah,' she said, sipping her pre-luncheon stengah, 'we had sacred cows mooing, and peacocks screaming, and elephants trumpeting at night. But sheep –! They are stupid creatures; and besides, they smell.'

And looking at her fine aquiline nose, her heavy mouth curled in disdain, I could imagine her speaking in exactly the same terms of the non-white population of India.

I stood at the break of the poop and looked down at the dingy mass.

At first they had all looked alike, but now I could pick out individuals: the old chap with the curly horns who used their sharp points like a pick to dig his way through to the food and water troughs; the wether with one eye missing, perhaps gouged out by one of those cruel horns; another with its horn broken off at the base, leaving a raw-looking hole.

When once a sheep got down, whether it fell from weakness or slipped in the filth on the deck, it was soon trampled to death. Many more would have died in this way if it had not been for the only other passenger, young Deborah, a schoolgirl going home to Malaya for the long summer holidays.

Her parents lived on a rubber plantation. She had been up and down this coast a dozen times, several times on the same ship. She knew most of the crew, and she shrieked at the seamen in Cantonese when she thought they were neglecting the sheep. If it had not been for her almost proprietorial care, a great many more woolly corpses would have gone overboard to the sharks.

There was something rather horrible about seeing a dead sheep disposed of. Two bare-footed seamen would pick up the stiff body by its legs, give two swings and heave it over the rail. The other sheep would then spread thankfully into the extra space.

I was reminded of the story I'd heard about an extremely hot passage of the Red Sea, when eight elderly passengers died one after the other and were buried over the side; soon the sharks were following like a pack of wolves.

Deborah was still about the decks even when the adult passengers were deep in their afternoon siesta. With her short brown hair blowing in the wind, her thin brown legs protruding from brief blue shorts, she would climb over the hurdles and prod sheep out of the way until a panting, far-gone animal could reach the water troughs.

When we ran into a tropical storm, the rain falling in solid sheets which were at first warm, then bitterly cold, she forced her way in among the obstinately miserable sheep. If an animal was down, lying in the brown mess of dung and water and straw on the deck, she wrestled to get it on its feet again. She came out wet and muddy and smelling of sheep, but triumphant. She had saved a life.

Once through the Sunda Straits, with all the interesting sights left behind – Java Head, and Krakatoa puffing out smoke like a giant smoking a pipe – the bored passengers gathered to look at the sheep on the welldeck. We were traversing the muddy green waters of Bangka Strait, between low mangrove swamps with an occasional lighthouse or the skeleton jetties of native fish traps away on the horizon.

'Look at the poor brutes!' cried the Englishwoman, her dewlap shaking. 'Disgusting, I call it. Look at that poor animal with its head caught through the rail! Boy! Boy! Lookee sheepee!' She pointed wildly and waved at an uncomprehending seaman.

'These wretched boys only pretend to be deaf,' said the Anglo-Indian woman, who was convinced that Cantonese sailors should understand perfectly when she shouted at them in Hindustani.

'Gad, they must be hot! Look how they're panting! Why can't they kill the poor brutes first, and then ship them as frozen mutton?' asked the Englishman.

'It's for Ramadan,' explained the Australian. 'The big Muslim feast in the New Year. They have to be killed just before they're eaten, and in the prescribed way, or they're unclean and the natives won't eat them.'

'I suppose worse things have been done before in the name of religion,' I said.

'Yes, but hardly so long drawn out. Ten days of torment, if they survive the trip, and their throats cut at the end of it. Perhaps those that go overboard are luckier.'

The next day great canvas air-scoops were rigged to funnel cool air down into the stifling holds. I wondered how many had died down below before they decided on this move.

That night I stood and looked down at the patient mob on the afterdeck, being borne over the sea to a certain death. They were quiet but for an occasional distressed 'Bah-ah!' as the ship, which was pitching in a head sea, gave a particularly violent lurch. We were out in the South China Sea, with a gale warning ahead.

I looked back at the stars dancing up and down in the rigging, the bright Pointers and Canopus, and thought of old Omar five hundred years ago: *Into this Universe, and why not knowing....*

Here was a symbol of humanity, carried through space on a mysterious course, from an obscure beginning to an unimaginable end; a few getting their

heads through the rails, and, from a glimpse of the moving sea, inferring some purpose in the voyage; others buried deep in the ship's hold without a clue; but all carried steadily towards death under the eyes of indifferent or impotent gods.

'We're all in the same boat,' I thought, and went below, where the cockroaches scuttled about my cabin as I turned on the light.

The steadily rising note of the wind made my sleep uneasy. When I got up soon after dawn, the ship was bucking and plunging like a terrified horse.

The sheep up for'ard were being drenched in spray, while those near the stern staggered about as the counter lifted and kicked in midair.

First the bows would rise on a tremendous wave. Up, up they climbed, and then began the downward plunge. Smack! and the seas came aboard. Then the stern began to lift. As the rudder came out of the water she gave a violent sideways twist. A shudder shook the whole ship; the bows rose again, the stern plunged down into the water, and the helmsman corrected the sideways lurch, so that we moved in a series of twisting leaps. The sheep uttered a kind of groan at each plunge. Several more died that morning.

By midday the wind had abated a little, though the seas were just as high. Our motion had eased considerably, and no more water came aboard. The engines were down to dead slow; we just moved through the water.

It was 'for the comfort of the passengers', the captain assured us blandly at lunch, but no one was fooled. We knew it was for the sake of the sheep. The losses were beginning to worry somebody.

I was happy if it meant an extra day at sea. But the Englishman, who had to make a connection with a boat at Penang, began to grumble. He 'didn't mind how much the old tub bucked as long as she got there on time', and besides he was anxious to hear the results of the last Test match. He held forth at length about the iniquity of ship's wireless officers who hadn't even the decency to pick up the Test scores.

But this was nothing to the angry stream of words which burst from him when we were told next morning of the change of schedule. We were approaching the Singapore Roads; Malay prahus and Chinese fishing junks sailed over the glass-green water, their sails a rich russet in the early sunlight.

'I say, have you heard the latest?' he boomed at me as we met on the boat-deck before breakfast. 'Not even callin' at Penang, except on the way back, because they want to land these blasted sheep first. Got no sense of proportion, these fellers' – he waved his hand to include all non-British shipping lines – 'we pay our fare, and they expect us to play second fiddle to a lot of stinkin' sheep.'

'Well, at least it will cut short their sufferings,' I said, wondering whether to risk a reference to *poor dumb creatures*, for I saw his wife coming up with an aggrieved air. 'They're pretty low after that storm, apparently.'

'Means we have to take all our stuff ashore – trunks, God knows what – and go overland from Singapore,' he said as if he had not heard.

'Yes,' said his wife, 'and train travel always makes me sick. As if another two days would have hurt the wretched sheep!'

And she looked down malevolently at the silent, dun-coloured mass, where Deborah was already at work, heaving, exhorting, and prodding, her young thin face obstinately set against death.

THE LOAD OF WOOD

FRANK HARDY

1917–

THE six relief workers toiled slowly and methodically, each in turn skil-
fully spreading a shovelful of gravel. They wore guernseys or old waist-
coats for, despite the efforts of the sun to drive the frosty air out of the
valley, the weather was cold. Two empty tip drays stood by the road, the horses
nibbling the dew-white grass.

'Better make this the last heap before dinner,' said Murphy, the council fore-
man, who was supervising the work. 'It's nearly twelve o'clock.'

The biggest man in the group – massive and rough-hewn – threw his shovel
into one of the drays. 'Here's one Darky that's not spreadin' another shovelful
before dinner,' he said, running a toil-hardened hand through his mass of un-
combed black hair: 'Think you was payin' us a tenner a week, 'steada the dole.'

Taking a newspaper-wrapped lunch and a bottle of cold tea from a tattered
coat hanging on the post-and-rail fence, he stretched himself comfortably on an
empty chaff bag, his huge figure bursting out of a red and black football guern-
sey and patched dungaree trousers.

'Please yourself, Darky,' Murphy continued timidly. 'I got a job to do, you
know that.'

'Yer getting well paid for it, too, Spud. Buzz orf and have yer dinner. We'll
spread it after.'

'Mr Tye's goin' crook about how slow youse blokes is workin' that's all.'
Murphy wheeled his bike from the fence and cocked his leg over the saddle.
'Better spread some of it before dinner.'

Murphy was past middle age, and his bent figure seemed at home only on a
bicycle. As he rode slowly away – heels on pedals – Darky called after him:
'Tell Tye to come and have a go himself if he's in such a hurry.'

The other shovellers worked on until Murphy melted into the elm tree near
the little town, which lay morosely at the other end of the valley – sullen, as if

resenting the sorrow brought to its people by the depression.

'I'd like to see Tye 'ere shovellin' gravel,' said Darky as the others sprawled on the heap near by and began eating. 'We'd keep him joggin', I'll bet.'

They all laughed at the thought, and Darky raised himself to one elbow. 'I met him in front of the Co-op store the other day, and he says to me, "How are yer, Darky?" "None the better for your askin'," I says. Then I says, "Listen," I says, "as far as I'm concerned, there's only two bastards in this town." "And who are they?" he asked me. "Type, the Shire Secretary and Tye, the Shire Engineer," I says. And he didn't like it, either.'

'Yer didn't expect him to like bein' called a bastard, did yer?' spoke up 'Sniffy' Connors, wiping his nose with the back of his hand.

'Stickin' up for Tye now, are yer?' snapped Darky.

'I'm not sticking up for him. Just said you didn't expect him to like being called a bastard.'

Darky took a big swig of tea and lay back, attacking a thick jam sandwich ravenously.

'Yer know,' he said presently, looking at the sky, 'if a workin' man voted Nationalist, it'd be as bad as scabbin', wouldn't it?'

'I ain't never voted Nationalist,' Sniffy answered nervously.

'I ain't sayin' yer have,' said Darky looking in his direction. 'I just said that if a workin' man voted Nationalist he'd be a bloody scab, that's all.'

The men continued eating in awkward silence, until Ernie Lyle, a young married man and father of a new baby, changed the subject. 'Jees, it was cold last night, wasn't it? I nearly froze to death.'

'Eight white frosts in succession,' interposed one of the dray drivers, 'and we haven't got a stick of wood in the house. The issue only lasts a few days. We been burnin' palin's off the back fence and the landlord's threatening to kick us out, 'less we replace 'em.'

'Me and Liz, have been goin' to bed straight after tea,' said Sniffy. 'The little bit we get does the cookin'. And we're nearly out.'

'Went along the creek to get some last night, but she's too wet since the floods last month,' said another.

'We gotta get some wood from somewhere, or we'll freeze,' came back Ernie Lyle. 'The baby's got an awful cough. That old house is enough to give anybody pneumonia, without a fire.'

The other driver, the oldest man in the group, stood up and stretched his legs. 'We're buggered, too – burnin' the floor boards orf the dunny,' he said.

Darky threw his last crust savagely into the grass. 'Ar, I got no sympathy for youse blokes. I'm battlin', same as you are. But I got plenty a'wood. I got a shed full of it.'

'There's been a lot of wood goin' orf from yards round the town lately,' said Sniffy, looking slyly at Darky. 'I s'pose you been gettin' some of it?'

'I ain't sayin' as I'm gettin' it or not. But if I was, I'd be takin' it from the big heads and people that can afford it. You blokes give me the willies. Yer moan 'cause you've got no wood, and there's paddicks of wood all around yer. Acres of it. Why don't you get a lend of a truck one night, and get a load?'

'That'd be stealin',' answered Sniffy. 'You know what happened to "Beano"

Jackson, when he got caught. I don't want to go to jail.'

'You'd be no worse orf in jail than you are now, would yer? Here's one Darky that'll risk gettin' pinched, before he'll let his kids freeze.'

'Darky's right,' said Ernie Lyle. 'We orta risk it.'

'No, he ain't. I've never stole nothin' in me life and I'm not starting now,' contested Sniffy. 'I reckon we should see Coulson about it,' he added referring to the local Nationalist member of Parliament.

'What's the good a seein' Coulson? What's he ever done for the workers? I'd rather freeze than ask 'im anyway,' replied Darky, standing up. 'Last election time he offered me a drink. I'm standing outside the pollin' booth, handin' out Labor tickets, see; and he comes out after votin' for hisself, and he says, "Come and have a drink, Darky." "I'm fussy who I drink with," I says. "Aw," he says, "come on Darky. There's no hard feelin's as far as I'm concerned." I says, "There is as far as I'm concerned."' Darky spat on the ground, as if spitting out Coulson's name. 'Ask Coulson – not bloody likely.'

He took a tobacco tin from his hip pocket and rolled himself a smoke with sharp, savage movements. 'If youse haven't got the guts to pinch a load, then I can't be worried. I got plenty of wood.'

'I reckon we orta give it a flutter,' said Ernie Lyle. 'We gotta have a fire. It's risky, but we gotta have a fire.'

'I won't have nothin' to do with it,' dissented Sniffy.

'I need the wood,' said the man who had been burning his lavatory floor, 'but it's too risky for my liking, Darky.'

'The wife's old man has promised us a load,' lied another.

'You're a bloody lot of squibs,' said Darky, disgusted. 'But I'll tell you what I'll do. I'll borra Bert Spargo's truck and get a load, if one of youse will come with me. I got plenty of wood, but I'll take half the load and sell it. And you blokes can split the other half between yer.'

The men looked at each other hopefully, then all eyes, except Sniffy's, turned to Ernie Lyle, who hesitated before saying uncertainly: 'All right, Darky, I'll be in it. I'll be in it.'

'I'm not doing this to help you blokes, see? I look after this Darky here,' Darky replied, tapping his enormous chest. 'I'll make a few quid outta my half, see? An' you blokes keep yer traps shut. I'll see Spargo this evenin' about the truck and me and Ernie'll get a big load tomorrow night.'

Suddenly, he turned towards Sniffy again. 'Are you going to be in the swim? Do you want some wood?'

'I need the wood badly, Darky, but I don't want no stolen property.'

'So yer won't even take it as a present?' He grasped Sniffy by the shirt collar with great gnarled hands, and dragged him to his feet. 'Well, keep yer trap shut. If yer squeal about this, I'll kick yer bloody guts in!'

'I w-won't squeal, Darky,' said Sniffy, scared. 'You know that – I won't squeal.'

'Yer better not,' said Darky, releasing him. 'Yer better not. Here comes bloody old Spud. We better start workin'. Now, keep yer mouths shut. I'll hand the word round tomorrow.'

On the following night, the frost draped Benson's Valley like a white sheet

'If youse haven't got the guts to pinch a load, then I can't be worried. I got plenty of wood.'

as Ernie Lyle walked quickly down a side street to keep his appointment with Darky on the outskirts of the town at midnight.

Hope Darky's not late, he thought, digging deeper into his overcoat pockets and looking furtively over his shoulder, each breath forming a cloud in front of him.

Footsteps approached and Ernie crossed the road hurriedly. The wife was right, he thought. I should have stopped home. We might get caught.

No sooner had he arrived at the rendezvous than an old truck approached. 'Hop in,' said Darky, keeping the engine running. 'I had a job to start it, I think the battery's flat.' He wore faded black clothes and a battered hat, with his neck muffled in an old red scarf.

'By Jees, it's cold, isn't it?' he added, as Ernie got in.

'Where are you goin' to go?' inquired Ernie, as the tumbledown vehicle leapt forward under Darky's inexpert handling of the clutch.

'To that paddick of old Squatter Fleming's, a couple of miles up the river road. Pleny of good timber there.'

'But you know what old Fleming is. His house is only about a mile over the hill from that paddock. He'll jail us if we're caught.'

'He's gotta catch us first, and if he comes pryin' into our affairs, I'll throw him in the creek.' Darky laughed uproariously at his own joke, but Ernie was not amused.

Darky began whistling 'Pretty Red Wing', out of tune but plaintively, and Ernie watched the steering wheel quivering in his hands as he endeavoured to steer the rattling vehicle between the potholes of the rough road.

Surely Darky's scared, but he don't seem to be. Wish to hell I hadn't said I'd be in it. If we're seen, we'll go to jail, brooded Ernie. And as he thought of his wife and baby, Darky's apparent unconcern suddenly rankled him.

'For chris'sake stop whistlin',' he snapped. 'Anyone would think we were goin' to a picnic.'

'Aint's scared, are yer?'

'My bloody oath I am.'

'No need to be. I'm too cunnin' for the mugs in this town,' Darky replied reassuringly, then began whistling again.

As they neared their destination, the truck crossed a little bridge over the creek and the loose boards rattled. To Ernie these sounded like the rumblings of thunder and he sank lower in his seat, as if he thought the night itself had ears and eyes, for the nearest habitation was nearly three-quarters of a mile away.

They reached the paddock gate: Ernie opened it with desperate haste. 'What's that sign on the tree over there,' he whispered, getting back into the truck, 'just near the light on your side?'

Darky alighted and, by the simple process of bending one of the battered mudguards upwards a little, focused the light on a sign high up on a tree and read it half aloud: 'Trespassers will be prosecuted. Anyone removing timber from this property will be severely dealt with. By order, John Fleming.'

Without a word, Darky took an axe from the back of the truck, spat on it, and began cutting a saw break in the tree with the sign on it. It was a big, dry gum with huge limbs – made to order for firewood. The sound of the axe cracked the frosty air while Ernie sat in the truck nearly petrified with fear.

Darky came back, put his hat, scarf and coat on the seat, went to the rear and returned with a cross-cut saw.

'Come on,' he said, switching out the lights. 'We can work in the dark till we get her down.'

'I think we orta go home, Darky, we're a moral to get nabbed.'

'Come on, we won't get nabbed if we work fast. And for chris'sake stop shiverin', yer give me the creeps.'

Ernie shed his overcoat reluctantly and, after becoming accustomed to the darkness, they started sawing. To Ernie the saw seemed to say, 'We'll go to jail. We'll go to jail.' He was quaking with fright and this interfered with his sawing efficiency.

'I don't mind you having a ride on the saw, but for gawd's sake keep your feet off the ground,' cracked Darky, spitting on his hands and guffawing loudly.

Ernie made no reply and they began sawing again. They'll hear us down at the house, he thought, and old Fleming will come and put the police on to us. Darky's too game, that's the trouble. The wife was right, I shouldn't have had anything to do with it. Better work fast, anyhow. He swung into the sawing in an endeavour to match Darky's powerful strokes, and soon the trunk was almost severed.

'I think she's nearly right,' said Darky, feeling the tree. He switched on the lights and, after starting the truck with some difficulty, focused them on the tree.

'Just a few more strokes,' he added, coming back. And soon the tree crashed on the dewy ground, tearing the night in halves.

'Gawd,' muttered Ernie, 'they will hear that back in the town.'

Over the hill, in the direction of the Fleming farmhouse, a dog barked in the distance.

'Hurry, get the other axe,' whispered Darky, 'we'll cut all the dry limbs orf and fill the truck as quick as we can. And don't be too fussy.'

'Don't worry, Darky, I won't be too fussy. I just want to get home. We'll be nabbed, for sure.'

'A man can't tell whether you are shivering with fright or with the cold. Yer a Jonah, if ever there was one. Hop into it, and stop moaning.'

They worked hastily and unceasingly for nearly an hour, desperation and frenzy driving Ernie to emulate Darky's mighty swings; then Darky stopped and wiped his forehead on his arm. 'This sign will make a fine piece of kindling,' he said, hacking the stern warning off the tree trunk and throwing it into the truck. But Ernie paid no heed.

They were hot and sweating in spite of the freezing air, but after another hour the truck was loaded high above the sides, and when Darky tied the load with a stout rope, they were ready to leave – much to Ernie's relief. But the motor did not respond to Darky's cranking! He ran to and fro adjusting the spark and choke, swearing and blaspheming. He grunted, and cranked and swore, but to no effect, while Ernie peered through the night apprehensively.

'She's as cold as a maggot, and the battery's flat,' Darky said. 'We'll have to turn her round and run her down the hill there.'

They pushed, Darky steering with one hand. And when the truck gathered impetus, he jumped in and the old vehicle vibrated as he manipulated the clutch. It careered erratically between trees, over bumps and stumps before the engine started hesitantly, then revved loudly as Darky turned in a huge half-circle and drove out the gate.

Wiping the dew from the windscreen at intervals, they had reached the out-skirts of the dark, silent town when Darky roared out with uncontrolled raucous laughter.

'What the hell are you laughin' at?' asked Ernie.

'I'd like to see old Squatter's face when he sees what's left of that tree in the mornin',' answered Darky, and when his laughter subsided, he added, 'We'll deliver "Matches" Anderson's first. And remember, I'm taking half the load to sell. I ain't doing this for the good of me health.'

'she's as cold as a maggot, and the battery's flat. We'll have to turn her round and run her down the hill there.'

Darky swung the trunk into a sparsely inhabited back street and pulled up at the side of Anderson's house.

'Be careful we're not seen,' Ernie muttered.

'There's no danger of us bein' seen,' Darky said. They go to bed with the chooks in this town, and it's after two o'clock now.'

Lights switched off, engine still running – they threw several logs over the fence, handling the wood gingerly with chilled hands; then suddenly, a light glowed through the side window and a face peered through the curtain for a moment before the light went out again.

'That'll be enough,' whispered Ernie, 'there's five of us to half the load, you know.'

'Another couple for the road,' replied Darky, heaving two more big logs into the yard. 'Now old Matches won't have to burn his dunny in the fire!'

They delivered wood to three more houses without detection, Darky in each case throwing 'an extra couple for the road'. His apparent unconcern continued, and Ernie's nervousness was somewhat replaced by his urgent desire to get the job done, until he saw a man walk by in the shadows!

'Who was that?' he exclaimed. 'Was it the new copper?'

'No,' answered Darky, peering through the back of the cabin, 'only Clarrie Simpson going home from the bake-house. He wouldn't wake up. Hasn't got enough brains to give hisself a headache.'

'He mighta seen who it was.'

'Do you think he can see in the dark? Ah, you're a dingo, if ever there was one.'

'I'll be glad when we deliver the rest to our houses and get to bed. And even then we might get found out.'

Darky's only reply was to begin whistling again changing the tune to 'Mother Machree'. He seemed absent in reverie and misjudged the turn into the narrow lane behind Ernie's house. The truck's side scraped loudly on the fence.

'Be careful, Darky, d'yer want to wake the neighbours?'

'They wouldn't wake up if you drove in their front door and out the bloody back,' replied Darky nonchalantly, halting the truck against Ernie's back fence, its wheels crackling in a frozen puddle of water.

'You've thrown orf over half the load already, Darky.'

'Ar, I got plenty've wood, I told yer that. You blokes'd freeze to death if I'd let yers.'

A good supply soon thudded into Ernie's backyard. 'That'll keep me goin',' he said.

'Better have a couple more than the other squibs. You come with me, didn't yer?' grunted Darky, heaving two enormous logs over together with apparent ease. 'Better have the sign, too,' he added, throwing the broken signboard into the yard.

'Break it down, Darky.'

'Garn, it'll do yer for kindling in the morning. We'll slip back and leave the rest at my place. Better hurry and get finished before daylight. Then I'll drop yer here and return the truck to Spargo.'

As they drove away, skirting Main Street, they passed the house of an old widow pensioner.

'Bet that poor old bitch ain't had a fire for weeks,' said Darky. 'We orta chuck a few logs over.'

'Yer won't have much left to sell if you do.'

'I got a shed full of wood, and there's still a good bit in the truck – won't miss a couple of logs.'

As Darky threw three big pieces unceremoniously into the middle of a well-tended flower garden, the front door opened and a pyjama-clad grey-haired woman peered from behind a kerosene lamp.

'Who's that?' she asked in a shrill, frightened whisper, then apparently comprehending the scene, she blew out the lamp and closed the door.

'Jees, I bet we gave her a fright,' said Darky. 'Aw, well, even if she ain't got anyone to sleep with, she'll have a fire to keep her warm.' And he laughed heartily at his own coarse joke, as always.

'You've got me beat, Darky. I'm scared to death and sick in the guts. For God's sake deliver yours and get me home.'

The truck swung into the street where Darky lived and the dim lights shone on the dilapidated dwelling which the recalcitrant Sniffy Connors occupied with his wife and three children.

'I'll bet the snifflin' bastard's snorin' away in there while we get wood. And he wouldn't even take some as a present!'

'Ar, poor ol' Sniffy ain't a bad fella,' defended Ernie.

'He's a bloody scab at heart, I'm tellin' yer. He voted for the Nationalists, didn't he?'

'You're not sure of that, Darky. Anyway, where did votin' Labor get us?'

'He's a bloody scab at heart, I'm tellin' yer. But I s'pose a man can't blame his wife and kids for it. I'll bet they're freezin' to death. A man orta chuck a few logs in.'

'You've only got about half a dozen logs left for yourself.'

'Aw, well, even if she ain't got anyone to sleep with, she'll have a fire to keep her warm.'

'I keep tellin' yer, I got a shed full of wood,' snapped Darky impetuously swinging the truck around. 'And I ain't shorta dough, either. I picked a place card last Saturday.'

No one stirred as they unloaded, and Darky drove out of the lane snarling with a show of savagery: 'An' I hope he burns his bloody self to death with it.'

'Be daylight shortly,' said Ernie, as they halted in front of Darky's old house.

'I won't be a minute,' replied Darky, alighting hurriedly, 'there are only two or three logs. I'll just throw them in the front garden.'

'Better take 'em round the back. Someone might see 'em in the garden and we'll get pinched. I'll give you a hand.'

'I'll be right. Think a man's a bloody weaklin' like yourself?'

'They're heavy logs, I'll help yer.'

'I'll be right, I said,' snapped Darky.

And in spite of Ernie's continued protests, he went to the back of the truck and, with tremendous effort, took the biggest log under one arm and the two smaller ones under the other, and staggered down the side path.

The first glimmer of frozen dawn peeped as Ernie waited.

Darky's a funny bloke, he thought. I wonder if he has got any wood in that shed?

THE HOMECOMING

NENE GARE
1919-

EVERYONE said Milly was a good old stick. She'd been with her white man going on six years now. Done his cooking an washing an kept his camp clean, never gone with other fellers even the times when she could have got away with it. Sometimes Con was gone two or three days, though if it came to that you never knew when he might be back and it was a lot less trouble just to do like he said and keep herself to herself except, of course, for a bit of a game with the cards and a bit of a yarn.

She and Con had moved into the old pensioner's place. Felt a bit funny after dark still. Milly never could forget that old pensioner and the way he'd come out and yell at them for using his front tap – as if it hurt him for them to get their water there. His fault if they left the tap on too, coming up behind them an yelling. He'd been dead a long time now, that ole man, and she and Con and the littlies had his house, empty and dry inside, not like the old tarp over your head, lettin the drips through when it rained, an the wind cold on you all night long, and the kids' noses snotty, an the coughing keepin a feller awake, even if you wasn't too cold to sleep.

It had felt good. Two rooms and a front veranda and a WC of their own in the backyard. And she'd done her best to keep out all those others who'd wanted to camp there too, once they saw what a good place it was, and how there was no need to be afraid. Con made her keep them out. Never liked sharing, Con didn't. Liked a bit of quiet, he said. Kept out everyone but Dolly, she had, an she'd let Dolly come because ya couldn't be too bloody hard and even if it was a white man's camp Dolly needed some place to go. Had some fun with Dolly, looking back. Right back to when they was kids together. Now this had ta happen. Wasn't Con's fault but. Con hadn't wanted anyone else there at all cept a few visitors of course, an having a game or something. Her own damn fault, an she'd done the lot of it herself just about. After so many years but, an after thinking Dolly was a real good friend who wouldn't go an take a woman's man away.

She still had the house. The two of them had gone off, that was all. Con might even come back. She didn't expect that. She'd like it, but she didn't expect it. No! That one would keep him now she got him. He'd been a good ole man ta have, too. Given her a few dollars now an then, which was more than some did. Take Eva. Gave her nothing an treated her rough too, her bloke. Con never treated her rough, nor he didn't touch her dowment neither. Let her have the lot, even if one of the kids was his. Fond of them kids too. Might miss them, even if he didn't miss her. Come back maybe ta see how they was getting on. Fond of the whole four of em. Treated em the same as if he owned the lot.

Another side ta this business too. Soon as everyone knew Con was off with Dolly, what hopes of keeping the place to erself. Hard enough keeping em out when he was there. Milly's jaw clenched. An it was still a white man's camp.

They didn't have no right ta move into a white man's camp less he said so. If only the willies wasn't coming back on er, nights, with no man there. Milly didn't fancy nights. Maybe after a while she might have ta let a few camp with er so's there'd be a man—some man not scared of ghosters. When she knew for sure Con wouldn't be back.

That was the reason she was out now: that old pensioner. Even in the daytime, when the kids was off at school an that, it was too quiet. Noises, too. Might be anything. Might be him coming back to do some more yelling because she was living in his house. Better off getting out of the place, an a nice walk down past the hospital to the town.

Who the hell was this? A hand yanking her coat half off her. A voice in her ear that she knew. Mrs Yorick, camped across the hill from her.

'Not feeling friendly today, h'nh? An don't tell me ya didn't hear because I been yellin me guts out fa half an hour at ya.'

'Didn't hear ya. Me feet hurt.'

'Ya look as if ya feet hurt ya. Why ya wear them damn man's shoes? Too big for ya. Splay footin along there.'

'Con left im behind. Still got good soles on em. Keep out the wet when it rain.'

'Con left im behind?' A quizzical look. 'Con gone an left ya?'

Milly cursed her tongue. Have to come out soon but. 'Gone off with that Dolly.'

'I told ya, didn't I? Serve ya right. What ya worryin bout but? Ya don't wanta worry bout losin no man. You want a man you come with me an I get ya a man. Mens everywhere. No shortage a bloody men. Ya have *my* ole man, ya wantim. Got any money?' Sharply.

'Nup!'

'Shout ya a ice-cream first shop. An take that look offa ya face. Maybe ya might get im back an if ya don't what's ta worry bout? Wisht I could get mine off me back. Follerin me round, sendin the kids after me just when I got a lucky streak an look like winnin. Always comin an standin over us an puttin a blight on everyone with is sour face.' She mimicked, '"Come awn. Time ta get home. Kids want their tucker." Gawd! Ya lucky, you are.'

'Con not like that. Con liked his game well as me. Play all night some nights.' Wistful.

'Yeah! They all the same but. Grisel guts! Better off without em. Besides, I got me pension now. What I want with any ole mans?'

Mrs Yorick fished out all the money she could find in her pockets and bought ice-creams. They licked them going up the street. Two middle-aged women, both plump, in step with each other, their heads bobbing up and down, their shoulders rounded, their behinds sticking out from the drape of their coats that fell almost to their ankles, Mrs Yorick's greying waves plopping about, Milly's hair lanker, longer.

'What say we go up the risserve? Git a game? Cheer ourselfs up?'

'Couldn't get in a game. No money. Terrible long way ta walk up that hill. I'm damn hungry too. That ice-cream didn't fix im. Me stomach's pinchin me, it's that empty.'

'Get us a feed too. Someone up there bound ta have some tucker. Don't I give em plenty when I got some? Can damn well gimme it back now. An we not walkin. What's wrong with a taxi? Owe im the money.'

They were into the long main street now. Passing a crony or two, slowing to greet them, stopping for a yarn with the group edging the footpath near the barber shop. 'Can't go in there askin for change now,' Mrs Yorick observed. 'Hafta buy chewies now. E as ta change it then. Cheek, tellin me ta change me money at the bank.'

And to a grinning man who formed one of the group. 'Look who's here, well? Last time I seen im e's runnin up the hill quicker than a emu. Mighta got is ead carved off im with a spade if e didn't. H'nnnh!' The brown eyes sparked malicious enjoyment.

'Aah! Should keep that ole man a yours locked up,' the discomfited one countered.

'Better man than you,' Mrs Yorick said sharply. 'E teached you ta go roun twistin a girl's arm off nearly.' She turned to the others, a broad smile replacing the spark. 'Gawd, I hadda laugh but. There was me, inside on me bed an I hear all this shriekin an callin out an me ole man yellin an I come out an everyone's flyin off up the road and I dunno why they's runnin, but I'm in the lead a *them*. An when I ask someone I find it's im,' pointing, 'been havin another go at that pore creacher's livin with im. That Eva. So me ole man does is block an goes for im with a spade.' She directed a hard stare at the uneasy man an licked her smiling lips, daring him with her eyes to contradict her tale. To defend himself.

Johnny, already on the outside of the group, turned his head away, hunched his shoulders higher and dove his hands deep into his pockets, directing a casual glance up the street. He moved off and the eyes of the group followed him.

'Bastard,' Mrs Yorick snorted. 'Come on, Milly, we gotta see bout that taxi.'

She poked her head in at a taxi driver. 'We want a lift up the risserve. All right?'

'Cost ya a dollar.'

'See ya dowment day,' Mrs Yorick said cheerfully, opening the front compartment and sliding over the seat towards the taxi driver. 'Come on, Milly. In front ere with me case this feller tries ta get too friendly. C'mon!' The two women managed to compress their plumpness sufficiently to shut the door. 'An that's enough a that,' Mrs Yorick cautioned. 'Keep both them hands on the wheel, ya don't mind. You'll get paid—don't you worry bout that—good hard cash.'

The taxi man dropped them off at the end of the long wattle-bordered path that led to the reserve. Milly's face had brightened. You couldn't stay down in the dumps long with Mrs Yorick. Didn't give damn for anything, her ole man, the rest of the mob; not even the monarch or the partment man.

'An if it looks like an off day,' Mrs Yorick was murmuring, 'far as tucker's concerned, just have to get in a game somewhere an start winnin.'

There was a circle around an old rug the second house down. The two women greeted the players and moved into the circle of sprawlers. Mrs Yorick's eyes watched the play intently while she exchanged snippets of gossip. Mrs Mungo was still annoyed about what had happened the night before. 'That taxi driver, the one with the big blue Holden, come up here again an dumped some men off, three of them little Indians offa the boat. Two of em went down ta Doreen's place an hung aroun. An one feller, cheeky brute, come up ta my place. Seen Diana, an come after er. Couldn't get im offa the place an Diana inside shoutin, "Tell im ta go away, I don't want him. Tell im I'm gettin married nex month an I don't want im." And im callin out to er, "Come on, darling. I'll give ya ten dollars an four to ya mother." An I tole im, "I don't want ya bloody money", an im saying, "Why won't ya come with me. Ya the same colour I am. I wouldn't hurt ya, darling. Just wanta talk to ya." Talk to er's right. Only it was dark I coulda got that taxi man's number. Will next time.'

'Ya get rid of im, the little Indian?' Mrs Yorick asked.

'E saw I mean what I say when I get me broom out an give im a shove,' Mrs Mungo glowered. 'Dirty black nigger.'

'Listen ta Snowdrop speaking,' Mrs Yorick chuckled, and even Milly laughed.

'Put us in, come on,' Mrs Yorick said, and as there was a shuffling but no response, she added, threateningly, 'Come on now, put me in at least. Someone give us a dollar. I give it ta youse plenty times.'

'Mrs Mungo grudgingly threw some money. Mrs Yorick was in. The expression on her face altered. Her attention was for the cards now, falling light as feathers on the old rug.

'Four twos,' Mrr Yorick said with satisfaction. 'Beats ya full hand, don't it?' She snapped up the money in the centre, picked out the big silver and pushed the smaller stuff over to Milly. 'Come on, deal.'

It was one of Mrs Yorick's good days, to begin with anyway. And she went on picking out the big money and passing the rest over the Milly. Milly had a pocketful of coins in less than an hour. After a while she sat back a bit and watched the players' faces. Her thoughts reverted to Dolly. She'd been mistaken there all right. And tonight there she'd be by herself again. In the dark with all the kids asleep and noises all round. Mice or something it must be. Not the old pensioner. Funny how you got used to a man's big, warm body alongside, and the way you got to sleeping in the same position every night, him hunched up an you behind him, keeping his back warm, he said. Wasn't the same, sleeping with the kids. Gawd, some nights ya wouldn't say no to anyone, not even the little dark men offa the boat. Just so long as they could make ya forget the dark and the creaking.

Her stomach was troubling her still. Really biting at her. Empty as the little house now Con was gone. And she couldn't be cheeky like Mrs Yorick an ask for tucker. Didn't need to now anyway. The money in her pocket jingled pleasantly as she moved.

She rose and straightened her skirts. 'I'm off,' she said.

'Count that money I been givin ya,' Mrs Yorick said, without looking up. 'See how much. Might want it back, ya never know.'

'Dollar ninety cents,' Milly said after a while.

'Gawd! Better get goin before I start askin for a stake. I'm startin ta lose.' Milly moved off. Mrs Yorick called after her. 'An if ya see that ole man a mine headed this way you tell im I went from here before, see?'

A gust of laughter rose from the group as Milly trudged off.

Milly bought a good feed at the delicatessen shop on the way home. The man there knew her. Knew she wasn't particular if it meant getting a bit more for the money. Ends of paloney, stuff like that.

Two full loaves of crusty bread too. The smell of it was enough. As soon as she was on the hospital road she stopped and tore off a crust, stuffing great chunks of it into her mouth, chewing with gusto, a look of dreamy content on her face.

The kids were home. She heard them from a way off, shouting and laughing, the barks of the two dogs adding to the noise. Two dogs? That was Dandy's bark, wasn't it? Con's dog, that he'd taken with him. Milly gulped and swallowed and coughed.

It was Con all right. Playing with the kids, pretending to fight them, pretending they'd winded him and he couldn't fight any longer. Staggering away with them after him and all over him.

Milly stopped at the broken gate and Con looked over at her. Milly smiled. 'Ya back.'

Con's eyes fastened on the packages. 'Tucker! Gawd, I'm hungry. Couldn't find a bloody thing inside. Was nearly goin off again. Some place a man can get a feed when e's hungry.'

Milly went down the path and in through the front door. 'P'loney,' she said as she passed him. 'An two loaves a bread.'

THE GLASS BOY

GWEN HARWOOD
1920–

MY friend Alice and I were forbidden to go anywhere near the creek, but we had taken some lollies saved for a secret feast to one of our caves in the lantana, where God could not see us through the tangles. Our refuge was near a grassy hollow overhung by the creek bank, sometimes flooded but now dry. We heard voices, and looked down, unseen. What we saw astonished us.

One of our Sunday School teachers was squashing Poor Myrtle. He was lying right on top of her and kissing her plump dollface. He must have been tickling her to make her giggle so much. No doubt we would have watched to see what they did next, but Alice sneezed. Fearful of discovery we scuttled back through the lantana tunnels, past the chow's cabbage field, and in through my back fence to the orange orchard. There we lay on the grass and played at squashing, giving one another kisses flavoured with Jersey toffee. We were giggling so much we did not hear my grandmother approaching.

'Get up, you naughty, rude little girls. You'll have to be put back to First Babies. How dare you play such silly games!'

She gave us both a good smacking. Alice began to whinge. 'I'll tell my mother you smacked me.'

'When you are left for me to mind, I'll smack you when you need it.'

I was enchanted by the rhythm of this, so like 'Speak roughly to your little boy, and beat him when he sneezes.' Were there special smacking poems? Blubbering, Alice gave away our secret. 'We saw Harold Rubin lying on top of Poor Myrtle.'

Where had we seen this? We got another smack for going near the creek, but Granny seemed more worried than cross. The day was turning melancholy. She spoke to my father, who was chopping wood for the stove. He put down his axe and went indoors. My mother came out of the house and took Alice to be brushed and tidied and returned home. I was given my tea early and put to bed with another scolding.

That night there was a kind of meeting at our house. It was not an evening, with music and cards. Without understanding, I heard that Myrtle was four months already and that there were five or six of them. They ought to be in jail. But they were only boys, a voice said. 'If they can do *that* they're not boys,' my grandmother said.

What was *that*? The big boys teased poor simple Myrtle continually. They would give her presents and surprises which turned out, when she unwrapped them, to be a dog's turd, a fish head, a skinned frog. Myrtle was unteachable. It was because her father had been killed in the war, right at the beginning, before she was even born. The shock had been too much.

She ought to go to Wooloowin, a voice said. But my grandmother cried, 'No, no, no. Why should the Micks have her. It's not her fault. The misery of that

place would kill her.' I had heard about Holy Cross. Had even, on my naughty days, been threatened with it and with what the Sisters of Mercy would do to teach me better behaviour.

One of the big girls at school said that Holy Cross had 13 windows across the front, the Devil's number, and a pit where the nuns buried their babies in quick-lime. The voices went on as I drifted into sleep. Myrtle would stay at home with a lock on the gate. My mother said she could have the clothes Little Joe had grown out of. Veronica had her midwifery and would be there when she was needed.

Veronica was everyone's favourite. She was a nurse who lived with her old great-aunt. Every morning she got up very early, washed and dressed Aunty, and put her out in the sun with her breakfast and her two sticks 'to watch the world go by'. Only the odd horse and cart went by along our dusty road, but the neighbours would look in on Aunty while Veronica was at work in a private

'VERONICA was beautiful, kind and sweet-smelling.'

hospital. Aunty always spoke her mind, which was sharp and savage. She told everyone that Myrtle was far better off at home than working in the steam laundry for the bloody Pats.

Veronica was beautiful, kind and sweet-smelling. One morning she came in on her way to work and said that Myrtle had a lovely boy, the finest she had ever seen. An easy birth, a perfect child. Then Veronica asked a favour. She had a special friend, and she would like to ask him down to Mitchelton on her next day off, but we knew how cantankerous Aunty was. Aunty didn't like her friend, whom Veronica had met while she was nursing his dying mother. He was clever and handsome. She hoped they would get engaged. Handsome is as handsome does, said Granny, but she invited Veronica to bring him for dinner. Big Joe would be taking my mother and Little Joe out in the sulky for a picnic. What a choice! I decided to stay with Granny and meet Veronica's friend, who was an accountant and had a university degree.

'I hear you are going to entertain Mr I Always,' said the old great-aunt next morning. What a curious name, I thought. Was his name Isaac Always? Ivan Always? Isaiah Always? 'I've told her,' continued Aunty, 'she won't get the house if she marries him. He's a mother's boy. He wants another mother.'

When the day came I helped Granny prepare the chook for Mr Always. We set the table in the sitting room instead of on the back veranda. Veronica met Mr Always at the station and brought him up our front stairs to be introduced. His name was Mr Cecil Stitt. How could Aunty have made such a mistake? We sat on the front veranda with glasses of mandarine juice. I wanted to read to Veronica from my *Children's Encyclopaedia*, but she said it would be rude, and we must make conversation. When she and Granny went in to the kitchen I made conversation with Mr Stitt.

'Dinner will soon be ready.'

'You mean lunch.'

'Did you have a pleasant journey down on the train?'

'No. I always say trains are a dirty way to travel.'

'Do you have any little girls?'

'Certainly not.'

'Any little boys?'

'Certainly not. I am not married.'

'God gave Myrtle a little boy and she's not married.'

'I always say children shouldn't speak until they are spoken to.'

'Do you keep chooks?'

'Certainly not.'

I did not think him handsome. His face was stern and tight. I began to give him my grandmother's lecture on poultry. They were good company. They gave you eggs and a nice dinner when they were too old to lay. And feather pillows. You could use them all except the head and the claws. I knew where the heart was. And the lights. And the gizzard.

Dinner was served. Granny carved some white meat for Veronica and was beginning to put dark meat on Mr Stitt's plate when he said, 'I should like some breast, please. I always prefer the breast.' I saw Granny's lips compress, but she carved him some breast. White meat for the ladies, dark meat for the gentlemen, and drumsticks for the children. Had nobody taught him? I ate carefully with my big knife and fork and saw that Mr Stitt was mashing up his dinner as if it were being prepared for Little Joe. He mashed peas into the gravy and potato into the peas and stuffing into everything. I would not have dared to do it in company. He left a lot of good food on his plate, and did not say it was delicious. When the ladies went out to wash up I resumed my lecture.

He barked at me, 'I always say having children at the table makes them bold.'

I replied boldly, 'Only babies mash their dinner.'

He insisted on leaving far too early for the train, and made Veronica go.

'He hates fowls,' I told Granny.

'Sometimes education cuts people off,' she said.

Veronica married him quietly. The great-aunt spoke her mind finally by dying just before the wedding and leaving her house to a great-nephew who sold it and gambled the money away. Myrtle's boy continued to thrive. I heard Veronica telling Granny on one of her now rare visits that Myrtle treated him like a doll and often forgot about him. Myrtle's mother reared him as she had reared Myrtle, on milk arrowroot biscuits and condensed milk. Veronica seemed thinner and sadder, though she was as beautiful and kind as ever.

Granny told my parents that Veronica was far from happy. He would not let her go to work. He made her account for every penny. He worked at home a lot and expected her to be there when he was. Nobody called him Cecil, or Mr Stitt. It was always He, like Jehovah.

One day Granny and I were invited to dinner, which Veronica now called lunch, at her home in Ascot. The house was huge, dark and gloomy. It smelt unfriendly. Veronica had the table set for four, but he came in and asked for lunch in his study. He did not bother to talk to the visitors. I found a water-closet which fascinated me utterly, and was repeatedly pulling the handle, which had the word PULL embossed in black letters on ivory, when he appeared and said, 'I always say children should be left at home.'

A maid took away our luncheon dishes and brought us tea, and we began to talk about old times. He appeared again and asked us to talk outside, so we took our tea on to the shady veranda. I tried to roll on the lawn, but the buffalo grass was too scratchy, so I found a corner where I could hear what Veronica was telling my grandmother. She felt like a prisoner. There was nothing to do. She had an ice chest and the laundry went out to Holy Cross and came back so starchy you had to tear it apart. He had kept his mother's house exactly as it was, and kept his mother's cranky, bossy maid, who put things back if Veronica tried to rearrange them. 'Well, my dear,' said Granny, 'it is for better or worse. You knew you're always welcome with us. You might have a child.'

'He doesn't want one. He can't abide children.'

Time passed as usual at Mitchelton, until something terrible happened. Myrtle's mother left the gate unlocked and Myrtle wandered off with her little boy. She took him down to the creek and forgot all about him. He rolled into the water and drowned. Veronica came down for the funeral, and afterwards sat with my grandmother. I was in my darkened room. That evening I was to be allowed up to listen to a new crystal set my father had built, so I had to lie down for a horrible enforced afternoon rest. I heard Veronica telling Granny how she had tried for one last time to get things right. 'We took a shack at Humpybong for a few days. I thought we might talk things out by ourselves, but he didn't want to listen. I borrowed a dinghy and went out fishing, and got a bream, not very big but enough for tea, and found a beach with lovely polished stones. I felt like a child again, and thought of that poem you taught Gwenny:

> *White foam on the sea-top*
> *Green leaves on the tree-top*
> *The wind blows gay,*
> *Sing ho! sing hey!*

'I found one stone like a heart, and one with a face, and a brown one like a perfect egg. And in the seaweed a glass buoy covered in rope. I felt it was a sort of sign that things would be better, and put everything in the fishing bucket and rowed back. But when I got to our beach he was waiting, angry because his tea was late and he'd had enough of the seaside. He said the fish was too small, and tipped everything out of the bucket. I cried and cried. I felt like a helpless child.'

She cried again. No wonder, with such treasures lost. An egg, a face and a heart. And the wonderful glass boy. I saw him, translucent green, the colour of the marbles we used to stop the jam sticking to the kettle; he had his ropes taken off and was set on the windowsill to catch the morning light. Granny was getting four o'clock, and I went in to cuddle Veronica.

'The glass boy, were his arms joined to his sides, or did they move like a doll's? Was he a baby boy or a grown-up boy? Could you stand him up like an ornament? Was he hollow or glass all through?'

'Not that kind of boy,' she said. 'Bring me your book of words.' I brought the book, and she wrote down BUOY. 'It's something that keeps you afloat in the water. Or tells you there are dangers, like rocks underneath. This one was a ball of glass, hollow inside; not a doll, my darling.'

My friend Alice was brought in that night to hear the wireless. We sat in our nightgowns with one headphone each.

'What can you hear?' asked my father.

'A piano playing. Ladies singing.'

'What are they singing?'

Alice did not know, though we had learnt the song at school. Her family was not musical.

My father said wireless would change the world.

> *– Over the rolling waters go,*
> *Come from the dying moon and blow,*
> *Blow him again to me –*

I mourned for the green glass boy, born of a mistake in my head, floating on the waves in his net cradle as I lay before sleep listening to the stone-curlews. But I did not grieve for Myrtle's baby.

Our street was full of boys. It was nature's way of making up for the Great War.

'SHE cried again. No wonder, with such treasures lost. An egg, a face and a heart. And the wonderful glass boy.'

A HEDGE OF ROSEMARY

ELIZABETH
JOLLEY
1923–

No one knew where the old man went every night at dusk. He sat to his tea in his daughter-in-law's kitchen and ate up obediently everything she put before him. She was a sharp woman but quite kind, she called him Dad and stirred his tea for him as she put the cup beside him. She put it a bit towards the middle of the table so he would not knock it over.

'Mind your tea now, Dad,' she always said, and without looking up from his plate he answered, 'Thank you kindly, much obliged.' After the meal he would sit for a while with his boots off: he held them in both hands and studied the soles intently, sometimes shaking his head over them, and Sarah would get his dishes done out of the way.

Just about this time, as on other nights, his son John, who had a business in town, came in and he and Sarah had their dinner. When that and the necessary bits of conversation were over they all went into the lounge room and sat in comfortable chairs to watch the television. The house was very quiet with John's three boys all grown up and gone their ways, two to Sydney and one overseas. When the old man had sat a short while with John and Sarah in the lounge he put on his boots slowly and carefully and then, getting up carefully from his comfortable chair, he went out through the back veranda.

'Mind how you go, Dad!' Sarah called after him and he replied, 'That's right, that's right!' and went off into the dusk round the side of the house and through a door in a vine-covered trellis and down into the street. After he had gone Sarah wondered where he was going. On other evenings she had peered out into the dark fragrance to see if he had gone up to the end of the garden. She thought

he might have gone up to the shed for something. Sometimes she had looked in there and had even pushed open the door of the whitewashed place next to the shed thinking he might be ill in there. He never would use the one in the bathroom which was so much nicer. But he was never in either place. If she went out of the front door she could never see him: by the time she had picked her way across her neatly laid out suburban garden he was always gone from sight and all she could do was to peer up the street and down the street into the gathering darkness and go back into the house where John was absorbed in the television.

'I wonder where Dad's off to again,' she said, but on this night, as on all other nights, John was not listening to her.

'The Queen's not looking so well,' Sarah remarked as some activities of the Royal Family came on in the news. John grunted some sort of reply and they both sank into the next program and did not think too much about the old man walking off on his own into the night.

During the day the old man did practically nothing. He tidied the garden a bit and stacked wood slowly and neatly outside the veranda so Sarah had only to reach out an arm for it. Mostly he sat in the barber's shop. He went shopping, too, with his battered attaché case. He laid it on the counter in the Post Office and opened in with his trembling old hands. Glossy magazines lay in neat rows over the counter.

'Mind my magazines now, Dad!' the postmistress said, and he replied, 'That's right, that's right!' And when he had drawn his money he said, 'Thank you kindly, much obliged', and back to the barber's shop where the paint was peeling from the ceiling and the shelves were littered with old-fashioned hairnets and curlers and other toilet requisites long out of date and covered in dust. Faded advertisements hung on the walls, but no one ever read them.

Towards the end of the afternoon the shop filled with little boys from school and sometimes little girls came in and would take their turn in the chair unnoticed by the barber who did not do girls. The children ignored the old man and brushed past him to reach for old magazines and tattered comics which they read greedily, sprawled on the linoleum. The barber greeted every customer in a nasal drawling voice. He spoke to the old man.

'And how are they treating you, eh? Pretty good, eh?' He said the same thing to everybody, and the old man replied, 'That's right, that's right.' If the children had asked him he could have thought up stories about the Great Red Fox and Brother Wolf, but the children never asked him anything, not even the time.

Some days he wandered by the river watching the weaving pattern of children playing on the shore. They never took any notice of him and he sat half asleep in the shade of one of the peppermint trees that grew at intervals along the bank. He sat just a bit back from the sandy edges where the kind-hearted water rippled gentle and lazy and shallow. He was always sleepy at noon after his midday meal which Sarah gave him early, at half past eleven, so that she could get cleared up in the kitchen. The children never came to him to ask his advice or to show him things. He supposed he was too old. Yet he knew a good many things about the foreshore and about playing in the sand. Back at home he had three things better than plastic spades; he had an iron gravy spoon and an ash scoop and an old iron trowel. These had been for his grandchildren years ago when he had brought them down to the shore to play, minding them for Sarah so she could get on and do the house and the cooking and the washing. He never thought about these three things now; they lay somewhere at home behind the stove. He never thought about the Great Red Fox and Brother Wolf either. But if someone had asked him, he could have thought about them.

There was a little merry-go-round there, a corner of jangling music and laughter, a corner of enchantment. When the children went round and round on the little painted horses the old man forgot everything as he sat on a bench and watched them. They smiled and waved and he would nod and smile and wave and then shake his head because the children were nothing of his and were not waving to him. Once a child was crying on the path and he fished a penny out of his pocket and held it out, but she would not take it and hid her face in the uneven hem of her mother's dress.

'You can't get anything for a penny now, Gran'pa,' the mother said and, laughing quite kindly, walked on along the path.

When he went out in the evening he walked straight down the middle of the road, down towards the river. The evening was oriental, with dark verandas and curving ornamental rooftops, palm fronds and the long weeping hair of peppermint trailing, a mysterious profile sketched temporarily purple on a green and grey sky. Fingers of darkness crept across him as the moon, thinly crescent and frail, hung in the gum-leaf lace. Dampness and fragrance brushed his old face and he made his way to the river where the shores were deserted. The magpies caressed him with their cascade of watery music. This was their time for singing at dusk and all night if they wanted to. Down by the water's edge the old man crouched to rest and his voice sighed into a whisper sliding into the great plate of smooth water before him.

'No one should be alone when they are old.' His thought and his word and his voice were like dry reeds rustling at the edge of the gentle water.

When he had rested a few moments he walked on through the stranded ghosts of the swings and the merry-go-round. The little wooden horses, their heads bent and devout, were dignified in their silence. The old man walked by unnoticed, for why should the little horses notice him? – he walked this way so often. A little farther on he turned up the grass bank away from the river. The slope was hardly a slope at all but he had to pause more than once for breath. Soon his hand brushed the roughness and fragrance of rosemary and his nostrils filled with the sharper scent of geranium, and he fumbled the wooden latch of a gate and went in and along the overgrown path of a neglected garden. The hedge of rosemary was nearly three feet thick and sang with bees in the heat of a summer day. Geraniums like pale pink sugar roses climbed and hung and trailed at the gateposts, and again on either side of the crumbling woodwork of the veranda trellis. Later on the air would be heavy with the sweetness of honeysuckle, but the old man was not thinking of this. He fumbled again at the latch of the door and made his way into the darkness inside the familiar place which had been his home and his wife's home and his children's home for more years than he ever thought about now. In the kitchen he felt about with his old hands till he had candle and matches.

'THERE was a little merry-go-round there, a corner of jangling music and laughter, a corner of enchantment.'

Three years back he had been ill with pneumonia and fever and Sarah declared the place unhealthy and smelling of the river and drains, or lack of them; and herself finding it too much to come there every day to see to him and his house as well as her own house which took a deal of doing on her own. So she and John had come one Sunday afternoon in the car and fetched him to their place and had nursed him well and comfortable. And later, had sold his place to the owner of some tearooms further along the river, the other side of the swings and the merry-go-round. So far the man who had bought it had done nothing except sell the furniture, and even some of that, the shabby good-for-nothing stuff, was still there. As soon as the old man was better enough from his illness he had started to walk back to his place. At first he had only got as far as the barber's shop on the corner, and then to the postmistress where the road widened before turning down to the sandy wastes by the river. And then one day he managed to get to a bench at the merry-go-round, and after that strength was his to walk right to his place. And he went inside and sat in the kitchen and looked about him thinking and remembering. But he did not think and remember too much; mostly he rested and was pleased to be there. He laid his attaché case on the kitchen table and opened it with his trembling old hands, he unpacked his shopping into the cupboard by the stove. He had little packages of tea, sugar and matches. Then he took out his pipe and tobacco and he sat and smoked his pipe. Sarah objected to the smell of his cheap tobacco in her home, even if he smoked out on the veranda. She complained all the time afterwards, and went from room to room opening windows, shaking curtains and spraying the air with something pine-scented to freshen the place up, as she called it. So every night he walked down home and had his pipe there. He did not say where he was going because Sarah would insist that he stayed in her place to smoke and then all that airing and freshing up afterwards.

During the day he sometimes spent an hour tidying up the old tangled garden as much as an old man could. He stacked up some wood and split a few chips for the stove. People passing the rosemary hedge would wish him 'good day' if they saw him in the garden, but mostly people took no notice of him. They were busy with their children or with their thoughts or with each other. The old man came and went in peace and every night he came home to his place and smoked his pipe and sat and rested. He did not think very much because there is no use thinking over things when you can do nothing about them any more. His children were gone their ways, they mostly were like her. She had been a great reader and had sat reading her life away. She read everything the old post-mistress could get for her, novelettes they were called years ago. Bundles of them had come to the house. The children had mostly been like her and she had taken them with her into the kind of world she lived in.

He had come, as a very young man, from the Black Country in England, from the noise and dirt of the chain-making industrial area where people lived crowded and jostled together in indescribable poverty. The women there had muscles like men and they worked side by side with their men in the chain shops pausing only at intervals to suckle their babies. He had carried his younger sisters daily to his mother and had later cared for them in other intimate ways as he minded them in the blue-brick backyards and alleys which were the only playgrounds. When he had come to Australia he had gone straight to the country where he had been terrified by the silence and loneliness. He was afraid of the heat and the drought too, but more than that he could not stand the still quiet nights in the bush when he was alone with the silence. And the white trunks of the gum trees were like ghosts in the white light of the moon. He had longed to hear the chiming of city clocks through the comforting roar of the city and the friendly screech of the trams as they turned out of the High Street into Hill Street. He missed the heave and roar of the blast furnace and the nightly glow on the sky when the furnace was opened. All his life these had been his night light and his cradle song. So he went from the country to the town and found work in one place and then in another and later was employed to look after the foreshore. There was the house there for him too and, though it was quiet, the city and the suburbs were spreading towards him reassuringly.

If any one had said, 'Tell me about the chain shop', he could have told them about it and about a place he once visited as a boy where, in the late afternoon sunshine, he had walked with his father down a village street. Standing on the village green were twelve geese. They were so still and clean and white. Beautiful birds, his father had said so. It was the stillness of the geese in his brief memory of the countryside that had made him leave the hustled, crowded life among the chain makers and come to Australia. But no one ever asked him about it so he never really thought about it any more except perhaps for a moment while he sat smoking, but only for a moment.

So on this night as on all the other nights he sat and rested and smoked his pipe in the neglected old house which had once been his place. He was so comfortable there he forgot it had been sold. Though Mr Hickman, the man who had bought it, had called once when the old man was doing the garden. Mr Hickman had said he was having the place demolished in a week or two because he wanted to start building.

'You've got some fine roses there,' Mr Hickman had said after the pause which had followed his previous statement.

'That's right, that's right,' the old man had replied and they had stared at the roses together while the bees hummed and sang in the hedge of rosemary.

'THEY had stared at the roses together while the bees hummed and sang in the hedge of rosemary.'

But this had been nearly a year ago and the old man did not think about it because there was nothing he could do about it. So just now he sat and rested and enjoyed his pipe and was pleased to be there. When his pipe was finished he remembered he must walk back. He got back to his son's place just after nine and Sarah said, 'How about a nice cup of tea before bed, Dad', and he replied, 'Thank you kindly, much obliged.' And he sat down in the kitchen and took his boots off carefully and stared at the soles of his boots. He shook his head a bit very slowly and set the boots down beside his chair. Sarah stirred his tea and put the cup down towards the middle of the table.

'Mind your tea now, Dad,' she said.

'Thank you kindly, much obliged,' he replied.

'Have a good walk, Dad?' John asked him.

'That's right, that's right,' the old man said and he drank up his tea.

'Good night, Dad,' Sarah said.

'Good night, Dad,' John said.

'Good night, good night,' the old man said and he took up his boots and he went off to his bed.

THE BEAUTIFUL CLIMATE

ELIZABETH
HARROWER
1928–

THE Shaws went down to the cottage on Scotland Island every weekend for two years. Hector Shaw bought the place from some hotel keeper he knew, never having so much as hinted at his intention till the contract was signed. Then he announced to his wife and daughter the name of a certain house, his ownership of it, its location, and the fact that they would all go down every Friday night to put it in order.

It was about an hour's drive from Sydney. At the Church Point wharf they would park the car, lock it up, and wait for the ferry to take them across to the island.

Five or six families made a living locally, tinkering with boats and fishing, but most of the houses round about were weekenders, like the Shaws' place. Usually these cottages were sold complete with a strip of waterfront and a jetty. In the Shaws' case the jetty was a long spindly affair of grey wooden palings on rickety stilts, with a perpendicular ladder that had to be climbed getting in and out of the boat. Some of the others were handsome constructions equipped with special flags and lights to summon the ferryman when it was time to return to civilisation.

As Mr Shaw had foretold, they were constantly occupied putting the house in order, but now and then he would buy some green prawns, collect the lines from the spare-bedroom cupboard, and take his family into the middle of the bay to fish. While he made it obligatory to assume that this was a treat, he performed every action with his customary air of silent, smouldering violence, as if to punish misdemeanours, alarming his wife and daughter greatly.

Mrs Shaw put on her big straw sunhat, tied it solemnly under her chin, and went behind him down the seventy rough rock steps from the house. She said nothing. The glare from the water gave her migraine. Since a day years before when she was a schoolgirl learning to swim, and had almost drowned, she had had a horror of deep water. Her husband knew it. He was a difficult man, for what reason no one had been able to discover, least of all Hector Shaw himself.

Del followed her mother down the steep bushy track, not speaking, her nerves raw, her soundless protests battering the air about her. She did not *want* to go, nor, of course, could she want to stay when her absence would be used against her mother.

They were not free. Either the hostage, or the one over whom a hostage was held, they seemed destined to play for ever if they meant to preserve the peace. And peace had to be preserved. Everything had always been subordinated to this task. As a child, Del had been taught that happiness was nothing but the absence of unpleasantness. For all she knew, it was true. Unpleasantness, she knew, could be extremely disagreeable. She knew that what was irrational had to be borne, and she knew she and her mother longed for peace and quiet – since she had been told so so often. But still she did not want to go.

Yet that they should not accompany her father was unthinkable. That they should all three be clamped together was, in a way, the whole purpose of the thing. Though Del and her mother were aware that he might one day sink the boat deliberately. It wasn't *likely*, because he was terrified of death, whereas his wife would welcome oblivion, and his daughter had a stony capacity for endurance (so regarding death, at least, they had the upper hand): but it was *possible*. Just as he might crash the car some day on purpose if all three were secure together in it.

'Why do we *do* it?' Del asked her mother relentlessly. 'You'd think we were mental defectives to way we troop behind him and do what we're told just to save any trouble. And it never does. Nothing we do makes sure of anything. When I go out to work every day it's as if I'm out on parole. You'd think we were hypnotised.'

Her mother sighed and failed to look up, and continued to butter the scones.

'*You're* his wife, so maybe you think you have to do it, but I don't. I'm eighteen.'

However, till quite recently she had been a good deal younger, and most accustomed to being used in the cause of peace. Now her acquiescence gnawed at and baffled her, but though she made isolated stands, in essence she always did submit. Her few rebellions were carefully gauged to remain within the permitted limits, the complaints of a prisoner-of-war to the camp commandant.

This constant nagging from the girl exhausted Mrs Shaw. Exasperation penetrated even her alarming headaches. She asked desperately, 'What would you do if you *didn't* come? You're too nervous to stay in town by yourself. And if you did, what would you do?'

'*Here*. I have to come *here*, but why do we have to go in the boat?' On a lower note, Del muttered, 'I wish I worked at the kindergarten seven days a week. I dread the night and weekends.'

She could *think* a thing like that, but never say it without a deep feeling of shame. Something about her situation made her feel not only passively abused, but actively surprisingly guilty.

All her analysis notwithstanding, the fishing expeditions took place whenever the man of the family signified his desire for some sport. Stationed in the dead centre of the glittering bay, within sight of their empty house, they sat in the open boat, grasping cork rollers, feeling minute and interesting tugs on their lines from time to time, losing bait and catching three-inch fish.

Low hills densely covered with thin gums and scrub sloped down on all sides to the rocky shore. They formed silent walls of a dark subdued green, without shine. Occasional painted roofs showed through. Small boats puttered past and disappeared.

As the inevitable pain began to saturate Mrs Shaw's head, she turned gradually paler. She leant against the side of the boat with her eyes closed, her hands obediently clasping the fishing line she had been told to hold.

The dazzle of the heavy summer sun sucked up colour till the scene looked black. Her light skin began to burn. The straw sunhat was like a neat little oven in which her hair, her head and all its contents, were being cooked.

Without expression, head lowered, Del looked at her hands, fingernails, legs,

at the composition of the cork round which her line was rolled. She glanced sometimes at her mother, and sometimes, by accident, she caught sight of her father's bare feet or his arm flinging out a newly baited line, or angling some small silver fish off the hook and throwing it back, and her eyes sheered away.

The wooden interior of the boat was dry and burning. The three fishers were seared, beaten down by the sun. The bait smelt. The water lapped and twinkled blackly but could not be approached: sharks abounded in the bay.

The cottage was fairly dilapidated. The walls needed painting inside and out, and parts of the veranda at the front and both sides had to be re-floored. In the bedrooms, sitting room and kitchen, most of the furniture was old and crudely made. They burnt the worst of it, replacing it with new stuff, and what was worth salvaging Mrs Shaw and Del gradually scrubbed, sanded and painted.

Mr Shaw did carpentering jobs, and cleared the ground near by of some of the thick growth of eucalyptus gums that had made the rooms dark. He installed a generating plant, too, so that they could have electric light instead of relying on kerosene lamps at night.

Now and then his mood changed inexplicably, for reasons so unconnected with events that no study and perpetuation of these external circumstances could ensure a similar result again. Nevertheless, knowing it could not last, believing it might, Mrs Shaw and Del responded shyly, then enthusiastically, but always with respect and circumspection, as if a friendly lion had come to tea.

These hours or days of amazing good humour were passed, as it were, a few feet off the ground, in an atmosphere of slightly hysterical gaiety. They sang, pumping water to the tanks; they joked at either end of the saw, cutting logs for winter fires; they ran, jumped, slithered, and laughed till they had to lean against the trees for support. They reminded each other of all the incidents of other days like these, at other times when his nature was in eclipse.

'We'll fix up a nice shark-proof pool for ourselves,' he said. 'We own the waterfrontage. It's crazy not to be able to cool off when we come down. If you can't have a dip here, surrounded by water, what's the sense? We'd be better to stay home and go to the beach, this weather.'

'Three cheers!' Del said. 'When do we start?'

The seasons changed. When the nights grew colder, Mr Shaw built huge log fires in the sitting room. If his mood permitted, these fires were the cause of his being teased, and he liked very much to be teased.

Charmed by his own idiosyncrasy, he would pile the wood higher and higher, so that the walls and ceiling shone and flickered with the flames, and the whole room crackled like a furnace on the point of explosion. Faces scorching, they would rush to throw open the windows, then they'd fling open the doors, dying for air. Soon the chairs nearest the fire would begin to smoke and then everyone would leap outside to the dark veranda, crimson and choking. Mr Shaw laughed and coughed till he was hoarse, wiping his eyes.

For the first few months, visitors were non-existent, but one night on the ferry the Shaws struck up a friendship with some people called Rivers, who had just bought a cottage next door. They came round one Saturday night to play poker and have supper, and in no time weekly visits to each other's house were established as routine. Grace and Jack Rivers were relaxed and entertaining company. Their easy good nature fascinated the Shaws, who looked forward to these meetings seriously, as if the Rivers were a sort of rest cure ordered by a specialist, from which they might pick up some health.

'It was too good to last,' Mrs Shaw said later. 'People are so funny.'

The Rivers's son, Martin, completed his army training and went down to stay on the island for a month before returning to his marine-engineering course at a technical college in town. He and Del met sometimes and talked, but she had not gone sailing with him when he asked her, nor was she tempted to walk across the island to visit his friends who had a pool.

'Why not?' he asked.

'Oh, well ....' She looked down at the dusty garden from the veranda where they stood. 'I have to paint those chairs this afternoon.'

'*Have* to?' Martin had a young, open, slightly freckled face.

Del looked at him, feeling old, not knowing how to explain how complicated it would be to extricate herself from the house, and her mother and father. He would never understand the drama, the astonishment, that would accompany her statement to them. Even if, eventually, they said, 'Go, go!' recovering from their shock, her own joylessness and fatigue were so clear to her in anticipation that she had no desire even to test her strength in the matter.

'THEY sang pumping water to the tanks; they joked at either end of the saw, cutting logs for winter fires; they ran, jumped, slithered, and laughed till they had to lean against the trees for supports.'

But one Saturday night over a game of cards, Martin asked her parents if he might take her the next night to a party across the bay. A friend of his, Noel Stacey, had a birthday to celebrate.

Del looked at him with mild surprise. He had asked her. She had refused.

Her father laughed a lot at this request as though it were very funny, or silly, or misguided, or simply impossible. It turned out that it *was* impossible. They had to get back to Sydney early on Sunday night.

If they *did* have to, it was unprecedented, and news to Del. But she looked at her father with no surprise at all.

Martin said, 'Well, it'll be a good party', and gave her a quizzical grin. But his mother turned quite pink, and his father cleared his throat gruffly several times. The game broke up a little earlier than usual, and, as it happened, was the last one they ever had together.

Not knowing that it was to be so, however, Mrs Shaw was pleased that the matter had been dealt with so kindly and firmly. 'What a funny boy!' she said later, a little coyly, to Del.

'Is he?' she said indifferently.

'One of the new generation,' said Mr Shaw, shaking his head, and eyeing her with caution.

'Oh?' she said, and went to bed.

'She didn't really want to go to that party at all,' her mother said.

'No, but we won't have him over again, do you think? He's got his own friends. Let him stick to them. There's no need for this. These fellows who've been in army camps – I know what they're like.'

'She hardly looked at him. She didn't care.' Mrs Shaw collected the six pale-blue cups, saucers and plates on the wooden tray, together with the remnants of supper.

With his back to the fire, hands clasped behind him, Mr Shaw brooded. 'He had a nerve though, when you come to think of it. I mean – he's a complete stranger.'

Mrs Shaw sighed anxiously, and her eyes went from one side of the room to the other. 'I'm sure she didn't like him. She doesn't take much interest in boys. You're the only one.'

Mr Shaw laughed reluctantly, looking down at his shoes.

As more and more of the property was duly painted and repaired, the Shaws tended to stop work earlier in the day, perhaps with the unspoken intention of making the remaining tasks last longer. Anyway, the pressure was off, and Mrs Shaw knitted sweaters, and her husband played patience, while Del was invariably glued to some book or other.

No one in the district could remember the original owner-builder of their cottage, or what he was like. But whether it was this first man, or a later owner, *someone* had left a surprisingly good library behind. It seemed likely that the builder had lived and died there, and that his collection had simply been passed on with the property from buyer to buyer, over the years.

Books seemed peculiarly irrelevant on this remote hillside smelling of damp

earth and wood smoke and gums. The island had an ancient, prehistoric, undiscovered air. The alphabet had yet to be invented.

However, the books *had* been transported here by someone, and Del was
pleased to find them, particularly the many leather-bound volumes of verse.
Normally, in an effort to find out why people were so peculiar, she read nothing
but psychology. Even after she knew psychologists did not know, she kept reading it from force of habit, in the hope that she might come across a formula for
survival directed specifically at her: *Del Shaw, follow these instructions to the letter! ...*
Poetry was a change.

She lay in a deckchair on the deserted side veranda and read in the mellow
three o'clock, four o'clock, sunshine. There was, eternally, the smell of grass and
burning bush, and the homely noise of dishes floating up from someone's kitch-
en along the path of yellow earth, hidden by trees. And she hated the chair, the
mould-spotted book, the sun, the smells, the sounds, her supine self.

And they came on a land where it was always afternoon.

'It's like us, exactly like us and this place,' she said to her mother, fiercely
brushing her long brown hair in front of the dressing-table's wavy mirror.
'Always afternoon. Everyone lolling about. Nobody *doing* anything.'

'My goodness!' Her mother stripped the sheets off the bed to take home to the
laundry. 'I thought we'd all been active enough this weekend to please anyone.
And I don't see much afternoon about Monday morning.'

'Active! That isn't what I mean. Anyway, I don't mean here or this weekend.
I mean everyone, everywhere, all the time. Ambling round till they die.' Oh,
but that wasn't what she meant, either.

Mrs Shaw's headache look appeared. 'It's off to the doctor with you tonight,
Miss!'

Del set her teeth together. When her mother had left the room with her arms
full of linen, still darting sharp glances at her daughter, Del closed her eyes and
raised her face to the ceiling.

Let me *die.*

The words seemed to be ground from her voiceless body, to be ground,
powdered stone, from her heart.

She breathed very slowly; she slowly righted her head, carefully balancing its
weight on her neck. Then she pulled on her suede jacket, lifted her bag, and
clattered down the uneven stone steps to the jetty. It always swayed when anyone set foot on it.

When the cottage had been so patched and cleaned that, short of a great
expenditure of capital, no further improvement was possible, Hector Shaw
ceased to find any purpose in his visits to it. True, there was still the pool to be
tackled, but the summer had gone by without any very active persuasion, any
pleading, any teasing, from his wife and daughter. And if *they* were indifferent,
far be it from him....

Then there was another thing. Not that it had any connection with the place,
with being on Scotland Island, but it had the side effect of making the island
seem less – safe, salubrious, desirable. Jack Rivers died from a heart-attack one
Sunday morning. Only fifty-five he was, and a healthier-looking fellow, you

couldn't have wished to meet.

Since the night young Martin Rivers had ruined their poker parties, they had seen very little of Jack and Grace. Sometimes on the ferry they had bumped into each other, and when they had the Shaws, at least, were sorry that it had all worked out so badly. Jack and Grace were good company. It was hard not to feel bitter about the boy having spoiled their nice neighbourly friendship so soon before his father died. Perhaps if Jack had spent more time playing poker and less doing whatever he did do after the Saturdays stopped....

On a mild midwinter night, a few weeks after Jack Rivers's funeral, the Shaw family sat by the fire. Del was gazing along her corduroy slacks into the flames, away from her book. Her parents were silent over a game of cards.

Mr Shaw took a handful of cashew nuts from a glass dish at his side and started to chew. Then leaning back in his chair, his eyes still fixed on his cards, he said, 'By the way, the place's up for sale.'

His wife stared at him. 'What place?'

'*This* place.' He gave her his sour, patient look. 'It's been on Dalgety's books for three weeks.'

'What for?' Del asked, conveying by the gentleness of her tone, her total absence of criticism. It was dangerous to question him, but then it was dangerous not to, too.

'Well, there isn't much to do round here now. And old Jack's popped off –' (He hadn't meant to say that!) Crunching the cashew nuts, he slid down in his chair expansively, every supra-casual movement premeditated as though he were playing *Hamlet* at Stratford.

The women breathed deeply, not with regret, merely accepting this new fact in their lives. Mrs Shaw said, 'Oh! ....' and Del nodded her comprehension. Changing their positions imperceptibly, they prepared to take up their occupations again in the most natural and least offensive ways they could conceive. There was enormous potential danger in any radical change of this sort.

'Ye-es,' said Mr Shaw, drawing the small word out to an extraordinary length. 'Dalgety's telling them all to come any Saturday or Sunday afternoon.' Still he gazed at his handful of cards, then he laid them face down on the table and, with a thumb, thoughtfully rubbed the salt from the cashews into the palm of his other hand. It crumbled onto his knees, and he dusted it down to the rug, seeming agreeably occupied in its distribution.

'Ye-es,' he said again, while his wife and daughter gazed at him painfully. 'When and if anyone takes the place, I think we'd better use the cash to go for a trip overseas. What do you say? See the Old Country.... Even the boat trip's pretty good, they tell me. You go right round the coast here (that takes about a week), then up to Colombo, Bombay, Aden, through the Suez, then up through the Mediterranean, through the Straits of Messina past some volcano, and past Gibraltar to Marseilles, then London.'

There was a silence.

Mr Shaw turned away from the table and his game, and looked straight into his wife's grey eyes – a thing he rarely did. Strangers were all right, he could look at them, but with relations, old acquaintances, his spirit, unconscious, was ashamed and uneasy.

'*THE island had an ancient, prehistoric, undiscovered air. The alphabet had yet to be invented.*'

'Go away?' his wife repeated, turning a dreadful colour.

He said, 'Life's short. I've earned a holiday. Most of my typist've been abroad. We'll have a year. We'll need a year. *If* someone turns up on the ferry one day and *wants* the place, that is. There's a bit of a slump in real estate just now, but I guess we'll be okay.'

And they looked at each other, the three of them, with unfamiliar awe. They were about to leave this dull pretty city where they were all so hard to live with, and go to places they had read about, where the world was, where things happened, where the photographs of famous people came from, where history was, and snow in cities, and works of art, and splendour . . . .

Poetry and patience were discarded from that night, while everyone did extra jobs about the cottage to add to its attractiveness and value. Mrs Shaw and Del planted tea-trees and hibiscus bushes covered with flowers of palest apricot, and pink streaked with red. Mr Shaw cemented the open space under the house (it was propped up on columns on its steep hillside) and the area underneath was like a large extra room, shady and cool. They put some long bamboo chairs down there, fitted with cushions.

Most weekend afternoons, jobs notwithstanding, Del went to the side veranda to lean over the railing out of sight and watch the ferry go from jetty to jetty and return to Church Point. She watched and willed, but no one ever came to see the house.

It was summer again, and the heatwave broke records. Soon it was six months since the night they had talked about the trip.

Always the island was the same. It was scented, self-sufficient; the earth was

warm underfoot and the air warm to breathe. The hillside sat there, quietly, rustling quietly, a smug curving hillside that had existed for a long time. The water was blue and sparkled with meaningless beauty. Smoke stood in the sunny sky above the bush here and there across the bay, where other weekend visitors were cooking chops, or making coffee on fuel stoves.

Del watched the ferries and bargained with fate, denying herself small pleasures, which was very easy for her to do. She waited. Ferries came and went round the point, but never called at their place.

They lost heart. In the end it would have been impossible even to mention the trip. But they all grieved with a secret enduring grief as if at the death of the one person they had loved. Indeed, they grieved for their own deaths. Each so unknown and un-understood, who else could feel the right regret? From being eaten by the hillside, from eating one another, there had been the chance of a reprieve. Now it was evidently cancelled, and in the meantime irretrievable admissions had been made....

At the kindergarten one Tuesday afternoon Miss Lewis, who was in charge, called Del to the telephone. She sat down, leaning her forehead on her hand before lifting the receiver.

'Hullo?'

'Del, your father's sold the cottage to a pilot. Somebody Barnes. He's bought the tickets. We've just been in to get our cabins. We're leaving in two months.'

'What? ... A pilot?'

'Yes. We're going on the *Arcadia* on the 28th of November. The cabins are lovely. Ours has got a porthole. We'll have to go shopping, and get injections and passports –'

'We're *going*?'

'Of course we are, you funny girl! We'll tell you all about it when you get home tonight. I've started making lists.'

They were going. She was going away. Out in the world she would escape from them. There would be room to run, outside this prison.

'So we're off,' her mother said.

Del leant sideways against the wall, looking out at the eternal afternoon, shining with all its homey peace and glory. 'Oh, that's good,' she said. 'That's good.'

MENA ABDULLAH
1930–
AND
RAY MATHEW
1929–

WHEN I was little everything was wonderful; the world was our farm and we were all loved. Rashida and Lal and I, Father and our mother, Ama: we loved one another and everything turned to good.

I remember in autumn, how we burnt the great baskets of leaves by the Gwydir and watched the fires burning in the river while Ama told us stories of Krishna the Flute-player and his moving mountains. And when the fires had gone down and the stories were alive in our heads we threw cobs of corn into the fires and cooked them. One for each of us – Rashida and Lal and I, Father and our mother.

Winter I remember, when the frost bit and stung and the wind pulled our hair. At night by the fire in the warmth of the house, we could hear the dingoes howling.

Then it was spring and the good year was born again. The sticks of the jasmine vine covered themselves with flowers.

One spring I remember was the time of the peacock when I learnt the word *secret* and began to grow up. After that spring everything somehow was different, was older. I was not little any more, and the baby came.

I had just learnt to count. I thought I could count anything. I counted fingers and toes, the steps and the windows, even the hills. But this day in spring the hills were wrong.

There should have been five. I knew that there should have been five. I counted them over and over – '*Ek, do, tin, panch*' – but it was no good. There was one too many, a strange hill, a left-over. It looked familiar, and I knew it, but it made more than five and worried me. I thought of Krishna and the mountains that moved to protect the cowherds, the travellers lost because of them, and I was frightened because it seemed to me that our hills had moved.

I ran through the house and out into the garden to tell Ama the thing that Krishna had done and to ask her how we could please him. But when I saw her I forgot all about them; I was as young as that. I just stopped and jumped, up and down.

She was standing there, in her own garden, the one with the Indian flowers, her own little walled-in country. Her hands were joined together in front of her face, and her lips were moving. On the ground, in front of the Kashmiri rose-bush, in front of the tuberoses, in front of the pomegranate tree, she had placed little bowls of shining milk. I jumped to see them. Now I knew why I was running all the time and skipping, why I wanted to sing out and to count everything in the world.

'It is spring,' I shouted to Ama. 'Not nearly-spring! Not almost-spring! But really-spring! Will the baby come soon?' I asked her. 'Soon?'

'Soon, Impatience, soon.'

I laughed at her and jumped up and clapped my hands together over the top of my head.

'I am as big as that,' I said. 'I can do anything.' And I hopped on one leg to the end of the garden where the peacock lived. 'Shah-Jehan!' I said to him – that was his name. 'It is spring and the baby is coming, pretty Shah-Jehan.' But he didn't seem interested. 'Silly old Shah-Jehan,' I said. 'Don't you know anything? I can count ten.'

He went on staring with his goldy eye at me. He *was* a silly bird. Why, he had to stay in the garden all day, away from the rooster. He couldn't run everywhere the way that I could. He couldn't do anything.

'Open your tail,' I told him. 'Go on, open your tail.' And we went on staring at one another till I felt sad.

'Rashida is right,' I said to him. 'You will never open your tail like the bird on the fan. But why don't you try? Please, pretty Shah-Jehan.' But he just went on staring as though he would never open his tail, and while I looked at him sadly I remembered how he had come to us.

He could lord it now and strut in the safety of the garden, but I remembered how the Lascar brought him to the farm, in a bag, like a cabbage, with his feathers drooping and his white tail dirty.

The Lascar came to the farm, a seaman on the land, a dark face in a white country. How he smiled when he saw us – Rashida and me swinging on the gate. How he chattered to Ama and made her laugh and cry. How he had shouted about the curries that she gave him.

And when it was time to go, with two basins of curry tied up in cloth and packed in his bag, he gave the bird to Ama, gave it to her while she said nothing, not even 'thank you'. She only looked at him.

'What is it?' we said as soon as he was far enough away. 'What sort of bird?'

'It is a peacock,' said Ama, very softly. 'He has come to us from India.'

'It is not like the peacock on your Kashmiri fan,' I said. 'It is only a sort of white.'

'The peacock on the fan is green and blue and gold and has a tail like a fan,' said Rashida. 'This is not a peacock at all. Anyone can see that.'

'Rashida,' said Ama, 'Rashida! The eldest must not be too clever. He is a white peacock. He is too young to open his tail. He is a peacock from India.'

'Ama,' I said, 'make him, make him open his tail.'

'I do not think,' she said, 'I do not think he will ever open his tail in this country.'

'No,' said Father that night, 'he will never open his tail in Australia.'

'No,' said Uncle Seyed next morning, 'he will never open his tail without a hen-bird near.'

But we had watched him – Rashida and Lal and I – had watched him for days and days until we had grown tired of watching and he had grown sleek and shiny and had found his place in the garden.

'Won't you ever open your tail?' I asked him again. 'Not now that it's spring?' But he wouldn't even try, not even try to look interested, so I went away from him and looked for someone to talk to.

The nurse lady who was there to help Ama and who was pink like an apple and almost as round was working in the kitchen.

'*THEN it was spring and the good year was born again. The sticks of the jasmine vine covered themselves with flowers.*'

'The baby is coming soon,' I told her. 'Now that it's spring.'

'Go on with you,' she laughed. 'Go on.'

So I did, until I found Rashida sitting in a windowsill with a book in front of her. It was the nurse lady's baby book.

'What are you doing?'

'I am reading,' she said. 'This is the baby book. I am reading how to look after the baby.'

'You can't read,' I said. 'You know you can't read.'

Rashida refused to answer. She just went on staring at the book, turning pages.

'But you can't read!' I shouted at her. 'You can't.'

She finished running her eye down the page. 'I am not reading words,' she said. 'I know what the book tells. I am reading things.'

'But you know, you know you can't read.' I stamped away from her, cranky as anything, out of the house, past the window where Rashida was sitting – so cleverly – down to the vegetable patch where I could see Lal. He was digging with a trowel.

'What are you doing?' I said, not very pleasantly.

'I am digging,' said Lal. 'I am making a garden for my new baby brother.'

'How did you know? How did you all know? I was going to tell *you*.' I was almost crying. 'Anyway,' I said, 'it might not be a brother.'

'Oh yes, it will,' said Lal. 'We have girls.'

'I'll dig, too,' I said, laughing, and suddenly happy again. 'I'll help you. We'll make a big one.'

'Digging is man's work,' said Lal. 'I'm a man. You're a girl.'

'You're a baby,' I said. 'You're only four.' And I threw some dirt at him, and went away.

Father was making a basket of sticks from the plum tree. He used to put crossed sticks on the ground, squat in the middle of them, and weave other sticks in and out of them until a basket had grown up round him. All I could see were his shoulders and the back of his turban as I crept up behind him, to surprise him.

But he was not surprised. 'I knew it would be you,' he said. I scowled at him then, but he only laughed the way that he always did.

'Father –' I began in a questioning voice that made him groan. Already I was called the Australian one, the questioner. 'Father,' I said, 'why do peacocks have beautiful tails?'

He tugged at his beard. 'Their feet are ugly,' he said, 'Allah has given them tails so that no one will look at their feet.'

'But Shah-Jehan,' I said, and Father bent his head down over his weaving. 'Everyone looks at his feet. His tail never opens.'

'Yes,' said Father definitely, as though that explained everything, and I began to cry: it was that sort of day, laughter and tears. I suppose it was the first day of spring.

'What is it, what is it?' said Father.

'Everything,' I told him. 'Shah-Jehan won't open his tail, Rashida pretends she can read, Lal won't let me dig. I'm nothing. And it's spring. Ama is putting out the milk for the snakes, and I counted –' But Father was looking so serious that I never told him what I had counted.

'Listen,' he said. 'You are big now, Nimmi. I will tell you a secret.'

'What is secret?'

He sighed. 'It is what is ours,' he said. 'Something we know but do not tell, or share with one person only in the world.'

'With me!' I begged. 'With me!'

'Yes,' he said, 'with you. But no crying or being nothing. This is to make you a grown-up person.'

'Please,' I said to him, 'please.' And I loved him then so much that I wanted to break the cage of twigs and hold him.

'We are Muslims,' he said. 'But your mother has a mark on her forehead that shows that once she was not. She was a Brahmin and she believed all the stories of Krishna and Siva.'

'I know that,' I said, 'and the hills –'

'Monkey, quiet,' he commanded. 'But now Ama is a Muslim, too. Only, she remembers her old ways. And she puts out the milk in the spring.'

'For the snakes,' I said. 'So they will love us, and leave us from harm.'

'But there are no snakes in the garden,' said Father.

'But they drink the milk,' I told him. 'Ama says –'

'If the milk were left, the snakes would come,' said Father. 'And they must not come, because there is no honour in snakes. They would strike you or Rashida or little Lal or even Ama. So – and this is the secret that no one must know but you and me – I go to the garden in the night and empty the dishes of milk. And this way I have no worry and you have no harm and Ama's faith is not hurt. But you must never tell.'

'Never, never tell,' I assured him.

All that day I was kind to Lal, who was only a baby and not grown up, and I held my head up high in front of Rashida, who was clever but had no secret. All of that day I walked in a glory full of my secret. I even felt cleverer than Ama, who knew everything but must never, never know this.

She was working that afternoon on her quilt. I looked at the crochet pictures in the little squares of it.

'Here is a poinsettia,' I said.

'Yes,' said Ama. 'And here is –'

'It's Shah-Jehan! With his tail open.'

'Yes,' said Ama, 'so it is, and here is a rose for the baby.'

'When will the baby come?' I asked her. 'Not soon, but when?'

'Tonight, tomorrow night,' said Ama, 'the next.'

'Do babies always come at night?'

'Mine, always,' said Ama. 'There is the dark and the waiting, and then the sun on our faces. And the scent of jasmine, even here.' And she looked at her garden.

'But, Ama –'

'No questions, Nimmi. My head is buzzing. No questions today.'

That night I heard a strange noise, a harsh cry. 'Shah-Jehan!' I said. I jumped out of bed and ran to the window. I stood on a chair and looked out to

'ALL of that day I walked in a glory full of my secret. I even felt cleverer than Ama, who knew everything but must never, never know this.'

223

the garden.

It was moonlight, the moon so big and low that I thought I could lean out and touch it, and there – looking sad, and white as frost in the moonlight – stood Shah-Jehan.

'Shah-Jehan, little brother,' I said to him, 'you must not feel about your feet. Think of your tail, pretty one, your beautiful tail.'

And then, as I was speaking, he lifted his head and slowly, slowly opened his tail – like a fan, like a fan of lace that was as white as the moon. O Shah-Jehan! It was as if you had come from the moon.

My throat hurt, choked, so that my breath caught and I shut my eyes. When I opened them it was all gone: the moon was the moon and Shah-Jehan was a milky-white bird with his tail drooping and his head bent.

In the morning the nurse lady woke us. 'Get up,' she said. 'Guess what? In the night, a sister! The dearest, sweetest, baby sister .... Now, up with you.'

'No brother,' said Lal. 'No baby brother.'

We laughed at him, Rashida and I, and ran to see the baby. Ama was lying, very still and small, in the big bed. Her long plait of black hair stretched out across the white pillow. The baby was in the old cradle and we peered down at her. Her tiny fists groped on the air towards us. But Lal would not look at her. He climbed on to the bed and crawled over to Ama.

'No boy,' he said sadly. 'No boy to play with.'

Ama stroked his hair. 'My son,' she said. 'I am sorry, little son.'

'Can we change her?' he said. 'For a boy?'

'She is a gift from Allah,' said Ama. 'You can never change gifts.'

Father came in from the dairy, his face a huge grin, he made a chuckling noise over the cradle and then sat on the bed.

'Missus,' he said in the queer English that always made the nurse lady laugh, 'this one little fellow, eh?'

'Big,' said Ama. 'Nine pounds.' And the nurse lady nodded proudly.

'What wrong with this fellow?' said Father, scooping Lal up in his arm. 'What wrong with you, eh?'

'No boy,' said Lal. 'No boy to talk to.'

'*Ai! Ai!*' lamented Father, trying to change his expression. 'Too many girls here,' he said. 'Better we drown one. Which one we drown, Lal? Which one, eh?'

Rashida and I hurled ourselves at him, squealing with delight. 'Not me! Not me!' we shouted while the nurse lady tried to hush us.

'You are worse than the children,' she said to Father. 'Far worse.' But then she laughed, and we all did – even the baby made a noise.

But what was the baby to be called? We all talked about it. Even Uncle Seyed came in and leant on the doorpost while names were talked over the over.

At last Father lifted the baby up and looked into her big dark eyes. 'What was the name of your sister?' he asked Uncle Seyed. 'The little one, who followed us everywhere? The little one with the beautiful eyes?'

'Jamila,' said Uncle Seyed. 'She was Jamila.'

So that was to be her first name, Jamila, after the little girl who was alive in India when Father was a boy and he and Uncle Seyed had decided to become

friends like brothers. And her second name was Shahnaz, which means the Heart's Beloved.

And then I remembered. 'Shah-Jehan,' I said. 'He can open his tail. I saw him last night, when everyone was asleep.'

'You couldn't see in the night,' said Rashida. 'You dreamt it, baby.'

'No, I didn't. It was bright moon.'

'You dreamt it, Nimmi,' said Father. 'A peacock wouldn't open his tail in this country.'

'I didn't dream it,' I said in a little voice that didn't sound very certain: Father was always right. 'I'll count Jamila's fingers,' I said before Rashida could say anything else about the peacock, '*Ek, do, tin, panch*,' I began.

'You've left out *cha*,' said Father.

'Oh yes, I forgot. I forgot it. *Ek, do, tin, cha, panch* – she has five,' I said.

'Everyone has five,' said Rashida.

'Show me,' said Lal. And while Father and Ama were showing him the baby's fingers and toes and telling him how to count them, I crept out on the veranda where I could see the hills.

I counted them quickly, '*Ek, do, tin, cha, panch*.' There were only five, not one left over. I was so excited that I felt the closing in my throat again. 'I didn't dream it,' I said. 'I couldn't dream the pain. I did see it, I did. I have another secret now. And only five hills. *Ek, do, tin, cha, panch*.'

They never changed again. I was grown up.

THE ONLY SPEAKER OF HIS TONGUE

DAVID MALOUF
1934–

HE has already been pointed out to me: a flabby, thickest man of fifty-five or sixty, very black, working alongside the others and in no way different from them – or so it seems. When they work he swings his pick with the same rhythm. When they pause he squats and rolls a cigarette, running his tongue along the edge of the paper while his eyes, under the stained hat, observe the straight line of the horizon; then he sets it between his lips, cups flame, draws in, and blows out smoke like all the rest.

Wears moleskins looped low under his belly and a flannel vest. Sits at smoko on one heel and sips tea from an enamel mug. Spits, and his spit hisses on stone. Then rises, spits in his palm and takes up the pick. They are digging holes for fencing-posts at the edge of the plain. When called he answers immediately, 'Here, boss', and then, when he was approached, 'Yes, boss, you wanna see me?' I am presented and he seems amused, as if I were some queer northern bird he had heard about but never till now believed in, a sort of crane perhaps, with my grey frockcoat and legs too spindly in their yellow trousers; an odd, angular fellow with yellow-grey side-whiskers, half spectacles and a cold-sore on his lip. So we stand face to face.

He is, they tell me, the one surviving speaker of his tongue. Half a century back, when he was a boy, the last of his people were massacred. The language, one of hundreds (why make a fuss?) died with them. Only not quite. For all his lifetime this man has spoken it, if only to himself. The words, the great system of sound and silence (for all languages, even the simplest, are a great and complex system) are locked up now in his heavy skull, behind the folds of the black brow (hence my scholarly interest), in the mouth with its stained teeth and fat, rather pink tongue. It is alive still in the man's silence, a whole alternative universe, since the world as we know it is in the last resort the words through which we imagine and name it; and when he narrows his eyes, and grins and says 'Yes, boss, you wanna see me?', it is not breathed out.

I am (you may know my name) a lexicographer. I come to these shores from far off, out of curiosity, a mere tourist, but in my own land I too am the keeper of something: of the great book of words of my tongue. No, not mine, my people's, which they have made over centuries, up there in our part of the world, and in which, if you have an ear for these things and a nose for the particular fragrance of a landscape, you may glimpse forests, lakes, greater snow-peaks that hang over our land like the wings of birds. It is all there in our mouths. In the odd names of our villages, in the pet-names we give to pigs or cows, and to our children too when they are young, Little Bean, Pretty Cowslip; in the nonsense rhymes in which so much simple wisdom is contained (not by accident, the language itself discovers these truths), or in the way, when two consonants catch up a repeated sound, a new thought goes flashing from one side to another of your head.

All this is mystery. It is a mystery of the deep past, but also of now. We recapture on our tongue, when we first grasp the sound and make it, the same word in the mouths of our long dead fathers, whose blood we move in and whose blood still moves in us. Language *is* that blood. It is the sun taken up where it shares out heat and light to the surface of each thing and made whole, hot, round again. *Solen*, we say, and the sun stamps once on the plain and pushes up in its great hot body, trailing streams of breath.

O holiest of all holy things! – it is a stooped blond crane that tells you this, with yellow side-whiskers and the grey frockcoat and trousers of his century – since we touch here on beginnings, go deep down under Now to the remotest dark, far back in each ordinary moment of our speaking, even in gossip and the rigmarole of love words and children's games, into the lives of our fathers, to share with them the single instant of all our seeing and making, all our long history of doing and being. When I think of my tongue being no longer alive in the mouths of men a chill goes over me that is deeper than my own death, since it is the gathered death of all my kind. It is black night descending once and for ever on all that world of forests, lakes, snow-peaks, great birds' wings; on little fishing sloops, on foxes nosing their way into a coop, on the piles of logs that make bonfires, and the heels of the young girls leaping over them, on sewing needles, milk pails, axes, on gingerbread moulds made out of good birchwood, on fiddles, school slates, spinning tops—my breath catches, my heart jumps. O the holy dread of it! Of having under your tongue the first and last words of all those generations down there in your blood, down there in the earth, for whom these syllables were the magic once for calling the whole of creation to come striding, swaying, singing towards them. I look at this old fellow and my heart stops, I do not know what to say to him.

I am curious, of course – what else does it mean to be a scholar but to be curious and to have a passion for the preserving of things? I would like to have him speak a word or two in his own tongue. But the desire is frivolous; I am ashamed to ask. And in what language would I do it? This foreign one? Which I speak out of politeness because I am a visitor here, and speak well because I have learnt it, and he because it is the only one he can share now with his contemporaries, with those who fill the days with him – the language (he appears to know only a handful of words) of those who feed, clothe, employ him, and whose great energy, and a certain gift for changing and doing things, has set all this land under another tongue. For the land too is in another language now. All its capes and valleys have new names; so do its creatures – even the insects that make their own skirling, racketing sound under stones. The first landscape here is dead. It dies in this man's eyes as his tongue licks the edge of the horizon, before it has quite dried up in his mouth. There is a new one now that others are making.

So. It is because I am a famous visitor, a scholarly freak from another continent, that we have been brought together. We have nothing to say to one another. I come to the fire where he sits with the rest of the men and accept a mug of their sweet scalding tea. I squat with difficulty in my yellow trousers. We nod to one another. He regards me with curiosity, with a kind of shy amusement, and sees what? Not fir forests, surely, for which he can have neither

'WHEN I think of my tongue being no longer alive in the mouths of men a chill goes over me that is deeper than my own death, since it is the gathered death of all my kind.'

picture nor words, or lakes, snow-peaks, a white bird's wing. The sun perhaps, our northern one, making a long path back into the dark, and the print of our feet, black tracks upon it.

Nothing is said. The men are constrained by the presence of a stranger, but also perhaps by the presence of the boss. They make only the most rudimentary attempts at talk: slow monosyllabic remarks, half-swallowed with the tea. The thread of community here is strung with a few shy words and expletives – grunts, caws, soft bursts of laughter that go back before syntax; the man no more talkative than the rest, but a presence just the same.

I feel his silence. He sits here, solid, black, sipping his tea and flicking away with his left hand at a fly that returns again and again to a spot beside his mouth; looks up so level, so much on the horizontal, under the brim of his hat.

Things centre themselves upon him – that is what I feel, it is eerie – as on the one and only repository of a name they will lose if he is no longer there to keep it in mind. He holds thus, on a loose thread, the whole circle of shabby-looking trees, the bushes with their hidden life, the infinitesimal coming and going among grassroots or on ant-trails between stones, the minds of small native creatures that come creeping to the edge of the scene and look in at us from their other lives. He gives no sign of being special. When their smoking time is up, he rises with the rest, stretches a little, spits in the palm of his hand, and goes silently to his work.

'Yes, boss, you wanna see me' – neither a statement nor a question, the only words I have heard him speak....

I must confess it. He has given me a fright. Perhaps it is only that I am cut off here from the use of my own tongue (though I have never felt such a thing on previous travels, in France, Greece, Egypt), but I find it necessary, in the privacy of my little room with its marble-topped washbasin and commodious jug and basin, and the engraving of Naomi bidding farewell to Ruth – I find it necessary, as I pace up and down on the scrubbed boards in the heat of a long December night, to go over certain words as if it were only my voice naming them in the dark that kept the loved objects solid and touchable in the light up there, on the top side of the world. (Goodness knows what sort of spells my hostess thinks I am making, or the children, who see me already as a spook, a half-comic, half-sinister wizard of the north.)

So I say softly as I curl up with the sheet over my head, or walk up and down, or stand at the window a moment before this plain that burns even at midnight: *rogn, valnøtt, spiseskje, hakke, vinglass, lysestake, krabbe, kjegle....*

OUTRAGEOUS BEHAVIOUR

MORRIS LURIE
1938–

HE had never slept in before, not ever, not once. Six mornings of the week he was gone before Moses woke up, out of the house just after seven, wearing, every day of the year, summer and winter, his gabardine coat, spotty, baggy, likewise his shapeless hat, and in his left hand his famous Gladstone bag, the sides so broken from years of flinging it to the ground that it hung down from its handle like an accordion (on the ground it was a leather puddle, with rubbed-raw patches and deep cracks and the shiny handle foolishly swimming somewhere in the middle). On the seventh day, Sunday, Moses would wake to the clatter of the lawn-mower on the lawn just outside his window, the old hand mower, on wet mornings to the high whirr of the blades spinning uselessly, the wheels locked and skidding, gouging deep scars in the grass, to sounds of puffing, grunting, a savage kick to get the wheels free, red-faced, impatient sounds, lasting rarely more than ten minutes, perhaps fifteen, the lawn an obstacle to be got over, finished, done, never mind the cruel scars, the untouched clumps, the wild, waving edges. He claimed he did it for pleasure, but the evidence was no. Or was impatience his style? Noisiness certainly was. He was noisy in the kitchen (this woke Moses up, if the lawn-mowing hadn't), banging cupboards, slamming drawers, rattling cutlery and plates. When he clapped the kettle down on to the stove it rang like a cymbal. He ate noisily too. Listen to him drinking tea! He slept sometimes on Sunday afternoons – a *drimmel*, he called it, a little dream – hunched under a plaid rug on the settee in the front room, the rug pulled up tight, almost over his head. Then he would wake up, slouch to the bathroom, wash his face – another noisy business – run his fingers through what was left of his hair, and then, hands in pockets, walk around the house, poking his nose into every room, and then outside, a slow circuit, proprietorial, proud, a landowner surveying his property, checking out that everything was in order, nodding to a neighbour, looking up at the sky. And then he made some tea. His habits, his ways. But he had never slept in before, not ever, not once, and though Moses sensed there was something wrong he didn't know what to do.

'Dad?' Moses called softly. 'Dad? Are you all right?'

Sunday morning. Ten o'clock. A hot Melbourne morning in February, going to be hotter. Moses stood in the doorway of his father's room. 'Dad?'

He was barely visible. His head had slipped down, almost off the pillow, the big European feather pillow Moses's mother had brought from Poland thirty years ago, just the top, the very top, of his head showing over the lumpy eiderdown (she had brought that too), grizzled, grey. The pillow on the other side of the bed, her pillow, was untouched. Moses's father never ventured to that side of the double bed, never encroached a centimetre, hadn't from the day Moses's mother went to hospital, a year ago. Where, twenty days ago, finally, wasted, exhausted, frail beyond belief, having lasted longer than anyone had thought

possible, the doctors, the specialists, the endless consultants – but not Moses; Moses believed nothing they said, they were just words, this was his *mother* – she had died.

Moses called again. Now his father began to sit up. 'Hey, you slept in,' Moses said, smiling foolishly, coming into the room.

There *was* something wrong. He looked dazed. His eyes were bleary, distant, not quite in focus. Moses had never seen his father like this before.

'What's the time?' his father said. 'It's late. I'll be late for work.'

There was something wrong with his voice too.

'Dad,' Moses said. 'It's Sunday. You don't go to work today.' Out came another foolish smile. 'It's Sunday,' he said again. 'You slept in.'

He looked pale, veined, his skin like antique porcelain crazed under the glaze, like the thinnest paper. His cheeks were frosted with bristles. His lips were dry. He frowned, not looking at Moses, ignoring him. He sat up properly. He pushed the eiderdown away. His feet, his white feet, touched the carpet by the side of the bed. 'Late,' he said, and then he moaned. His hand came up to his brow. 'Headache,' he said. 'Terrible headache.'

'Go back to bed, Dad,' Moses said. He heard his own voice coming out strange too, too high, too thin. 'Would you like some aspirin? I'll bring you a

cup of tea. Go back to bed. Please.'

Moses hurried to the bathroom, then to the kitchen. Aspirin. Water. The kettle on the stove. Moses spilt tea-leaves, couldn't see the milk. The kettle whistled, pluming out steam. Sugar. A spoon. He made the tea, put everything on a tray, lifted it carefully, but when he came back to the bedroom, his father had gone.

Then Moses heard the front gate banging and when he ran outside he saw that his father was already halfway down the street, wearing his gabardine coat, his shapeless hat, his accordioned Gladstone bag hanging from his customary left hand.

Mr Harris next door was washing his car, Mr Williamson in the next house was clipping his hedge, the Slaters were out, the Beatons, scrawny old Mr Thurgrove in number nine was standing in his garden in a dirty singlet with his arms crossed, squinting into the sun. Everyone was out and busy and looking and talking as Moses went down the street, eyes down, trying not to run. Someone said 'Good morning', someone called, someone waved. Moses ignored them all, his face on fire as he hurried past.

He caught up with him outside the Millers', jaunty Mrs Miller in a shiny bikini snipping at roses, the rhinestones on her sunglasses flashing. Moses put his hand gently on his father's arm. 'Where are you going, Dad?' he said. 'It's Sunday. You don't go to work today.'

His father turned and looked at him, blankly, his eyes puzled, vague, as though he had never seen Moses before. His mouth opened but no words came out.

'Come home, Dad,' Moses said softly, keeping his hand on his father's arm, turning him round, and together they walked back up the street, Moses not looking at anyone, his father not saying a word.

Moses helped his father off with his cost, his jacket, back into his pyjamas. His father pulled the eiderdown up and was asleep at once. For a full minute Moses stood and looked down at his father, hardly daring to breathe, and then he tiptoed out. In the hall he stared at the telephone, stared and stared, but how could he call the doctor, how, what could he say, just twenty days after his mother had died?

Doctor Rose said he'd come at once, be there in an hour. Moses wanted to go outside and stand in the street, but he couldn't with the neighbours there. He tiptoed to his father's doorway, saw that he hadn't moved, was still asleep, and then tiptoed away. Where? The kitchen? The front room? He went out to the garden at the back. He stared at the lawn, at the scars, at the clumps. He wondered should he mow it, it was something to do, but he thought, no, not now. He checked on his father again. Still asleep. He sat on the back step and smoked a cigarette, and then another, and finally he heard a car, and then a knock on the front door, and as he went past his father's room to let the doctor in, Moses saw that his father had once again gone.

Doctor Rose, good Family Doctor Rose, wearing a gaudy Hawaiian-type sports shirt loose outside his trousers, wearing canvas espadrilles and no socks, wearing a thoughtful frown, caressed his thick black moustache with the edge of a thumbnail and said it was flu. He said if he didn't eat anything, not to worry, that was all right. He said to give him liquids, tea, orange juice, water, but only if he asked for them. He said aspirin, maybe, but don't wake him up especially. Let him sleep, he said. The best thing was just to let him sleep. He said he'd look in again in the morning, and in the meantime not to worry.

'But he keeps getting dressed,' Moses said. 'He keeps putting on his clothes and taking his bag and going off to work. He doesn't even know it's Sunday. He doesn't seem to know anything.'

'Watch him,' Doctor Rose said.

Moses watched him. The house was still. Moses sat in the front room, in the kitchen, in his room, smoking, trying to read, just sitting, every ten minutes tiptoeing to his father's doorway and looking in. His father slept and slept. The afternoon waned. Moses wondered should he phone someone, an uncle, a family friend, to tell them what was happening, but he couldn't bring himself to pick up the telephone. He didn't, somehow, trust his voice. And what was there to tell? That his father was asleep? Why alarm everyone? The doctor said it was flu. He said to let him sleep. He said he'd be all right.

But he looked at me, Moses said to himself, and he didn't know who I was.

He didn't even know I was there.

The house, as the afternoon waned, as the sun retreated, as night began to fall, grew even stiller. The public, outside sounds – cars, hoses, mowers, people talking and laughing, children running, people walking past – gone now, replaced by private, inside sounds – Mrs Harris next door in her kitchen humming to herself as she washed up, a radio, someone's muffled TV. A door opened somewhere on an argument, and then closed again with a bang. Moses sat in the front room and felt the stillness deepening, spreading around him like ink.

Silence.

The whole past year had been silent, but in a different way, a different kind of silence. A busy silence. Hospital visits. Going there. Coming back. Silent meals. Silent thoughts. And then, suddenly, twenty days ago – nothing. Suddenly nowhere to go, nothing to do. All those things, those routines – yes, they *had* become routines – taken away. Moses and his father sat in the house, like strangers on a ship, forced into each other's company. Moses didn't know what to say. His father said nothing. Another kind of silence. A vacuum. A void.

And now this silence.

Moses stood up. Oh, for God's sake, he told himself, he's only got the flu! He snatched up his cigarettes, lit one, blew smoke. His hands, he saw, were trembling. Stop it! he told himself. He went quickly to his father's room and stood in the doorway.

'Dad?' he said.

He was awake. He was looking up at the ceiling, not moving, his brow creased. The room smelled stale, close.

'You're awake,' Moses said. 'Do you want anything? How's your headache? Do you feel better?'

His father mumbled something but Moses didn't catch what it was.

'Stay there,' Moses said. 'I'll bring you a cup of tea.'

Moses helped his father sit up. His father brought his hands out from under the eiderdown and reached for the tea. His eyes were still dazed, bleary. He took two sips, three, and then fell back on to the pillow. He mumbled something. 'What?' Moses said, leaning closer to hear. 'What did you say, Dad?'

'I want....' his father said, and then he was sick. He was violently sick, on the eiderdown, on the carpet, on Moses's hand. And then he fell back again, moaned, and closed his eyes.

Moses phoned Doctor Rose. He was there in twenty minutes, still wearing his gaudy Hawaiian-type shirt, but tucked inside his trousers now, a jacket over it. He had also put on socks. Moses's father was awake, but didn't say anything while Doctor Rose examined him, listened to his heart, looked at his eyes. 'He had some tea,' Moses said, 'but only a few sips....' Doctor Rose went past him and into the hall. 'I'll use your phone,' he said.

Moses sat with Doctor Rose in the front room, waiting for the ambulance. Moses smoked a cigarette. 'I know how you feel,' Doctor Rose said. Moses looked down at his feet.

———

It was the same hospital, the same wing. Moses was asked to sign some forms. A nurse asked if he wanted a cup of tea. Moses shook his head. He waited in a corridor. Nurses and sisters walked past quickly on the cold, squeaky floor. Twenty minutes passed, thirty. Then someone called Moses's name, and then a doctor, Moses didn't catch his name, a tall man with tired eyes, told Moses that his father had suffered a brain haemorrhage, something about pressure, impossible to do anything just at the moment, but he was comfortable, the best they could do. The doctor said to go home, get some sleep, come back in the morning. Moses asked when visiting hours were. The doctor said he could come any time.

Will he die? Will my father die? Is my father going to die? Impossible! Of course not! Don't be stupid! Moses refused to let the idea, the possibility, enter his head. Or, if it did, he pushed it immediately away.

He made himself busy. He made phone calls. He repeated, endlessly, what the doctor had told him, to uncles, cousins, family friends, everyone he could think of to call, standing in the hall at home, trying to be efficient, brisk. When he phoned Mrs Salter, an old family friend, and she began to wail, Moses tried to cut her short. 'They told me he's comfortable,' he said, and started to hang up, but she went on and on, and he couldn't. He tried not to listen, staring down at his feet, her wails and moans boring into his ear, impossible to escape, but finally she finished, and Moses, quickly, phoned someone else.

Who else? Who have I forgotten?

They were all his mother's family, the people Moses phoned, the uncles, the cousins, and the friends too, people Moses's father had never really liked, had never really had any time for, had tolerated at best, sitting uncomfortably in their houses, restless, impatient, or when they came here, the same, berating them when they had gone, mocking them, bored by them, but never to their faces, because who else was there, what else was there to do? He had no family here – his were in Israel, a brother, two sisters, cousins, a complicated family tree Moses had never been able to unravel properly and his father had never bothered to explain, a private world he kept to himself, reading their letters almost secretly, and never out loud. He had come here in the thirties, alone, intending to stay just one year, make some money, go back. Instead, lonely, friendless, a rough, wide-shouldered young man, already balding, already grey, whose pleasure was in his body – in Israel, or Palestine as it was then, he had worked in a quarry, splitting rocks in the sun, 'A beautiful life,' he told Moses over and over, 'a real life' – he married. Moses thought of getting in touch with Israel, a phone call, a cable, but he wasn't exactly sure how to go about it, whom to contact, and somehow all that seemed too dramatic. Not now. It was after midnight. Moses brushed his teeth and went to bed.

He phoned the hospital at eight the next morning and was told that his father's condition was unchanged. 'I'll be there in half an hour,' Moses said. He splashed water on to his face, didn't waste time shaving or having breakfast, ran down the street for a taxi. When he got to the hospital, hurried along endless corridors, past endless doors, and then slowed down, stopped, stepped carefully

'HE had come here in the thirties, alone, intending to stay just one year, make some money, go back.'

into the ward, he saw that overnight his father had changed.

His eyes were no longer bleary. There was colour in his cheeks. He was sitting up, or trying to. There was a nurse by the side of the bed, her hands on his shoulders, trying to get him to lie down. Moses's father was shouting at her, telling her to leave him alone. His language was coarse and obscene. Moses came slowly forward, not sure what to do.

The nurse turned and saw him. She was a small woman, in her forties, with a sharp, mousy face. 'Who are you?' she snapped at Moses.

'That's my father,' Moses said. 'I've come to see him.'

'Oh,' she said. Her face fell, but only for a second. 'Well, he's behaving *abominably*,' she said, her face hardening again. 'Dreadful man. He's upsetting everyone in the ward.'

'Dora! Dora!' Moses's father shouted. 'I'm coming! I'm getting out of this stinking place!'

'Listen to him,' the nurse said. 'I'm going to get the doctor.'

'Yes,' Moses said.

Moses advanced to the side of his father's bed. There were rails on it, like a child's cot. 'Dad,' he said softly. 'You mustn't shout. You'll only make yourself worse.'

His father ignored him, didn't even look at him. 'They can't keep me here!' he shouted to the ceiling. 'I've been here long enough! I'm coming, Dora! I'm coming!'

He fell back on to his pillows. He laughed. He shouted some dirty words. And then he began to sing. Moses stood speechless by the side of the bed. Then someone tapped him on the shoulder, and a doctor, a new doctor, asked him to step out into the corridor.

There was nothing they could do. The pressure was still there. They were waiting, hoping to take an X-ray. Something about tests. Meanwhile.... The doctor said it was all right if Moses smoked.

When Moses went back into the ward, his father was quiet again. His eyes were open, but he wasn't looking at anything. He didn't seem to know that Moses was there. Moses sat on a chair by the side of the bed. At twelve o'clock a nurse told him to go and have some lunch.

———

Now they began to arrive, the uncles, the cousins, the people Moses had phoned. Moses's father seemed delighted to see them. He sat up. He laughed. He sang. His face was very red, his eyes faded but clear.

'Ah, the fat pig!' he shouted at Moses's Uncle David. 'How are you, you thief, how's business? Don't buy from him,' he told everyone in the ward. 'He's a *ganef*! Black market. Stolen goods!' He laughed. 'Well, you're not going to steal from me,' he told Uncle David. 'You're too late. I'm going. Dora? Can you hear me? I'm on my way!'

He berated, he ridiculed, he mocked. 'Ah, the little *pisher*! he greated Moses's Uncle Abe. 'You've come just in time. He thinks he's a hot-shot,' he told the ward, 'a gambler. Ha! His whole card-playing isn't worth a *fortz!*'

Mrs Salter crept into the ward, a handkerchief to her eyes. 'The dirty tongue

'HOW are you, you thief, how's business? Don't buy from him. He's a ganef! *Black market. Stolen goods!'*

236

has come,' Moses's father said. 'Well, I don't need dirty tongues. You know what your dirty tongue can do?' He told her.

'Oi oi,' wailed Mrs Salter, 'what is he saying? He doesn't know what he is saying any more.'

Moses's father chuckled, and then he moaned. He was obviously in great pain, but he wouldn't lie down, he wouldn't stop. He seemed somehow very happy. Mrs Salter began to cry. A nurse came and asked her to leave.

'You better go too,' she said to Moses. 'Let him rest.'

'I'm all right here,' Moses said, not moving from his chair by the side of the bed.

The nurse drew the screem around the bed, sealing it off from the ward. Moses sat alone with his father. 'Dad?' he said. 'Dad?' His father stared up at the ceiling and didn't say a word.

Because I never mowed the lawn? Moses said. Because I never helped him in the garden? Is that why? Is that why he won't speak to me, or even look at me, not even once, just to see that I'm there? But he speaks to everyone else. And he hates them. Why not to me?

But it was no *pleasure* to work with him, Moses said. He never did anything properly. Bang, smash, he didn't care how anything looked. Chewing up the lawn. Weeds all over the place. And whenever I went out to straighten things up, he'd walk away. Or stand there, criticising me. 'Where's your muscles? You call that an arm? Ha! I've seen better muscles on a *chicken*!'

What did he want from me? What did he want me to be?

Like him? Did he want me to be like him? I can't. That's just not me. He's got no ambition, he never wanted to be anything. Breaking rocks in a quarry in Palestine. I can't do that.

Moses sat and stared down at his hands. And there came to him a morning a long time ago – five years ago? six? – a cold morning, close to rain. Moses and his father were chopping down a tree. It was an old tree, probably dead, or if not, certainly dying, and anyhow it was in the way. It was where they were going to put a washing line. First his father chopped, and then Moses took the axe, and in ten minutes, working together, they had it down. It was hard work and they were both in a sweat. Rain began to spit. Then Moses's mother came out and saw them both standing there, and the tree on the lawn. She looked alarmed. She always looked alarmed. 'Moses,' she cried, 'it's raining! Put on a jumper! You'll get a cold!' 'Don't worry, Mum,' Moses said, 'I'm all right.' He laughed. 'A bit of rain never hurt anyone,' he said. Then Moses's father clapped Moses on the shoulder and said, 'Not bad shoulders he's got, uh?'

'I'm sorry, Dad,' Moses said, sitting in the dark. 'I'm sorry. I'm sorry.' He felt, suddenly, that spot on his left hand where his father had been sick, where he had brought up the tea. His hand, just there, felt scraped, scalded, burnt.

Moses came every morning, stayed all day, sat and sat. There was nothing the doctors could do. He slept longer and longer, waking up to laugh and sing and shout at whoever was there. He called them thieves, liars, gluttons, and worse. His face was tight with pain. He didn't once speak to Moses, and when he happened to turn that way, his eyes were blank.

———

Six days, seven days, eight.

On the ninth day he was asleep all the time, though once or twice he moaned, softly, with almost no power or strength. The doctors still hadn't been able to do anything. A nurse brought Moses a cup of tea. It grew cold on the floor by his feet.

At eight o'clock on the tenth morning Moses came into the ward and saw his father lying curled on one side, his eyes squeezed tight. Moses sat down beside him. The ward was very quiet. His father looked as though he was trying to push something out of his way, a massive boulder, a gigantic rock. He was pushing with every part of his face. His cheeks blossomed with thin red veins, a network, a map. He was like that for an hour, exactly the same, straining and pushing, but never once moving, and then his eyes came open a fraction. A nurse came in and very softly began to draw the screens around the bed.

In the corridor a doctor, a very young doctor, his stethoscope poking out of the pocket of his crisp, white jacket like a badge to an exclusive club, put his hand on Moses' shoulder and said he was very, very sorry. He asked Moses would he like to sit down quietly for a while. Moses shook his head.

Outside, on the steps, the trees across the road moving like smoke, Moses saw someone hurrying towards him. It was Mrs Salter. She was carrying, in one hand, a large black handbag, an enormous thing, and in the other a string bag filled with fruit. She saw Moses and her eyes turned instantly weepy and wet.

'What's happened?' she said. Moses didn't say anything. 'Oi oi,' wailed Mrs Salter, fussing for something in her handbag. 'Why didn't you phone me?' Out came a handkerchief. 'He's gone, he's gone, such a beautiful man,' she wailed. 'When will we see such a beautiful man again?' She dabbed at her eyes, her nose, but looking at Moses all the time. 'And what will happen to you now, a boy, all alone in the world? Oi oi.' Her hand took hold of the lapel of Moses' jacket. 'But why didn't you phone me, tell me, so someone could be with him there? From the family?'

Moses stared at Mrs Salter's face. He stared at her crabbed mouth, at her pinched, hard eyes, her sudden tears. Her hand on his lapel felt like a claw. He felt something rising inside him. He felt himself swelling and trembling. He saw himself pushing Mrs Salter, savagely, flinging her aside, her string bag of fruit flying down the steps, and her vile black handbag, and Mrs Salter too, her falsely snivelling face, her deceitful eyes, down the steps she crashed. He saw himself shouting at her as she fell. 'Hypocrite! Dirty mouth! Liar! Filth!'

And then he felt on his hand that spot where his father had been sick, that scald, that burn, that chastisement he knew then he would feel for ever.

His eyes fell. 'Excuse me,' he said to Mrs Salter, or maybe he didn't even say that. He went past her, his eyes on fire but not with tears – they would come later, when he was alone, when there was no one to see. Eyes lowered, he walked quickly away, down the steps.

MOTEL MIDNIGHT

FRANK
MOORHOUSE
1938–

As I sat there up on the stage my mind was gnawed by the possibility that something would interfere with and thwart my getting to bed with Julia who was sitting out there in the auditorium surrounded by an audience made up heavily of men without women.

When Markham got up to open attack on my paper, I found that my vulnerability had gone away. The stockade I'd built of inner preparation and outer preparation to meet public assault now faced the wrong way. I sent the soldiers home. I had said my piece and my anxieties were gnawing on Julia.

Markham went to the microphone with a stagey jauntiness. He was an experienced academic lecturer but the conference world was another place. The jauntiness was an attempt to meet it. Trying not to be too academic but not wanting the audience to forget his status, a performer but not a clown.

He used a quotation from Johnson, 'My old mate Sam', adding, 'not, of course, our old mate Ben', which got an uncertain, generous laugh from the auditorium who'd probably long forgotten which was which, if they'd ever known.

The educator trying to lightly teach.

He said that I could 'cut a colossus from a rock; but could not carve heads upon cherry stones'. Which I took to mean that my general line was sound but that I handled some sub-arguments badly. Or that I went for the Grand Hypothesis when I should have worried about smaller questions, or detail. But essentially, the quotation was dragged in by its scruff.

He said he would now go on to 'pick some nits'. Why does that phrase tickle so many academics?

He adopted a Reformer position against my 'pluralism of the system'. I wanted many channels of media, many radio stations, TV channels, and journals servicing beliefs, sub-cultures, communities and so on. He argued for mainstream media – few central channels, newspapers – but carrying extended diversity. He saw this as a forced feeding into the mainstream of society a diversity of ideas – preventing what he saw as the hiving off of society into cultural ghettoes.

As he spoke I saw something about my position that I had not before realised.

I was a pluralistic conservative. I wanted a recognition of the existing, and developing, diversity and an arrangement of media to service them. This would reinforce the prevailing situation. I saw that Markham, and other reformers, wanted a competing pluralism – but only to permit the emergence of a superior single set of values and ideology. Theirs. They wanted eventually a unified society, unified their way.

Maybe the difference was that I had no long-range picture, no world vision.

I hadn't seen myself like that before.

During the open discussion there were no attacks. There were the few dec-

'*MAYBE the difference was that I had no long-range picture, no world vision I hadn't seen myself like that before.*'

larations of heartfelt concerns.

A woman stood up and made a women's movement declaration and it was inept. The women's movement analysis had moved a long way and this woman hadn't kept up. She was still 'conspiring in a male reality'.

I noted myself making allowances for this woman – the contemporary 'difficulties' of women. It was an unpalatable and unmentionable fact that women through conditioning, which they have so thoroughly analysed themselves, function poorly in some situations. Not only male situations. And not all women. But it is only by accident of upbringing (accident of temperament, oddball parents, say) that some women have escaped the pernicious effects of female conditioning. There is an awkwardness which comes, too, from the woman recognising the conditioned limitations. Functioning is impaired when the woman works against the conditioned personality and tries to supplant it with a liberated model.

All this, then, sometimes produces an artificial relationship where the man treats the woman 'as a theoretical equal' while not feeling it. Where the man tries not to let the woman's conditioning, or personal limitation, shape his reaction to her. He behaves with ideological correctness.

At the end of the session Markham leant over and said, 'Hope I wasn't too rugged.'

I mumbled something about its not being the first time I'd been compared with Milton.

I moved away quickly towards Julia through the crowd, stopped on the way by people who wanted to take things up. Julia seemed to be for ever across the foyer as I tried to keep my mind on the things people were saying to me.

Maybe the impulsiveness on both our parts to have dinner had been replaced by second thoughts and she would say that 'maybe it wouldn't be a good thing'.

At last I reached her.

'Still interested in dinner?'

The old euphemism.

'Of course, aren't you?'

We avoided the bar bistro of the motel where a lot of us were staying and found a cafe unknown to both of us. We tried to do an assessment of it from the outside – did it have a specialised menu, as against the 'international and Australian cuisine', did it have tableclothes, did it have its own decor or instant decor, did its name imply its aspirations, was it 'trying'?

The cafe, we agreed, passed our tests and we went in. But the meal was poor. The dinner was best described as two bottles of wine with food.

As we walked back to the motel Julia commented on how much salt I used.

'You're not becoming a food freak, are you?' I said.

'No – but I think a lot of our problems come from too much salt.'

I didn't take up the subject.

At the lift door I said, with all the gaucheness I was out to avoid, 'Your room or mine – as they say in *Playboy*?'

'You know, *Playboy* was quite good about equality – it doesn't deserve its bad name,' Julia said. 'My room – my cigarettes are there.'

I think we were both drawing on leftover intimacy of the affair we'd had a couple of years earlier. We needed, or at least I did, some of the intimacy, the familiarity anyhow, to get relief from the fatiguing unfamiliarity of everything around us.

We were pleased to find in bed that there was some of the intimacy left, and we were able to relax each other. The sex itself, though, was more caressing than passionate. In the after-sex rambling and candour, we talked about earlier times. We had worked together once on the same magazine.

Julia lay there with her inevitable cigarette, I with a drink, in the after-sex aroma.

It was all broken by a burst of knocking at the door.

Julia's inclination was to ignore it. She lay there smoking, but the knocking went on. A telephone or knock at the door in a strange city is usually irresistible. She may have guessed who was knocking. But then she got up abruptly and put on a robe, calling out 'Hold on', and going to the door. I was concealed from the sight-line of the door in the other arm of the L-shaped room. I knew, though, the voice.

It was Newell Smith, who was something of a current escort of Julia's. He liked women journalists.

After some exchange with a reference to 'an understanding', Newell Smith's voice became quite formal and said good night in a very correct voice which, given the circumstances, was also a miffed voice.

She came back and grimaced, a little embarrassed, and said, 'Newell Smith.' Or was it a boasting flush she had? I-am-rather-popular.

'The old bull.'

I deflected an unworthy, self-congratulatory feeling of having 'beaten' another man to a woman. The feeling did, however, cross over me.

'He likes lady journalists,' I said, unnecessarily diminishing Newell Smith.

'Don't I know it.'

'There should be conference ladies,' I said, 'but professional ladies probably think intellectual conferences aren't interested. Only businessmen.'

'... and conference studs for us girls,' Julia amended.

We resumed talking, resting more on old times than on intimacy. She made remarks about trying to get some 'stability' into her life and about being now a more 'purposeful' person. I thought she was trying to establish that she did control her life – to escape the suggestion that she depended on the chance of midnight callers.

'I have a proposition,' she said, as she went about making instant tea.

'Yes?'

'I don't want to live with a man – I've been through all that – but you and I – we might be able to come to an arrangement – we're the same age ... we get along....'

'An arrangement?' I was dozy and boozed.

'Maybe we could see each other once a week, say – if this appeals to you – say for a movie or meal. Nothing heavy.'

I pulled myself out of my doziness, Julia was being serious about her life.

She added, 'It's just nice sometimes to wake up with a warm body.'

It was nicely offered, and it could, in a way, have been feasible.

She knew my scene back home. It wasn't a competitive strike. No, it was a nice offer.

I said, 'The proposition is very attractive ... but ....'

'... but ...' she said, 'the nasty *but*.'

'No, not like that. You know what it is – I don't think I have enough room in my life. I really find it hard to just get time alone in my life. I know it might sound, well, as if I'm flaunting 'a rich, full life'. But I don't mean it like that.'

'If you've got it, baby, flaunt it,' she broke in, joking, but a little cutting.

'I just don't think I have the energy for ... new situations ... except for a passing night ... a conference. There are physical limits too'—I laughed—'as we get older.'

Until that conversation I hadn't thought of having a life that was 'full up'. I realised that I did have to think before I tried to fit new people into my life. I supposed it was a problem of a life which had shaped up.

'In a way I know what you mean,' she said, bringing the tea. 'I think I made the suggestion to you because, because you're not new.' She leant over and lightly kissed me. 'We wouldn't have to go through a questionnaire about each other. Well, if you ever have a vacancy let me know.'

I kissed her shoulder.

I began to think of going back to my own room to sleep. Our intimacy might be just too small to sustain a night; and with the inevitable sobering up, without wine, the morning could be just irritable good manners. I also felt that if I stayed it would be for the wrong reason. I'd be 'compensating' for having rejected the proposal rather than staying for good old honest desire.

I was thinking of saying something like this when the door knocking began again.

I thought – Newell Smith has come back to plead his case again.

What would happen if I'd already gone?

Putting on her robe, this time irritated and embarrassed, she went to the door.

This time it was also a voice I knew. Not Newell Smith. It was Easton, the visiting American lecturer who'd been the cause of the demonstration earlier that day.

She called him by his first name – 'Jerry'.

'I'm sorry, Jerry,' she said, and then to halt his entry, 'Jerry, I'm in bed.'

He suggested that he himself was ready for bed, her bed. 'One hell of a day.' The tone was full of confident, pushing expectation.

I hadn't even realised that she knew Easton, except from a dinner party on the first night, and then they'd seemed like newly met acquaintances.

Odd.

He persisted and then went away with more good grace than Newell Smith.

All very odd.

She returned, blushing. 'I guess you heard that.'

'I didn't know you knew him.'

'I met him in the States last year.'

'You've known him *that* long?'

'Remember, I went over on a State Department grant – a few journalists had them.'

I turned it all over in my mind.

'Is there anything in it – about him being CIA?' I asked, pondering.

'That's all nonsense,' she said. 'He's travelling on his own pocket – he's what's known as a voluntary speaker. He just offers his services around.'

'You don't think he's CIA then?' I repeated, although the question had a foolish insistence.

'No – he's a political innocent. Really,' she said, agitated, either by the questions or by the complications of the night.

'It's a randy time of night,' I said.

'Anyhow what's your interest in Chile and all this?' she asked aggressively, walking about, agitated, smoking.

Chile? Had I mentioned Chile? No.

'Well an interest in the first socialist government freely elected that tried to maintain free speech and personal freedom,' I said.

A formula answer. She snorted.

I dressed and she didn't ask me to stay the night, which relieved me.

We said an affectionate good night, but there had been an unpleasant, skidding return to sobriety brought about by it all.

As I walked down the motel corridor I thought first about the limitations I had realised in my life. I had passed from the time of unknown capacity, of undrawn boundaries, of boundless possibilities – to knowing, generally, what was possible in my life. I was shaping up to being *staid*. I didn't welcome it: I didn't regret it. It was just a fact of life. A fact of my life.

About Easton I was suspicious. I recalled that Julia had sent articles back on Chile but they'd been straight up and down – as I remember. About Allende, the overthrow and the aftermath.

It was all too late at night.

But I wasn't too preoccupied or boozed to forget to take down my breakfast order.

THE SPIDER

GEORGIA
SAVAGE

19 —

BETWEEN Brook's death and the time I reconciled myself to it there were terrible days to get through. Some were worse than others but the day his ashes arrived from the crematorium and the day I went to the compensation hearing in Melbourne were the worst of the lot.

I collected his ashes in Gorrangher at the sweet little red-brick post office where roses hang over the fence. Inside, the man who handed me the parcel was so embarrassed he couldn't look at me. While I was signing for it he kept his eyes firmly on the wall behind my head.

The ashes were in a grey plastic box. I put it on the front seat of the car and drove to the place in the bush where I'd decided Brook would like to be. Apart from the box I was alone and it was a weird feeling having it beside me. Brook was 185 cm, the box was no more than 20 cm. I felt as if I'd somehow got into a science fiction story and that if I spoke to the box it would answer me in an electronically controlled voice.

I didn't drive all the way to the place where I meant to leave the ashes. For some reason it seemed to me that it would be disrespectful to Brook to arrive there by car, so I got out and walked the last couple of kilometres into the bush. I had the box in one hand and a hammer in the other.

It took me a long time to get the box open. The plastic was made to last. I managed in the end and I scattered the ashes in the bush in a place where I thought I wouldn't mind being myself. It was among ironbark trees on the top of a rise with a view of the mountains in the east. The day was hot and I couldn't hear any birds but I knew they'd be there. I knew there'd be kangaroos, too, in the evenings.

People have told me since that you don't get the right person's ashes; that at the crematorium they put all the ashes in a pile and fill the plastic boxes with a shovel so that you get a mixture. Perhaps that's true. It makes sense. I don't think it matters much. At the time I was sure the ashes were Brook's and I did the best with them I could.

I go now and then to the place where I put them and I always feel that it's a good place to be. With the tall trees and the sudden whipping cry of birds it seems to me to have the essence of the land which Brook loved perhaps more than he loved anything else.

I should be able to tell how I felt while I was scattering the ashes in the bush that day but I can't. The point is that I didn't feel anything at all. Some things which happen to you are so bad that you cross a threshold and come out into a wasteland where there is nothing. That feeling of nothing is the worst feeling of all. I knew, though, that life would never be as bad again. In theory, at least, I'd able to meet anything front-on and not give a damn. That was almost true but not quite for, after that day, it took me a long time to learn to sleep quietly at night.

I thought the day of the compensation hearing would be one of the occasions when I'd be able to meet things front-on. I wasn't stupid enough to think it would be pleasant. I knew it wouldn't be. When I'd done the business with Brook's ashes at least I'd done it in private. The hearing would be in public and I'd already learnt how inquisitive people are about grief. More than that, I'd learnt that there are people who enjoy watching it. I decided the only way to handle the day would be to shut myself off and act the part of a woman who'd been widowed too early.

Up till that day I fancied myself as an actress. When I was a child I didn't expect to be anything but an actress. Once, when I was home from school with the mumps, Irene, my mother, who was a film fiend, dragged me off to a matinee of *Anthony Adverse*. She wound a woollen school scarf around my neck, dosed me with Aspros and took me there on the tram. I don't know whether I fainted or what but the only thing I remember of the film is the gouty duke's young wife slipping out of the chateau to meet her lover. She wore a crinoline with a cape over it and her lover was dressed in what I thought were highwayman's clothes. They met beneath a huge tree and fell into each other's arms. I had no idea what lovers did after they'd kissed. As a child I was particularly naive about sex. I suppose I thought they collapsed into the sweet grass and swooned with bliss.

Anyway, when I got over the mumps, I spent a lot of time acting out the scene from the film. I used to deck myself in one of Irene's evening dresses and a postman's blue serge cape which had somehow found its way into our laundry, then I'd rush into the garden and swoon as I met my lover. We didn't have the right kind of tree in our garden so I made do with the bougainvillea.

Irene told me that in the film the lover in the highwayman's clothes was run through with a sword by the duke so, whenever I was tired of swooning with bliss, I acted out his death. It sounds as if I'm trying to be funny but when I was a kid I acted out those scenes with great seriousness and in the weeks leading up to the court case I was crazy enough to believe that all the rehearsing in childhood would help me through the real thing.

Brook was an engineer who worked for an American construction company. They were building bridges across the big irrigation channels in the Maryston Valley. The day Brook died someone had left a live electric lead on the ground and someone else had rolled a steel drum on to it. When Brook went on duty he grabbed the drum to move it out of the way and died as soon as he touched it.

His union had an inspector from the city at the site within two hours. He took statements from all of Brook's work mates and then came to our house to tell me that the union would arrange and pay for a case against the construction company.

I had one meeting with my solicitor before the day of the case. He was a young Italian with a handsome, pitted face and cynical eyes. We met again in the foyer of the court building in Melbourne and before the lift shot us skywards he told me Brook's employers had admitted liability and that the case wouldn't be defended.

The building was one of those windowless, air-conditioned places so high you feel you'll be on the moon when you reach the top. In fact it was much as I've always imagined the headquarters of the CIA would be like in Washington – muted voices, people scurrying about with files and, hanging over everything, an air of secrecy. On our way to the briefing room we passed several groups of people and in each group there was an injured person, either bandaged or in a wheelchair. They looked as if they'd just returned from a hopeless mission. I remember thinking that in my borrowed clothes and with my world-weary escort I probably looked like a spy too.

For half an hour Frank and I sat in a tiny airless room, making embarrassed conversation while more of the wounded limped past the door. And that's where my acting career ended. The next part of the day is a blank. It must have been bad for, no matter how hard I've tried, no matter how long I've spent in willing myself to remember, not one incident of the courtroom experience returns to me. I don't even remember going into the courtroom, let alone remember what happened while we were there. I know I was the only woman present but I'd have to undergo hypnosis to remember anything else.

When my mind started working again I was on another level of the building and talking to the registrar of the compensation board. He was telling me it was not his custom to see people immediately after a case but that as I'd travelled a distance of 200 kilometres he'd decided to grant me an interview. Then he asked me what assets I had.

I asked him what he meant.

He must have thought I was trying to be funny because his jaw muscles tightened and he said: 'I'm trying to determine your financial position. Unless we can manage to do that today, you'll have to come back some other time. The court has awarded you the full amount of compensation to which Victorian law entitles you. You've been awarded $13,600 but before we can advance any of it to you, we must determine your financial position.'

I thought to myself that the sum of $13,600 was an incredibly small one in return for all the things Brook had been. Four hundred million might have been nearer the mark. I sat thinking about it for a long time and in the end I worked out that, as the man who'd presided over the court had no way of knowing what Brook was worth to me, I had no right to hold the paucity of the sum against him.

The registrar was still speaking. He was saying: 'Of course we don't give you the money. We hold it in trust and if you need part of it you make application either by letter or by phone and the board considers your request.'

I said, 'I beg you pardon?'

By then the registrar had decided he was dealing with an idiot. Patiently he explained that widows awarded compensation weren't allowed to handle the money in case they blew it on some doe-eyed fag. He didn't use those words but that's what he meant.

I was appalled. I'd imagined myself going back down in the life with the full $400 million hanging out of my pockets.

When I didn't speak the registrar said: 'Of course it's a very old law. One day it'll be changed. But in some ways it works in your favour. When you're old enough to get the widow's pension, the moneys held in trust by us won't be taken into consideration and when you remarry....'

'I was appalled. I'd imagined myself going back down in the life with the full $400 million hanging out of my pockets.'

I cut him off by saying, 'I won't be remarrying.'

He smiled and his face was flooded with Father-Knows-Best condescension. I knew he was about to tell me that of course I'd remarry and I knew there was no point in telling him that I wouldn't; that when I'd married Brook I'd married him for good. So instead I said: 'Your name's Butterfield, isn't it?'

He nodded. 'Yes, Thomas Butterfield.'

'The man who married us was called Butterfield too. That's funny, isn't it?'

I'd embarrassed him and he concentrated on the pile of forms lying on his blotter, so I told him quickly that my assets were a small weatherboard cottage in Gorrangher and a 10-year-old car. I told him how much money I had left in the bank and then I stood up, said 'Goodbye' and went out of his office.

Frank was waiting outside for me so we went to a pub near the court and had a beer and a sandwich. When we were sitting down I told him how I'd expected to leave the court with my pockets bulging with dollar bills.

He tried to find something sympathetic to say. 'You'll marry again, you know.'

Instead of arguing with him I asked what had happened inside the court-room.

For a moment he didn't know what I meant and when he'd worked it out he said, 'Was it as bad as that?' I knew he didn't expect me to answer so I waited and he went on. 'We were only there a short time. The judge asked you if you could prove you were Brook's wife. You said "Yes" and handed the clerk of the court your marriage certificate. Then the judge asked you if you were, to your knowledge, Brook's only dependent. You said you were.

'The young bloke who was representing Brook's employers stood up and told the court they admitted liability and didn't wish to defend the case and the judge said you were entitled to full cmpensation.'

I said: 'If I were a man and I'd been awarded compensation for an injury, would they have given me the money or held it in trust?'

'You'd have got the money.'

'A bit archaic, isn't it?'

'Yes, but remember that if you were a man whose wife had been killed at work you'd have got nothing.'

'That's even more archaic.'

He smiled. 'So don't bitch, eh?'

'Well, not at you,' I said, and turned the talk to other things.

On the way back to Gorrangher that evening the train was full of soldiers travelling to Puckapunyal. None of them looked to me to be more than 12 years old. The one sitting next to me was a bit pissed. He kept asking me if I'd get out at Seymour with him and go to a dance.

I told him I was married, but he looked so much like Potsie in the television show *Happy Days* that I felt I knew him and, as I spoke, I couldn't help laughing.

He waggled a finger at me and said, 'Now don't tell lies. You're not married. I know.'

I asked him how he knew.

'Because the bloke who put you on the train at Spencer Street wasn't your husband.'

'How do you know that?'

'I could tell by the way he was looking at you.'

There was silence in the carriage as his mates waited to see what I'd say. They'd all stopped drinking to listen.

'No. He was my solicitor.'

The boy beamed. 'Then you're getting a divorce?'

'Something like that.'

'So you can come to the dance with me.'

'I can't, y'know.'

'Why not?'

'Because if I do, you'll be named as co-respondent.'

He leant back, nursed his beer can and tried to work out how much truth there was in my words. In the end the problem was too much for him and he said, 'Vinnie, I *like* you.'

Someone passed me a can and I started drinking too. My friend in the next seat didn't take his eyes off me and every so often he interrupted the conversation to ask again if I'd go to the dance. Finally I agreed to dance with him in the corridor of the train.

Pissed or not, he danced like an angel. I'd expected that we would lurch around in the corridor like disco dancers, shooting our hips and looking cool. But it wasn't like that at all. As soon as were in the corridor he took me in his arms and, humming an Aznavour song, began to waltz. His body was young and boneless. He seemed scarcely to be holding me at all but we melted together and danced as if we'd been dancing together all our lives. Neither the movement of the train nor its noise bothered Neil. He was a boy who could have done a breathtaking tango in a row-boat.

It seemed that we danced for hours. We danced together so easily that in the end he stopped humming and we just danced. We used the open doorways of carriages for turns and sometimes we danced into carriages and out again. Each time we did that we were greeted by a cheer which came over us and vanished. I heard my skirt seam rip at the knee and danced on.

In the end, exhausted, I leant against the window and Neil, still holding me, leant against me.

'Where did you learn to dance?' I gasped.

He said, 'Where did you?' – and he wasn't even out of breath.

'At school. Dancing school. I wanted to go on the stage.'

'I learnt at home with Mum. We used to dance every Friday and Saturday night. We had a lot of old records and a wind-up gramophone.' As an afterthought he added, 'My Dad's a cripple.'

I was still out of breath. The train whistled. I knew that we were close to Seymour. I moved my head to look out the window but Neil stopped me by kissing me. It was a sweet, young and, to me, sexless kiss but it went on for so long there in the rocking corridor that I suppose he came in his army underpants.

The train slowed. People began to push past us. Neil put his chin on the top of my head and, still holding me, said, 'Will you come down to Seymour and

'WE danced together so easily that in the end he stopped humming and we just danced. We used the open doorways of carriages for turns and sometimes we danced into carriages and out again.'

dance with me?'

Knowing I never would, I said 'Yes' and he let go of me and rushed back to the carriage for his beret and bag.

The evening train stops at Seymour for 20 minutes so I got out with Neil and stood watching him as he went towards the gate with his mates. The rest of the crowd rushed to the cafeteria for tea and railway cake. At the archway he turned and saluted me, then he was gone.

It was dark by the time we pulled into Gorrangher. I'd tried to sleep after leaving Seymour but too many images chased themselves through my head and I hadn't been able to.

My friend Hannibal met me. She had a funny look on her face as if she couldn't make up her mind whether the moment called for laughter or for tears.

Instead of hullo I said, 'What's wrong?'

'When the train whistled, I was buying petrol. I backed out in a hurry and hit the bowser behind me. The side of my car's smashed in.'

'Are you hurt?'

'No. I hit the passenger side.'

Looking at her I realised she'd spent the evening blow-waving her hair and decorating her face so she'd look her best when I got off the train. We stood together on the bleak little railway platform with the battered VW on the other side of the wire fence and I remembered the time when she was eight years old and had looked out the east window of my house and said, 'I love the railway station at night. I like the lights. They look exciting.'

Exciting, for Christ's sake. The lights! There were five of them.

To find her waiting for me with what looked like an entire jar of Vegemite on her eyelashes repaid me for a lot of the things that had happened that day. I wanted to tell her so, but instead I hit her softly with my bag and said, 'It's like a movie, isn't it? Court cases, railway stations, smashed-up cars.' Hannibal loved movies more than anything in the world. All the time when her mother was at work and thought Hannibal was at school she was home instead watching old movies on television.

She laughed then and said, 'You're a fool, Vinnie.' But I knew she felt better and we went to her car and both crawled in through the driver's door.

As she started the engine, Hannibal sniffed and said, 'You smell of beer.'

I told her about the soldiers on the train and how one had asked me to dance with him.

We were already travelling on the dirt road towards my place but Hannibal turned to gape at me. When she was a fat little girl no one wanted much, Brooke treated her like Grace Kelly and she loved him. She meant to go on loving him, I'm sure, for the rest of her life.

While she was gaping at me we hit the railway track where it crossed the road. It took her a few moments to get the VW under control. When she did she said, 'You kissed him, didn't you?'

It was my turn to gape. 'How did you know?'

'You kiss everybody. When you get pissed, you'd kiss a horse.'

'Oh come on, for Christ's sake. I don't *know* anyone, let alone kiss them.'

'You find them.'

'WHEN she was a fat little girl no one wanted much, Brooke treated her like Grace Kelly and she loved him. She meant to go on loving him, I'm sure, for the rest of her life.'

'I guess I'm one of the Great Kissers of the World,' I said, referring to an old joke of ours.

She didn't answer and I said, 'It wasn't anything. He was only a kid. If you want to know, it was like kissing Christopher Robin.'

She took the corner near my house as if she were leading the field at Le Mans. The car lights picked up my dog waiting at the gate. As we shot towards her she leapt for her life, then we flew into the drive and skidded to a halt under the pergola.

Hannibal cut the motor and switched off the lights. 'Listen,' I said, 'sometimes things get out of hand. Today was like that.'

She thought about it while Billie scrabbled at the door. Finally she said, 'Okay, but I don't want to talk about it' and got out of the car.

As I climbed out through the driver's door, Billie grabbed my bag and ran into the orchard with it. Hannibal chased her and in a second they'd both vanished in the dark.

I went alone into the house. I turned on the light in the back hall and the first thing I saw was a huntsman spider clinging to the Chinese wall-hanging; right in the centre of it, as if he'd been embroidered there. He was the biggest spider I'd seen and must have spanned 15 cm. He was a soft cocoa colour with a paler head and his eyes were black.

I went close and stared at him. He watched me. I knew he was thinking 'Friend or foe?' and that his legs which could run at 100 kilometres an hour were ready to move.

Before he knew what I was doing, I'd snatched off my shoe and hit him. He fell on his back on the floor with most of his legs already folded on his belly. One leg remained out straight. The leg twitched twice and I thought, 'God, he's going to die slowly. I'll have to hit him again.' But with what seemed to me exquisite grace he folded the leg so that it formed a pattern with the others on his belly. Then he was still.

I was horrified at what I'd done. I stooped and picked him up in my hand. In death he was tiny, made of velvet like some exotic seed pod. I wanted him to be alive again and fast and menacing.

Without warning the dam inside me broke. The tears I hadn't cried when Brook died came and I cried as I'd never cried in my life before. And Hannibal came in and stood beside me and didn't know what to do.

MURRAY BAIL
1941–

BREAKING into light, this long silver bus. It comes rumbling from its concrete pen. Grunting away. It reaches North Terrace by stopping and yawning; its full length swings.

Yawns left, climbs past Rosella, hesitates at Maid 'n Magpie, take the left, roads are empty, petrol stations are empty, car yards are empty, shops are empty, hold her steady, chassis doesn't pitch then, there are couples behind curtains, there's a dog, watch him, man on a bike, shiftworker in a coat probably. Now the road's stirring, milkman turns a corner, leaves the road open, driver taps the steering wheel rim, enormous view of life in the morning, foot taps contented by it.

The bus had PARADISE printed on the front, sides and back. It was a long run to the suburb. At the outer reaches it specialised in young married women with prams; and Merv Hector had to smile. From his position in the driving seat he could see the new generation hair-dos, skirts, worried eyebrows. Gentle, slow-eyed Hector waited for them, was happy to be of service. When one of them waved between stops he would stop the great silver machine every time. His conductors were quick to see they were riding with a soft heart. Straightforward characters, they were quick to assert themselves. 'Be an angel, Merv. Stop at the shops there for some smokes.' They also went to him when sick of things.

This time his conductor was Ron. His voice, tightly pitched. 'Getting up at this hour really makes me wonder. We're not carrying a soul. Look, it really makes me sick.'

Merv shook his head. Through the pure windscreen the road was alive ahead of him. Below his feet the bus was really travelling. It made you feel alive.

'There's the people we get on the way back,' Merv said.

He made a long sentence of it, as he did when contented, and heard Ron's breath come out dissatisfied.

'There's too bloody many then. We should have two here serving then. All the school kids; they never have to pay properly. What time is it?'

They were entering Paradise. As usual Hector waited to be thrilled by it, he stared and was ready, but a disappointment spread like the morning shadows. Streets were golden but it seemed more like a finishing sunset than the beginning of a day. When he stopped the bus it seemed to be further away – Paradise did. New tiles pointing in the sky spoilt the purity. But Paradise could be close by. It felt close by. The air light, bright; he was at the edge of something. Hector's stubborn fifty-four-year-old eyesight produced these messages for his heart but he was required to turn the bus, and he turned the bus around.

'Hell, we're going to really get hot and crowded.'

It was Ron running his finger around his collar.

'She'll be right,' said Hector.

'Hang on a sec. Let us out at the shop. You want some chewy?'

Stopped. Merv Hector was mild cheese from Norwood. At the MTT he was considered slow and forgetful. But he was dependable enough, and voiced no objections to the long early morning runs. His moon wife was stupefied by his sincerity. He was older. Their garden grew weeds. His watch was inaccurate, and he stumbled near the garden. 'Dear?' he sometimes said to Enid and faded out. The distance to Paradise, with the great screen framing all kinds of life, gave him this gentle advice: move, slow down, stop, let them get on, move, see, Paradise. The world was beautiful. It was plainly visible.

'THE distance to Paradise, with the great screen framing all kinds of life, gave him this gentle advice: move, slow down, stop, let them get on, move, see, Paradise.'

Now Ron said something again.

'Look at all the bloody kids. Just what I need. All right! Move down the back!'

The bus grew squatter and fatter with the weight of everybody. Ron battled through, and the air was hot and human. They were now channelled by houses near the city, yet it was confusing.

A green bread van turned while Merv wondered. The shape was smacked by the metal at Merv's feet and the whole green turned over and over like a dying insect, a round pole came zooming forward, Hector's world entered it and splintered. Glass splattered. A crying uniform over Hector's shoulder cracked the windscreen.

There was the crash, Hector remembered. And the memory of Paradise persisted. If there was a beautiful place he could watch for like that.

He was wrinkling and gave a twitch.

He found other work.

'Morning.'

'Morning. Six, thanks.'

'Six, and?'

'Eight.'

'Right there.'

'Two for me.'

'Back a bit, sir. Up we go.'

Inside a driver's uniform again. They hold their breaths and stare at lights blinking. 4,5, feel the altitude moving below the toes, 6, blink, blink, 7,8, turn the lever, doors further up: whrrp! abrupt stop, men breathe into ears, business face veins, Windsor knots left-right-centre. Right this little lift will help, reach the top, an essential task in the latest glass architecture.

I'll go to Heaven.

Merv Hector settled on his stool in the lift. Shuffling and throat-clearing squashed the space into a noise box. Like the run to Paradise, he was at the entrance with a mild face, helping them: they stepped out at certain vertical intervals, sped down horizontal tunnels for special meetings. These repetitions gave him the most gentle pleasure. He was in the centre of activity and happily assisting. His placid role in giving this regular service, regular service, settled his features.

In the mornings a lemon-headed man unlocked the building and the lifts.

'How are you today?'

'What are you this early for?' the caretaker answered.

'Well –' Hector began.

The caretaker cut him off. 'If the others come here late, you've got to get here at this hour.'

'It's a good building you've got,' Hector suggested, in all seriousness.

'What's good about it? You don't have to live in it.'

And Hector had to take some keys to him one morning right up to the eighteenth floor. He was touched by the high silence. Outside the wind scratched at the glass. Inside currents of cold air tugged at his sleeve like the mysterious breathing of a giant snowman. It was some height, near the clouds. God. Hector marvelled. His veins, his eyes seemed to be swelling. Was this pleasure? It must be nearer to heaven, or Paradise, up there.

'What's your trouble?'

The caretaker came up behind.

'Give us the keys, and scoot. They're buzzing you.'

Merv ran back to the lift.

'Is it all right if I bring my lunch on the roof?' he called out.

'Christ Almighty!' the watchman said.

Why, the roof was high. It was peaceful. He could watch noises made by the street-people below. And clouds closed in; could almost touch me. And someone had placed pot-plants along the edge, and wind trembled their green. Did the lonely caretaker put them there? The slow question gently surrounded him with pleasure, and near the clouds he chewed on Enid's sandwiches.

The lift was always crowded. He kept going up down, up down, all day. Now he preferred going up to down. Going down it was back to the street, hot and old. So he kept going up, and late one morning kept going, kept going, and wondering, crashed into the ceiling. Roof hit roof – or there were springs to stop him. But it was enough to jump him off the stool, and the caretaker arrived.

'No one's ever done that before, you bloody fool.'

'Strike,' said Hector.

He was dazed.

Merv Hector continued. His hour on the roof was something to look forward to. I'm very near it, he said in the silence. Full of pretty, dazed visions he slept past two, and was immediately fired by the caretaker.

'Even if you come here early,' said the caretaker, signalling up and down with his arm. 'Useless, useless.'

Hair on Hector's head looked electrocuted. It was fifty-four-year-old stuff flaking and greying: always looked as if he had left a speedboat. He wore brown eye-glasses. Sometimes he touched his lips with his fingers vibrating, exactly as though they played a mouth organ.

Home with Enid she carried on a bit.

But she noticed something. He had been weeding the garden. One finger was cut by a buried piece of china – a broken pre-war saucer of some description – and self-pity moved him to silence. He seemed to dry up. More or less alone, he shaved vaguely. He didn't say much.

He was not his cheery self, she said.

'Why don't you get another job, dear? We can settle down after.'

Hector agreed.

'You sit there,' the young man pointed. 'The phone goes, write down what they say. Just sit here. The Bureau rings about every half-hour. Arrange the switches like so. You can make any words they tell you. At the moment it's RAIN DEVELOPING.'

Hector looked through the tiny window, looked across the wall of the building and there, in enormous lights, were the words RAIN DEVELOPING.

'If we had an automatic system,' the young man said, 'you wouldn't have to mess around with all these switches. But it's easy enough.'

'Yes,' admitted Hector absently.

So this is how the weather lights work, he thought.

This is what I do.

The room was tiny, concrete: enough to depress anybody. It was high in the dead part of the building, ignored by the air-conditioning. A plastic ashtray sat on the small table.

The black phone gave a sudden ring. A voice told him to change the message to RAIN. 'Right, then,' said Hector. He fiddled with switches, concentrating, then turned them on. Through the window he saw the sudden change in the message and automatically wondered what the people below thought. Would they believe in that? Would they notice his sign? How many would be caught without coats, umbrellas, rudimentary shelter?

But there was no rain – not a drop. Standing at the window he became concerned. Merv looked at his message. He looked down at the people-shapes moving casually. Then, miraculously it seemed, rain began hitting and splashing. His sign shined in triumph; and the thought that his warning had saved people flooded him with specific pleasure. It was good, and he clenched himself. He

looked up then at the clouds. They seemed to be pressing down on his room, around his life, down his mouth, showering his vision with rain. God, he wondered.

Down on the street depressed figures ran from point to point. The shining traffic remained queued, steam rose, and three silver buses waited bumper to bumper. It recalled certain mornings behind the steering wheel, the giant screen wipers scanned repetitiously like radar, squish-a-squish. Now he stared through the glass window, up at the clouds, up into the heart of the rain. He felt settled, sure, safe, glad to be there; he thought of home, the maroon chair, and his Enid.

Nothing's the matter, he said. I'm fine, he wanted everyone to know. On the panel he moved across and switched the message to FINE.

The huge bright lights said FINE as the rain kept splashing down. Altogether, Merv Hector marvelled at every single thing. He stared at his sign. It was true. He loved the clouds. It was another world, and he was there. The phone began to ring.

SUMMER ON ICE

BEVERLEY
FARMER
1941–

THE first time Caroline goes skating the cold shocks her, such motionless cold and in summer. Her breath fumes. The building, a hollow barn she remembers from her childhood, is uglier, darker, older than ever. Long drops of water fall from the ceiling to make blue lumps on the ice. She has been imagining ice like deep glass, bluish and with long needles of air frozen in it, but no: it is frosted, slashed and scarred, although no one else is there. A net hangs behind where the hockey goal was last night. She regrets having come.

A grinning boy hands her a pair of skates. She laces them tight as she has read she should, and clumps to the swing door, on to the ice. She slithers, clinging with both frozen hands to the fence to drag herself along. Her feet sting with the cold then go numb. After a dogged hour she can propel herself with one hand. No one else has turned up. Records of rock songs boom now and then over the loudspeakers. A cone of sun burns through a skylight. Dark trees flicker at its glass. When there is no music her skates scrape and thump and she remembers how her skis thumped on the hard snow of a sunlit mountain top the first time she dared go so high; her terror then as she crouched curling down and down.

She prances out of the rink on suddenly light feet, pleased with herself. The bay is opaque olive green this morning. Yachts on it flutter their wet sails. In the haze of the western shore, the towers of Melbourne are grey slabs, tombstones. In a week it will be Christmas.

———

A scrawled postcard in her letter box, the first: the Statue of Liberty and a New York postmark.

My darling,

Remember how we lay and drank champagne and dreamed of being here together? I miss you terribly – a million things to tell you. Found you some books you'll adore in the Gotham – not telling what – and mailed them yesterday. They should arrive soon after I do, some time in mid-Feb., I hope. It's freezing here....

He gives the address of a post office in Greenwich Village where she can write to him, and signs off: *'Take care, sweet.'*

———

Has he remembered that they quarrelled then as they lay and drank champagne? He hasn't, it seems.

'I wish you were coming with me,' he murmured.

'Well, I would. I could afford the affair.'

'What did you say?'

'The fare. I could afford the fare.' They both laughed.

'Will you wait for me, Caro?'

'Oh, probably.'

'Eight weeks.' His eyes were fixed in anger. She sat up.

'All right, it's not eternity. I know. Eight weeks is eight weeks – of jaunts and sensual joy in the Big Apple while I sit waiting.'

'It won't be joy. I'll be thinking of you the whole time. You know that.'

'I'll think of you.'

'Promise you'll wait?'

'No! What gives you the right to ask?'

'Caro, listen. I can't not take her. She's been looking forward to it all year. All our friends know we're coming over. I can't *do* it to her.'

'But I don't *want* you to. Have I ever said I did?'

'But you won't wait?'

'Won't promise to. I can't. On principle I can't. It's something time will tell.'

'I see. Yet another of those somethings of yours that time will tell.'

'Yes. Like: "I told you so."'

He started to dress, talking over his shoulder.

'You claim to love me.'

'Yes. Not the point, though, is it?'

'I think it is.'

'You love me, you claim. You're going with her.'

'She *is* my wife.'

'Yes. *That's* the point.'

'I'm coming *back*.'

'I'll be here.' She shrugged.

'Will you? Alone?'

'As far as I know.'

With a gasp of anger he walked out. She cried, but noticing he'd kept his key she didn't lose hope. The next day she sent (to his work address) a card with a Pre-Raphaelite Ophelia afloat in skirts like a peacock's tail, on the back of which she had written: '*Look in my face; my name is Might-have-been. (D. G. Rossetti – SONNET 98)*'. On the third day he came. They lay in bed all afternoon and listened to a broadcast of the New World Symphony. He promised they'd live together when he got back. She promised to wait.

———

Against her will, as one who prides herself on being free of possessiveness – relatively free – Caroline imagines him arm-in-arm with his wife, a jolly figure though faceless, strolling along Fifth Avenue. Caroline has never been to America. She buys a book of photographs of New York and studies the sunset skyscrapers, the squirrels and snowdrifts of Central Park, slums in the Bronx on fire. In one photograph a small tree of grey twigs on some avenue is spun all over with webs of white lights, for Christmas, she thinks. Has he seen it?

She finds a photograph in her book of a man at a block party in the Village, swaggering on a stoop, thumbs in his belt and his curled chest bare. A glass of beer in one fist. His stance, though not his face, reminds her of her lover and she puts a marker at that page. Soon the book starts opening there of its own

accord. She takes the marker out.

Am I compulsive? she writes in her diary. Am I old-maidish? I'm thirty-two. Am I becoming a tedious woman? I was never so mild and quiet, such a mouse. Be fearless and joyful. Make him love me.

She takes over her sister's flat near the beach. Her sister is working in Sydney. Packing and scrubbing out the old flat and moving her things keeps her too busy for a couple of days to feel lonely. She has told him her sister's number but no calls come. Is he trying and not getting through? She writes to him about the flat, Poste Restante. What, she worries, if in a new flat she seems like a stranger to him? She does to herself.

———

At last he rings her from a coin phone in Manhattan in a downpour. For her it's another sultry Melbourne night. They spar and hedge, off-key, and say nothing in the end.

'I do miss you, Caro. Really.'

'Oh, good. Now and then would be nice.'

'All the time. Was that a laugh?'

'A cynical snort, more like it.'

'Undeserved.'

'Is it? I miss you too.'

'Good.'

'Darling, it's four in the morning! If I'm not making sense, make allowances.'

'I wanted to catch you in. I hoped you wouldn't mind.'

'I don't. You're sure of your welcome.'

'Actually, I'm not. Far from it.'

'You always seem sure.'

'It's the best policy.'

'Better than honesty?'

'Much.' He pauses. 'You seem sure yourself.'

'I do? What do I seem sure of?'

'Me, for one.'

'Baby, you gotta be kidding.'

'Well, you can be.'

'Yeah?'

'Hey, I'm the one should talk American. Yeah.'

'Put it down to my sceptical nature.'

In no time the three minutes are up. She lies on her bed with the lamp on, wishing she had let the phone ring. He is standing bitter in the rain now, he who hates rain. She has lost ground, and lies wondering with a chill of panic if she has ever believed that he loves her, and what does a married man mean by saying he loves her, anyway?

'SHE has lost ground, and lies wondering with a chill of panic if she has ever believed that he loves her, and what does a married man mean by saying he loves her, anyway?'

Anyway, darling, the flat's in a narrow street with a little yellow-grey Gothic church at one end and at the other is the bay. From the balcony you can see right across. Now and then today a shifting wind has been blurring the sea. Then it comes still and clear again as if a glass dome had been put back on. The façade of the old baths is intact, and the one domed white turret that I can see from here looks like a whitewashed chapel on some island. Mykonos, Ios. In the evening I lie getting brown on the sand. I hope you like your women brown? I eat down there and before I come home sow my handful of crumbs although only one gull is even in sight – far out at sea, circling. In a long swoop it comes crying and others follow and stalk around. They arch their grey wings like scythes, ruffle themselves and jab the sand.

The lights go on in the city and along the bridge – a sudden golden bow. Freighters at sea flick on their white lights.

I close the French window and see my room move with the glass across the darkening sea and sky: a yellow lamp, a table with books, a chair on a white rug.

The second time she goes skating the lights and the plant have been turned off. No one is there but two boys cleaning up. Water swills glittering around the blades of her skates. She wavers, anxious not to fall and be soaked, so half an hour passes before she lets go of the fence. She hovers over the hockey circles, trying to balance on one foot at a time but never daring. There is music, then the needle sticks and it is switched off. The two boys circle, sweeping off the ice. She imagines him, back from New York earlier than he said, coming here to find her: herself catching sight of his smile of admiration and pride. She will be gliding, whirling in her mist of breath, in the spotlight that the sun makes falling on the creamy ice.

'You'll fall flat at his feet,' she says aloud, amazing the boys. Her laugh echoes.

After the turkey and Christmas pudding at her mother's farm, the family goes on drinking in the garden while she and her mother wash up. This year, though, they leave the dishes to soak, and walk to the apple orchard. Her mother is worried, Caro can tell, and wants her to talk about him. What is there to say? As she talks on, her mother breathes sunlit smoke; watching it, not Caro.

'Is he going to leave his wife for you?' she interrupts.

'Only if she consents,' says Caro.

'Consents? Oh, Caro darling! You and your dream world!'

There are days when Caro does feel as if she is living a dream. She is not real; or she is fading, becoming invisible; or is left behind by time. She lies awake all night. No one knows that they are – were? – lovers. Are we? Were we? she wonders.

Another postcard, the Chrysler building this time.

... So you're learning to skate these holidays, my darling? There's an open-air rink here at the Rockefeller Centre. Center. Some of the skaters are serious and waltz eyeball-to-eyeball as in their young days in old Prague and Budapest. The young guys clown around pretty girls in tutus who loftily ignore them. Lovely to think of my darling in a tutu. Had any falls yet? Take care, as they all say here. I love you ....

He mentions that he has been to see a revival of 'West Side Story' on Broadway. He always writes 'I' not 'we'. She is reminded of one morning when, arriving unexpectedly, he found her still in bed and joined her there and later got up to make coffee. Naked at her little stove he swayed and sang 'I feel pretty', a cigarette dangling. His smile when she laughed was full of innocent bafflement. She wonders if he was reminded too: he doesn't mention it. She tries not to feel hurt.

She writes in her diary: *Is he thinking, poor little Caroline, writing his postcards? Caroline, stop it.*

Caroline has started indulging in exotic foods. Am I trying to sublimate desire?

she wonders. She buys a smoked fish in its cloth of gold, sullen-mouthed and swarthy. Creamy avocadoes in coarse black shells. Pumpernickel like sour plum pudding. Cheese crusted with black peppercorns or riddled with blue mould in crumbs or dimly veined with wine. A round Edam in red wax like a toffee apple. She eats her cheese with morello cherry jam by the saucerful. She buys quantities of Turkish coffee and tart Chianti in straw. At one sitting she eats a whole jar of peanut butter. She bakes a tray each of pumpkin and sweet potato in the oven of her new flat, filling it with smoke in which lurk the ghosts of other tenants' burnt dinners, her sister's probably. In reaction she eats nothing for a week but fruit: mandarines with spongy skins, bananas and sour early apricots and plums. She buys a gloosy oval crimson fruit which a poster in the shop names a tamarillo. It looks like the glowing eggs baked into plaits of bread in Greek shops over Easter. Cut, it is orange, studded with dark seeds in a butterfly shape. It tastes of passionfruit and pawpaw together and Caroline savours every bite. The tamarillo, she reads, is a winter fruit.

She takes herself off to various good restaurants with a book and a half-bottle of fine wine. She reads *Pale Fire, A Lost Lady, Washington Square*. She orders Chicken Maryland, Manhattan Clam Chowder, Pastrami, things he must be eating. She is a slow eater and a fast reader. She keeps her head down. She hopes people are not looking at her in sly amusement.

I'm not a bold person, she writes in her diary. Not an innovator or a rebel. Not the life of the party. But I am self-sufficient and don't much mind if strangers patronise me.

He'll forget me. Worse, I'll seem drab and dull when he gets back. I listen to concerts recorded in San Marco's in Venice, in New College, Oxford – places I've been to – and wonder how my life can have shrunk so small. Someone vivid will catch his eye. He'll drop me.

In an Italian restaurant she eats little sea creatures stewed in wine and tomatoes: whole baby squids and mussels, scallops, shrimps and clams tangled on the plate in what looks like red seaweed. She drinks her green Italian wine. It is raining, a summer storm. From her window table she sees puddles begin to swarm with rain. Restaurants in New York have glassed-in verandas like train carriages flush with the footpaths. She has seen them in her book. She imagines she is with him inside the golden glass of one of them, rain shivering down it and people rushing past, heads bent, smiling in at them from a black and silver Manhattan street. The waitress brings fruits, grapes and peaches and watermelon, unasked with the coffee. He said so in a letter. A candle, she thinks; a bowl of autumn fruits, a green bottle; our hands clasped on the red cloth. Afterwards, running home in this rain. No. On iced footpaths, sidewalks, slithering, hand in hand, our breath white: like skaters.

The third time there is a mist over the ice. Two other women are there practising leaps and figures. They smile sympathetically at Caroline's wobbles. The sunlight is a bobbin wound with gold mist and, dazzled, she can easily imagine that she is not here but in Central Park. Or the Rockefeller Centre. Center. In a letter he has mentioned smoking pretzel carts and puffs of steam from under the

streets like white balloons hovering; or on a windy day flung shredded between glass walls, fluttering in the mirrors the walls make. She weaves – but in blue jeans, not a tutu – through the mist. She will amaze him at the Rockefeller Center one day, one day.

After two hours she can go round and round the rink quite fast without ever holding on and the two women smile and say how well she's doing.

He writes a lot. He writes, for example, about the hotels he (they) stay at, in rooms on the thirtieth and fortieth floors. 'Like in a helicopter, a huge ferris wheel. You sleep among stars.' She imagines him (them) high up at the summits of glass towers all gold and silver light, webbed with their long lamps and hung among stars. To make love up there, she dreams, though heights freeze her with terror. And what if they sway in the wind? She goes to Luna Park and grimly rides the ferris wheel above the glittering city.

Then he writes that he's moved to the Village now, to a friend's apartment.

Greenwich Village has all these red tenements caged with fire escapes. Basement rooms with lamps on all day. You've read Washington Square, *haven't you? I was there today. The fountain was empty, just a skin of grey water and dead leaves. A pale boy was sitting on the rim gazing in, his feet bloated, red raw. I've never known such cold. You must have in Europe. There were trees, lamps, lonely wanderers. Puddles of sleet dark red as night fell, and then red-lit coffee shops with guitarists (of a sort), bright fruit shops and souvenir and book shops: one day we'll browse in the Strand together. Again no letter from you today. Write to me, Caro, will you?*

New Year she spends in her flat waiting for him to ring but he never does. She tints her hair Granada Muscat so that it glows unexpectedly with a crimson burnish and shocks her when she meets it in plate glass windows. She has dinner with old friends, drinks too much and talks too much about him. She apologises too much, and they say not to be silly, what on earth are friends for?

'What I like about skating,' she assures her friends, 'is that I'm really getting somewhere, I'm making progress. I'm not just waiting for the time to pass. I'm getting results. I'm growing, I'm improving. Aren't I? It's visible progress.' Giggling, she waves her brandy balloon. 'It's all in the balance!' They just look, concern on their faces.

Caroline, who has been so sure that certain afternoons were really unforgettable, finds they have gone. Like a film only intermittently in focus, all the rest a mist. In dreams she relives moments and wakes burning and overjoyed. The dreams fade quickly. If he's forgetting too, she thinks in a panic, what is there left?

She looks at the five photographs, all that she has of him. Whenever she thinks of him now his face is in one or other of the five expressions. Is she forgetting what he looks like? When she sees him again, will she find herself trying to match his face to the photographs? She goes over old conversations. They are being eroded, and the expressions don't fit them at all. If only I'd written them down, she thinks.

She writes in her diary: *Write things down*. She finds scribbled lines:

> *Look in my face; my name is Might-have-been;*
> *I am also called No-more, Too-late, Farewell ...*
>
> D. G. Rossetti.

She goes out in the simmering streets and sees him on this corner or the next. He's back and he hasn't told her. It's always – well, of *course* it is! – someone else. She goes to the rink most days. Cats doze on verandas, on a sprouting old settee left out as garbage, on brick walls. A tortoiseshell cat and a snail-coloured tabby cat, coiled and humped and with ears like horns, follow her then vanish. One day she finds a caterpillar with sparse long black fur and a hump, arching hurriedly on a wall. It looks like a tiny moulting kitten. Days later there it is again, yards further on. She is absurdly pleased. The next day it is deep under grey layers of a spider web. So what was she expecting? Immortality? Brown broken glass glows. Vomit lies on the hot footpath in clots.

She writes to him about all this and hopes he will understand. She tells him she is thinking of getting a cat: for company, she adds. So he'll know she's alone. She tells him she loves him.

She imagines that he is walking towards her. He stops to talk, seeing that she has seen him. With a smile more like a wince, out of pure courtesy he tries to chat. His shirt is open at the neck. She could lean forward and touch her lips to the hairs of his chest, except that he doesn't want her to. She remembers on a beach the hairs of his belly and groin all sunlit. Shadows of a dark tree broke over him.

'I must go, sweet,' he would say as soon as he could. 'We'll have a lunch one day, will we?'

'IN dreams she relives moments and wakes burning and overjoyed. The dreams fade quickly. If he's forgetting too, she thinks in a panic, what is there left?'

———————

One night, five weeks now since he left, the phone is suddenly ringing. His voice is heavy, blurred, and she is vague from sleep. The operator tells her to wait while he drops quarters in a coin phone. 'Darling, I can't stand it any longer,' his stifled voice is saying. 'I'm going to have to tell her. It can't go on like this. She can tell there's something wrong. I can't go on saying there's nothing *wrong* day in day out –'

'Oh, but listen. Wait!' Is he as drunk as he sounds?

'We'll get a flat,' he said. 'Look for a flat. She can have the house. Don't tell me you've changed your mind now?'

'*No*. Let's not be rash. Let's wait till you get back and we can talk about it. We never *have*. We need time –'

'"Time will say nothing..." How does it go again?'

'Oh, darling.'

'Don't want me now. I see.'

'I *do*. You know I do.'

'Your three minutes are up,' the operator says. 'Are you extending your call, sir?'

Caroline persuades him to ring her again right away, reversing the charges.

'Lady ain't tired a me yet, you hear her?' he drawls to the new operator, who sniffs. He is determined, truculent, heavily offended that she is raising objections now. They ring off, both promising a letter that will explain everything. 'My mind's made up,' he insists. 'I'm going ahead and telling her tonight.'

Caroline lies awake. His too-eager eyes urge her and on their brown surface she doesn't recognise herself. Justify this, they are saying. Justify me, seduce me, adore me. Be what I dream. Am I having to pay a great price all for nothing? Her heart thudding, she lies rigid all night.

That day she rings her mother, who is both pleased and horrified. She tells the friends she had dinner with and looks up Flats To Let in the newspaper. She waits for his letter, but none comes. She tries to write to him and can't. She skates, walks in the hot streets, swims when the bay is clean. No more phone calls wake her.

———

A week later there is a letter from New York: a funny recycled New Year card mailed weeks ago. He writes of having gone to Mass on Christmas Eve at St Patrick's. Long before you reach it, he says, you can see reflections of a white spire.... And she sees it jagged, a white spire curling and melting, swooning in glass. In a marble nave he gracefully genuflects as if in a dance. She, raised a Protestant, has never learnt to genuflect, or to dance for that matter. Her movements are not fluid but tight and graceless as a chilled swimmer's.

Wine is a help, she thinks. Wine does help, it warms and frees me. Remember to drink wine before he comes, she writes in her diary, and be bold and wild, sinuous! With the help of Chianti she answers his letter from the past. Her memory is starting to jam on times when things went wrong between them. This is fatal, she tells herself. At the moment of doubt the skater falls.

Darling,

When your letter came, your New Year card, I went to the little church at the end of my street. I bought guava jelly at the stall they were holding, and went through an archway with a cool tree and lilies. From outside, the windows are embroideries of iron on glass; from inside, saints in robes of flame on their deep sky. The stone is draped like vines in Tuscany. How I wish it could bud in spring and be warmly hung with golden leaves and grapes in autumn, like the mast of Dionysus's ship – holding out its fruit in the darkness ...

Tell me, do the skyscrapers (but did the hotels is what she meant) sway in a high wind? And is there skating in summer at the Rockefeller Centre? I can skate now. I haven't fallen yet. I won't, I refuse to. I'll show you!

It's probably too late for her letter to reach him before he leaves New York, but she mails it anyway, backdating it to before his phone call. Then she sits eating guava jelly with a spoon, regretting the letter. It reads like an essay. What has its voice to do with her voice on the phone or with his? Is there any point at which their lives touch now?

Will we be happy living together (she writes in her diary)? The only time he could stay all night wasn't a success. We were nervous and drank too much. I felt his disappointment, though he hid it courteously, without knowing what I'd done. Two days later he told me.

'You're such a selfish lover,' he added.

'But of course I care if you're not satisfied!' I protested. 'You mean you faked?'

'Well, I had to. You were so damn happy.'

'I spent $300 on new bedcovers for one night, does that look like I didn't care?'

Again that gasp of impatience, his hand in that gesture of despair or anger: okay, let's just forget it. On the night I just lay there in an anguish of propitiation. I thought he was feeling guilty. He left earlier in the morning than he needed to. Yet we got over this. We were overcoming our misunderstandings. Surely we'll come through?

Don't tell me he's having religious scruples now. I don't believe this!

One hot afternoon the phone rings and she grabs it wildly, but it's her mother full of news about a neighbour's grassfire turned back just in time, a dog lost and found lame. A rooster crows on the farm, miles away, glossy and smug under gum trees heavy with dust. Sheep are grizzling on all the dry hills. To splash on horseback, she thinks, through shadows at the amber creek.

'Caroline. Is he back yet?'

'No. Well, I don't know.'

'You haven't heard at all? The bastard. He hasn't rung you?'

'He will soon, I expect.'

'Well, come up to the farm, why don't you? Come and pick apples. What's the use of languishing alone?' She laughs. 'Sorry. Mother hen. Anyway, you know. Always welcome and all that.'

'I will come up. Yes, I will. But not yet. Who have you got lined up for me now?'

She puts the phone down before her mother can think up a denial. Checkmate. Her mother will be smiling now by the west windows, the phone still in her hand. Smiling herself, Caroline takes *Couples*, a towel and a bag of nectarines and lies on the hot sand, and swims, and dries off in the late red sun.

———

A postcard then – the Lincoln Center by night – but all it says is that he's coming back on schedule, two days from the day she gets it. He can't say what flight. She is elated at first and then succumbs to a frenzied panic. What does that mean: *can't say what flight?* She doesn't, of course, dare go to the airport on the day. She waits at home. He doesn't come or ring. Speechless with dread she drags through the night and the next day. At five he knocks: he hasn't a key to this flat. They embrace, but tentatively. He is certainly himself and she has not been forgetting him at all. He exclaims how brown she is and how much thinner. He has brought cuttings, book reviews for her to read. She pours what's left of the Chianti that has got her through these last two days into glasses full of ice cubes. The ice glows red round the glittering splinters of its tiny bubbles. The glasses mist over. She tries to read while he sips and smokes and listens to a new record she has bought for the occasion, the New World Symphony. Then he gets up to go. She gazes at him.

'I can't stay, darling.' He is discomforted rather than apologetic. 'It's this welcome-back party we're going to. God, I'm a zombie from jetlag. Don't look like that. I'll stay longer some other time.'

'But we haven't talked.'

'Darling, some other time.'

She nods and tries to smile, jiggling her red ice. 'What you said on the phone? Can't you tell me what's happened?'

'Nothing's *happened*.'

'It *has*. You don't love me now.'

'Sweet, that's *not* true.'

'*Please?*'

'I got by. It wasn't wasted. Wasted. I learnt to skate.'

He sits down sighing. 'I don't know. I was sure I did. I even told her so, for God's sake, once when I was blind drunk. Oh, you know, I rang you. We went through hell for days after that, all over Manhattan. But we came through. You know, I think we're closer now than we've ever been. Hell, Caro, you don't want to listen to this. Sorry. Was it a good summer, sweet? Tell me about you.'

'I got by. It wasn't wasted. *Wasted.* I learnt to skate. Wait till you see Caro on ice!' But he is shaking his head. 'Let me guess: the deal is you give me up?'

He nods. 'A clean break.'

'Oh, right. Keep it clean. What did you tell her about me?'

'Not much. What could I? We don't talk about it any more. Though she did ask today –'

'Does she know you're here now?'

'No. She did ask today if I had any regrets about – you know. "Breaking with Caroline." I said no. No regrets.'

'Not a bad curtain line. Delivered with more conviction.'

'I meant it, Caro.'

'At the time.'

He looks at the time. 'God, *look* at the time,' he says, and stands up. 'It was fun, though, wasn't it? Caro, you were great.' At light kiss, and he is gone.

She drinks her wine, pulls thick woollens and gloves on. then wanders out on to the sunny Esplanade. Palms stoop and swish, sails shake on the foam of the bay. Leaves, torn off the trees, rise and sink about her as if in a fire. Summer is as good as over. And no bones broken either. Already Caro can see herself glide, a long blue shape on the ice among the other skaters, flaring through the sun's path with dust and mist and veils of snowy breath behind her; dazzled, transfigured, she turns and glides.

THE LIFE OF ART

HELEN GARNER
1942–

My friend and I went walking the dog in the cemetery. It was a Melbourne autumn: mild breezes, soft air, gentle sun. The dog trotted in front of us between the graves. I had a pair of scissors in my pocket in case we came across a rose bush on a forgotten tomb.

'I don't like roses,' said my friend. 'I despise them for having thorns.'

The dog entered a patch of ivy and posed there. We pranced past the Elvis Presley memorial.

'What would you like to have written on your grave,' said my friend, 'as a tribute?'

I thought for a long time. Then I said, '*Owner of two hundred pairs of boots.*'

When we had recovered, my friend pointed out a headstone which said, *She lived only for others.* 'Poor thing,' said my friend. 'On *my* grave I want you to write, *She lived only for herself.*'

We went stumbling along the overgrown paths.

My friend and I had known each other for twenty years, but we had never lived in the same house. She came back from Europe at the perfect moment to take over a room in the house I rented. It became empty because the man – but that's another story.

My friend has certain beliefs which I have always secretly categorised as *batty*. Sometimes I have thought, 'My friend is what used to be called "a dizzy dame".' My friend believes in reincarnation: not that this in itself is unacceptable to me. Sometimes she would write me long letters from wherever she was in the world, letters in her lovely, graceful, sweeping hand, full of tales from one or other of her previous lives, tales to explain her psychological make-up and behaviour in her present incarnation. My eye would fly along the lines, sped by embarrassment.

My friend is a painter.

When I first met my friend she was engaged. She was wearing an antique sapphire ring and Italian boots. Next time I saw her, in Myers, her hand was bare. I never asked. We were students then. We went dancing in a club in South Yarra. The boys in the band were students too. We fancied them, but at twenty-two we felt ourselves to be older women, already fading, almost predatory. We read *The Roman Spring of Mrs Stone*. This was in 1965; before feminism.

My friend came off the plane with her suitcase. 'Have you ever noticed,' she said, 'how Australian men, even in their forties, dress like small boys? They wear shorts and thongs and little stripey T-shirts.'

A cat was asleep under a bush in our back yard each morning when we opened the door. We took him in. My friend and I fought over whose lap he would lie in while we watched TV.

My friend is tone deaf. But she once sang *Blue Moon*, verses and chorus, in a talking, tuneless voice in the back of a car going up the Punt Road hill and down again and over the river, travelling north; and she did not care.

My friend lived as a student in a house near the university. Her bed was right under the window in the front room downstairs. One afternoon her father came to visit. He tapped on the door. When no one answered he looked through the window. What he saw caused him to stagger back into the fence. It was a kind of heart attack, my friend said.

My friend went walking in the afternoons near our house. She came out of lanes behind armfuls of greenery. She found vases in my dusty cupboards. The arrangements she made with the leaves were stylish and generous-handed.

Before either of us married, I went to my friend's house to help her paint the bathroom. The paint was orange, and so was the cotton dress I was wearing. She laughed because all she could see of me when I stood in the bathroom were my limbs and my head. Later, when it got dark, we sat at her kitchen table and she rolled a joint. It was the first dope I had ever seen or smoked. I was afraid that a detective might look through the kitchen window. I could not understand why my friend did not pull the curtain across. We walked up to Genevieve in the warm night and ate two bowls of spaghetti. It seemed to me that I could feel every strand.

My friend's father died when she was in a distant country.

'So now,' she said to me, 'I know what grief is.'

'What is it?' I said.

'Sometimes,' said my friend, 'it is what you expect. And sometimes it is nothing more than bad temper.'

When my friend's father died, his affairs were not in order and he had no money.

My friend was the first person I ever saw break the taboo against wearing striped and floral patterns together. She stood on the steps of the Shrine of Remembrance and held a black umbrella over her head. This was in the 1960s.

My friend came back from Europe and found a job. On the days when she was not painting theatre sets for money she went to her cold and dirty studio in the city and painted for the other thing, whatever that is. She wore cheap shoes and pinned her hair into a roll on her neck.

My friend babysat, as a student, for a well-known woman in her forties who worked at night.

'What is she like?' I said.

'She took me upstairs,' said my friend, 'and showed me her bedroom. It was full of flowers. We stood at the door looking in. She said, "Sex is not a problem for me."'

When the person ... the man whose room my friend had taken, came to dinner, my friend and he would talk for hours after everyone else had left the table about different modes of perception and understanding. My friend spoke slowly, in long, convoluted sentences and mixed metaphors, and often laughed. The man, a scientist, spoke in a light, rapid voice, but he sat still. They seemed to listen to each other.

'I don't mean a god in the Christian sense,' said my friend.

'It is egotism,' said the man, 'that makes people want their lives to have meaning beyond themselves.'

My friend and I worked one summer in the men's underwear department of a big store in Footscray. We wore our little cotton dresses, our blue sandals. We were happy there, selling, wrapping, running up and down the ladder, dinging the register, going to the park for lunch with the boys from the shop. *I* was happy. The youngest boy looked at us and sighed and said, 'I don't know which one of youse I love the most.' One day my friend was serving a thin-faced woman at the specials box. There was a cry. I looked up. My friend was dashing for the door. She was sobbing. We all stood still, in attitudes of drama. The woman spread her hands. She spoke to the frozen shop at large.

'I never said a thing,' she said. 'It's got nothing to do with *me*.'

I left my customer and ran after my friend. She was halfway down the street, looking in a shop window. She had stopped crying. She began to tell me about ... but it doesn't matter now. This was in the 1960s; before feminism.

My friend came home from her studio some nights in a calm bliss. 'What we need,' she said, 'are those moments of abandon, when the real stuff runs down

My friend cut lemons into chunks and dropped them into the water jug when there was no money for wine.

My friend came out of the surgery. I ran to take her arm but she pushed past me and bent over the gutter. I gave her my hanky. Through the open sides of the tram the summer wind blew freely. We stood up and held on to the leather straps. 'I can't sit down,' said my friend. 'He put a great bolt of gauze up me.' This was in the 1960s; before feminism. The tram rolled past the deep gardens. My friend was smiling.

My friend and her husband came to visit me and my husband. We heard their car and looked out the upstairs window. We could hear his voice haranguing her, and hers raised in sobs and wails. I ran down to open the door. They were standing on the mat, looking ordinary. We went to Royal Park and flew a kite that her husband had made. The nickname he had for her was one he had picked up from her father. They both loved her, of course. This was in the 1960s.

My friend was lonely.

My friend sold some of her paintings. I went to look at them in her studio before they were taken away. The smell of the oil paint was a shock to me: a smell I would have thought of as masculine. This was in the 1980s; after feminism. The paintings were big. I did not 'understand' them; but then again perhaps I did, for they made me feel like fainting, her weird plants and creatures streaming back towards a source of irresistible yellow light.

'When happiness comes,' said my friend, 'it's so thick and smooth and uneventful, it's like nothing at all.'

My friend picked up a fresh chicken at the market. 'Oh,' she said. 'Feel this.' I took it from her. Its flesh was pimpled and tender, and moved on its bones like the flesh of a very young baby.

I went into my friend's room while she was out. On the wall was stuck a sheet of paper on which she had written: 'Henry James to a friend in trouble: "throw yourself on the *alternative* life ... which is what I mean by the life of art, and

'MY friend sold some of her paintings. I went to look at them in her studio before they were taken away. The smell of the oil paint was a shock to me: a smell I would have thought of as masculine.'

which religiously invoked and handsomely understood, *je vous le garantis*, never fails the sincere invoker – sees him through everything, and reveals to him the secrets of and for doing so.'''

———

I was sick. My friend served me pretty snacks at sensitive intervals. I sat up on my pillows and strummed softly the five chords I had learnt on my ukulele. My friend sat on the edge of a chair, with her bony hands folded round a cup, and talked. She uttered great streams of words. Her gaze skimmed my shoulder and vanished into the clouds outside the window. She was like a machine made to talk on and on for ever. She talked about how much money she would have to spend on paint and stretchers, about the lightness, the optimism, the femaleness of her work, about what she was going to paint next, about how much tougher and more violent her pictures would have to be in order to attract proper attention from critics, about what the men in her field were doing now, about how she must find this out before she began her next lot of pictures.

'I want a man who'll look after me and love me. I want a grown-up.'

'Listen,' I said. 'You don't have to think about any of that. Your work is *terrific.*'

'My work is terrific,' said my friend on a high note, 'but *I'm not.*' Her mouth fell down her chin and opened. She began to sob. 'I'm forty,' said my friend, 'and I've got *no money.*'

I played the chords G, A and C.

'I'm lonely,' said my friend. Tears were running down her cheeks. Her mouth was too low in her face. 'I want a man.'

'You could have one,' I said.

'I don't want just any man,' said my friend. 'And I don't want a boy. I want a man who's not going to think my ideas are crazy. I want a man who'll see the part of me that no one ever sees. I want a man who'll look after me and love me. I want a grown-up.'

I thought, If a could play better, I could turn what she has just said into a song.

'Women like us,' I said to my friend, 'don't have men like that. Why should *you* expect to find a man like that?'

'Why shouldn't I?' said my friend.

'Because men won't do those things for women like us. We've done something to ourselves so that men won't do it. Well – there are men who will: But we despise them.'

My friend stopped crying.

I played the ukulele. My friend drank from the cup.

READING THE SIGNS

MICHAEL
WILDING
1942–

I T grew under the apple tree. It got a start because nothing much else
ever grew there. We did try potatoes occasionally, but you caught your fork
in the tree roots trying to dig them up. So that from the apple tree to the
fence at the right was my garden, and from the apple tree to the path at the left
was my sister's. She put in rocks and moss and things for the fairies.

It grew there with its stubby wooden stem and its bushy branches of leaves
and then this amazing pinkish-purplish bugle of a flower. We let it grow
because we had never seen anything like it; even before the flower, it had this
presence, this numinousness. But the flower was a clarion of mystery. Then the
seedpod formed, green and spiky at first, and then it darkened and became
rounded and leathery.

We asked everybody what it was, and no one knew. Even Dad must have
accepted some of its mystery, because he never pulled it up. Even though under
the apple tree was not productive and even though he didn't believe in stripping
off all unplanted vegetation like some of the people in the avenue, the bigger
weeds got pulled up and put on the compost heap.

So nobody knew, and we picked the seedpod and kept it in a little fish-paste
jar in the kitchen window, sitting in the fish-paste jar like an egg in an eggcup
on the windowsill above the sink, among the rubber rings that sealed the fruit
we bottled in jars, and the hairpins, and the used razor blades, and countless
other things. Sometimes the robin would hop in through the open window and
peck around. Year after year the windowsill was in the robin's territory.

The seedpod cracked open, and we kept the dark-brown seeds in the bottom of
the fish-paste jar through the winter, and they stayed on the windowsill with all
the other accreted things and got forgotten. The plant died beneath the apple
tree, and the dried stem was tossed on to a bonfire.

The next year, it came again. But the next year it had come all over the rest of
England, too. Neighbours had them. The newspapers reported its mysterious
appearance throughout the country. The Californian thorn apple, they called it.
Jimsonweed. *Datura stramonium*. Said to be deadly poisonous.

'Wonder you didn't poison the lot of us,' Dad said. Poisonous, they all said.
No one said it was a hallucinogen. But they stamped them out and burnt them
just the same.

Once the plant was everywhere and had been named, we didn't know what
else to do. We knew there was a mystery, but the naming and the reported
spread of it were made to do service for the revelation. We never did take any of
it, boiled or brewed or powdered or smoked or rubbed into the skin. The newspapers never suggested you could do that. That sort of knowledge hadn't sur-
vived. It was about this time Mum had her fortune read at the village fête and
was told that in a few years she'd be doing the same herself: reading fortunes.
She was always able to read the signs. If she dropped a big knife it would be a

tall visitor coming, and a little knife a short visitor. The magpies would fly over the fields, one for sorrow, two for joy. But the uses of the thorn apple had been stamped out in the witch burnings. Everything comes in threes was another of Mum's sayings. But the third year the thorn apple didn't come back. And the seeds had got thrown on the fire because of everyone's saying how poisonous it was. I think that was a mistake, not keeping the seeds.

'That flying saucer you saw,' I asked Mum.

'Oh, Michael, did we?' she says. 'I can't remember now.'

It was like this when I needed my precise time of birth for the astrological chart. 'Here we are. Five. One. Or was that the date? Wait until I find my specs.'

'When we were living up the avenue. You remember?'

The avenue was a row of twenty-seven houses, with fields in front of us – because they hadn't built on the other side of the road – and fields behind. They stopped building when the war started. The prisoners of war used to hoe in the fields at the back.

'We were in the back garden talking one evening and it just came across,' Mum said. 'I can't remember if it was our back garden, even.'

'And it just came over the garden?'

'I think so,' Mum said. 'It wasn't very high. It was just like a bright light. It had a sort of tail, I think.'

'And where did it go?'

'It just vanished. It just went. It wasn't there any more.'

'No,' said Dad. 'No, no, no, it was in the front of the houses. We were standing in the road. It was going up the river. It was a meteorite. It was going up the river.'

'What, following it along?'

'That's what it looked like.'

Dad wrote to the paper. 'As an iron-moulder, it seemed to me like a glowing red ball of molten iron.'

Sometimes he would be at home with burns on his hands or feet from molten iron that had spilt. Now he is at home dying of emphysema from the foundry dust.

'It was just like the molten iron when it comes out of the furnace.'

Mum was furious, embarrassed. She went red.

'I never expected them to print it,' Dad said. 'I just wrote it as information for them.'

Other people in town had sighted it. There were other letters.

'You might have known they'd print it.'

'No, I didn't, so that's that,' said Dad.

Mum was mortified. On the forms at school we wrote 'Engineer', not 'Iron-moulder'. Filling in the forms for university, I went off to a private place and my stomach wrenched for a long time and for 'Father's Profession or Occupation' I crossed out 'Profession' and wrote 'Iron-moulder'.

The man at the appointments board, just before I left, congratulated me.

'Well, well,' he said, 'you're tipped for a first, you edited the university paper, you've done very well for an iron-moulder's son.'

Dad said, 'It went along up the river glowing like molten iron and then it exploded. It was a meteorite.'

'There wasn't any noise,' Mum said.

'I didn't say there was any noise,' Dad said. 'It exploded in a big flash.'

'But explosions usually make a noise,' Mum said.

I don't know whether Dad clipped the letter or not. I've had letters in print that were not intended for print. I think I kept them but kept them beneath dark stacks of things.

'People who've seen them don't seem to talk about them much,' I said.

'That's right,' Mum said. 'We didn't talk about it much, did we?' she said to Dad.

What they talked about was the letter. The shame of being a manual worker and the ridicule for having seen a flying saucer and the breaking of the taboo in revealing these things in print.

PETER CAREY
1943–

THE soldier has been on the line for two weeks. No one has come. The electrified fence stretches across the desert, north to south, south to north, going as far as the eye can see without bending or altering course. In the heat its distant sections shimmer and float. Only at dusk do they return to their true positions. With the exception of the break at the soldier's post the ten-foot-high electrified fence is uninterrupted. Although, further up the line, perhaps twenty miles along, there may be another post similar or identical to this one. Perhaps there is not. Perhaps the break at this post is the only entry point, the only exit point – no one has told him. No one has told him anything except that he must not ask questions. The officer who briefed him told the soldier only what was considered necessary: that the area to the west could be considered the United States, although, in fact, it was not; that the area to the east of the line could be considered to be Australia, which it was; that no one, with the exception of US military personnel carrying a special pass from Southern Command, should be permitted to cross the line at this point. They gave him a photostat copy of an old pass, dated two years before, and drove him out to the line in a Ford truck. That was all.

No one in the United States had briefed him about the line – its existence was never mentioned. No one anywhere has told him if the line is part of a large circle, or whether it is straight; no one has taken the trouble to mention the actual length of the line. The line may go straight across Australia, for all the soldier knows, from north to south, cutting the country in half. And, even if this were the case, he would not know where, would not be able to point out the line's location on a map. He was flown from the United States, together with two cooks, five jeeps, and various other supplies, directly to the base at Yallamby. After they landed there was no orientation brief, no maps – he waited fifteen hours before someone came to claim him.

So, for all he knows, this line could be anywhere in Australia. It is even possible that there are two parallel lines, or perhaps several hundred, each at thirty-mile intervals. It is even possible that some lines are better than others, that not all of them stretch through this desert with its whining silence and singing in the line.

The road crosses the line, roughly, at a right angle. The fact that it is not exactly a right angle has caused him considerable irritation for two weeks. For the first week he was unable to locate the thing that was irritating him, it was something small and hard, like a stone in his boot.

The bitumen road crosses the line at the slightest angle away from a right angle. He has calculated it to be, approximately, eighty-seven degrees. In another month those missing three degrees could become worse.

The soldier, who is standing on double white lines that run the length of the road, kicks a small red rock back into the desert.

The soldier sits inside the door of the caravan, his eyes focused on the dusty screen of his dark glasses, his long body cradled in his armchair. He was informed, three weeks ago, that he would be permitted to bring a crate of specified size containing personal effects. From this he gathered some ill-defined idea of what was ahead of him. He is not a young soldier, and remembering other times in other countries he located an armchair that would fit within the specified dimensions. The remaining space he packed with magazines, thrillers, and a copy of the Bible. The Bible was an afterthought. It puzzled him at the time, but he hasn't thought of it or looked at it since.

He had expected, while he put the crate together, that he would have a fight on his hands, sooner or later, because of that armchair. Because he had envisaged a camp. But there was no camp, merely this caravan on the line.

The soldier polishes and cleans his dark glasses, which were made to prescription in Dallas, Texas, and stands up inside the caravan. As usual he bumps his head. His natural stoop has become more exaggerated, more protective, because of this caravan. He has hit his head so often that he now has a permanent patch that is red and raw, just at the top, just where the crewcut is thin and worn like an old sandy carpet.

But this is not a caravan, not a real caravan. It resembles an aluminium coffin, an aluminium coffin with a peculiar swivelling base constructed like the base of a heavy gun. The soldier has no idea why anyone should design it that way, but he has taken advantage of it, changing the direction of the caravan so that the front door faces away from the wind. Changing the view, is what he calls it, changing the view.

No matter which way you point that door the view doesn't alter. All that changes is the amount of fence you see. Because there is nothing else – no mountains, no grass, nothing but a windmill on the western side of the line. The corporal who drove him out in the Ford said that things grew in the desert if it rained. The corporal said that it rained two years ago. He said small flowers grew all over the desert, flowers and grass.

Once or twice the soldier has set out to walk to the windmill, for no good reason. He is not curious about its purpose – it is like the road, an irritation.

He took plenty of ammunition, two grenades, and his carbine, and while he

walked across the hot rocky desert he kept an eye on the caravan and the break in the wire where the road came through. He was overcome with tiredness before he reached the windmill, possibly because it was further away than it appeared to be, possibly because he knew what it would look like when he got there.

The day before yesterday he came close enough to hear it clanking, a peculiar metallic noise that travelled from the windmill to him, across the desert. No one else in the world could hear that clanking. He spat on the ground and watched his spittle disappear. Then he fired several rounds in the direction of the windmill, just on semi-automatic. Then he turned round and walked slowly back, his neck prickling.

The thermometer recorded 120 degrees inside the caravan when he got back.

The walls are well insulated – about one foot and three inches in thickness. But he has the need to have the door open and the air-conditioner became strange and, eventually, stopped. He hasn't reported the breakdown because it is, after all, of his own making. And, even if they came out from Yallamby and fixed it, he would leave the door open again and it would break down again. And there would be arguments about the door.

He needs the air. It is something he has had since he was small, the need for air coming from outside. Without good air he has headaches, and the air-conditioner does not give good air. Perhaps the other soldiers at the other posts along the line sit inside and peer at the desert through their thick glass windows, if there are any other soldiers. But it is not possible for him to do that. He likes to have the air.

He has had the need since he was a child and the need has not diminished so that now, in his forty-third year, the fights he has fought to keep windows open have brought him a small degree of fame. He is tall and thin and not born to be a fighter, but his need for air forced him to learn. He is not a straight fighter, and would be called dirty in many places, but he has the ability to win, and that is all he has ever needed.

———

Soon he will go out and get himself another bucket of scorpions. The method is simple in the extreme. There are holes every two or three inches apart, all the way across the desert. If you pour water down these holes the scorpions come up. It amuses him to think that they come up to drink. He laughs quietly to himself and talks to the scorpions as they emerge. When they come up he scoops them into a coffee mug and tips them into the blue bucket. Later on he pours boiling water from the artesian bore over the lot of them. That is how he fills a bucket with scorpions.

To the north of the road he marked out a rough grid. Each square of this grid (its interstices marked with empty bottles and beer cans) can be calculated to contain approximately one bucket of scorpions. His plan, a new plan, developed only yesterday, is to rid the desert of a bucket full for each day he is here. As of this moment one square can be reckoned to be clear of scorpions.

The soldier, who has been sitting in his armchair, pulls on his heavy boots and goes in search of yesterday's bucket. The glare outside the caravan is considerable, and, in spite of the sunglasses, he needs to shade his eyes. Most of the glare comes from the aluminium caravan. Everything looks like one of those colour photographs he took in Washington, over-exposed and bleached out.

The blue bucket is where he put it last night, beside the generator. Not having to support the air-conditioning, the generator has become quiet, almost silent.

He takes the blue bucket which once held strawberry jam and empties a soft black mass of scorpions onto the road, right in the middle, across those double white lines. In another two weeks he will have fifteen neat piles right along the centre of the road. If you could manage two bucketfuls a day there would be thirty. Perhaps, if he became really interested in it and worked hard at it, he could have several hundred buckets of scorpions lined up along those double lines. But sooner or later he will be relieved from duty or be visited by the supply truck, and then he will have to remove the scorpions before the truck reaches the spot.

He walks slowly, his boots scuffing the road, the blue bucket banging softly against his long leg, and enters the caravan where he begins to search for a coffee mug. Soon he will go out and get himself another bucket of scorpions.

———

The sun is low now and everything is becoming quieter, or perhaps it is only that the wind, the new wind, suggests quietness while being, in fact, louder. The sand which lies on the hard rocky base of the desert is swept in sudden gusts and flurries. Occasionally one of these small storms engulfs him, stinging his face and arms. But for all the noises of sand and wind it appears to him that there is no sound at all.

He stands in the middle of the road, his shoulders drooping, a copy of *Playboy* in his hand, and gazes along the road, as far as he can see. Somewhere up towards the western horizon he can make out an animal of some type crossing the road. It is not a kangaroo. It is something else but he doesn't know exactly what.

He gazes to the west, over past the windmill, watching the slowly darkening sky. Without turning his legs he twists his trunk and head around to watch the sun sinking slowly in the eastern sky.

He squats a little, bending just enough to place the copy of *Playboy* gently on the road. Walking slowly towards the caravan he looks once more at the windmill which is slowly disappearing in the dark western sky.

The carbine is lying on his bunk. He clips a fresh magazine into it, and returns to his place on the road, his long legs moving slowly over the sand, unhurriedly. The noise of his boots on the roadway reminds him of countless parades. He flicks the carbine to automatic and, having raised it gently to his shoulder, pours the whole magazine into the sun which continues to set in the east.

———

He lies on the bunk in the hot darkness wearing only his shorts and a pair of soft white socks. He has always kept a supply of these socks, a special type pur-

chased from Fish & Degenhardt in Dallas, thick white socks with heavy towel-
ling along the sole to soak up the sweat. He bought a dozen pairs from Fish
& Degenhardt three weeks ago. They cost $4.20 a pair.

He lies on the bunk and listens to the wind in the fence.

There are some things he must settle in his mind but he would prefer, for the
moment, to forget about them. He would like not to think about east or west.
What is east and what is west could be settled quickly and easily. There is an
army issue compass on the shelf above his head. He could go outside now, take
a flashlight with him, and settle it.

But now he is unsure as to what he has misunderstood. Perhaps the area to
the geographical east is to be considered as part of the United States, and the
area to the west as Australian. Or perhaps it is as he remembered: the west is the
United States and the east Australian; perhaps it is this and he has simply
misunderstood which was east and which west. He was sure that the windmill
was in the United States. He seems to remember the corporal making some joke
about it, but it is possible that he misunderstood the joke.

There is also another possibility concerning the sun setting in the east. It
creeps into his mind from time to time and he attempts to prevent it by blocking
his ears.

He had been instructed to keep intruders on the outside but he is no longer
clear as to what 'outside' could mean. If they had taken the trouble to inform
him of what lay 'inside' he would be able to evaluate the seriousness of his
position. He considers telephoning the base to ask, and dismisses it quickly, his
neck and ears reddening at the thought of it.

It is hot, very hot. He tries to see the *Playboy* nude in the dark, craning his
head up from the pillow. He runs his dry fingers over the shiny paper and thinks
about the line. If only they had told him if it was part of a circle, or a square, or
whatever shape it was. Somehow that could help. It would not be so bad if he
knew the shape.

Now, in the darkness, it is merely a line, stretching across the desert as far as
his mind can see. He pulls his knees up to his stomach, clutching his soft socks
in his big dry hands, and rolls over on his side.

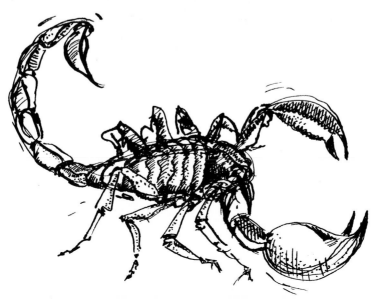

Outside the wind seems to have stopped. Sometimes he thinks he can hear the windmill clanking.

———

The alarm goes at 4.30 a.m. and, although he w   instantly, his head is still filled with unravelled dreams. He does not like   member those dreams. A long line of silk thread spun out of his navel, and   he spinner, could not halt the spinning. He can still taste the emptiness in his stomach. It is not the emptiness of hunger but something more, as if the silk has taken something precious from him.

He bumps round the caravan in the dark. He does not like to use the light. He did not use it last night either. He is happier in the dark. He spills a bottle of insect repellent but finds the coffee next to it. With his cigarette lighter he lights the primus.

He could go outside, if he wanted, and take boiling water straight from the artesian bore, but he is happier to boil it. It makes a small happy noise inside the caravan which is normally so dense and quiet, like a room in an expensive hotel.

It will become light soon. The sun will rise but he doesn't think about this, about the sun, about the line, about what the line divides, encircles, or contains, about anything but the sound of boiling water.

The blue flame of the primus casts a flickering light over the pits and hollows of his face. He can see his face in the shaving mirror, like the surface of a planet, a photograph of the surface of the moon in *Life* magazine. It is strange and unknown to him. He rubs his hands over it, more to cover the reflected image than to feel its texture.

The coffee is ready now and he dresses while it cools off. For some reason he puts on his dress uniform. Just for a change, is what he tells himself. The uniform is clean and pressed, lying in the bottom of his duffle bag. It was pressed in Dallas Texas and still smells of American starch and the clean steam of those big hot laundries with their automatic presses.

In the middle of the desert the smell is like an old snapshot. He smiles in soft surprise as he puts it on.

———

He stands in the middle of the road. It is still cold and he stamps up and down looking at the place where the horizon is. He can make nothing out, nothing but stars, stars he is unfamiliar with. He could never memorise them anyway, never remember which was the bear or the bull, and it had caused him no inconvenience, this lack of knowledge.

He stands in the middle of the road and turns his head slowly around, scanning the soft horizon. Sooner or later there will be a patch, lighter than any other, as if a small city has appeared just over the edge, a city with its lights on. Then it will get bigger and then it will get hot, and before that he will have settled one of the questions concerning east and west.

He turns towards the east. He looks down the road in the direction he has known as 'east' for two weeks, for two weeks until he was crazy enough to watch the sun set. He watches now for a long time. He stands still with his hands behind his back, as if bound, and feels a prickling along the back of his neck.

He stands on the road with his feet astride the double white line, in the at-ease position. He remains standing there until an undeniable shadow is cast in front of him. It is his own shadow, long and lean, stretching along the road, cast by the sun which is rising in the 'west'. He slowly turns to watch the windmill which is silhouetted against the clear morning sky.

It is some time later, perhaps five minutes, perhaps thirty, when he notices the small aeroplane. It is travelling down from the 'north', directly above the wire and very low. It occurs to him that the plane is too low to be picked up by radar, but he is not alarmed. In all likelihood it is an inspection tour, a routine check, or even a supply visit. The plane has been to the other posts up 'north', a little further along the line.

Only when the plane is very close does he realise that is is civilian. Then it is over him, over the caravan, and he can see its civilian registration. As it circles and comes in to land on the road he is running hard for the caravan and his carbine. He stuffs his pockets full of clips and emerges as the plane comes to rest some ten yards from the caravan.

What now follows, he experiences distantly. As if he himself were observing his actions. He was once in a car accident in California where his tyre blew on the highway. He still remembers watching himself battle to control the car, he watched quite calmly, without fear.

Now he motions the pilot out of the plane and indicates that he should stand by the wing with his hands above his head. Accustomed to service in foreign countries he has no need of the English language. He grunts in a certain manner, waving and poking with the carbine to add meaning to the sounds. The pilot speaks but the soldier has no need to listen.

The pilot is a middle-aged man with a fat stomach. He is dressed in white: shorts, shirt, and socks. He has the brown shoes and white skin of a city man. He appears concerned. The soldier cannot be worried by this. He asks the pilot what he wants, using simple English, easy words to understand.

The man replies hurriedly, explaining that he is lost and nearly out of petrol. He is on his way to a mission station, at a place that the soldier does not even bother to hear – it would mean nothing.

The soldier then indicates that the pilot may sit in the shade beneath the wing of the aircraft. The pilot appears doubtful, perhaps thinking of his white clothing, but having looked at the soldier he moves awkwardly under the wing, huddling strangely.

The soldier then explains that he will telephone. He also explains that, should the man try to move or escape, he will be shot.

'HE slowly turns to watch the windmill which is silhouetted against the clear morning sky.'

He dials the number he has never dialled before. At the moment of dialling he realises that he is unsure of what the telephone is connected to: Yallamby base which is on the 'outside', or whatever is on the 'inside'.

The phone is answered. It is an officer, a major he has never heard of. He explains the situation to the major who asks him details about the type of fuel required. The soldier steps outside and obtains the information, then returns to the major on the phone.

Before hanging up the major asks, what side of the wire was he on?

The soldier replies, on the outside.

It is two hours before the truck comes. It is driven by a captain. That is strange, but it does not surprise the soldier. However it disappoints him, for he had hoped to settle a few questions regarding the 'outside' and 'inside'. It will be impossible to settle them now.

There are few words. The captain and the soldier unload several drums and a hand pump. The captain reprimands the soldier for his lack of courtesy to the pilot. The soldier salutes.

The captain and the pilot exchange a few words while the soldier fixes the tailboard of the truck – the pilot appears to be asking questions but it is impossible to hear what he asks or how he is answered.

The captain turns the truck round, driving off the road and over the scorpion grid, and returns slowly to wherever he came from.

'THE captain turns the truck round, driving off the road and over the scorpion grid, and returns slowly to wherever he came from.'

The pilot waves from his open cockpit. The soldier returns his greeting, waving slowly from his position beside the road. The pilot guns the motor and taxis along the road, then turns, ready for take-off.

At this point it occurs to the soldier that the man may be about to fly across the 'inside', across what is the United States. It is his job to prevent this. He tries to wave the man down but he seems to be occupied with other things, or misunderstands the waving. The plane is now accelerating and coming towards the soldier. He runs toward it, waving.

It is impossible to know what is the 'inside'. It would have been impossible to ask a captain. They could have court-martialled him for that.

He stands beside the road as the small plane comes towards him, already off the road. It is perhaps six feet off the road when he levels his carbine and shoots. The wings tip slightly to the left and then to the right. In the area known as the 'west' the small aeroplane tips on to its left wing, rolls, and explodes in a sudden blast of flame and smoke.

The soldier, who is now standing in the middle of the road, watches it burn.

He has a mattock, pick, and shovel. He flattens what he can and breaks those members that can be broken. Then he begins to dig a hole in which to bury the remains of the aeroplane. The ground is hard, composed mostly of rock. He will need a big hole. His uniform, his dress uniform, has become blackened and dirty. He digs continually, his fingers and hands bleeding and blistered. There are many scorpions. He cannot be bothered with them, there is no time. He tells them, there is no time now.

It is hot, very hot.

He digs, weeping slowly with fatigue.

Sometimes, while he digs, he thinks he can hear the windmill clanking. He weeps slowly, wondering if the windmill could possibly hear him.

THE MANAGERESS AND THE MIRAGE

ROBERT DREWE
1943–

Y father wasn't in his element in party hats. His head was too big; the mauve crepe-paper crown stretched around his wide forehead looked neither festive nor humorous, just faintly ridiculous. Annie and David and I sat embarrassed in silly hats as well. They were compulsory fun, Dad was definite about them. We'd always worn them at home and the normal Christmas dinner routine was being followed wherever possible.

There was one major difference this Christmas: because our mother had died in July we were having dinner at the Seaview Hotel instead of at home. Consequently we were observing several other minor variations on our traditional dinner – we ate roast turkey instead of the usual chicken and ham, we children were allowed glasses of pink champagne alongside our glasses of lemonade, and the plum pudding contained plastic tokens like Monopoly symbols – obviously poked into the pudding later – rather than real threepences and sixpences cooked into it.

When Dad suggested that we eat dinner at the hotel we agreed readily enough. Since July we'd had a middle-aged woman, Gladys Barker, housekeeping for us. Dad called her Glad to her face, but to us he sometimes called her Gladly – as in the hymn 'Gladly My Cross I'd Bear' – because of her sighs around the house and air of constant martyrdom. We thought this was funny, but at the time we thought he was saying 'Gladly, My Cross-Eyed Bear' so we

had it wrong for five or six years. Glad's cooking was unexceptional, a depressing prospect for Christmas dinner, and anyway, without anyone spelling it out, this Christmas we wanted to keep the family unit tight and self-contained.

I caught Annie's and David's eyes from time to time, but they showed only a vague self-consciousness as we sat in the hotel dining room in our party hats and school uniforms, picking at our meals, gingerly sipping pink champagne and pulling crackers. Dad was becoming increasingly amiable, however, even hearty. It was clear to us that he was making an effort. He made jokes and we laughed at them, for him rather than with him, out of mutual support.

'Remember I was travelling the other week to a sales conference down at Albany?' he said. 'Well, I stopped overnight at Mount Barker. I went down to dinner in the hotel dining room and on the menu was rabbit casserole. I said to the waitress, "Excuse me, dear, is that with or without myxomatosis?"'

'"I wouldn't know," she said, very po-faced. "It's all in the gravy."'

He was trying hard for all our sakes. It had not dawned on me before that I loved him and the realisation was slightly embarrassing.

Soon he became the dining room's focus of attention. Selecting a plastic whistle from the cracker debris, he blew it gamely. Other nearby guests, observing us and seeing the lie of the land, smiled encouragingly at us and followed suit. An old fellow gave Annie his cracker toy. A fat man tickled his wife's nose with a feathered whistle; she balanced a champagne cork on his sunburnt head. Crackers popped and horns tooted. Above these antics a fan slowly revolved.

Beyond the high expanse of windows the ocean glistened into the west, where atmospheric conditions had magically turned Rottnest Island into three distinct islands. Annie was struck by the mysterious asymmetry of this illusion.

'It's gone wrong,' she said loudly, pointing out to sea. The other guests began murmuring about the phenomenon. Annie's plaits looked irregular; one was thicker than the other; Dad still hadn't mastered them. 'The lighthouse has gone,' she said.

'No, it's still there,' Dad said, and tried to explain mirages, mentioning deserts and oases, with emphasis on the Sahara. I knew the horizon was always twelve miles away, but I couldn't grasp the idea of shifting islands or the creation of non-existent ones. So thirsty people in deserts saw visions of water – why would people bursting with food and drink see visions of land?

As our plates were being removed our table drew special attention from the hotel manageress. A handsome dark-haired woman in her thirties, she clapped her hands authoritatively for more champagne, and more crackers for us to pull, and joined us for a drink, inquiring about out presents with oddly curious eyes. Dad introduced us.

She announced to me, 'You do look like your father, Max.' She remarked on Annie's pretty hair and on the importance of David looking after his new watch. Sportively, she donned a blue paper crown and looked at us over the rim of her champagne glass. As the plum pudding was being served she left the table and returned with gifts for us wrapped in gold paper – fountain pens for David and me, a doll for Annie. Surprised, we looked to Dad for confirmation.

He showed little surprise at the gifts, however, only polite gratitude, intoning several times, 'Very, very kind of you.'

'Rex, it gave me pleasure,' the manageress said. 'They're a credit to you.' She called him Rex, not Mr Lang. His eyes were moist at her compliment. He lit a cigar and leant back in his seat, crown askew, like Old King Cole.

After the plum pudding (he and the manageress had brandies instead) and another cracker pulling we thanked her again for our presents, on his instructions, and he sent us outside while he paid the bill.

'Get some fresh air, kids,' he said.

We trooped out to the car park. Before today the car park had been the only part of the Seaview Hotel familiar to us. Sometimes on Saturday mornings we'd languished there, watching the ocean swells roll in, dying for a swim, squabbling in the Ford's back seat or desultorily reading Shell road maps from the glovebox while Dad had a drink or two.

'I have to see a chap about something,' he'd say, bringing us out glasses of raspberry lemonade. A frightening hubbub sounded from the bar, yet he would turn and stride back into this noise and smoke and beer-smell with all the cheer in the world.

Outside, the mirage persisted. Rottnest was still three oddly attenuated islands which seemed to be sailing south. The afternoon sea breeze was late and the temperature lingered in the nineties. The heat haze smudged the definition of the horizon and the Indian Ocean stretched flat and slick to Mauritius and beyond before curving into the sky.

David said, 'Did you smell her perfume?' and made a face. He loosened his tie and farted from the champagne. Annie poked at her doll's eyes. 'I've got one like this called Amanda,' she said. We presumed who had given her the other doll yet by unspoken agreement no one mentioned her. I knew the others were thinking that normally at this time we'd be unwrapping presents from the tree. She would play cheery Christmas records on the radiogram and run from the kitchen bringing us mints and nuts and little mince pies.

Eyes remained dry as we walked to the car. The car park was almost empty because of the bars being closed for Christmas. Asphalt bubbled, a broken beer glass from Christmas Eve sat on the veranda rail and the smell of stale beer settled over the beer garden. Around the garden's dusty, worn lawn, red and yellow hibiscuses wilted in the heat. Christmas was running short of breath. One after another, David, Annie and I snatched off our party hats, crumpled them and threw them on the ground.

The imaginary islands, showing smoky silhouettes of hills and tall trees, kept sailing south. From the car you could see into the manageress's office. She was combing his hair where his party hat had ruffled it. He came out whistling 'Jingle Bells' and the stench of his cigar filled the car.

BEING HERE NOW

ANGELO
LOUKAKIS
1951~

I sit outside the theatre and can do nothing but exercise my memory. As I wait to see if he will live (they tell me this open-heart stuff has a ninety-five per cent success rate), I make him young again. I find him in another life. The late fifties, early sixties, they were his salad days.

Say Christmas around 1960.

My memory lets me down on this, but, on the theory that there were always heatwaves in our little Arncliffe, I would say this was a week of heat. Why not? I can remember nearly everything else.

He comes up from the yard behind the shop, in his singlet. It's soaked in sweat.

'We can do nothing about this heat. We have to live with it. Open the doors, close the doors, what's the difference? We are baking in hell.'

'Doesn't matter,' I say. 'Christmas is soon. Aren't we gonna put up decorations? All the big shops have decorations, why can't we have some?'

'*Kala. Pare* six bob from the till. Six bob only. Go up the paper shop. But listen, don't bring me back rubbish.'

I take at least eight bob and go via Frank's Milk Bar so I can play the pinball first. The Hawaii machine, two games for one shilling, replay for lucky number. And only then do I go, two doors up, to the paper shop and buy glass baubles and tinsel and a cardboard Santa. Mrs Mack wraps it up in brown paper, and after that I start back to our Mixed Business.

I always hate the bits of footpath with no awnings in the summer because it's always so stinking hot. And so I run the last little bit to our place, and finish up red and panting anyway. But I have to get inside quick, don't I?

He doesn't look in the parcel straight away. He always thinks I never do as I'm told. So he just asks, and I tell him what I got. He doesn't say anything else, so I must have done right, probably....

'But still we have to get the trees don't forget,' I say.

'Tomorrow.'

The sister comes and calls me, because they are wheeling him out of the operating theatre and into intensive care. How is he? Reasonable. It was a bit complicated. A couple of things the surgeon wasn't expecting. He is stable, however.

When I see him, he doesn't recognise me. He is doped up and will remain that way for a couple more days, they tell me.

The next day when I come to visit he is asleep, and I wait in a chair by his bed. Where was I? I was going to go to the markets today, to buy the trees.

I had this pet thermometer which I bought at the chemist and carried around with me everywhere. No doubt I had it in my pocket that December morning. I do up the button on my shirt pocket so it doesn't fall out when we push the Renno around the corner. I help him do this every day so it can roll down the hill and get started. There's something wrong with the battery. There's always something wrong with the battery.

And it's hot again today. In the car, I look at the temperature on my thermometer. Eighty degrees at nine a.m.

I love it at the markets, the Haymarket, the way he knows everybody, their names, and everybody knows him.

'We go to the Chinese man for Christmas trees, but first we got to get fruit and vegetables,' he says. He sends me to get a trolley. Then he lets me wheel it to the first stand, and then it starts to get full, and then he takes over.

A box of lettuce, a box of tomatoes, a half-case of cucumbers, a sack of onions....

'Enough until after Christmas,' he says. I know we don't sell much. He pushes all the stuff back to the car and I help him put it in. I watch the muscles move on his arms. He's got big hands too. (I look at mine and compare them to his as he lies there, still groggy, twenty-four hours after they slit his chest open. His hands are still large. Mine are still small. Except for them, every part of him seems wired to something, and there are drips in his forearms.)

Then he says –

'Go to the Chinese man, you know the one, and wait. I'll be there in a minute for the trees.'

I know what he does. When he sends me to wait somewhere at the markets, it's so he can go to one of the pubs and have a couple of quick ones. I don't care. Only I'm not supposed to tell my mother what he does, he told me once.

When he comes back, he's smiling at me, looking like it's *him* that's done something wrong for a change. But not really wrong, and we're both in it together, aren't we? He kisses me, even though he knows I don't like him doing it when anybody is around.

And now, twenty years later, he's lying in this hospital bed. He's been coming round for the last hour or two. Finally, he moves his arm, meaning that I should come closer.

'What time it is?'

'Two in the afternoon.'

'I woke up so quick,' he says slowly.

He is thinking it is the afternoon of the day of his operation.

'It's not the same day. It's two o'clock the next day. It's Wednesday today,' I tell him. He nods and then closes his eyes again. He seems so incredibly tired. I stay a little longer, then leave to go back to the office.

Today, three days after his operation, they tell me he is going to be right. I settle back to pass the time while he sleeps, playing my game, putting it all back together again. There was a time when he wasn't such a mess. I wish it were still here, that time.

———

Mr Chin starts up like he always does –
  'Is he a good boy?'
  'Yes, he's a good boy,' my father answers.
  'Help his father?'
  'Yes, he help his father.'
  Mr Chin smiles at me.
  'Help your father, son. Jackie here works hard. I work bloody hard myself.'
  Mr Chin calls everyone Jackie. My father's name is Pavlos. 'Help your father, son,' I keep thinking as he picks out three small trees. I take out my thermometer as we head back to the car. Ninety today. How are we gonna get the trees in the car? The ends will have to stick out the window, he says.
  We pull them out of the car first when we get back. One is for us, one is for Mrs Riley, and one is to put in the shop for sale – only one because our customers usually get their trees from the big fruit and veg. up the road.

———

Christmas Eve? I would have delivered the tree that was ordered, like I always did. My father puts our own tree in an old five-gallon ice-cream tin with some water, and carries it into our living room behind the shop. He puts some Christmas paper around the tin to hide it. Then I'm allowed to put the decorations up.

———

Christmas morning 1960? Presents. Some clothes, a model airplane kit from Phil, son of the lady who cleans the shop once a week. And I get a Meccano set from my parents. This part I like. But then my father says Kosta and Maria and Dimitri and some other friends of my mother's are going to come around in the afternoon – same as every Christmas. They'll make Greek food, which I like, but they'll play records on the radiogram too, which I don't. Her records are always whining ones, and everyone is always singing high notes. And that's how it was.

———

And I'm thinking maybe after lunch I'll remind him of those times. He likes to hear stories about the past, not much less than he likes telling them.
  I watch him eat, slowly cutting up his cottage pie and piling small amounts of potato on to his fork. I know he doesn't like this sort of food. He likes plenty of *salsa*, lamb and beans done Greek style, everything juicy. He pushes the bowl of custard with half an apricot on top to one side. He does like tea, however, which he eventually drinks leaning back against the pillows.
  'Almost Christmas.... Are you feeling sentimental?' I ask him.
  An ironic smile, and he points to the dressing on his chest.
  'Here is my present,' he shakes his head, and then tears well in his eyes.

'I've been thinking of Christmas when I was a kid.... Do you remember when I was always at you to buy the decorations? And I came to the markets to buy trees? Remember? Every year I used to....'

'Not *every* year,' he says. 'You come a couple of times.'

'I used to deliver them to your customers.'

'Sometimes....' He smiles again. 'You didn't like to make the deliveries. You complained. I want to go out! I want to ride my bike! ... You forget.'

'Remember the trouble we used to have with those old Rennos? Trying to get them started to go to the markets?'

He grins again. 'The Renno was a good car.'

'That's not what I thought,' I say, knowing that when he interrupts me like this, I may as well give up. He's not in his listening mood. Anything you say he just takes as a cue for himself.

'The doctors say everything is OK, You are going to be right.'

I hold his hand but he doesn't seem to notice. He seems to drift off for a few moments, then he says –

'Yes. The surgeon come to see me before. Same thing, he said.'

'It's a pity you won't be out for Christmas.'

'Pah. I don't care about Christmas. You know that.'

'Not even if you were in Greece?' I say, trying to get him on to his favourite subject.

My old man lives in his mind, and always, for as long as I've been aware of these things, has done. It's the only way he can cope with his life, which he hasn't liked for years, but hasn't been able or willing to fix either. In recent years I've spent plenty of energy trying to find things we could talk to each other about – although he himself has never bothered to do the same. I haven't been able to find too many. My father is a very selfish man.

'If I had stayed in Greece, I never would be sick. In Australia everybody gets sick, doctors, hospital all the time.'

'It's the change of diet. Too much animal fat. No exercise. Too much stress. All those things have....'

'No, it's the water,' he says. 'And the climate. All my life here, forty years, I never had a drink of water taste good. Clean water. From the mountains, and cold. I remember still the taste.... You telling me before about Christmas when you was a kid. When I was young, not just twenty, but *fifty* years before, I can remember, and I can tell you.'

'So tell me.'

'We had plenty holidays. St Nicholas Day and Christmas and New Year and *Ta Fota*. We play cards, everybody get together and we play cards on the eve of New Year – *ti Kali Hera*, we call it. In winter don't forget, I'm talking about. In the village we kill one or two pigs and make sausages. Only one time a year we had sausages. That was Christmas time. And the smell, and the taste, mmm....'

'Did it snow where you were?'

'Yes, sometimes it snow too.'

The nurse comes to take pulse and blood pressure readings, and while she's doing that I go for a walk down the corridor.

'ONLY one time a year we had sausages. That was Christmas time. And the smell, and the taste, mmm....'

I am so tired of humouring him, even as sick as he has been. I've humoured him for years, and I'm doing it now. I wonder when it's going to end. Probably never.

I've been looking after him for years, although he doesn't seem to realise, or want to acknowledge the fact. I've arranged for this operation. I'm paying his bills. And what's my return? Nil. He doesn't really care about me.

He switched off years ago. When he decided that fate had dealt him blows he just hadn't deserved, he cut everyone out. My mother, myself, everyone. He couldn't cope, so he made life a misery for everyone else.

As I walk back towards his part of the ward, I see the nurse exit.

'How are they, Mr Krinos's readings?'

'They're fine. He's doing well.'

When I get to his bed he says –

'You didn't go. I thought maybe you go back to work.'

'No, I'm still here.'

'I remember some more. You talk before about Christmas, what you did. And I tell you about snow in the old country?'

'Yes.'

'I remember something more.... One time, near Christmas, or end of the year – I'm talking maybe 1927, '28 – my father tell me he have a job for me – to take some potatoes, a sack of potatoes he grow himself, to my uncle up in Varvisa. Varvisa is the village high up from us in the mountains. I was twelve, thirteen *chronos*. I never been to that place by myself before – but I know where it is. That's what I say to myself. The donkey I been riding everywhere else, so my father say, take the donkey, put the potatoes in the pack, and take him up to Varvisa.

'It was afternoon when he tell me to do this job. Really, it takes one day to go up to Varvisa and come back down. He gives me only half-day. But I love my father and I do what he say. I take the donkey and start to go to my uncle in Varvisa.

'The road is very long. Ten kilometres. Twelve kilometres, maybe more. And....'

He can't find the word, and tilts his hand upwards instead.

'Steep,' I say.

'Steep. Yes. Steep.... Only times before I went to this village I went with my father. And this time I think to myself, I know how to go there. So, I'm going. One hour. Two hour. Should be about three hour. But three hour pass and no *horio*, no Varvisa. Then four hour. It's after four o'clock. It's late. Then I see I am lost. I am lost. I have to think what to do. What can I do? I turn around and come back down.

'And I am very upset. All the way I come back down I think how stupid I am, how every time I do wrong thing. My father send me to do the job, like man, and I can't do it.

'Anyway, I am back in Ritopolis, oh, after dark, and I put the donkey in the shed, and quietly I take potatoes and pack off him. I am doing this and my father hear the noise and he come to the shed. He has the lamp with him, because it is dark in there, and he see me. Me and the potatoes.'

'What did you say?'

'I say nothing. I am very upset. I remember even now. I start to cry. He say to me, "I send you to do job, to your uncle, and you come back like this. What's the matter with you? Where you been?" He ask me questions and questions, and me, I am crying.'

And my old man's eyes, which had been welling up as he was speaking, finally spill over.

'It's all right,' I say to him. 'It's all right. That was a long time ago. It's all over now. All over. Come on. You're all right.'

I take his hand, and the tears start to subside.

'You've been through a lot,' I say. 'The operation was hard, I know. But you're going to be better now.'

He nods hopefully. He just nods. Looking like the kid he really is. And immediately succeeds in turning me off again. He is so self-indulgent it is unbelievable. How I am going to put up with his old age is beyond me. There's no one else to look after him. He's only in his sixties and already he's a fond old fool. I don't know what the answer is. I know I can't go on resenting him like this. I'll finish up with some disease myself.

I think there's nothing I can do but just put up with it. Depressing as that prospect is. I decide I should leave him for today.

'I'm going now,' I try to tell him, but he's so tired, he's already falling asleep. A meal and fifteen minutes' talk is enough to wipe him out at this stage of his recovery.

I walk away from the ward. The answer is to try not to think what things might be like tomorrow. Being here now is what I should be aiming at. Great.

NEIGHBOURS

TIM WINTON
1960–

WHEN they first moved in, the young couple were wary of the neighbourhood. The street was full of European migrants. It made the newly-weds feel like sojourners in a foreign land. Next door on the left lived a Macedonian family. On the right, a widower from Poland.

The newly-weds' house was small, but its high ceilings and paned windows gave it the feel of an elegant cottage. From his study window, the young man could see out over the rooftops and used-car yards the Moreton Bay figs in the park where they walked their dog. The neighbours seemed cautious about the dog, a docile, moulting collie.

The young man and woman had lived all their lives in the expansive outer suburbs where good neighbours were seldom seen and never heard. The sounds of spitting and washing and daybreak watering came as a shock. The Macedonian family shouted, ranted, screamed. It took six months for the newcomers to comprehend the fact that their neighbours were not murdering each other, merely talking. The old Polish man spent most of his day hammering nails into wood only to pull them out again. His yard was stacked with salvaged lumber. He added to it, but he did not build with it.

Relations were uncomfortable for many months. The Macedonians raised eyebrows at the late hour at which the newcomers rose in the mornings. The young man sensed their disapproval at his staying home to write his thesis while his wife worked. He watched in disgust as the little boy next door urinated in the street. He once saw him spraying the cat from the back step. The child's head was shaved regularly, he assumed, in order to make his hair grow thick. The little boy stood at the fence with only his cobalt eyes showing; it made the young man nervous.

In the autumn, the young couple cleared rubbish from their backyard and turned and manured the soil under the open and measured gaze of the neighbours. They planted leeks, onions, cabbage, brussels sprouts and broad beans and this caused the neighbours to come to the fence and offer advice about spacing, hilling, mulching. The young man resented the interference, but he took careful note of what was said. His wife was bold enough to run a hand over the child's stubble and the big woman with black eyes and butcher's arms gave her a bagful of garlic cloves to plant.

Not long after, the young man and woman built a henhouse. The neighbours watched it fall down. The Polish widower slid through the fence uninvited and rebuilt it for them. They could not understand a word he said.

As autumn merged into winter and the vermilion sunsets were followed by sudden, dark dusks touched with the smell of wood smoke and the sound of roosters crowing day's end, the young couple found themselves smiling back at the neighbours. They offered heads of cabbage and took gifts of grappa and firewood. The young man worked steadily at his thesis on the development of

the twentieth century novel. He cooked dinners for his wife and listened to her stories of eccentric patients and hospital incompetence. In the street they no longer walked with their eyes lowered. They felt superior and proud when their parents came to visit and to cast shocked glances across the fence.

In the winter they kept ducks, big, silent muscovies that stood about in the rain growing fat. In the spring the Macedonian family showed them how to slaughter and to pluck and to dress. They all sat around on blocks and upturned buckets and told barely-understood stories – the men butchering, the women plucking, as was demanded. In the haze of down and steam and fractured dialogue, the young man and woman felt intoxicated. The cat toyed with several heads. The child pulled the cat's tail. The newcomers found themselves shouting.

But they had not planned on a pregnancy. It stunned them to be made parents so early. Their friends did not have children until several years after being married – if at all. The young woman arranged for maternity leave. The young man ploughed on with his thesis on the twentieth century novel.

The Polish widower began to build. In the late spring dawns, he sank posts and poured cement and began to use his wood. The young couple turned in their bed, cursed him behind his back. The young husband, at times, suspected that the widower as deliberately antagonising them. The young wife threw up in the mornings. Hay fever began to wear him down.

Before long the young couple realised that the whole neighbourhood knew of the pregnancy. People smiled tirelessly at them. The man in the deli gave her small presents of chocolates and him packets of cigarettes that he stored at home, not being a smoker. In the summer, Italian women began to offer names. Greek women stopped the young woman in the street, pulled her skirt up and felt her belly, telling her it was bound to be a boy. By late summer the woman next door had knitted the baby a suit, complete with booties and beanie. The young woman felt flattered, claustrophobic, grateful, peeved.

By late summer, the Polish widower next door had almost finished his two-car garage. The young man could not believe that a man without a car would do such a thing, and one evening as he was considering making a complaint about the noise, the Polish man came over with barrowfuls of wood scraps for their fire.

Labour came abruptly. The young man abandoned the twentieth century novel for the telephone. His wife began to black the stove. The midwife came and helped her finish the job while he ran about making statements that sounded like queries. His wife hoisted her belly about the house, supervising his movements. Going outside for more wood, he saw, in the last light of the day, the faces at each fence. He counted twelve faces. The Macedonian family waved and called out what sounded like their best wishes.

As the night deepened, the young woman dozed between contractions, sometimes walking, sometimes shouting. She had a hot bath and began to eat ice and demand liverwurst. Her belly rose, uterus flexing downward. Her sweat sparkled, the gossamer highlit by movement and firelight. The night grew older. The midwife crooned. The young man rubbed his wife's back, fed her ice and rubbed her lips with oil.

And then came the pushing. He caressed and stared and tried not to shout. The floor trembled as the young woman bore down in a squat. He felt the power of her, the sophistication of her. She strained. Her face mottled. She kept at it, push after push, assaulting some unseen barrier, until suddenly it was smashed and she was through. It took his wind away to see the look on the baby's face as it was suddenly passed up to the breast. It had one eye on him. It found the nipple. It trailed cord and vernix smears and its mother's own sweat. She gasped and covered the tiny buttocks with a hand. A boy, she said. For a second, the child lost the nipple and began to cry. The young man heard shouting outside. He went to the back door. On the Macedonian side of the fence, a small queue of bleary faces looked up, cheering, and the young man began to weep. The twentieth century novel had not prepared him for this.

INDEX OF
AUTHORS

with brief biographies and select bibliographies

MENA ABDULLAH

MENA ABDULLAH was born in 1930 at Bundarra, New South Wales, of Indian extraction. Her father was a sheep farmer and she was brought up in the country. She was educated at Sydney Girls' High School. She worked in an administrative post with the Commonwealth Scientific and Industrial Research Organization in Sydney. She collaborated with Ray Mathew (q.v.) in writing a collection of stories, *The Time of the Peacock* (1965). Her stories reflect the joys and sorrows of an Indian family accepting and sometimes rebelling against Australian life.

The Time of the Peacock, 1965.

Pages 220–225

MURRAY BAIL

MURRAY BAIL was born in 1941 at Adelaide. He lived in India from 1968–70 and then spent four years in England and Europe. In London he wrote for *Transatlantic Review* and the *Times Literary Supplement*. A collection of stories, *Contemporary Portraits*, was published in 1975 and established his reputation as an original and subtle writer, a reputation consolidated by his novel *Homesickness* (1980). His work has been published in England and the USA. He has a deep interest in art, and for some years was a trustee of the Australian National Gallery. In 1981 he published a monograph on the painter Ian Fairweather. He lives in Balmain, Sydney.

Contemporary Portraits and Other Stories, 1975.

Pages 252–256

MARJORIE BARNARD

MARJORIE BARNARD was born in 1897 at Ashfield, Sydney, and was educated at Sydney Girls' High School and the University of Sydney, where she took first-class honours in history. Her father would not let her take up a graduate Oxford scholarship. She became friends with Flora Eldershaw, with whom she later wrote books under the pseudonym M. Barnard Eldershaw. Other literary friends included Frank Dalby Davison, Vance and Nettie Palmer and Miles Franklin. Barnard worked until 1935 as a librarian at the Sydney Technical College. She has been a noted historian and critic as well as a writer of fiction under her own name and in collaboration with Flora Eldershaw. She was awarded the AO in 1980, and won the Patrick White Literary Award in 1983. She lives at Point Clare, NSW.

The Persimmon Tree and Other Stories, 1943. With Flora Eldershaw, *A House is Built*, 1929; *Tomorrow and Tomorrow*, 1947; an uncensored version was published in 1983 as *Tomorrow and Tomorrow and Tomorrow*.

Pages 79–82

BARBARA BAYNTON's origins were for many years romanticised. She claimed to have been born in 1862, the result of an elopement of a young married woman with an Indian Army officer. In fact she was born in 1857 at Scone, NSW, the daughter of a carpenter. She married a selector, Alexander Frater, in 1880; after she had borne him three children he left her for a servant. Divorced in 1890, she married Thomas Baynton, a retired surgeon. In 1896 her first story was published in the *Bulletin*. In 1902–3 she was in London, where her collection of stories, *Bush Studies*, was published. Dr Baynton died in 1904, leaving her well-off and able to move between England and Australia. In 1921 she embarked on a brief marriage with Lord Headley. Baynton's grim stories of the bush are oddly different from most of her life.

Bush Studies, 1902.

Pages 17–22

LOUIS BECKE was born George Lewis Becke in 1855 at Port Macquarie, NSW. From 1869 to 1894 he wandered the Pacific as sailor and trader; once he was supercargo with the pirate 'Bully' Hayes. In Sydney in 1893 he met J.F. Archibald, who helped him turn his yarns into stories that could be published in the *Bulletin*. Becke said that Archibald 'taught me the secrets of condensation and simplicity of language'. In 1894 a collection of his Pacific stories, *By Reef and Palm*, was published in London with a preface by the Earl of Pembroke, who had himself co-authored a celebrated book of Pacific adventures, *South Sea Bubbles*, by The Earl and The Doctor. Becke wrote thirty-five books, and is one of the most esteemed of writers about the Pacific. He died in poverty in Sydney, in 1913.

By Reef and Palm, 1894; *The Ebbing of the Tide*, 1896; *Pacific Tales*, 1897; *Under Tropic Skies*, 1904; *The Call of the South*, 1908.

Pages 12–16

DAVID CAMPBELL was born in 1915 at Ellerslie station, Adelong, NSW. He was educated at The King's School, Parramatta, and at Jesus College, Cambridge, where his tutor in English was the well-known scholar E.M.W. Tillyard. Campbell represented the University in boxing and played football for England. He served as a pilot in the RAAF in World War II, and was awarded the DFC and bar, reaching the rank of Squadron-Leader. He lived on various properties for most of his life, giving his time to farming and to poetry. He is one of Australia's finest lyric poets, and received a number of awards in recognition of his poetry. He published two volumes of short stories. *Evening Under Lamplight* is about growing up on a sheep station. Campbell died in 1979.

Evening Under Lamplight, 1959; *Flame and Shadow*, 1976.

Pages 172–176

PETER CAREY

PETER CAREY was born in 1943 at Bacchus Marsh, Victoria. He was educated at Geelong Grammar School and Monash University where he studied science. After leaving university he worked in advertising in Melbourne and London and Sydney. Carey began writing fiction in his early twenties, when he completed three unpublished novels. His short stories began appearing in the literary magazines and in the 1970s two volumes of these were published. He won the New South Wales Premier's Literary Award in 1980. His novel, *Bliss*, was published in 1981; in 1985 came *Illywhacker*, which was short-listed for the Booker Prize and has won some major awards in Australia. A notable film was made from *Bliss*. Carey lives in Sydney, and gives his time to working in advertising and writing fiction.

The Fat Man in History, 1974; *War Crimes*, 1979.

Pages 278–286

NANCY CATO

NANCY CATO was born in 1917 in Adelaide, SA, where she worked as a journalist and art critic on the *News*. She married the motor racing driver Eldred Norman, and has three children. She has published poetry as well as fiction. One of her favourite subjects, both in verse and prose, has been the Murray River. Her trilogy of novels with the Murray as background was reworked and brought together in one volume, *All the Rivers Run* (1978). This has been translated into several languages and has become a best-seller in many countries; a television mini-series was made from it. Nancy Cato lives in Queensland. In 1984 she was awarded the AM for services to literature.

The Sea Ants and Other Stories, 1964.

Pages 183–186

PETER COWAN

PETER COWAN was born in 1914 in Perth of an old Western Australian family. A grandmother, Edith Cowan, was the first woman member of an Australian parliament; Cowan has written a biography of her. His first job was as an insurance clerk, and he spent several of the Depression years working as an itinerant farm labourer. In 1938 he enrolled at the University of Western Australia, where he took an Arts degree. In World War II he served in the RAAF. He has taught English at Scots College, Perth, and at the University of Western Australia. Cowan has published seven collections of short stories and two novels. Much of the best of his fiction deals with the rigours of life on the land, but he also writes well about the tensions of life in the city. A self-effacing man, he lives in Perth where he is co-editor of the literary magazine *Westerly*.

Drift, 1944; *The Unploughed Land*, 1958; *The Empty Street*, 1965; *The Tins*, 1973; *New Country*, 1976; *Mobiles*, 1979; *A Window in Mrs X's Place*, 1986.

Pages 163–171

FRANK DALBY DAVISON was born in 1893 at Glenferrie, Victoria. He was chris-
tened Frederick Douglas, but when he began writing he called himself Frank
Dalby to distinguish himself from his father Frederick, a real estate business-
man who also ran a journal, the *Australian*. Davison left school at twelve and
worked on farms, before moving with his family to the USA in 1908, where he
was apprenticed to a printer. He travelled in North America and the Caribbean
before enlisting in the British Army in World War I. After the War he spent
four years as a soldier settler in the Maranoa district, and then joined his father
in Sydney, where two of his novels were serialised in the *Australian*. He could not
find a publisher for *Man-Shy*, his novel about a wild red heifer, so he printed it
and peddled it himself around Sydney householders. It won the Australian
Literature Society's medal in 1931 and has been in print ever since. He believed
his major work to be the very long novel *The White Thorntree* (1968), a study of
sexuality in suburban life. Davison died in 1970, on the farm in Victoria where
he had lived for some twenty years with his second wife, Marie.

The Woman at the Mill, 1940; *The Road to Yesterday*, 1964.

Pages 64–72

ROBERT DREWE was born in 1943 in Melbourne. He accompanied his family to
Western Australia where he was educated and began work as a journalist. He
has worked for the *West Australian*, the *Australian*, the *Age* and the *Bulletin*, and
has won several awards for journalism, including the Walkley Award in 1976
and 1981. He has published a number of short stories, and two novels, *The
Savage Crows* (1976) and *A Cry in the Jungle Bar* (1979). Some of his best short
stories deal with the beach culture of life in places like Bondi. Drewe has retired
from journalism to write fiction, and now lives in Melbourne.

The Bodysurfers, 1983.

Pages 287–290

BEVERLEY FARMER was born in 1941 in Melbourne and was educated at Mac-
Robertson Girls' High School and the University of Melbourne. She has worked
at a large variety of jobs, and for three years lived in Greece, where she taught
English and helped run a seaside restaurant. She has been a writer-in-residence
at the University of Tasmania. Her first novel, *Alone*, was published in 1980.
Her collection of stories, *Milk* (1983) won the New South Wales Premier's Literary Award. She has a fourteen-year-old son, and lives partly at Point Lonsdale
and partly in Melbourne.

Milk, 1983; *Home Time*, 1985.

Pages 257–268

FRANK DALBY
DAVISION

ROBERT DREWE

BEVERLEY
FARMER

NENE GARE

NENE GARE was born in 1919 in Adelaide and educated at the Adelaide Art School and the Perth Technical School. Her first stories appeared in the *Western Mail*, edited by Malcolm Uren, and she has written a number of novels. Her marriage to Frank Gare, former Director of Aboriginal Affairs in Western Australia, brought her in touch with Aboriginal people in many places in the state. Her profound sympathy with Aborigines and part-Aborigines, and her fine ear for the cadences and rhythms of their speech, are evident in her best-known work, *The Fringe Dwellers* (1961), which has been many times reprinted and has recently been made by Bruce Beresford into a feature film.

Bend to the Wind, 1978.

Pages 195–199

HELEN GARNER

HELEN GARNER was born in 1942 at Geelong, where she was educated before going on to the University of Melbourne, graduating in 1965. She taught in secondary schools until she was dismissed in 1972 for answering students' questions about sexual matters. Since then she has worked as a freelance journalist and critic, and as a writer of fiction. Her novel, *Monkey Grip* (1977), won a National Book Council Award in 1978, and was made into a feature film in 1981. Garner is a French scholar, and lived in Paris 1978–79. She has received several fellowships from the Literature Board of the Australia Council, and has worked as writer-in-residence at various Australian universities and in Tokyo.

Honour and Other People's Children, 1980; *Postcards from Surfers*, 1985.

Pages 269–274

FRANK HARDY

FRANK HARDY was born in 1917 at Bacchus Marsh, Victoria. (It is odd that this little country town should have produced two of Australia's best-known writers, Hardy and Peter Carey). Hardy comes from a widespread Victorian Catholic family. He left school at thirteen and worked as a seaman, fruit-picker, grocer, and on the roads; he has also been a cartoonist. He joined the Communist Party in 1939 and the army in 1942. While stationed in the Northern Territory he produced a camp newspaper, the *Troppo Tribune*, to which he contributed most of the text and all of the art-work. After working with the army magazine, *Salt*, he became a journalist in Melbourne. Always a keen betting man, he was ideally suited to research the life and times of the millionaire former SP-bookie, John Wren. His novel *Power without Glory* (1950) led to his prosecution for criminal libel. The case drew a lot of sympathy for Hardy all around Australia; he was acquitted after a trial that lasted nine months. *Power Without Glory* has been translated into many languages, and was made into an ABC TV mini-series.

The Man from Clinkapella, 1951; *Legends from Benson's Valley*, 1963; *The Yarns of Billy Borker*, 1965; *Billy Borker Yarns Again*, 1967.

Pages 187–194

ELIZABETH HARROWER was born in Sydney in 1928 and spent most of her first eleven years in Newcastle. Educated at public and private schools, she worked as a clerk until she went to London in 1951 and lived there until 1959. There her career as a writer began. Returning to Sydney, she was employed by the ABC and by a publishing firm. Elizabeth Harrower has written four novels, of which the finest is probably *The Long Prospect* (1958), based on her early years in New-castle, called Ballowra in the novel. Her short stories have been published in many journals, but not collected in book form. She lives in Sydney.

Pages 211–219

GWEN HARWOOD was born in 1920 at Taringa, Brisbane. She studied music, and was organist at All Saint's Church in Brisbane. She has taught music, and written librettos for Larry Sitsky's operas, and also written lyrics for music by James Pentherby and Ian Cugley. In 1945 she married a linguist, William Har-wood, and moved to Tasmania where she still lives. She is best known as a poet, and has won a number of awards, including the Patrick White Literary Award in 1978. There is no collection of Gwen Harwood's stories.

Pages 200–204

BRIAN JAMES was born John Tierney in 1892 at Eurunderee in the Henry Law-son country of NSW. His father taught Lawson. James was educated at Eurun-deree School and Sydney University. He lived in England 1922–24 and took a Diploma of Education at Oxford, then followed in his father's profession and for thirty-seven years was a teacher in high schools in the country and in Sydney. He later acquired a small farm. In 1942 he sent his first short story to Douglas Stewart at the *Bulletin*, and he received firm support from Stewart and Norman Lindsay over the years. His novels and stories are predominately about farming and school life. His novel *The Advancement of Spencer Button* (1950) is a shrewd and deeply ironic account not only of the career of a schoolteacher but of the whole education system of New South Wales. After retiring from teaching, James lived on his orchard farm. He died in 1972.

First Furrow and Other Stories, 1944; *Cookabundy Bridge*, 1946; *The Bunyip of Barney's Elbow*, 1956; *The Big Burn*, 1965.

Pages 51–55

ELIZABETH JOLLEY was born in 1923 in Birmingham, England, and was educated in England and in Europe. She served as a nurse in World War II. She came to Western Australia in 1959, where she worked as a teacher. She emerged as a fully-fledged writer of a remarkable range of fiction in the late 1970s, and has already published several award-winning volumes of stories and novels. She also writes radio plays, six of which have been broadcast on the ABC and the

BBC. She has been a tutor and writer-in-residence at the Western Australian Institute of Technology. She lives in Perth.

Five Acre Virgin and Other Stories, 1976; *The Travelling Entertainer*, 1979; *Woman in a Lampshade*, 1983; *Stories*, 1984.

Pages 205–210

HENRY LAWSON

HENRY LAWSON was born in 1867 on the goldfields at Grenfell, NSW. His father, Niels Larsen, who called himself Peter Lawson, was a Norwegian ex-sailor; his mother, Louisa, was a pioneer radical feminist, publisher and journalist. After Henry's birth the family returned to New Pipeclay (Eurunderee), near Mudgee, where, apart from a break at Gulgong, they worked a poor selection until 1883, when Louisa moved to Sydney. Peter Lawson died in 1888. Henry's first poem was published in the *Bulletin* in 1887, and his first story in 1888. Lawson worked as a coach-painter and then as a journalist in Albany, WA, and in Brisbane. In 1892 J.F. Archibald provided the funds for Lawson to go to Bourke, where he worked as a house-painter; he then humped a swag to Hungerford and back. It was a time of drought and economic depression and scarred Lawson for life. In 1893 he went to New Zealand for seven months. In 1896 he married Bertha Bredt; in 1900, with their two children, they left for London from which they returned poverty-stricken in 1902, with the marriage in ruins. Lawson's drinking problem, which had begun in the 1880s, led to several terms in prison between 1905 and 1910. In 1916 he was granted a sinecure to live in Leeton, a prohibition area. Lawson died in 1922. He was the first Australian writer to be granted a State funeral.

Short Stories in Prose and Verse, 1894 (published by Louisa Lawson); *While the Billy Boils*, 1896; *On the Track*, 1900; *Over the Sliprails*, 1900; *Joe Wilson and His Mates*, 1901; *Children of the Bush*, 1902.

Pages 23–31

ANGELO LOUKAKIS

ANGELO LOUKAKIS was born in 1951 in Sydney, of a Greek migrant family, and educated in Sydney. His short stories and articles have been published in a number of journals, and he has written plays and scripts for film and television. He is also the author of a children's book about Greek migrants in Australia, and a travel book on Norfolk Island. He has held a fellowship from the Literature Board of the Australia Council.

Vernacular Dreams, 1986.

Pages 291–297

MORRIS LURIE

MORRIS LURIE was born in 1938 in Melbourne, son of Jewish migrants from Poland. He studied architecture, and for a time worked in advertising with

Barry Oakley and Peter Carey. In 1965 he went overseas and lived in Europe, North Africa and New York until returning to Melbourne in 1973. He says that he grew up in 'a strange bubble of isolation', his parents being exiles from Poland and alien to Australia. But Lurie had always been one to see the humour as well as the pathos of the situation. He is the only Australian writer with that rich Jewish sense of the comic that is so marked in American fiction. Many of Lurie's stories have appeared in journals in England and the USA, such as *Punch*, the *New Yorker*, *Esquire* and the *Transatlantic Review*. He has published four novels. He lives in Melbourne.

Happy Times, 1969; *Inside the Wardrobe*, 1975; *Running Nicely*, 1979; *Dirty Friends*, 1981; *Outrageous Behaviour*, 1984; *The Night We Ate the Sparrow*, 1985.

Pages 230–238

DAVID MALOUF was born in 1934 in Brisbane; his father was Lebanese and his mother English. He was educated in Brisbane and at the University of Queensland, where he taught for two years before leaving for England and Europe in 1959. He stayed away for nine years, mostly working at teaching in schools in London and Birkenhead. He returned to Australia to lecture in English at the University of Sydney (1968–77) and resigned in order to work full-time as a writer. He has a house in Tuscany and he works part of the year there and part in Australia. He has published six volumes of verse and three novels. He is a theatre critic, and wrote the libretto for Richard Meale's opera on Patrick White's novel *Voss*, first performed in 1986. He has won a number of awards.

DAVID MALOUF

Antipodes, 1985.

Pages 227–229

CECIL MANN was born in 1896 at Cudgen, NSW, and was educated in state schools. He fought with the AIF at Gallipoli and in France in World War I, and also saw active service in World War II. He worked as a reporter on newspapers along the north coast of New South Wales, the scene of many of his best stories, and then on the *Sydney Morning Herald*. He was on the literary staff of the *Bulletin* from 1925 until his retirement in 1960; he edited the Red Page, and was associate editor of the magazine. Mann died in 1967.

CECIL MANN

The River and Other Stories, 1945; *Three Stories*, 1963.

Pages 73–78

ALAN MARSHALL was born in 1902 at Noorat in western Victoria, and educated at nearby Terang. At the age of six he was crippled by what was then known as

ALAN MARSHALL

infantile paralysis. He later wrote about coming to terms with being a cripple in *I Can Jump Puddles* (1955), which has sold over three million copies and been translated into many languages. After learning accountancy at a business college he worked as accountant for a shoe factory, an experience which provided the background for *How Beautiful Are Thy Feet* (1949). After the shoe company closed down in 1935 he became a freelance writer. His columns in *Woman* and the *Argus* had a large following. At the same time he began to publish short stories in various journal. Marshall was awarded the OBE in 1972 and the AM in 1981. He died in 1984.

Tell Us About the Turkey, Jo, 1946; *How's Andy Going?*, 1956; *Short Stories*, 1973; *Hammers over the Anvil*, 1975; *Festival and Other Stories*, 1975; *The Complete Stories of Alan Marshall*, 1977.

Pages 83–90

RAY MATHEW

RAY MATHEW was born in Sydney in 1929 and educated at Sydney High School and the Sydney Teachers' College. He taught for several years in country schools and left teaching to take a variety of casual jobs, then becoming a tutor with the University of Sydney before he left Australia in 1961 to live in London, Italy, and finally New York. He wrote and published plays in the 1950s, as well as three volumes of verse, short stories, and novel (*The Joys of Possession*, 1967).

A Bohemian Affair, 1961; *The Time of the Peacock* (with Mena Abdullah), 1965.

Pages 220–225

FRANK MOORHOUSE

FRANK MOORHOUSE was born in 1938 at Nowra on the south coast of NSW. He worked as a journalist in Sydney on the *Daily Telegraph*, and then on country newspapers at Wagga Wagga and in the Riverina. In 1963 he edited the *Australian Worker*, and was a union organiser for the Australian Journalists' Association. Later he served a term as President of the Australian Society of Authors. His stories began to appear in the late 1950s. By the 1970s he was publishing his characteristic linked short fictions which he calls 'discontinuous narrative'. Moorhouse did not invent this literary technique, but he has made it characteristically his own. He has written screenplays and many articles and columns, especially for the *Bulletin*, some of which were collected in a book he edited, *Days of Wine and Rage* (1980). Moorhouse has for some years lived in Balmain, an area favoured and written about by various friends and Moorhouse himself.

Futility and Other Animals, 1969; *The Americans, Baby*, 1972; *The Electrical Experience*, 1974; *Conference-ville*, 1976; *Tales of Mystery and Romance*, 1977; *The Everlasting Secret Family and Other Secrets*, 1980; *Room Service*, 1985.

Pages 239–243

MYRA MORRIS was born in 1893 at Boort in western Victoria, and grew up in the Mallee district. She was educated at a convent in Rochester, and then went to live near Frankston where she worked as a freelance writer of verse, articles and short stories. She published two novels and two collections of poems. She died in 1966.

The Township, 1947.

Pages 56–63

JOHN MORRISON was born in 1904 at Sunderland, England. He migrated to Australia in 1923 and earned his living as a bush worker. When he married in 1928 he settled in Melbourne, where he worked for ten years as a wharfie, and for the rest of the time as a gardener. He has written many stories about the wharves, and one of his finest long stories, 'The Battle of the Flowers', is about two ardent lady gardeners. He began publishing stories in the 1940s; he has published two novels and a collection of memoirs and essays. His work has been translated into ten languages. John Morrison lives in Melbourne.

Sailors Belong Ships, 1947; *Black Cargo*, 1955; *Twenty-Three*, 1962 (awarded the gold medal of the Australian Literature Society); *Selected Stories*, 1972; *Australian by Choice*, 1973; *Stories of the Waterfront*, 1984; *This Freedom*, 1985.

Pages 99–105

VANCE PALMER was born in 1885 at Bundaberg, Queensland, the youngest of a family of eight. His father was a schoolmaster, and during Vance's childhood the family moved around Queensland country towns. He was educated at Ipswich Grammar School, and in 1905 departed for London where he described his existence for two years as that of a 'Grub Street hack'. Travelling by way of Russia and Japan he returned to Australia, where he worked as a tutor and bookkeeper on Queensland stations, with a spell as a drover in the north-west. In 1910 he returned to London, where A.R. Orage, the influential editor of the *New Age*, took him under his wing and encouraged his development as a writer. In 1914 he married Janet Higgins, who as Nettie Palmer became one of the liveliest of Australian critics. They were a formidable partnership. Palmer served in the AIF in World War I. In 1925 the Palmers went to live in Caloundra, a fishing village in Queensland, where Vance wrote novels and Nettie articles and reviews. After further travels, the Palmers settled in Melbourne where Vance became a regular and well-loved broadcaster on the ABC. He died in 1959.

Separate Lives, 1931; *Sea and Spinifex*, 1934; *Let the Birds Fly*, 1955; *The Rainbow Bird and Other Stories*, 1957.

Pages 46–50

HAL PORTER

HAL PORTER was born in 1911 at Albert Park, Melbourne. His family moved to Bairnsdale in Gippsland when he was six, and he was mainly educated there. He lived in Williamstown 1927–37, working as a school-teacher. He married in 1939 and was divorced in 1943 and did not remarry. In 1939 he was badly injured in a traffic accident which prevented his joining up; ironically, the life thus perhaps saved was eventually destroyed by another traffic accident in 1983, which left him in a coma until he died in 1984. During the war Porter taught in private schools in Adelaide and published his first collection of stories. After working as a teacher with the Occupation Forces in Japan (1949–50) he was librarian at Bairnsdale and Shepparton (1953–61). He then devoted all his time to writing, holding a number of Fellowships from the Commonwealth Literary Fund and the Literature Board. He published three novels, three collections of poetry, and one of the finest of modern autobiographies, in three volumes. He also published plays, history and criticism. He won many awards and was awarded the AM in 1982.

Short Stories, 1942; *A Bachelor's Children*, 1962; *The Cats of Venice*, 1965; *Mr Butterfry and Other Tales of New Japan*, 1970; *Selected Stories*, 1971; *Fredo Fuss Love Life*, 1974; *The Clairvoyant Goat*, 1981.

Pages 117–125

KATHARINE SUSANNAH PRICHARD

KATHARINE SUSANNAH PRICHARD was born in 1883 at Levuka, Fiji; her father was editor of the *Fiji Times*. Her childhood was spent in Tasmania and Melbourne, where she was educated at South Melbourne College. She worked as a governess on stations in Gippsland and western New South Wales. Between 1908 and 1916 she spent six years in London working as a writer and journalist. Her first novel, *The Pioneers*, about Gippsland, was published in 1915 and made into a film in 1916. In this year she returned to Australia. She married Captain Hugo Throssell, VC, in 1919 and went to live in Western Australia. In 1920 she became a founding member of the Communist Party of Australia and was an early feminist. *Coonardoo*, about an Aboriginal woman, is the finest of her eleven novels. She also wrote poetry, plays, an autobiography, and numerous pamphlets and journalistic pieces. She died in 1969.

Kiss on the Lips, 1932; *Potch and Colour*, 1944; *N'Goola*, 1959; *On Strenuous Wings*, 1965; *Happiness*, 1967.

Pages 41–45

HENRY HANDEL RICHARDSON

HENRY HANDEL RICHARDSON is the pseudonym of Ethel Florence Lindesay Robertson (*née* Richardson) who was born in 1870 in Melbourne and educated at the Presbyterian Ladies' College there. Her father, Walter Lindesay Richardson, was a medical practitioner who came from Ireland to the Ballarat goldfields. Her most important work, *The Fortunes of Richard Mahony*, gives a penetrating portrait of him and describes her family's fluctuating fortunes. First published in three separate volumes—*The Fortunes of Richard Mahony* (1917), *The Way Home* (1925), and *Ultima Thule* (1929)—the trilogy was issued in one volume in 1930. When she was 17, HHR was taken by her mother to Europe to study as a pianist, and in Leipzig she met J.G. Robertson, a Scottish student of German literature, whom she married in 1895. Her first novel, *Maurice Guest*, was published in 1908. Living in London (where her husband became Professor of German Literature in the University of London), she led a secluded and protected life devoted to her writing. She returned only once to Australia for a brief visit in 1912—'to test my memories'. She died in 1946.

The End of Childhood and Other Stories, 1934; *The Adventures of Cuffy Mahony and Other Stories*, 1979.

Pages 38–40

ROLAND ROBINSON was born in 1912 in County Clare, Ireland, and came to Australia at the age of nine. He left school early to work as a rouseabout on a sheep station near Coonamble, NSW. He has worked at many jobs, including railway fettler, boundary rider, factory-worker, ballet dancer, literary and ballet critic for the *Sydney Morning Herald*, golf-course groundsman. In his years in the bush he spent long periods with Aborigines, from the Roper River to northern New South Wales, and wrote down many of the legends and stories they told him. His identification with outback Australia and his sympathy with the Aborigines has given his many volumes of poetry a strength of belonging unique in Australian literature. In the 1970s he published an autobiography in three volumes. He lives at Belmont in New South Wales.

ROLAND ROBINSON

Legend and Dreaming, 1952; *The Feathered Serpent*, 1956; *Black-feller, White-feller*, 1958; *The Man Who Sold His Dreaming*, 1965; *Aboriginal Myths and Legends*, 1966.

Pages 160–162

PADDY ROE was born about 1912 on an old sheep station, Roebuck Plains, near Broome in the north-west of Western Australia. Of mixed ancestry, his white relations go back to John Septimus Roe, first Surveyor-General of Western Australia. When he was a small boy his Aboriginal mother took him out to the bush to save him from being forcibly removed to what were known as schools for half-castes. On one occasion she rolled him in a blanket and sat on him when police visited her camp looking for half-caste children. He worked as a drover and windmill repairer and is now patriarch of a large family in Broome. With a deep knowledge of traditional society, he has been described as 'a kind of ombudsman' negotiating between governmental agencies and the Aboriginal communities of the Broome region. Dr Stephen Muecke, a linguist at the South

PADDY ROE

Australian College of Advanced Education, has written two books with Paddy Roe, recording his stories and journeys through his spirit country.

Gularabulu, 1983; *Reading the Country*, 1984.

Pages 153–159

STEELE RUDD

STEELE RUDD (Arthur Hoey Davis) was born in 1868 at Drayton on the Darling Downs in Queensland. His father was a blacksmith who selected land at Emu Creek, where he took his family to live in 1868. Rudd left school before he was twelve and worked on properties and in shearing sheds until 1885 when he secured a job in the Public Service in Brisbane. About 1890 he began to contribute humorous pieces about rowing to the Brisbane *Chronicle*, under the pseudonym of 'Steele Rudder', the first name taken from the English essayist. In 1895 his first story about selection life appeared in the *Bulletin* with the surname reduced to Rudd. The selection stories soon became immensely popular. Rudd believed that this caused his retrenchment from his job of under-sheriff in the justice Department in 1904. He then founded an illustrated monthly, *Steele Rudd's Magazine*. In 1909 he bought a farm near Emu Creek. The great success of Bert Bailey's and Edmund Duggan's stage adaptation of *On Our Selection* brought little financial benefit to Rudd, who had money troubles all his life. Several silent and talking films were made from his work. All the stage and film versions coarsened and degraded the original family of *On Our Selection*, which was by no means entirely based on Rudd's own family. Rudd died in 1935.

On Our Selection, 1899; *Our New Selection*, 1903; *Sandy's Selection*, 1904; *Back at Our Selection*, 1906; *Dad in Politics and Other Stories*, 1908; *Stocking Our Selection*, 1909; *From Selection to City*, 1909; *The Rudd Family*, 1926.

Pages 32–37

GEORGIA SAVAGE

GEORGIA SAVAGE was born in Tasmania, and was educated at the Methodist Ladies' College in Launceston. She worked for a number of years in Victoria as a tax consultant. In 1950 she left work and went to live in Queensland as a full-time writer. At the end of 1984 she moved back to Melbourne where she now lives. She published a novel, *Slate and Me and Blanche McBride*, in 1984. Georgia Savage has not published a collection of short stories.

Pages 245–251

E.O. SCHLUNKE

E.O. SCHLUNKE was born in 1906 at Reefton, near Temora, NSW. His ancestors were Lutheran German settlers from the Barossa Valley, SA. He farmed his own sheep and wheat property, Rosenthal, near Reefton in the Riverina. He published three novels and many short stories, most of which originally appeared in the *Bulletin* and the *Sydney Morning Herald*. Schlunke had a powerful talent for depicting the landscape of the Riverina and the impact of the strict Lutheran faith on the German farmers. But his horizons were wider, for he had a shrewd satiric eye for the smart salesman, for the city and the politician.

The Man in the Silo, 1955; *The Village Hampden*, 1958; *Stories of the Riverina*, 1965.

Pages 106–116

CHRISTINA STEAD

CHRISTINA STEAD was born in 1902 in Sydney. Her mother died in 1904. Her father, David Stead, was a distinguished naturalist and Fabian socialist who married again in 1907 and sired a large family. Although Stead's greatest book, *The Man Who Loved Children*, is set in the USA, it is in fact based on the Stead household at Watson's Bay on Sydney Harbour. Stead graduated from Sydney Teachers' College in 1921 and taught for three years. She then worked as a secretary, saving up to go abroad. She worked in London in 1928–29, but became seriously ill as a result of some years of inadequate diet and overwork. In her convalescence she wrote her novel *Seven Poor Men of Sydney* (1934), which with *For Love Alone* (1944) is based on her Sydney experiences. With her husband William Blake, a banker, she moved to Paris in 1929 where she worked for five years in a bank. From 1937–47 the Blakes lived in the USA, returning to Europe in 1947 and settling in England in 1953. William Blake died in 1968 and in 1974 Stead returned to live permanently in Australia, where she died in 1983.

Ocean of Story, 1985.

Pages 91–98

DAL STIVENS

DAL STIVENS was born in 1911 at Blayney, NSW. He was educated at Barker College, Sydney, and worked in a bank, as a freelance journalist and as a public servant before serving in the army education service 1943–44 and in the Department of Information 1944–49. In 1949–50 he was Press Officer at Australia House, London. He worked in publishing after returning to Sydney and then became a full-time writer. Stivens has been very active in the Australian Society of Authors, becoming its foundation president in 1963. He is also a naturalist and a painter who has had a number of exhibitions of his work. He won the Miles Franklin Award in 1970 for his novel *A Horse of Air*, and the Patrick White Award in 1981. He has published four novels. He lives in Sydney.

The Tramp and Other Stories, 1936; *The Courtship of Uncle Henry*, 1946; *The Gambling Ghost and Other Tales*, 1953; *Ironbark Bill*, 1955; *The Scholarly Mouse and Other Tales*, 1957; *Selected Stories*, 1969; *The Unicorn and Other Tales*, 1976; *The Demon Bowler and Other Cricket Stories*, 1979.

Pages 126–132

JUDAH WATEN

JUDAH WATEN was born in 1911 in Odessa, Russia, of Jewish parents. The family emigrated to Western Australia in 1914, and he was educated in state schools in Perth and Melbourne. His father travelled around as a hawker. Waten worked as a schoolteacher, journalist, cook, mail-sorter and clerk, and joined the Communist Party with which, although remaining a Communist, he had a long and stormy relationship. In 1921–23 he was in England and Europe. He was arrested in a demonstration of the Unemployed Workers' Movement and sentenced to three months imprisonment in Wormwood Scrubs. Waten began writing at an early age, but first achieved recognition with a collection of stories, *Alien Son* (1952). He published seven novels and several autobiographical works. Waten gave a lot of his time to helping other writers in the Fellowship of Australian Writers and when serving on the Literature Board of the Australia Council. He died in 1985.

Alien Son, 1952; *Love and Rebellion*, 1978.

Pages 133–140

PATRICK WHITE

PATRICK WHITE was born in 1912 in London, on a visit there by his parents, who returned to Australia when he was six months old. He comes from a family long connected with the land in New South Wales. He was educated at private schools in New South Wales before being sent to Cheltenham College in England. On his return to Australia in 1929 he spent two years as a jackeroo on stations on the Monaro and near Walgett in New South Wales. He returned to England to read modern languages at King's College, Cambridge, where he graduated in 1935. He then lived in London writing novels, stories, plays and dramatic sketches. His first novel *Happy Valley*, appeared in 1939 and was well received in England and the USA, although White will not allow it to be reprinted. He served in the RAF in World War II as an intelligence officer. He spent a year in Greece after the war, and in 1948 returned to Australia with a Greek friend, Manoly Lascaris, with whom he settled near Castle Hill, New South Wales, to breed goats and schnauzer dogs. In 1964 he moved to Centennial Park in Sydney, where he still lives. He was awarded the AC in 1975 but rejected the honour in 1976 as a protest against the Government's introducing knighthoods to the Order of Australia. He has been awarded many Australian and English literary prizes, and in 1973 won the Nobel Prize for Literature. With the money for the Nobel Prize he established the Patrick White Literary Award. White has written many novels and plays and is regarded as the foremost of Australia's contemporary writers.

The Burnt Ones, 1964; *The Cockatoos*, 1974.

Pages 141–152

MICHAEL WILDING

MICHAEL WILDING was born in 1942 at Worcester, England, and educated at Oxford 1960–63. He became Lecturer in English at the University of Sydney in

1963, and returned to England 1967–68 to lecture at Birmingham University. In 1969 he returned to Sydney, where he is now Reader in English at the University. Wilding is the author of a number of scholarly works on Henry James, Marvell, Milton and Shakespeare, and he has published several works dealing with Marcus Clarke and William Lane of the New Australia settlement. He was involved with publishing in founding Wild & Woolley with Pat Woolley, and in the foundation of the short-fiction supplement, *Tabloid Story*. He is best known for his novels and short stories; he was part of the Balmain group that included Frank Moorhouse. He lives in Sydney.

Aspects of the Dying Process, 1972; *The West Midland Underground*, 1975; *The Phallic Forest*, 1978; *Reading the Signs*, 1984; *The Man of Slow Feeling*, 1985.

Pages 275–277

TIM WINTON was born in 1960 in Perth, WA, and was educated in Perth, Albany, and at the Western Australian Institute of Technology. He first achieved literary prominence as the joint winner in 1981 of the Australian/Vogel Award, for his novel *An Open Swimmer*. His second novel, *Shallows* (1984), won the Miles Franklin Award. He lives in the Perth suburb of Mount Hawthorn.

Scission, 1985.

Pages 298–301

TIM WINTON

JUDITH WRIGHT was born in 1915 at Thalgarrah station near Armidale, New South Wales, of an old-established pastoral family of whom she has written in *The Generations of Men* (1959) and *The Cry for the Dead* (1981). She was brought up on Wallamumbi station and educated by correspondence school before going to New England Girls' School and the University of Sydney. She visited England and Europe 1938–39, and back in Australia during the war she worked with her father on the land, her brothers having enlisted in the armed forces. In 1944–48 she worked as a secretary at the University of Queensland, where she met and married the philosopher J.P. McKinney. Her first book of poems, *The Moving Image*, was published in 1946. Since then she has become one of Australia's most eminent poets, and won many awards. She has also written children's books, history, and literary criticism. She has been a leading figure in the conservation movement and in organisations concerned with advancing the cause of the Aborigines.

The Nature of Love, 1966.

Pages 177–182

JUDITH WRIGHT

ACKNOWLEDGMENT OF SOURCES

Thanks are due to the publishers and copyright owners concerned for permission to include copyright material. For future editions, we should be grateful to receive any correction of sources wrongly credited.

MENA ABDULLAH AND RAY MATHEW

The Time of the Peacock: *The Time of the Peacock*, Angus & Robertson, 1965.

MURRAY BAIL

Paradise: *Contemporary Portraits and Other Stories*, University of Queensland Press, 1975.

MARJORIE BARNARD

The Persimmon Tree: *The Persimmon Tree and Other Stories*, Angus & Robertson, 1943.

BARBARA BAYNTON

The Chosen Vessel: *Bush Studies* (under the title 'The Tramp'), Duckworth, 1902.

LOUIS BECKE

A Truly Great Man: *By Reef and Palm*, Unwin, 1894.

DAVID CAMPBELL

Come On, Billy: *Evening Under Lamplight*, Angus & Robertson, 1959.

PETER CAREY

A Windmill in the West: *The Fat Man in History*, University of Queensland Press, 1975.

NANCY CATO

The Voyage North: *Southern Festival*, Rigby, 1960.

PETER COWAN

The Fence: *The Unploughed Land*, Angus & Robertson, 1958.

FRANK DALBY DAVISON

The Good Herdsman: *The Road to Yesterday*, Angus & Robertson, 1964.

ROBERT DREWE

The Manageress and the Mirage: *The Bodysurfers*, James Fraser, 1983.

BEVERLEY FARMER

Summer on Ice: *Milk*, McPhee Gribble/Penguin, 1983.

ACKNOWLEDG-
MENT OF
SOURCES

NENE GARE
The Homecoming: *Bend to the Wind*, Macmillan, 1978.

HELEN GARNER
The Life of Art: *Postcards from Surfers*, McPhee Gribble/Penguin, 1985.

FRANK HARDY
The Load of Wood: *Legends from Benson's Valley*, Werner Laurie, 1963.

ELIZABETH HARROWER
The Beautiful Climate: *Modern Australian Writing*, Collins/Fontana, 1967.

GWEN HARWOOD
The Glass Boy: The *Bulletin* Literary Supplement, 13 April 1982.

BRIAN JAMES
Gant and His Horses: *Cookabundy Bridge and Other Stories*, Angus & Robertson, 1946. Estate of the late John Lawrence Tierney.

ELIZABETH JOLLEY
A Hedge of Rosemary: *Stories*, Fremantle Arts Centre Press, 1984.

HENRY LAWSON
The Golden Graveyard: *Joe Wilson and His Mates*, Blackwood, 1901.

ANGELO LOUKAKIS
Being Here Now: *Vernacular Dreams*, University of Queensland Press, 1986.

MORRIS LURIE
Outrageous Behaviour: *Outrageous Behaviour*, Penguin, 1984.

DAVID MALOUF
The Only Speaker of His Tongue: *Antipodes*, Chatto & Windus, 1985.

CECIL MANN
The Pelican: *The River*, Dymock's, 1945.

ALAN MARSHALL
My Bird: *How's Andy Going?*, Cheshire, 1956.

FRANK MOORHOUSE
Motel Midnight: *Conference-ville*, Angus & Robertson, 1976.

MYRA MORRIS
A Woman Kind to Men: *The Township*, Angus & Robertson, 1947.

ACKNOWLEDG-
MENT OF
SOURCES

JOHN MORRISON
    Lena: *This Freedom*, Penguin, 1985.

VANCE PALMER
    The Rainbow Bird: *Sea and Spinifex*, Shakespeare Head Press, 1934.

HAL PORTER
    Francis Silver: *The Cats of Venice*, Angus & Robertson, 1965.

KATHARINE SUSANNAH PRICHARD
    Treason: *Kiss on the Lips and Other Stories*, Jonathon Cape, 1932.

HENRY HANDEL RICHARDSON
    The Bathe: *The Adventures of Cuffy Mahony and Other Stories*, Angus & Robertson, 1979.

ROLAND ROBINSON
    The Water Lubra and the Lotus Bird: *The Feathered Serpent*, Angus & Robertson, 1956.

PADDY ROE (with Stephen Muecke)
    Duegara: *Gularabulu*, Fremantle Arts Centre Press, 1983.

STEELE RUDD
    Cranky Jack: *On Our Selection*, Bulletin Newspaper Co., 1899.

GEORGIA SAVAGE
    The Spider: The *Bulletin* Literary Supplement, 30 June 1981.

E.O. SCHLUNKE
    The Garden of Dreams: *Stories of The Riverina*, Angus & Robertson, 1965

CHRISTINA STEAD
    The Milk Run: *Ocean of Story*, Viking/Penguin, 1985.

DAL STIVENS
    You Call Me by My Proper Name: *The Courtship of Uncle Henry*, Reed & Harris, 1946.

JUDAH WATEN
    Making a Living: *Alien Son*, Angus & Robertson, 1952.

PATRICK WHITE
    The Letters: *The Burnt Ones*, Eyre & Spottiswood, 1964.

MICHAEL WILDING
    Reading the Signs: *Reading the Signs*, Hale & Iremonger, 1984.

TIM WINTON

Neighbours: *Scission*, McPhee Gribble/Penguin, 1985.

JUDITH WRIGHT

The Vineyard Woman: *The Nature of Love*, Sun Books, 1966.

SOURCES OF ILLUSTRATION

p. 1 *Morning Tea*, Lionel Lindsay, c. 1924 NLA; p. 2 *Wet Afternoon*, Ethel Spowers, 1930 AGNSW and Mr Tom Quirk; p. 9 *The Artist's Wife*, Sali Herman, 1940 ANG; p. 12 ML; p. 13 John Oxley Library, SLQ; p. 15 ML; p. 17 ML; p. 19 *Cottage Macedon*, Frederick McCubbin AGNSW; p. 24 William Henry Corkhill, Tilba Tilba Collection NLA; p. 29 William Henry Corkhill, Tilba Tilba Collection NLA; p. 32 Fred Leist; p. 34 Fred Leist; p. 37 Fred Leist; p. 39 David Moore; p. 42 William Henry Corkhill, Tilba Tilba Collection NLA; p. 45 *Son of the Soil*, Cazneaux NLA; p. 47 Max Dupain; p. 52 *Peace After War & Memories*, Cazneaux, 1918, AGNSW; p. 57 *Rabbit Trapper*, David Potts, 1947, AGNSW; p. 60 William Henry Corkhill, Tilba Tilba Collection, NLA; p. 64 *Autumn*, Cazneaux, 1931, NLA; p. 69 *River Pastoral*, Cazneaux, NLA; p. 74 Robert McFarlane; p. 77 *Pelican Landing*, John Olsen; p. 78 Robert McFarlane; p. 81 *Leaf Study*, John Kauffman, 1930s, ANG; p. 82 Robert McFarlane; p. 85 Robert McFarlane; p. 88 *Black Swans, Wallis Lake NSW*, Margaret Preston, c. 1923, AGSA; p. 93 *Old Cottage*, Cazneaux, NLA; p. 98 William Henry Corkhill Tilba Tilba Collection, NLA; p. 101 Robert McFarlane; p. 104 David Moore; p. 109 *Joe's Garden of Dreams*, Russell Drysdale, Lady Drysdale; p. 118 *The Ferry*, E. Phillips Fox, c. 1910–1911, AGNSW; p. 127 Chapman Collection; p. 129 Kenneth D. Hastings; p. 133 *The Dispossessed*, Vic O'Connor, 1942 ANG; p. 134 Max Dupain; p. 137 ML; p. 142 *Madame Pfund*, Tom Roberts, 1887, NGV; p. 145 Mrs Helen Rutledge; p. 150 Mrs Helen Rutledge; p. 155 Vincent Serventy; p. 156 David Moore; p. 161 John Olsen; p. 162 John Olsen; p. 165 *Billy Meditation*, Cazneaux, 1906 AGNSW; p. 167 La Trobe, SLV; p. 173 Max Dupain; p. 174 Robert McFarlane; p. 177 Cedric Flower; p. 178 La Trobe, SLV; p. 185 David Moore; p. 187 SRA; p. 190 David Moore, J. Fairfax & Sons; p. 199 Jon Lewis; p. 201 *Portrait in Sunshine*, Cazneaux, 1931, NLA; p. 205 Robert McFarlane; p. 208 David Moore; p. 213 Kenneth D. Hastings; p. 218 Monte Luke; p. 224 Charles Blackman; p. 226 APL; p. 231 *Tired Man*, Bob Dickerson, NGV; p. 232 Grant Blackman; p. 241 Robert McFarlane; p. 244 Robert McFarlane; p. 254 David Moore; p. 256 *Control Tower*, Jeffrey Smart, 1969, AGSA; p. 259 APL; p. 263 David Moore; p. 270 Robert McFarlane; p. 277 David Moore; p. 279 *Painting 1978*, Pual Partos, NAB; p. 280 Max Dupain; p. 283 Joanna Collard; p. 289 Max Dupain; p. 292 Graham McCarter; p. 297 David Moore; p. 299 Joanna Collard; p. 300 Joanna Collard; p. 302 *Under the Jacaranda*, R. Godfrey Rivers, QAG.